More buzz about *Rivers*...

"Leslie Esdaile's story shines with hope and crackles with down-to-earth wisdom. She can conjure the power of sexual healing just as surely as she can tear across the jagged edge of a marriage gone bad. *Rivers of the Soul* is that rare thing: a delicious read and an inspiration. Leslie Esdaile keeps it real."
Lorene Cary, author of *Black Ice, The Price of A Child, and Pride.*

"Leslie Esdaile tells a compelling story about life in the 21st century as seen through the eyes of a single girl alone in the world. Esdaile's knack for mother wit and familiar colloquialism will give readers reason to smile; recalling tried and true advice from family elders that rings true even to this day. Her work is refreshing, redeeming and most of all realistic."
Denise Barnes, Feature Writer, *The Washington Times Newspaper*

Antoinette sat up and poured a new glass of pinkish liquid, never letting her vision stray from the page as she managed the wine with one hand. She took a deep breath through her nose with a luxurious sip. Lord, that man was making love to this woman the way it should be done! Have mercy.

As the lovemaking in the novel crescendoed, so did the ache that had crept between her legs. The heat rising from the bath became a constant nag that begged for attention. Bringing the side of the glass to her cheek, she reveled in the contrast of textures. The glass was cool, smooth—her face warm and moist. Just like she was on the beach. Just like she remembered Jerome… cool water ice in his mouth on a hot summer day connecting the chill to her neck, making it slip down her spine and burn her alive all at the same time.

Rivers of the Soul

by

Leslie Esdaile

Genesis, Press, Inc.

Indigo Sensuous Love Stories

are published by

Genesis Press, Inc.

315 Third Avenue North
Columbus, MS 39701

Rivers of the Soul

First Edition

Dedication

This book is dedicated to all those who said that "life ain't no crystal stairs"—but also reminded me to hang on, because "it was always darkest just before the dawn."

Those family griots, the parable keepers, the history collectors, the special women who held the torch of hope, and who are looking down on me from Heaven... they will always be the rivers of my soul:

My Mother, Helen Lena Thornton Peterson
My Aunt, Julia B. Peterson
And Julia's sister, my Aunt Hetti P. Jones
...and, of course both of my grandmothers.

Special Acknowledgements:

My deepest thanks to Dianne Miller and Mrs. Colom of Genesis Press for taking a chance on such a large project, and to Donna Hill for her encouragement, support, skill, and magic she shared in editing it! Also, my sincerest thanks go to my fellow sister-authors, Constance O'Day-Flannery, Diane McKinney-Whetstone, and Lorene Carey, for their friendship, support, and the refinement in the craft that I learned at their knees. Thanks, all, for being both patient and tough when it counted!

CHAPTER 1

Return to Philadelphia -- Day One

What was she doing here? She was thirty-seven, not seventeen, and definitely not supposed to be moving back home. Antoinette tried to chase away the mental demons that tortured her as she carefully walked up the icy front steps to cross the threshold to her new place in the world. She felt like Alice going through the looking glass. Everything was familiar, yet strange in so many ways. And everything had changed. Her independence was gone. Her husband was gone. Her finances were gone. Her figure was gone. Even her mother was gone.

Antoinette hesitated on the landing as self-confidence abandoned her again, just like her job and her husband had. She found herself peering at the reflection of an overweight, tired woman trapped within the frosted panes of the front door. What had happened, and why did it happen without warning? This was not who she had been ten years prior, when she seemed to have everything in the world going for her. Now, her tall brown form, with the additional bulk and layers from a heavy winter coat, made her want to run screaming into the street. But even a nervous breakdown was a luxury she couldn't afford, not with a four-and-a-half-year-old child to care for, and elderly parents to worry about.

She steadied herself and took a deep breath, bumping the sides of the building entrance with the overstuffed box as she made her way inside, and cursing the width of her hips in the process. Damn Brian Wellington, he'd promised to stay with her till death do you part.

The mover's question about where to situate her furniture felt like a slap in her face. How would she know where to put anything at the moment? This wasn't her split-level single home in Cherry Hill, New Jersey, with the manicured lawn. Nor did it have half the space she had become accustomed to. Everything would have to be squeezed and jockeyed into a workable position. Once they'd made their way to her unit, Antoinette glanced around the living room for a moment and let her breath out in a rush. Semi-dazed, she set down her load and took off her coat slowly, then wiped her hands on her sweat pants before running them through her hair.

The moving man gave her a look filled with agitation and repeated his question about the piece of furniture he was carrying. It seemed to take her too long to respond. She could tell his mood by the way he expelled a snort of annoyance—it was a sound that went well beyond sheer exertion as he dropped the heavy piece with a thud.

"I dunno," she murmured after a moment, "give me a minute." Even her once-executive brain was failing her. Each decision seemed to tax every mental faculty she could garner.

Adjusting the hair-scrunch that precariously held her shoulder-length ponytail, she stared back at the young moving man who assessed her like another heavy box to lift. Quickly making a mental note to buy a perm kit and a little rinse to chase away the gray, she studied the smooth dark face and flawless white smile that stood before her. She found herself wishing that she had at least worn some lipstick to preserve what was left of her feminine dignity.

The near-teenager simply shrugged and leaned against the wall as she thought about where to put the chair. Why his blasé non-response bothered her so, she couldn't determine. But, it did. Her only option was to force his casual gaze out of her head and to give him some instructions.

"Please set the Queen Anne in the living room," she said quietly, glimpsing how effortlessly he swept up the heavy piece, and noticing how the muscles in his back created a deep gorge as they narrowed into an invisible valley beneath his lifting belt. She was sure that this dark chocolate youth had a black man's sway back, that deep concave gully just before the muscles give rise to a firm, high, muscular butt. She closed her eyes briefly and turned away. Her girl-friends had been right; two years without a man was much too long. The kid before her was probably only twenty years old. Of course she looked like an overstuffed piece of furniture to him just like her ex-husband had once told her she would to any man.

"You got a nice spot, lady."

She didn't answer, ending the conversation by selecting a box to rummage through.

This wasn't home, or the place where her child-hood began and ended. Instead, it was a temporary bookmark in her life. This was just a place where she would bide her time until she figured out what to do next.

To avoid the hubbub that her friends were caus-ing as they talked cheerfully and moved about the condo with her stepmother and aunt, Antoinette mentally escaped through the window. She focused on the dull winter sky that felt like the color of her life, and forced herself to look away from the direc-tion of her father's home positioned just around the bend of the adjacent corner of the long block. The oppressive gray framed the barren trees. Each mature oak that lined the street below seemed to sway in unison as it creaked out its resistance to winter under the weight of glistening ice. Yes, she thought to herself, beautiful but harsh. She hated this time of year.

"Now isn't this just perfect, Toni? I mean, you and Lauren have all the space you two need, and the view of The City is wonderful," May said. "Plus, you're only around the corner from me and your father."

Her stepmother's voice chimed with an expectant tone as she began to unwrap and arrange Antoinette's paintings against the living room wall without asking Antoinette where she wanted the items placed. May stopped briefly to admire the view through the window, then went back to arranging the art. "I'm so glad that some of this awful snow is starting to go away. The City looks a mess after it has turned all brown and sloppy. But isn't this place wonderful?" she asked again, this time waiting for an answer.

"Just great, May," Antoinette returned flatly, pressing her hand against the cold glass pane and watching the fog around her palm fan out from the heat of it.

Okay, maybe she was still alive. Barely. Perhaps the walking dead. She was oddly surprised to find that her body still gave off perfunctory warmth, despite the hollow within it.

Deciding to busy herself with any task, instead of responding to what was bubbling inside of her,

5

Antoinette stepped away from the window and away from her momentary mental escape. She knew she would have to endure them all and talk to everyone sooner or later. She let out a deep sigh as she picked up the previously neglected box. "This was an answer to my prayers."

"Now, what's that supposed to mean?"

Instinctively, Antoinette forced a smile. With a grand sweeping gaze of the condo, she reluctantly lingered on the spaces that May was so proud of. The immaculate, newly-sanded hardwood floors, the fresh paint job May had ordered, the matching mauve drapes that May had custom made, and of course, the large bay-window that faced Center City. Today she hated mauve.

"Nothing. It's lovely," Antoinette muttered.

May eyed her suspiciously. "Not everybody gets to have the option to move into a place like this right after a divorce, especially when they don't have a job yet."

"May, I really do appreciate this." Common sense took over. Antoinette knew that May had detected a sheen of resentment in her tone, and had taken extreme exception to it.

"It's just great," Antoinette said, trying to sound deeply appreciative. "It's a lovely space, and a much better arrangement than me and Lauren moving in with you and Dad would have been. I mean, that would have crowded you newlyweds with my four-year-old just as your retirement fun was about to begin. This works much better. Thanks for allowing us to take over your condo."

She watched May's shoulders relax and her smile return brightly.

"I knew it from the beginning. That's why I told Matt this was how it had to be, and he needn't be here today. Not for this part, anyway. Decorating, and getting the cleaning done, is really women's work. Lauren needs a special environment, with her asthmatic condition, and you need to restart your life. In a month or two, when you begin paying rent, you won't have to bother about a security deposit, or getting the utilities turned on, and what have you, and your father and I will have a tenant in our property that we can trust. So, it's in everyone's best interest."

"It's a perfect solution. Better than crowding everyone into the old homestead." Antoinette would not allow her expression to change as she grabbed another box and turned away from May. "Yup. No sense in wallowing in self-pity, and looking at old high school pennants on the wall from a too small bed."

May laughed. "Oh, please. I had your room, and your sister's room redone six months ago. That old junk that was collecting dust would have been the least of your worries. But you're right. This is better."

Antoinette kept walking toward the hall closet although May's comment had nearly taken her breath while she was in mid-step.

"Re-did the room?" May's words trailed her down the narrow corridor and hovered over her, making it hard for her to breathe as the walls seemed to close in. She couldn't answer.

Yet, how could she blame May for redecorating? Any woman would have done that. How could May have known about the promises that her parents had made on her wedding day? That the tiny row house that she'd grown up in would always be home, that she could always return, and that she'd always be their baby no matter what. May hadn't been there then, nor could she ever understand how close they had all been. When her Mom died, it was the end of an era. Now a new queen resided where home used to be. There had been a changing of the guard.

Listening intently to the gaggle of female voices that emanated from the living room and kitchen where her friends Tracey, Val, and Cookie were working, Antoinette allowed her hand to reverently touch the taped seal on the large moving box before her. Although this one was unmarked, she knew its contents intimately. Where she had written on all the others with large visible print, this one had been left anonymous. Like Pandora's Box, it waited for her to summon the courage to break the seal on her past. It was the one that she had discretely taken from her stepmother and her Aunt Pearl's efficient hands, then hidden under piles of suitcases. It was the one that she didn't even want her friends to see.

No. This sarcophagus of buried hopes and plundered dreams required a solo evacuation. Stuffing the box into the bottom of the hall closet, she quietly closed the door on her past.

"Hey, T, you gonna help us get this place into shape, or what?"

She took a deep breath before answering her girlfriend Cookie's call. "Coming, coming, just trying to stuff as much into the closets as I can to get it out of the way for now."

Her Aunt Pearl had come into her secret hallway space, quietly moving behind her with the silence of a ghost before placing a supportive hand on her shoulder. Antoinette didn't start at the touch; somehow she had expected her Aunt to materialize. The gentle act didn't frighten her. It was Pearl's way, and she thanked God that her Aunt had heard her internal tears.

"Chile, that's no way to move in," Pearl said quietly, holding Antoinette's face between her arthritic hands as she moved in front of her. "You have to unpack and put things in their rightful place. Like you stayin' a while. Let go, and let God."

Antoinette just looked at her aunt and tried to smile before lowering her gaze to the floor. There was something strangely intimidating about looking into those kind bluish-brown eyes. Wisdom, and what felt like a hundred years of knowledge, emanated from a depth that went beyond their surface cataracts, making direct eye contact with her

9

Aunt Pearl too intense. Just a casual glimpse into them told her that they both knew the truth. She didn't want this.

"It's okay, baby... one day you'll be sure."

"Promise?"

"Promise."

Both women became very still as May approached. She ruptured their telepathy, fracturing the silent understanding that they shared, chasing away her Mother's spirit that always resided in those moments. And, as expected, May's response to being excluded from their quiet gathering in the hall was registered in the protest of her increasing gait. By the time she'd reached them, May had pulled her five-foot-one-inch frame up as tall as she could make it. Pointing her chin upward at them as she smoothed the front of her pink and green silk jogging suit, May was poised for battle.

"Regardless of Antoinette's lukewarm acceptance of this arrangement, and unless you think this move is temporary, Pearl-ine, and have a better option—my suggestion is that you stop babying her. I think this is a fair alternative, given the circumstances. Don't you?"

Her stepmother had obviously picked up the scent of their combined ambivalence. It was now going to be like fending off a Rottweiler.

Aunt Pearline just shook her head and moved toward the bedroom. On the surface, her aunt's demeanor hadn't changed, but Antoinette knew, just as May did, that May had better get out of Pearl's face. Fast.

"Temporary? It's all settled. Everything is fine," Antoinette said quickly, reading her aunt's unspoken closure on the subject.

"I would think so," May fussed in a testy voice, lingering where Pearline once stood. "Why in the world would we all be going through all of this trouble for you to just jump up again, without a plan, and irresponsibly wreak havoc in everyone's life? This has to be final. We've all had enough of your back-and-forth on this where-to-live issue."

For a moment Antoinette couldn't answer. She'd been attacked outright, all because she was sharing something special and unspoken with her aunt. She hated this contest, especially when May should have understood that it was futile to try to replace the affection she had for Pearline. If May would just back off, she'd give May her own new and different space to occupy within her heart. But never the same space. There were too many original bonds forged, rivers crossed, and too much water under the bridge. Just like moving into her parents' house and redecorating; it would still always be her mother's home.

Trying to steady herself before she spoke, Antoinette took a deep breath and stared at May. Common sense should have told the woman that a few brief years in her father's life could never eclipse the unconditional love and devotion her Aunt

Pearline showered on her. Ever. Just like nothing could suture the hole in her heart caused by having to give up her home and her marriage. It was all tied together in one complex ball of yarn. The emotions that ran through her were inexplicable. Why couldn't May just relent for once? Why couldn't she understand that moving in here meant that she'd lost two homes, not just one? Why couldn't she understand that Aunt Pearline was the only thing in her life that hadn't changed? And why in hell did she have to fight about that now!

Antoinette felt acid building on her tongue before she even spoke.

"No, May, this is permanent. I just want to get some order established before Lauren comes home. This move has been traumatic enough for my baby, and I don't want Lauren walking into her and Mommy's new place and having to step over boxes. Okay? So I pushed the ones that I don't have to unpack into the closets. I'll deal with it later. Aunt Pearl was just helping me. Period."

Upon hearing Antoinette's words, Pearline stopped, turned and re-entered the hall. Antoinette cringed inwardly as she stood between the two very formidable women. One tall and brown, one short and yellow; a show down was in the offing, and she knew that her aunt wasn't about to have a child of hers defend any position on her behalf. Aunt Pearline was well accustomed to speaking for herself, which meant May was on very thin ice, and way out of her league to mess in Pearline's private talks like this. Antoinette held her breath.

"Hey, Toni, where d' you want these canisters?" Valerie's gaze darted nervously between the three women hovering in the hallway as she rushed up and threaded an arm around Antoinette's waist, guiding her toward the kitchen. "I thought they would look pretty up on the counter top. You always keep your kitchen so nice. My house is always a pigsty. We'll have you back in business in no time."

"Did you hear the way she spoke to me, Pearline?" May's voice had become shrill. "I think Antoinette needs therapy, or something, for that repressed anger. I certainly didn't cause her life to turn out this way."

Antoinette could hear her stepmother's voice trail off as she walked forcibly down the hall. It was with no small measure of satisfaction that her Aunt only grunted a response. But now in the center of the action, the kitchen, she knew she would probably have to come between Cookie and Val. She assumed that was why Val had come to get her before Val lost her Mother-Earth charm and slapped Cookie. Obviously, Tracey-the-peacemaker, had given up her position, and was no longer able to keep Cookie and Val at bay. It had been that way for years. At least there was another constant in her life she could depend on.

Antoinette let out her breath slowly as she watched her two friends take their positions in her new kitchen. The stakes on this bout of who was the better friend were high, but at the moment she was so tired that she could barely stand. Refereeing this match was out of the question. The move alone, and the emotions that went with it, were draining enough. Now this?

Holding court, as usual, Cookie was knee deep in rhetoric by the time she and Val grabbed and opened another box. Perched on a kitchen stool, Cookie had one hand on her hip and a cigarette dangling between two perfectly manicured red talons. Antoinette watched as Val raced to put a paper cup beneath the ash that was about to drop in the sink, while a smile widened on Cookie's gaunt, brown face and Tracey cringed. Adjusting her stylish animal print head scarf, Cookie took another drag and dropped the butt in the sink, purposely missing the cup. Both Antoinette and Tracey sighed and exchanged a weary glance as Val set the paper cup down very precisely and tightened the rubber band that held back her clay-red, all natural Nubian locks, then moved away quietly to unpack a box sitting at the edge of the kitchen.

"Hey, lady. Where you want the bed?"

The sudden male voice and question jarred Antoinette, and she looked up quickly at the movers, drawing an exhausted breath before speaking.

"In the bedroom, I guess?" Antoinette stared at the two movers trying to jockey her king-sized bed past the kitchen arch and down the narrow hall, hoping that they wouldn't nick the fresh paint job.

The head mover grunted and dropped his end of the mattress. "I mean, what position? We're on the clock and only moving this monster once. Do you want it on the wall, facing the window, or what, lady?"

"It doesn't matter."

The two men let out a disgusted breath in unison.

"Put it against the window," May said with authority as she re-entered the hall, "so she can get a good dose of morning sun. Maybe that will improve her mood."

"In front of the window?" Cookie took a swig of beer and shook her head in defiance. "She's a bachelorette. Can't have all her bizness up in no dang window. Pulleeeze, May!"

"Cookie, please," Tracey murmured, going to find a box to occupy her.

"I'm not going to dignify that." Clearly disgusted, May huffed toward the back of the condo, motioning for the men to follow her.

"It doesn't matter," Antoinette said again firmly when the men didn't follow May.

"We ain't moving this till y'all decide. Drop your end, man."

The other end of the mattress hit the floor with a thud, and both men leaned against the wall for a moment until May's evil-eye grit made them stand away from the new paint job that she had been viciously protecting during the entire move.

"Look," Valerie said, her line of vision darting between Antoinette, Tracey, and Cookie then back to the movers, "this is Toni's space. We've been putting things up all afternoon, and nobody has really asked Toni where she wants any of it. Just give her a minute to decide."

Cookie looked up from her beer, and sucked her teeth. "She said it didn't matter, Val. Why are you always reading too much into everything? If you had a job, and didn't just do this full-time Mommy thing, you would understand about time and money. The chile is on a deadline. We gotta get this joint ship-shape before Lauren gets back here Sunday night. The girl don't care where the bed is going, cause that bed ain't seen, and knowing T, ain't gonna see, no action for a while. So she might as well put it by the window."

"What has my not working outside of the home got to do with me trying to be sensitive to Toni's needs, Cookie?"

"This is not the time, Cook," Tracey's voice pleaded. "C'mon, gurl." Tracey's wide brown eyes held a combination of anger and pity, and she positioned her petite, T-shirt and jeans clad form between Cookie and Val as she smoothed her freshly permed curls behind her ear.

The head mover looked at his watch. "Ladies, can we do this later, and just decide where this last big piece is going?"

"Want a beer, Val?" Tracey inched past the movers and went toward the refrigerator, making a wide-berth slice between Val and Cookie. When Valerie didn't respond, Tracey got two cold ones from the fridge, handed Valerie one and issued a warning glare at Cookie. "There's no need to argue about it. We can help her move the bed later if she doesn't like where it's set today. No problem."

"Are you crazy, Trace?" Valerie put down her beer and tucked one stray lock behind her cowry shell-laden ear. "The bed weighs a ton, and we'd have to move the dresser and armoire and everything else in the room. Toni has to decide, it's her room, her environment, and we haven't asked her anything all day."

"Well, at least we agree on something. And, yes, it does matter where the bed is put, which is what this whole decision is about, y'all," Cookie shot back, giving Valerie a sideways glance as she took a deep swig of beer.

"Well I wish one of y'all ladies would tell us where the bed is going, before we move it."

Antoinette looked at the movers and at her all female crew. "Put it next to the wall."

"Not the wall that adjoins the baby's room, guys," Cookie chuckled, appearing considerably mollified. "See, my girl has some sense left."

When the movers didn't respond and just picked up the mattress on the count of three, the potential combatants dispersed. Antoinette closed her eyes briefly and opened them, then looked around the ready-made condo. Almost everything was set in place. A place. Someplace. An efficient place. But nowhere that she would have put it.

Flanking Valerie, Tracey went to the far side of the room to finish unpacking the fine china, her Mother's treasures, and anything else that didn't have to go into the kitchen. The lines in the sand were drawn. The older women were in the back, working on the baby's room and her bedroom separately. Val and Tracey were working in the living room. That left her and Cookie to do the kitchen.

Time was wearing a hole in Antoinette's brain.

"Would somebody tell Valerie how to clean out a drawer before she puts the silverware in there?" Cookie hollered into the pass-thru between the kitchen and living room. "Although it might take a whole village to raise one child, I told you that you didn't need a whole tribe to move you in, Toni, just a few close friends because everybody does things differently."

"Look, Cookie, just because I got married early and my house isn't a museum, doesn't mean I don't know how to clean out a damned drawer." Valerie's oval cafe-au-lait face went beet-red, and she almost slapped herself with a rag as she slung it over her shoulder. Then tugging at her silver bangles, she pushed them up her wrist hard and folded her arms over her chest.

Cookie stared at Valerie for a moment then let out a howl of laughter. "Aw, sookie, sookie, now. The chile is gettin' serious. Let me shut up. I was just playin'." Turning on her heel, Valerie huffed past them. "I'll do the bathroom, Toni. Someone has to arrange your linen closet and put up some art or something in there."

Antoinette closed her eyes and rubbed her temples.

"Toni, what do you want us to do with all of your insurance sales awards? Do you want them on the wall over your roll-top desk in the living room?"

Antoinette shook her head without opening her eyes. Tracey's voice seemed so furtive. "No. Leave them in the box, I'll put them away in the closet."

"You can't do that! Cookie, talk to her." Tracey sounded appalled, and she walked back into the kitchen with the box in her arms, presenting the evidence. "You worked too hard for these awards. Just because Brian didn't appreciate your success doesn't mean that you shouldn't be proud of who you are."

"Were," Antoinette said flatly. She didn't want to discuss it, or think about the main contributing cause to the failure of her marriage. Success.

"Tracey, please, that was a long time ago." Antoinette could feel her voice quavering with emotion. She knew it; she should have moved in alone.

"See, Trace, you and Val are cut from the same piece of cloth." Cookie sucked her teeth hard and rolled her eyes upward as she passed by Tracey on the way to get another beer. "The girl is trying to restart her life. Any man that walks in here, seeing that she was a super-duper-sales-officionado, will first of all be intimidated, which means, no play, no nookie; successful women make their dicks limp. Second of all, they'll think our girl still has her long-bread job, and maybe try to work her. And Lord knows, T is naive about man-shit. She thinks that there is some good lurking about in every stray dog that comes by. Third of all, it ain't nobody's business. I understand my girl. She might be a dreamer about this Mr. Right thing, but she ain't as crazy as y'all make her out to be."

"You're just jealous because she has something to put on her walls, Cookie. And a very nice place to hang it." Tracey's expression was deadly, and her even, dark brown complexion soon offered a hint of red beneath it as she stood her ground and challenged Cookie.

"What, heifer? Jealous of Toni, and her situation?"

"Yeah. You have your own consulting business, Cook," Tracey quipped with icy defiance, setting the box down on the counter hard before making imaginary quotes in the air with her fingers as she spoke. "But I dare say it never earned what T used to make—and will make again—when she gets herself together. And at least Brian takes care of his kid." Heaving the grievous box into her arms again,

Tracey thrust her chin in the air as though to dare Cookie to respond.

"Are you speaking for Toni, or yourself? My consulting firm is doing very well, thank you. At least I had the presence of mind to stow away my own stash before Doug walked. The ex-men in my life don't have to take care of my kids. I can. What could you or Val do if your husbands walk? Not jack! And I didn't have to come home on a humble-beat to take no family bull because I didn't have enough to live on myself." Cookie cast a disparaging glance around the condo. "She couldn't have done this alone. Get real. Unlike you, I didn't go out looking for Mr. Goodbar every Friday night, praying that some knight on a white charger would save me, and marry me, and make some babies for me—like you and Val wasted time doing—only to wind up with the likes of Scoop and Buddy. I've always dealt with professional brothers. Mine come steady, regular, and they don't get no romance without the finance. Dig?"

This time, Antoinette visibly flinched as Tracey's eyes filled with moisture. She had promised herself that she would not referee any bouts today, but Cookie had gone too far, and Tracey was too wounded for her to stand by and not jump into Cookie's world.

"Back off, Cook. It has nothing to do with getting play, a man, men, or anything else. Okay? That was unnecessary. It has to do with the fact that I

21

don't need to be reminded that I put ten years into that insurance company, gave it my all, and when my daughter was born and went into the hospital for repeated asthma attacks as an infant, they laid me off. I don't want to think about how I stayed at home with my daughter for the first two years of her life, and Brian and I fought like cats and dogs over money, bills, just everything imaginable. Then Brian and I split up. After all I had done. After playing by the rules. After all of the sales records that I had busted for the region, I was still expendable then, just like I became expendable as a wife. Got it. Now, put the damned million-dollar-circle plaques in the closet, Tracey. That part of my life is over. I'm just a mom. Both of you drop it."

Tracey looked like she had been punched, and stood paralyzed with the box clutched against her chest. Antoinette walked over to their stunned comrade to help her with her disorientation, as much as to help her find a suitable place to store the subject of the debate. "You need to chill, Cookie. This move was a hard one."

Tracey's accusatory glare contained more than anger. Antoinette could see that it also included gall over Cookie's breach of trust. She'd known that they'd probably discussed her situation, ad nauseum. But, in keeping with the way things had always been handled when one of them had a problem, that reality was to have always remained an unspoken fact. It went with the package of their friendship. To have it tossed in her face was unforgivable. For now, she'd have to let it drop.

Strain made the beer in Antoinette's stomach feel like lava as it climbed back up her esophagus. The muscles in her neck and shoulders coiled into thick ropes until they began to throb. "I'm just tired, ladies. Tired of all of this crap... especially when..." Antoinette let her voice trail off. There was nothing else to say. Nothing further that she wanted to discuss.

Antoinette finished her beer to quell the building indigestion and held up her hand when Cookie took another breath as if to speak. She hadn't wanted to hear any derisive comments about anyone today, not even her ex-husband, his latest girlfriend, or her own stupidity for staying in a doomed marriage for so long. She didn't want anyone to argue about anything, or give her grief about anything. Her nervous system couldn't handle it. She didn't want to think about being a thirty-seven year old, ex-middle manager caught in corporate purgatory with a dwindling severance package, a four-year-old daughter, stretch marks and extra flab around her mid-section. She didn't want to hear it. Instinct and corporate practice had created the mask. She could be whatever she needed to be just long enough to get them to leave. Tough. Aggressive. Together. Sure. The problem was, that at this moment, she was none of those things. Which was exactly why she couldn't afford to let them see the tears that were blurring her vision now. Her mask was in severe jeopardy.

"Let it rest, Cook," Valerie said, moving to Antoinette's side and guiding her from the kitchen. Stopping briefly in the hallway as the movers passed, she looked up and gave them the last of the day's orders before turning back to Antoinette. "You know that grieving is not allowed in Cookie's or May's book— not for survivors who have caught their husband in the act. Don't blame Tracey, either. She has always wanted to be like you, or what she thought you were. Successful, upwardly mobile, and living in a nice house. OPP, girl. Other people's problems. You can't really blame any of them, even if they get on your nerves, right?"

Antoinette looked at her friend's warm smile and appreciated the tenderness offered. "I guess not, but what if Cookie's right? Maybe it is time for me to wake up and smell the coffee."

"That's right. No second thoughts. Not for strong, educated, feminist black women. Not for sistahs of the struggle who had read and seen *Waiting to Exhale*." Valerie's voice had become conspiratorial and mischievous as her smile widened. "Nor is crying over some no-good man to be tolerated. Even Pearline and Trace can't deal with that. Not when you've beaten him in court because he still has a high-profile job, which makes him vulnerable to spousal support to go along with child support. Never mind that he loves that child, and would have paid anyway. Never mind that he's offered a lot of concessions without having his arm legally twisted. Such talk of the bad-guy having some good qualities is sheer heresy. Today is supposed to be a time of vindication, rejoicing, of victory, of high-five, you go, girl solidarity! Get with the program."

"Then why do I feel like crying?" Antoinette smiled. She couldn't help it with Valerie's infectious grin two inches from her face.

"Because it's over." Valerie's expression remained tender as she peered at Antoinette. "So look, just be patient, and we'll be outta here soon. Then you can grieve for real, and cry, and wail because, God knows, if Buddy and I ever broke up, and my household fell apart, that's just what I'd do. No matter who was right or wrong."

She looked at Val for a long time, noticing a flicker of fear mixed in with the empathy that shone back at her. Two big tears forced themselves over the edges of Antoinette's lashes and she wiped them away quickly, shooting her gaze past Valerie toward the kitchen, then toward the bedrooms where the others furiously worked on getting her settled. "I don't want them to see me like this. He was wrong. I was wrong, at times, too, but I never wanted to be divorced." She swallowed hard as Valerie touched her face. "Why do things have to change?"

"Cookie isn't married anymore. She's still dating and doing wine-and-brie weekends of lust and romance after a Luther Vandross concert with a vengeance. Tracey's old man drinks and kicks her ass, did from day one. She never had anything close to what you and Brian had at one point, so she thinks today is your freedom move, and that you should be jumping for joy. A totally dysfunctional scene.

"And what can Cookie tell you after she blazed through a two year, in-name-only marriage, and had a baby when they never even had a joint bank account? Then she had a baby for some other wanna-be-millionaire who left her high and dry. Her kids are almost grown—and about to leave her, so she's got time to play. How's she supposed to trust after that? May and Pearl are from a different era. Your sister, Adrienne, is ten years your junior and not even on the same page. That's why Adrienne thought you had enough help today, because the girl is clueless about the impact of this move. Her thing was, she can't deal with May, but we could. Figured you had a big enough labor force to get the job done. Kid stuff, okay? Consider the sources. You, like me, were a lifer. We expected to be one like your Mom, to get thirty good years or more with the man you loved. So, if you go back to Brian, I'd be the last one to call you crazy. I'd understand."

She'd listened to Valerie's words intently, noticing that her dear friend had never answered her question about change, noticing that the fear in her eyes was now becoming clearly visible.

"I don't know if I can go back, Val. There was just too much disrespect, too much competition. He was too threatened by my success. But for Lauren, I would walk through hell. Now, it's too late. I called his bluff, divorced him, and he has a fiancée. A fiancée!"

"Come on," Val said quietly, moving her toward the bathroom. "It's all too fresh, and much too early to tell. You all might get back together, who knows? Some people divorce and remarry. He just needs to grow up. That so-called fiancée might just be a bluff to get you back. Say what you want, Brian still loves you."

Antoinette didn't respond to Valerie's hopefulness. She was too weary. She let her friend lead her down the hall to the bathroom, where she could wash her face and sit on the side of the tub while numbly watching Val's meticulous ordering of things. It was a good compromise. She'd be away from Cookie's glaring truths, Tracey's obsession with fighting know-it-all Cookie's stance, and she wouldn't have to collide with May and Pearl, who had found an uneasy truce by each working in a separate bedroom. She knew that she could get through another couple of hours, if she just tried hard enough, if she just focused on the task at hand. Unpack. Everything. Grieve later.

CHAPTER 2

Time passed in slow, excruciating motion as she waited for the older women in the crew to tire first and finish their tea, then for her S.W.A.T. team of girlfriends to ultimately smoke the last of their cigarettes and polish off their beers. She'd made sure she had waved cheerfully to everyone as they left her, offering hollow promises to come by or contact them in the morning. It was both an unspoken thank you, and a way to get them to leave her for her first night alone. Whatever mask they had required in order to believe that she was okay, any face they'd needed to see in order to get them to give her the private space she'd worn—all day long, until now.

Alone, at last, with her four-year-old safely stowed at her cousin's house and shielded from the trauma of the move, this final good-bye was a solo mission. A private purging, just as the end of her marriage had been a dignified private burial. Tucking her legs beneath her, Antoinette adjusted herself on the freshly mopped hardwood hall floor, and glanced around the condo one last time before yielding to the quiet whisper within the box and within her heart. Carefully retrieving it from the closet, for a moment, all she could do was stare at it.

An over-ripe tear hit the top of the tomb creating a large stain that darkened as it soaked into the cardboard. She traced the fallen tear and closed her eyes, remembering how she had packed the contents. Her wedding dress and veil were at the bottom, held in-state within vacuum sealed plastic. On top of it was her wedding photo album, exquisitely covered with antique white lace splattered with seed pearls that her Aunt had lovingly sewn on by hand. It contained one pristine, gold-monogrammed invitation. It was what she and her mother had joyously selected together. It was a memento of their last laughs together, their last private women's lunch together, along with the fragile parchment wedding program that hosted God's Cross on the front, and the 1 Corinthians 13 pledge of everlasting love within it. "Love is not spiteful, is not puffed up. . . rejoiceth not in unfairness. . . and of faith, hope, and love, the greatest of these is love."

Antoinette's breathing became labored as she realized that the most painful relic would necessarily greet her as she peeled away the surface tape on the box. Her childhood photo album would be on top of everything inside. She knew that memories would collide with memories until she couldn't bear it. But the need for catharsis drew her to it anyway.

Her hands trembled slightly as she peeled away the tape and lifted out the heavy book. Taking another deep breath to steady herself, she opened the deep burgundy cover and looked at the first page. A young girl in her teens stared back at her with a bevy of close companions squeezed into the shot and hanging on each other's shoulders in Fairmount Park at Belmont Plateau. The Crew. They had withstood the test of time. Babies, men, marriages, miscarriages, broken relationships, divorces, pap smear results and mammogram outcomes, new jobs, promotions, lay-offs, and the deaths of some of their parents. For richer, for poorer. In sickness, and in health... for all the days of their lives. That was the only thing that hadn't changed.

Antoinette focused on each bright face, remembering the dreams and fears that they had shared daily at the lunch table of their all-girls high school. She also remembered their goals and the things that they'd planned to accomplish during their lives. They all looked so young, so determined, so capable. Antoinette felt a smile come out of hiding. They'd had some wild days together.

Cookie stood front and center in the picture, and Antoinette touched her friend's face gently with the tip of her finger. "Girl you had it all goin' on, with your skinny, sexy self. Were gonna be the first one to get on the cover of *Black Enterprise Magazine*. Damn, girl, what happened? No wonder you're so angry. You were smarter than all of us–and worked the hardest. Got out of the projects, graduated college with honors and did it by yourself."

Hell, Valerie had a degree from Temple's Tyler School of Art, but had never gotten a shot at being the painter she wanted to be, despite the depth of her talent. A sudden and necessary marriage, along with a house full of kids, had eclipsed any dreams. Antoinette allowed a quick memory to wash over her as she thought about Valerie's middle-class Mount Airy parents, and their reaction to their daughter having to get married to someone other than a doctor or dentist, then banished it.

She let her fingers rove over Tracey's dancer-form image that posed next to Valerie's. Luminous brown eyes filled her friend's delicate almond-shaped face. Tiny, cute, and full of life, then—only to now be transformed into a harried woman with a crazy husband, and stuck in a dead-end collections agent job. "God, Trace... you should have been on Broadway by now." Antoinette closed her eyes for a moment. There was no one to blame—really. Tracey's parents had thought they were doing the right thing, sending her to every bogus modeling school posted on the predatory neighborhood billboards in Philadelphia, wasting money on headshots, and never pressing the academics or a college route. Their daughter had talent, and she was gonna be their star. Tracey was going to fulfill the hopes, dreams, and financial security that they hadn't been able to attain in their own lives. "God bless 'em," she whispered, "that's all they had to give you, Trace."

In the photo on Cookie's right, stood Francis, another business directed woman-on-a-mission. Her guidance was solid, and college had been paid for by fourth generation college graduated parents that Francis couldn't stand. So, her friend had left them all, escaping below the Mason Dixon line to go to school in Georgia. She wondered how Francis was doing, though. It had been a long time since they'd talked—really talked. Then, came Antoinette, standing on the end.

She studied Francis' warm, ebullient smile for a long time. Francis was a perfect fit for the highbred Atlanta society she now occupied. "At least Spellman did you well, hon. Too bad the Southern men didn't. But at least you got your own job place-ment firm out of the deal... and that precious Camille. We can't have everything, can we?" She murmured in question to her friend inabstentia, continuing to wonder how the one crew member that none of them had talked with in too long was faring?

Convincing herself that Francis was all right, and landing somewhere on her feet as usual,

Antoinette flipped the page without really looking at her own image in the shot. She made a mental note to call Francis and debrief her later. Much later.

Antoinette flipped another page expectantly, looking for a clue to who she had been. This time her image in a party scene photo stared back at her, and she wondered what that girl would have thought if she could see herself now? What would that young woman-child who wore a skin-tight, silver tube-top, sporting a giant Afro think if she saw this figure? she wondered, abruptly flipping passt-what used to be one of her favorite pictures.

But the image haunted her as she stared at the next photo. Then, her figure was hour-glass voluptuous. If memory served her right, she'd had a twenty-four inch waist, thirty-eight inch hips, and a bosom to match. In the day, she'd stopped traffic with regularity. Antoinette sighed and turned another page. Her stats were nowhere near those brick-house proportions now, and she couldn't even blame the change on having her daughter. No, in all honesty, childbirth had not been the issue, depression eating, and obsessive cooking, had. But, she had also wanted a good marriage full of boisterous, lively children, a home like Valerie's home; not a middle-class, yuppie house in the suburbs without abiding affection, like she'd had. She'd wanted a soulmate, not a husband. But, they'd all had dreams that hadn't come true, so who was she to throw a pity-party now? Perhaps May had a point. Not everybody crash-landed out of a marriage into this kind of safe haven. At least she had a roof over her head and people who cared about her.

Allowing faces to blend with memories, she strolled through her past listening to street traffic in the distance. The approaching sounds of night in the city were so different from her quiet, tree-lined past. Here, people cussed out loud, sirens became regular background noise, and students yelled at the tops of their lungs till all hours. It seemed that even the city had become something new to her, and it definitely had no space for her to fit in now.

The combination of the pictures clashed against the new sounds of her place of origin, making her feel like a displaced citizen.

As dusk began to eclipse the last of the sun's gray filter, she didn't bother to get up from the floor to turn on the ceiling light. The cloak of semi-darkness was comforting. She closed her eyes briefly and let the moisture dampen her lashes. Memories of her mother edged into her awareness with the approaching dusk. Mom. Fifty-four. Maybe she had seventeen good years left before she too would be consumed with fast-moving cancer like her mother had been... her best friend, and the most missed presence at the gathering of women today. She opened her eyes and steeled herself as she flipped the page, only to be confronted by a tuxedo-wearing ghost from her prom.

"Dear, God, it's Jerome Henderson," she whispered with reverence. The new awareness made her finally stand and go over to flip on the overhead light switch. Her chest felt tight as she gazed at the handsome face and warm smile. Leaning against the wall, she laughed out loud. "Look at that Afro! Oh, my God." Twenty years of time truncated instantly. He'd wanted to fly, go into the Air Force, then own his own chartered flight company... a Cesna or something, he'd told her once. Odd, but she couldn't remember, and she wondered what his life was like now? Sure, there were rumblings about Jerome and his wife having problems, but who had a perfect marriage?

The thought made Antoinette pause. Things had changed. She'd been steeped in denial while looking at the photos. Ever since she and Jerome broke up, the configuration of friendships had changed. Jerome and his new wife probably went with her friends, and their personal dramas unfolded in that safe haven. It was no different than what happened to her when she'd married. Soon Brian's friendships, and the wives that went with them, became the place where she'd interacted more than with even her home-girls. They'd probably gravitated to new social circles where there was common ground. Surely, she hadn't called Valerie to baby sit Lauren, because Val was a state away. The same held true for conversations, and career advice, and discussions about marital difficulties, which were mostly held within the new circles. Antoinette slowly covered her mouth with her hand. The old friendships hadn't been nurtured, and had become like extended family, people one saw occasionally once or twice a year. The awareness was staggering as she continued to stare at Jerome's photo. Her girls had responded to her emergency call to finally leave Jersey—based on history—but real talks about what was going on, day to day, had broken down. Did any of them really know each other like they once did? And Jerome... what did she really know about him?

After seventy-seven, they'd lost touch. But, she clearly remembered the way they'd met in the park during The Sons of Italy Walk-A-Thon for the March of Dimes. Every school had come out for the annual event in nineteen-seventy-six; The Bicentennial. Now looking at all the pictures was like looking at someone else's existence. Viewing her life in still Kodak moments was becoming an eerie out-of-body experience.

Antoinette turned the pages quickly, hoping that she had preserved another glimpse of the precious ebbing memories. She found him again several pages later, and smiled broadly at the bittersweet reward to her senses. Standing six feet three inches worth of fine in his high school, Penn Relays jogging suit, donning a mega Afro, wearing mirror aviator sunglasses—the sun reflecting off the silver lenses—and his high, chiseled cheekbones. They called him Reds. She remembered as their song popped instantly into her brain. Reasons, by Earth, Wind, and Fire. She hummed the melody with her eyes closed. "Yeah, that was it. He wanted to fly… and all the reasons disappeared."

A mental valve opened until everything her mind could scavenge about her first love poured out. The way he'd held her hand in public, unashamed of being claimed as a boyfriend. He was cool, but not phony with his vibe. Honest was more the word, and he'd made it his business to let people know that she was his lady, not just his woman. Pretty progressive in those days, she thought, as the easy memory made her chuckle. It all came back to her. Hanging on the steps in front of her parents' home, up at The Plateau, going to proms, the way they'd partied the paint off the walls in the basement, the way he always called her Princess when he looked into her eyes. Their first kiss, his urgent whispers on the basement sofa… and her first time. The way he'd asked her to marry him, and their pledge to wait for each other until she got out of school. "God, J, you were so fine."

Antoinette closed the album and walked into the kitchen, casting it aside on the counter. It had become unnecessary torture. What was the point? The last she'd heard from the grapevine, Jerome was solidly married, had four little kids, and a good-paying job in construction. He'd even been on the team that built The Convention Center or something like that. That's all she knew about this person who'd been such an important part of her life. Sure, her girlfriends had made occasional passing mention of the fact that his marriage was like theirs—troubled at times. But, again, what did that mean? Everybody's marriage was troubled.

When her marriage was crumbling, she'd made it a point to never ask about him, especially after time wore on. At first they'd ask her if she'd ever heard from Jerome again, and it had become obvious that the circles of friendships didn't intersect any longer. Their husbands spent about as much time with Jerome as she did with her girlfriends, not much. Any news they had to carry about him was probably pure speculation, she'd reasoned then. So, she hadn't wanted to hear about it during her own time of crisis.

Odd, now that she thought about it. All of her girlfriends seemed to know that the topic was taboo, and if it were broached, that was the only time she would turn really surly with them. Even Cookie backed off that one. It didn't matter anyway.

Besides, he was the married-forever-till-death-do-us-part kind. She didn't need to know where he was, and had missed the chance to be his forever a long time ago. She had chosen to go to school like her father told her to, and not to marry Jerome like he'd begged her to. Case closed. She had found an upper middle-class man, married him like her father wanted her to, and everybody was happy. Thank

God her mother had died long before the divorce.

There was no need to dredge her soul any more, she'd found the bodies. She didn't have to go through pictures of her ex-husband in his youth to see their incarnation during the college days, or to see the ex-Wellington family frozen in effigy during her wedding, especially not Mom Wellington—her second mother—her most cherished blessing, other than Lauren, that had come with the marriage. Now, Mom Wellington seemed as far away from her as her own natural mother did. Not because either of them wanted it that way, but just because it was time for them to move on. She missed her wisdom, her hugs, her Thanksgiving dinners. . . their private talks in the kitchen. . . the older woman's sense of knowing. It was time to close the album. It was also time to admit that her father wasn't the sole reason she'd decided not to marry Jerome, and to go with Brian instead. She'd made her bed, and she'd lain down in it for as long as she could.

As she began putting the memories away, it dawned on her that she wasn't sure of anything any longer. It was a frightening realization to admit that all of her past decisions and accomplishments were now being questioned by her own mind. That had always been the one thing she could count on: her own decision-making process. Now, she wasn't sure whether her decision to marry had been the right choice, her decision to divorce had been the right move at the right time. The choice of leaving

Jerome when she did seemed murky at best, and even her decisions about school and career choices seemed to swirl upon a sea of 'what ifs.'

But, what would have happened if each of them had followed their own dreams instead of doing what their families had expected? The question nagged at her insides. They had all probably paid a severe and personal price for going along with the program, so what could have been a worse outcome for doing things differently?

Antoinette allowed a deep exhale to answer the question for her. There was no perfect path or right road. She was a woman, and life, she assumed, just was not destined to be fair. If she'd chosen to be other than she had been, her reputation would have been at stake, her parents would have been in a lather, she would have still been financially strapped, she still might have had a baby to care for without an alimony check, and all hell would have eventually broken loose. But, at least she would have tried and failed on her own terms. She quickly banished that thought. It was too dangerous to consider at this juncture.

A deep chuckle found itself rising within her that felt like sudden hysteria. Now was not the time to be entering into a mid-life crisis, she more firmly told herself, as she chased the lurid thought of total freedom away from her being. She was black, female, and in America. Get real. But the one thing that kept sticking in her mind and in her craw was, why did all of her decisions revolve around what the men in her life wanted or did? Her father, Jerome, Brian, her bosses. When could a woman do what she wanted to do, without facing serious consequences? Was it like that for all women?

"Perish the thought," she murmured, as she more decisively put away her box of memories. The next issue was upon her without time to digest all of the rot that still needed mental review. So what that life wasn't fair. Had it ever been? She still had to find financial security without dependence on anyone but herself. That too had always been the case. In that regard, nothing much had changed. On Sunday, she'd buy a newspaper and start looking for a job again. She needed a plan. Motion. Money. Her own money. She could do this—now that she was back in Philly—just like she did it while living in marital limbo a state away.

She'd held herself together for the two-year separation by working as a substitute teacher, a jack-leg consultant, and doing sales temp work at small independent insurance companies. That's what she had to do now—piece together a string of little jobs that could provide her enough flexibility to be a mom with a sick child, and cover the most important bills. Utilities and the credit card bills would have to wait. Brian was not going to win this by starving her out, making her give in to being married to a man who thought it was his birthright to wander. That's all she'd wanted to get him to see. He couldn't wander, couldn't just roll in at all hours of the night, couldn't bleed their joint bank accounts to chase entrepreneurial dreams without it being a joint decision, and that she deserved to be respected.

Crisis was supposed to create opportunity. Funny, Jerome had told her that once. A man. She shook her head. Yeah, this was definitely a crisis. Yet, it was Pearline and her Mom who had told her, "God bless the child that has her own." Male-rhetorical logic versus female life-based wisdom. She needed her own. It was settled. She was a survivor. That much she also remembered.

Hunger tore at Antoinette's insides as she ransacked the half-empty cabinets. Damn, everything was in a can or frozen, but a delivered cheese steak could work. At least there was one thing in Philly that hadn't changed.

∞

Jerome Henderson looked up at the darkening sky, and he leaned his cement-breaking equipment against a stack of cinderblocks. The vibrations from the jack-hammer he'd cast aside still resonated in his bones as he wiped his brow with the back of his hand. He could feel grit fuse with his sweat as particles of earth and rock bit into his skin.

Damn the cold, and damn this airport job. He trained his gaze toward an ascending plane in the distance and imagined what it would feel like to lift off from the ground and fly away with that much engine power in one's hands?

So, Karen wanted a divorce... How and when had it come to this? Confusion clawed at his brain. Was she bluffing when she'd thrown out the comment when he was on his way to work? Was this another one of her in-house games to mess with his head, or what? But, if she was serious, then that meant he had to get serious. He had to find a lawyer, a place to live; and what about his kids? Where could he go to get some good advice about what to do anyway? His father? Karen's friends' husbands? His co-workers?

Jerome let out a long breath of disgust. His old friends, Buddy and Scoop, sure couldn't help him. Hell, they were all in the same boat, married to women that got on their nerves, and they were as trapped as he was. They hadn't found a way out either. But they all loved their kids, and took care of the bills. They did what they were supposed to do, as men. That's what he had to keep doing.

He struggled to focus on reality. "If wishes were fishes," he muttered, casting an appreciative gaze at the aircraft as it got smaller and smaller against the horizon, watching it become tiny then disappear from his view. Dreams.

But, what if she was serious? Buddy and Scoop had probably been through this crap, he guessed, and they were still married. They were still there for their kids. Anyway, the subject of daily arguments and power struggles didn't even come up in their conversations any longer, not that he and his home-boys saw that much of each other any more. Every brother he knew had the same answer to the question asked over a beer at the bar, "So, how you hanging, man?"

"Same old, same old," Jerome whispered, swallowing away both anger and hurt at the same time, and looking at his construction crew. He glanced at his watch. Quitting time was approaching as the sky gave way to blue-black night.

No, she had to be bluffing.

CHAPTER 3

"Sixteen hours workin' like a mule. Kiss my natural ass!" Jerome rested his head on the steering wheel of his Ford Bronco before starting the engine. Grime and sweat clung to his hands and the dust from blasted cement still made his lungs hurt.

Sitting up slowly, he reached into the breast pocket of his Eagles jacket and pulled out a box of Marlboro Lights. Eleven-thirty p.m. was too early to go home to deal with Karen. Not tonight. He'd worked too hard and didn't need to hear the mess. Flicking the lighter, he stared at the flame for a moment before bringing the tip of his cigarette to it. Hell, he was already at the airport for the job, what could it hurt to swing through West Philly for a drink? Couldn't a man go get a drink and look up his boys?

Cranking the engine, the Bronco almost drove itself. Some mysterious force seemed to pull at him, making the four-by-four turn off at the University City exit instead of Lincoln Drive. That was a good one—a mysterious force. He'd have to remember to tell Karen that yang when she threw a lamp at him. Chuckling to himself, he pressed down harder on the accelerator. What did it matter, he'd been sleeping on the sofa on and off for almost seven months anyway?

Before he knew it, he was negotiating the iced trolley tracks on Baltimore Avenue. When the sign for The Third World Lounge on forty-eighth came into view, he laughed. Yeah, he was gonna be in trouble anyway, so what the hell!

Parking in a tow-away-zone, he jumped out of the vehicle and pressed the remote alarm, listening for the connecting tone as he trudged toward the door of the bar. A warm blast of heat hit his face as he entered, and he hesitated a moment to let his eyes adjust to the blue lights. Immediately, throbbing bass line and heavy percussion pulsed in his veins, syncopating his mind to the beat of the music. He felt the tension drain from his body. It had been too long since he'd buzzed into what used to be his spot. Looking around cautiously, he edged into the terrain that was becoming foreign, noticing how many of the old gang were dwindling, dead, or gone. Taking a seat at the end near the door, he lit another cigarette and ordered a beer.

As the barmaid brought his order and took his money, he looked at her young face, wondering where Tosha, the one who used to serve him, had gone. Everybody in the place looked so young; where were all his boys? Even the bar stools were different. Newer. Updated. Seemed like everything was changing. Maybe he should have gone home, if he could call it that.

Glancing at the two brothers at the far end of the bar, who had been craning their necks in his direction, he felt the muscles in his right arm twitch. It was too early to start this crap, he thought, and he was definitely not in the mood to have to kick some young boy's ass. Damn. He should have gone home. When the short one with the bald head stood and moved toward him, conferring with the other who remained in the shadows, his senses went on red-alert. If they were packing a piece, he was glad he'd decided to stay by the door. Dag-gone young boys were such punks today, couldn't take it to the streets one-on-one like a man. Fatigue resettled in his bones, but pure adrenaline fought against it. Jerome took a drag on his cigarette and let the smoke out slowly. His grip tightened on the neck of the beer bottle. If it was gonna be some mess though, he'd attend to it.

"Yo, man, what's happening? Cherokee Red! Buddy, told chu it was our boy. Man, where you been at? Come on down and claim your old stool."

Relieved, Jerome stood and gave his friend

Scoop a big hug. "You shouldn't play like that, man! I thought you was some young punk lookin' at me. Where's your hair, bro? That's Buddy down there? Shoulda known."

Scoop laughed as he ushered Jerome to the other end of the bar. "Gerri-curl mess burnt it out. Had this big old horseshoe, so had to let it go. Doing a Jordan thang now, bro."

"Long time no see. Whatchu doing in West end? Whassup?"

Jerome broke into a wide grin as Buddy hailed him, and Scoop slid one seat over so he could sit between them. "You, brother." Moving to the empty seat, Jerome slapped Buddy on the back, and turned to give Scoop a high five. "Can't a man come home for a drink? I figured y'all'd be in here on a Friday night."

"Where else would we be, Reds? Ain't nothin' changed," Buddy chuckled, motioning for another drink. "Same old, same old. How you hangin', though?"

"Same old, same old," Jerome muttered, exchanging a look of understanding and solidarity as he raised his beer to his friend.

"Thought you was under house arrest, bro. Ain't seen you in almost a year," Scoop laughed as he motioned for the barmaid. "Pour my man some Cutty."

Jerome laughed with him and held up his hand. "Just a Miller, Sis."

Both of his friends looked at him with amazement, but Scoop seemed out-done. "A Miller? To chase the Cutty Sark, right?"

Buddy broke into the fray, waving a Guinness Stout. "Stop being cheap, Scoop. Git the man some Yak. Our long lost brother has returned."

"Naw, naw, no Cognac, y'all. See, I'm just trying to have a brew, then go home, which is where y'all should be in about an hour. I got to go way up The Drive, man. Can't be messin' myself up like Teddy Pendergrass did on them turns."

"Pour the man a double Cutty," Scoop laughed. "I remember," he added throwing a twenty on the bar, "straight without a chaser... oh, yeah, except his Miller. Ain't seen home-boy in a long time. But, he ain't no punk. This fool can drink."

"Come on, brothers," Jerome chuckled, taking a deep swig of his drink.

"Must be that Cherokee blood, Blood," Buddy joined in, slapping his back again and motioning for another. "We'll get you home, man. Stay for a while."

Jerome set down his glass, took a swig of his beer and made a face. "See, now, this is why I don't come in here. Y'all gonna get me put out. Got too much child-support to pay if I do, and couldn't leave my kids if I wanted to." Jerome contemplated the response to his comment, hoping that there would be a way to begin a serious conversation about the issue pressing in on his brain. Divorce.

"Yeah, man," Buddy said, taking a swig and giving him a slap on the back. "Can't be leaving them kids, even if the woman do get on your nerves."

Both men exchanged a knowing glance as Buddy tipped his beer in Jerome's direction and Jerome raised his glass of Cutty in salute. All right. He'd gotten his answer. A divorce was out of the question, and his boys had just confirmed what had been rumbling in his gut all day. It didn't make sense, for the sake of the kids.

"Too true," Jerome finally muttered. "Even if the woman do get on your nerves. Gotta suck it up," he added, then taking a long sip from his beer bottle.

"That's 'cause y'all don't have control of your castles." Scoop was indignant. "Need to kick Karen's tail from time to time, like I kick Tracey's. Then she wouldn't have nothin' to say whenever you come home."

Both Buddy and Jerome went still for a moment.

"You need to stop that mess, Scoop," Jerome said quietly through his teeth. The humor had left his voice and Buddy issued a sideways glance of concern.

"Been tellin' Scoop 'bout that mess for years, man. Ain't nothin' changed. Can't do nothin' with our brother." Buddy made a face as he downed his glass and frowned. "See, me, I love women."

"You love women? Sheeeeit. You need to tell her to use some damned birth control, is what you need to do. Five babies, Buddy? Five?" Scoop swayed as he held up his fingers.

Jerome's jaw dropped. Changing the subject before Buddy got really pissed, Jerome interjected, using his beer bottle to make his point. "Last I heard you had four like me, man. Congratulations. Boy or girl?"

"That crazy fool don't know, Reds. She poppin' 'em out so fast, every year, wit his black butt workin' round the clock cause he don't make her get a damned job. How he know? He better check to see if dey all his!"

Jerome refused to laugh so he wouldn't insult Buddy, but a grin forced its way out against his control. Instead, he opted to defend his friend. "You just mad cause our brother here is gettin' some regular, like. Man's gotta do, what a man's gotta do— work hard."

Buddy raised his beer to Jerome in appreciation. "Ain't no lie, good brother. Got m'boy, now. So I kin leave it be for a while, understand my drift?"

Before Jerome could respond, Scoop had hopped off his stool to come between them, leaning on both of their shoulders and making their eyes water with his breath.

"That's why y'all fools is working like dogs. Every time I see Buddy's Island behind, he on the way comin' or goin' to work. Don't know when the man got time to make them damned babies. And, you, when you get out? Ain't seen you nowhere."

Neither Buddy nor Jerome could answer for a moment. They stared at their drinks and took several deep sips. The groove had been blown by Scoop's bull. Damn. Things hadn't changed.

In that instant, it became immediately clear to Jerome why he didn't talk about his marital problems to his boys any longer, and why they hadn't been the source of his advice about what to do. Because nothing had changed, everything had changed. Walking into that bar was like walking into a time warp. His closest friends were still in the same places, mentally, as they had been during high school—the good old days. But, in his mind, he was miles away from there. Maybe Buddy had progressed and could offer some sound advice, but there was no way to tell that with Scoop hanging between them.

"Been tellin' Buddy he ought to make Val get a job. Girl got a degree in art and don't do jack with it," Scoop slurred on. "Makes babies, stays home, and makes more babies. And I'll tell you why," Scoop argued, returning to his stool with much effort, "...'cause her light-skinned lazy butt don't want to work. And our boy, Buddy, got his nose opened for yella tail and done been rope-a-doped. I'lln't care what color the women is, how fine dey may be, Scoop ain't working like a Georgia mule for no woman wit all dis free poontang out here in the world? Y'all's crazy."

Scoop threw more money on the bar, but Jerome

noticed that the barmaid was slow to retrieve it. One more, then he was outta there before something kicked off between him and Scoop.

"Yeah, dat's right. I work hard. 'Cause, I take care of me wife!" Buddy was on his feet, but nobody paid him any attention.

Tugging on Buddy's jacket sleeve, Jerome tried to get him to sit down, knowing that his friend was on the verge of a fight as Buddy's accent began to thicken with his increased rage.

"An' I don' take tea for da feva when it comes to speaking of me wife. Don't play dat wit me!"

"Ain't nothin' wrong with hard work, man. This here is a good brother," Jerome added, slapping his friend on the back to help calm him down.

Appearing mollified by Jerome's confirmation, Buddy eased onto his stool and took an unsteady sip of vodka, then a gulp of beer. "That's right," he said, glaring at Scoop. "I works me four jobs, and got a knot to show for it." Patting his pocket, Buddy looked at Jerome with a dazed expression. "Work for The School District during the day. Engineering."

"A glorified maintenance man," Scoop chuckled as he rapped his knuckles on the bar to get another drink.

Ignoring Scoop, Buddy went on. "Then I wear a beeper for three big condos around here. My night hustle. With the storm and all, lotta repairs needed. Tried to get Scoop's trifling ass to work with me to

53

catch da overflow. We coulda got paid during the storm, bro. But your boy over there don't do snow, or late hours, or nothin' else. Old man who works Garden Court is getting tired, so he calls me in to help. Wouldn't mind a partner."

"I wasn't even hardly going out in ball-biting cold to fix no old white lady's pipes for fifty dollars. You must be out your monkey-ass mind, Buddy." Scoop seemed so indignant at the thought that he almost fell off his stool when he leaned in toward Jerome. "Then your boy was complaining cause I wasn't out there trying to put a plow on the front of my four-by-four. Wasn't letting him mess up my transmission behind no chump change."

Jerome sat back in amazement. "You have a four-by-four, and you didn't make money during the snow? Hell, I was shoveling people out by hand for seventy-five a pop, cause I couldn't afford to buy the blade and attachments for the front of my Bronco. How many kids you got, Scoop?"

"Three."

Jerome shook his head. "See, that's your problem, man. You ain't got no incentive."

Encouraged, Buddy leaned in. "Reds, if you want, I'll cut you in. Some of them jobs go for a hundred, maybe a hundred and fifty. We do two or three in a night, and bam, we just got paid. Cash money, no taxes, under the table. All you need is a beeper, and be ready to work. I know you got tools."

"Now there's the problem. Karen ain't lettin'

him go nowhere. Girl hardly wants him to go to his day job. Now you talking about giving the man a beeper. And you know Antoinette done moved back home wit her kid—lives in one of them fancy buildings, that's where Tracey's butt been today behind that bull—talkin' 'bout she had to help her girl—being divorced now, and all. Toni's husband shoulda kicked her behind too, and made her stay. Like I said, you ain't being realistic, Buddy. Y'all's women is out of control. Need to stop pipe dreamin' and be real."

Jerome paused, polished off his Cutty, and set the glass down carefully. "Toni's back in Philly... with a baby?"

"Aw, man. Don't even think about it, bro. She's way out of your league now. Thangs is different, and like you said, you got too much child support to pay if you get put out. Karen will kick your punk bchind, and Toni's too."

Scoop's comment grated him. "How you going to tell me about what goes on in my house?" Jerome stood up. He'd had enough, it was getting late, and Scoop had rubbed his nerves raw. Putting his money down, he turned to Buddy. "Look, man, I need all the snaps I can get. Lemme know and I'll get a pager."

Extending his hand, Buddy stood up slowly and grabbed Jerome's, embracing him at the same time. "You in. Partners. Like the old days."

"You got it."

"No," Scoop said rapping for a drink that didn't come. "You the one who's gonna get it when Karen finds some beeper on you and you keeping strange hours. I'm tellin' you, brother. Buddy ain't being realistic and you need to sit your drunk butt down and have another drink." Scoop laughed at his own joke as he fished for more money.

"I'm out." Throwing another ten in Scoop's direction, Jerome nodded at Buddy. "Drive him home, man, and kill him if he hits my girl Trace."

⊗⊙

The neon-green clock on the Bronco dashboard made him shut his eyes as he pulled the car into his street. Two o'clock in the morning, and much liquor on his breath—yeah, a mysterious force made him do it. He almost laughed. This was going to be a good one. Jerome sat for a moment and took a deep drag on his cigarette. It had been a long time since he'd been out West with regularity, not since right after the Air Force days. That was ten years ago. Then his visits to the old neighborhood had become more and more infrequent, just as his conversations with his old friends had. How did twenty years whip past him like that? Ten years in the service, and ten years in construction. Deep.

He leaned his head back against the seat and looked up at the stars. In those days before The Air

Force, he could fly....

Damn. The bedroom light had flicked on and a silhouette appeared at the window. Just as abruptly, it snapped off. He let out a deep breath. What did it matter anyway? He took care of his kids, wasn't gonna leave, and miscellaneous street tail was too much trouble to chase these days. It was too expensive and now it could kill you. Yeah, the couch was calling his name.

"One more cigarette, then I'm going in, my brothers," he chuckled sadly to himself in the vacant space. The cold air felt good, and helped to sober him a little. Letting the smoke come out on a slow exhale through his nose, he continued looking at the stars. "What's the damned point?" It was always the same. He'd come in from working O.T. then get blamed for messing with whores that didn't exist. At least the alcohol would numb his senses and help him go to sleep with a hard-on. That always worked. But seven months was beyond ridiculous. Like his Pop always told him, getting another job was better than getting into trouble. He didn't need trouble, and dreams were nothing but that—trouble. He wrenched his gaze from the stars and looked at the bedroom window of his house, then closed his eyes briefly.

"I wanted to fly, Toni-girl, don't you remember?" he murmured into the quiet space before taking a last drag, crushing out the butt, and pulling his keys out of the ignition. The thought was stupid. Of course she didn't remember, much less know he was alive.

Never in a million years had he ever dreamed of being grounded so young.

CHAPTER 4

"Adrienne, I'm telling you, the girl is hurt bad. We need to pull together some kind of mobilization strategy for your sister." Cookie held the phone tightly in her grip and paced as she took a hard drag on her cigarette.

"You're making it sound like she's in a war, Cookie."

"It is!"

"With who? She just needs some time to heal."

"The girl don't have time! She's thirty-seven."

"So?"

"So!"

Adrienne shook her head at Cookie's over-exaggeration of the situation. Did age make people melodramatic, or something? She knew her sister; Toni was a survivor—always the best at everything.

Adrienne took another sip of carrot juice, readjusting the phone to a comfortable position in the crook of her neck. She could tell that this call from Cookie was gonna take time, and she glanced over at the seemingly lifeless male form sprawled out in the bed next to her as she stood and went into the kitchen.

"For real..." Cookie pressed on, "her money is all jacked-up. May is on her case like white on rice. She isn't even interested in the male species anymore. And, God help her, she's let her figure go so bad that she looks like a Holstein cow! We've all been watching it creep up on her during the two year separation, but the bulk of it must have jumped on her during that last few months while she was waiting for her papers. Girl, listen, I hadn't seen her in months, and had only talked to her on the telephone, but when I saw her, I couldn't believe it."

"C'mon, Cookie," Adrienne objected, looking at the row of vitamins on the counter. "Toni is still pretty, I'm sure. Plus, more important than anything, she has her health and strength, which gives her all the time in the world, and—"

"—And, she won't have time to find another husband soon! Time isn't on her side. Plus, she's scared to death of being by herself, being like me. She was never cut out for the single life. Your sister is the marrying kind, you dig. And, her prospects are going way down with every pound that she gains. It's like she's putting on some kind of protective armor, and doesn't even want to get back into the game. We can't let her do this to herself. She needs an intervention, kiddo."

Adrienne closed her eyes briefly and let out her breath, examining her glass of fresh carrot juice. "Stress can definitely take your life, Cookie," she said quietly, moving from the edge of the counter to get her vitamins, and going to the living room so she could flop down in the large orange captain's chair that she'd managed to wedge into her tiny studio apartment. "Saw it kill my mom. Stress breeds cancer in the body, then cancer takes you out. Okay. What can we do?"

"Finally, I'm talking to somebody that understands what I'm saying," Cookie huffed, sounding relieved, yet disgusted.

Adrienne let the giant tablets hit the back of her throat, and coughed as they slid down in a thick emulsion of juice.

"You okay?"

"Vitamins," Adrienne choked out, redirecting Cookie's inquiry. "What's the greatest source of Toni's stress, at the moment?"

"Aside from May... I guess it would be money, 'cause that's the only thing we can help with. There's nothing we can do about Brian having a fiancée, and there's nothing we can do about her insistence on grieving. Maybe we could baby sit from time to time, but she doesn't go anywhere! I don't know."

"Then, what are we supp-"

"The girl needs a real job, or a real business, not these little odd jobs that barely keep the wolf away from the door," Cookie cut in, stopping Adrienne's question. "Just like the weight, she hasn't gone back to her total potential. Then like a fool, she was satisfied with child support, and didn't pursue the alimony issue, all because she wanted everything done, pronto. She said she didn't want to go through a long court battle, and that if Brian helped to support Lauren that would be enough, she'd find a way to support herself. But, she's not, really."

"Yeah, true. All we can do is hold her hand while she gets being married out of her system, but the survival on one income issue will drive her insane. That's real."

"No, income, you mean!" Cookie's voice became more strident as her voice poured into the receiver. "You just ain' gettin' it, are you? Your sister is between even those odd jobs. Happened with the move. She just quit those temporary gigs with the idea to start totally fresh in Philly, and what Brian sends will just cover Lauren's daycare and a little food for the kid. May is, in this case, rightfully freaking out, because our girl ain't making sense. From what I understand, May's been divorced, and knows how serious all of this bull can be, so she's taken a tough-love stance, which is just further stressing Toni. I've tried it, too, giving her a tough-love dose of reality on the day we moved her in, but Val and Tracey made me back off. It's like your sister has sorta given up. I don't know what she's thinking. All I do know is that she held her own during the separation, but when the executed papers came a few weeks ago, she worked out the details of the final move, then just up and quit on everything."

"No income?"

"Yes, Adrienne... your sister doesn't have a job and her severance money is going fast... unemployment has been gone."

"What about Brian? Can't she haul him back to court to get the alimony part... what about her ex-husband's–"

"What about him? He only has to pay for Lauren. His child. Not an able-bodied adult woman with a solid job history. Child support and no alimony! Your sister's choice, and a botched negotiation for fast freedom! Could you live on five-hundred a month?"

Adrienne fell silent for a moment before questioning Cookie again. Didn't guys with good jobs have to pay for their babies and their wives? "But..." her voice trailed off as she felt suddenly foolish for not knowing the answer, and Cookie's knowledge of these issues held her hostage. For the first time in her life, she realized that maybe she wasn't as street-wise as she'd thought. Adrienne glanced at the calendar hanging precariously on a refrigerator magnet. Damn, she should have used birth control last night.

"So, Adrienne, what's the plan? You're the one with big contacts in LA, right?"

Fear of being found out to be an imposter halted Adrienne's words. None of them back home knew how badly she was doing, or that a lot of what she so-called had going on was only smoke and mirrors. Now, her sister's friends were coming to her to deliver what wasn't at her disposal to give. There were no big contracts, and all of her supposed contacts were fleeting glimpses of the rich and famous, maybe a lover or two in the mix, but no one dependable enough to entrust her sister's future with.

"I'll call her and get her to Fax an updated resume to me," Adrienne offered coolly. "If she gets back her independence, then maybe she'll feel more ready to address her heart. I don't know," she sighed. "She'd never move out here to LA with me, not even to get away from that toxic relationship with May and Dad. Can't Francis help her? She's got a placement firm in Atlanta, doesn't she?"

"Yeah, but Francis can get funny with you, you know?"

"This is an emergency. Or, is it my sister's pride that also won't let her call Francis?" She had to find a solution without opening her life to scrutiny or worry from her father and May. She knew that if Cookie had the least bit of information about her condition in LA, it would be on Eye-Witness-News-film at eleven. Francis had to handle this, she couldn't.

"I left a message with Francis," Cookie retorted, "but the heifer hasn't called me back yet. Like I said, she can get funny with people."

"Well," Adrienne hesitated, "if I know my sister, she has a plan. Have you asked her what she's gonna do? It's not like Toni to just fold."

"Toni's afraid, and not thinking about all her options yet. Sort of paralyzed, you know, A? You ain't old enough to have been this scared about what might, or might not, lie ahead of you. Shoot, at your age, you still think you got time to correct any mistakes. But, by the time you start approaching forty, you soon realize that time is running out."

"Oh, yeah," Adrienne scoffed, taking offense at Cookie's assumptions. "Like nothing makes me worry."

"I'm not talking about worry. I'm talking about fear. Pure terror. How could you know? You're still tall, thin, and beautiful with your whole life in front of you. Just wait till that fades, and you will know fear, darlin'. That's where your sister's at. Okay?"

"That's not true!" Adrienne's voice had become shrill against her futile attempt to remain calm. I do know what it's like to be scared. Aren't we all afraid of something? What did Cookie know? Terror was being a kid and watching cancer eat your mother alive. Fear was watching your sister, who was too young to fill the shoes of a sage, try to act like your mother. Scared-to-death was not knowing where to go, but knowing that you had to get away from home. Who the hell was Cookie to judge her! "She has to pull herself together. Period."

"For who?" Cookie shouted, "You, or herself?"

"That's not fair."

"None of this is fair."

Renewed tension wound its way between them in the silence as Adrienne stood up and went to the window. Cookie didn't know jack! The Los Angeles heat was insufferable, even early in the morning, and the stench from the garbage in the alley outside forced Adrienne back to her chair. She hated talking to her sister's friends. They all sounded like a bunch of old hags. They'd made their beds in life, and now had to deal with the consequences. You slow, you blow. Her sister was no different, and it was the source of their constant conflict. Antoinette had decided to stay and become a black June Cleaver.

She'd decided to leave dead-end Philly and seek her fortune and reach her dreams in LA. And they always assumed that she was livin' the life. What the hell did any of them know about her, or how hard it was to make it in this crazy city? Irony made Adrienne want to vomit. Different roads, same destination, landing her and her sister in the same hole—nowhere. After all of the drama between her and Toni about responsibility and keeping in touch with family, now, she was supposed to uproot her life and come running to Toni's side? No. Maybe it was time for her sister to really deal with the path she'd chosen just like she'd had to.

"I gotta go," Adrienne whispered. Yeah, sho' they right, she was livin' the life with a sexy, good-for-nuthin' laying in the next room taking up space in her bed. It was time her company got out of her space.

"I know," Cookie whispered, but not hanging up the line as she looked out of her kitchen window. She took a long drag on her cigarette, considering the younger woman's comments. Fear of returning, being sucked back into the black hole of family... Cookie could identify. Hadn't that been what had kept her from going back to the projects? She and Adrienne were cut from the same cloth, so how could she blame the girl? Both were runners from toxic waste. Something was wrong in LA. It had been a long time since she'd thought about fear, or allowed it residence in her soul. But, hearing Antoinette's pain, seeing the hurt and confusion in her dearest friends' eyes, had been like a flashback.

"I keep hearing her voice, A..." Cookie whispered as she tried to collect herself. "I keep hearing her sobs, that first day she called me when the papers finally came in. Your sister sounded like she was five years old, and she wailed like a baby for your mother. It took me going over to Jersey to find out what was wrong. When I got there, she just stared out the window for a long time, and said she wanted to go home, but couldn't because your Mom wasn't there." Swallowing away unshed tears with a deep inhale of smoke, Cookie steadied her voice. "I don't want to see her cry like that again, Adrienne. She scared me. I've never seen her like that, not even at your mother's funeral."

Pacing away from the window, Cookie left her small kitchen and hunted for her shoes within the tight confines of her overstuffed town house as she waited for Antoinette's younger sister to respond. She didn't give a damn if the girl was becoming unnerved, or what had gone down to drive the sisters apart. It was time for her to take a definitive stand and grow up. Cookie pulled on her cigarette with one hard drag and forced the air back out of her lungs. "Well?"

"You know," Adrienne began quietly, "everything in Toni's life is crumbling at the same time. The man, a sick kid, her looks, and now her job focus. If each of us shores her up, brick-by-brick, maybe... maybe, she won't be as afraid."

"We can't baby her, though," Cookie countered. "She has to do this herself."

"No, we can't. We'll never replace Mom. I even told her that myself when she tried to play that role with me. But, we can stand by her."

"Just ought to, since she stood by you."

"I don't do guilt, Cookie," Adrienne retorted.

"You ever consider that maybe she was so hard on you because she just didn't know what else to do, and she didn't want you failing on her watch?"

"My sister has a very rigid and outdated sense of

right and wrong, and I don't need that in my life at this—"

"So, she stayed on your butt till you got out of high school with no babies in tow, and leaned on you all the way until you graduated college, and never missed an event, a showcase, whatever. All I know is, your sister sat in the same seat your mother couldn't occupy. Yeah, heifer. Guilt, debt, call it whatever, that's still your sister, and you have a good one. You're luckier than most. So, did you ever consider that, maybe she was learning to fill too-big shoes?"

Cookie had murmured the question, as a dawning awareness struck her about her own way of handling people. This conversation was too close to home. She, like Antoinette, also raised brothers and sisters, and unlike Toni's sister, her siblings did fail on her watch. Every last one of them. "Maybe she'd promised your mother to look out for you while she was sick, but really didn't know how to raise a kid. She was almost a kid herself. Then when you did the teenage rebellion thing, maybe she buckled down on you a little too hard. Can you blame her? Look at you now. You made it out alive, and practically unscathed."

Silence was Adrienne's only answer, which allowed Cookie to press on.

"You know me, A. I've never been the one for the soft-touch. I'm more for a dose of reality--a bread-and-butter slap of get-yourself-together.

Wallowing, in my experience, only gets a girl stomped on. Getting it together, fast was the only thing that saved me when Doug walked, and Harold walked. It's the only reason my kids are okay today. I remember those terror years of being a single mother, and vowed to never go there again. Lost my brothers and sisters to that."

Grabbing her coat and her purse, Cookie surveyed her townhouse and let out her breath. "It was better that way. To count on just me. I got a lot of family, but no one to count on but me. Dig. Been that way since forever. So, Toni will get over it, but she needs somebody to talk to. I just figured you being her sister, you'd let by-gones be by-gones and be the one to call her. She didn't take the move well at all. You should have been there. Period."

"It never dawned on her that she'd ever be one of us. At risk, you know? She just always comes off so tough, with a plan," Adrienne admitted softly. "But, really, she's not used to being in this position. Guess it's our turn, huh, Cook, to give her whatever we can?"

"That's all I was trying to get you to see, A. None of us sisters are as tough as we try to make everybody believe. Superwoman is a dead concept."

"How much cash does she need?"

"I don't have any extra money that isn't already tied up in helping my kids and my crazy family, Adrienne... neither do you, really. Truthfully, I take back what I said earlier. Toni doesn't need cold cash, she needs a plan, a solid job, and to regain her self esteem so she can make her own money. Moral support."

Cookie stopped mid-stride to allow her words to sink in. She was used to fraud, and could smell it miles away through the phone. The comment was only designed to let Adrienne know that she knew the deal. Adrienne was obviously scuffling out there in LA. But, Adrienne's circumstance didn't matter to her now. She just wanted the girl to be there for Antoinette's emotional support, and to cut the bull. "My accounts have been slow, and I'm not liquid at the moment." Cookie hesitated again by the door and clutched her car keys in her palm. "Lord knows I wish I was, for her. My people drained it all two months ago. Gotta make the donuts."

"Yeah, maybe she doesn't just need money," Adrienne whispered. "Maybe she needs hope. Somebody to reshape her thinking about herself, and a little reinforcement. Maybe to help her get a job, so she can make her own money. Help her find her courage. Trace and Val can hold her when she cries." Adrienne let out a sad chuckle, "What can I really do? Go on a man-hunt for her?"

"Maybe, who knows?" Cookie said quietly.

"We all have our specialties."

Cookie chuckled sadly and shook her head. "Yup, we do. Well, girlfriend, that's the scoop. I'm going to the state-store now to find her some courage in a bottle. Then I'll drop it in her doorway, and leave her alone for a little while. I've already pissed her off. She's probably not even speaking to me. Everybody else is pissed too. Who cares."

"They'll get over it," Adrienne chuckled back. "They always do."

"Yeah, well... like I said. I've never been the soft-touch."

"You used to be..."

"And, where did that get me? All jerked around. Never again."

"Never say never, Cook. Life's too unpredictable. By the way, how is your new love?"

"The same. Living in his own, crazy space, and away from me. And only giving me a shot once a week when I can tolerate his whining crap. Girl, I don't see why Toni even wanted to try that happily-ever-after mess. Men are too much trouble. When the deal goes down, you only have your girls to back you up. She needs to find somebody stable like I did, who can make a good house-call on demand, then take his butt home. Know what I mean? Anyway, how's your young boy doing? And pulleeeze do not tell me you're in love. You've got your whole life ahead of you. Don't blow it on a man!"

"He's trying to make house calls three times a week, but I have work to do," Adrienne chuckled in a quiet tone that let Cookie know she had company.

"Girl, to have a twenty-five year old hunk wearing me out like that, I'd give my eye-teeth. Stop complaining."

"I'm too busy, hon." Adrienne laughed again sadly, and moving deeper into the apartment so she could talk. "Besides, he's not serious. He's just for fun. A good friend, but nobody to call a life-partner. If some serious stuff goes down, he won't be able to handle it," she whispered, glancing at the calendar again. "So, what's a girl going to do?"

"Take care of business, and build your career. Bottom-line."

"Yeah," Adrienne murmured, "and you have to pray to God that you can."

"We always do, don't we? Hey, what's the matter, hon? You sound blue all of a sudden."

Adrienne tried to summon a response for Cookie as her gaze swept her tiny studio. "Nah, not me. Just tired from being out late partying last night. Don't worry, I'll call T and find out if she's okay."

"Good," Cookie sighed. "Let me know how she is after you talk to her."

"Can't. My long distance is off."

"Then call me collect."

Adrienne hesitated then grunted an affirmative to Cookie's order. What did all the striving to succeed in the music industry mean anyhow? Pacing into the kitchen, she rummaged in the refrigerator for a piece of fruit. Loneliness claimed her. The truth was, her career was going nowhere, and she missed home. She missed a sense of permanency.

Yet, everybody thought that she was foot-loose and fancy-free out in LA. Not one of them knew how cold a place could be without roots to make it a home. She missed her sister who was too far away for her to help. She missed Pearline. She missed her mom. Tears of disappointment formed in Adrienne's eyes as she thought of her mom and Toni, the ones she'd fought with tooth and nail over everything, but who'd still loved her anyway.

"We all have to stick together. No matter what," Cookie insisted. "So call me, okay?"

"How's Tracey doing?" Adrienne countered, changing the subject before Cookie could absorb how bad off she was financially and emotionally. With Toni being in such a state, the last thing she wanted was for her sister to have to worry about try-ing to wire money.

"Huh?"

"Tracey," Adrienne went on, desperation clawing at her insides. "Are things better with her and Scoop?"

"Pulleeeze," Cookie scoffed. "She's still into those kids, and allowing Scoop to kick her behind every other Friday night just cause she's scared to go it alone. Everything boils down to money."

"Tracey is good with kids. She's kind, gentle, and deserves better. If she had money... support, do you think she'd leave Scoop?"

"Wouldn't any woman? But, her work history is a mess. She's never finished school, and you'd have to be a magician to find her a good-paying job in this economy."

"Yeah," Adrienne whispered, expelling the comment with a sigh. "At least Toni is viable, from an employment standpoint, and had the sense to leave Brian when things got really bad between them. Is Val okay?"

"Yeah, still the same pain in my neck, but okay. That ugly bulldog, Buddy, works like a demon for her, so what's she got to worry about? That's why I say we start first with getting T a better job. Once she's financially stable, then she won't have to worry about May, or Brian, or anything else for a while. That's our girl, and I won't see her go out like this. After she gets her money and head straight, I'll try to pull her into the business. She'd make a great consultant, if she could just stop being scared of her own possible success long enough."

"Yeah." Fatigue tugged at Adrienne's vocal cords, and she struggled to fight against the nausea building in her stomach from the combination of vitamins without food mixed with disappointment. She couldn't go home now. She'd waited too long to decide that she couldn't make it in LA. Now the choice was May's house or LA. She'd starve before going back to what used to be her mother's home. Staying with her sister and her niece had always been an option. Now that place she'd always taken for granted, was gone.

Adrienne sat down slowly on a kitchen stool and

rested her hands in her lap, smoothing her silk peach kimono as her mind wandered. "I love you, Cook. Tell everybody who's still speaking to you, that I said, 'Hi.' Let Toni know that I'll call her in a few days. We have a big gig going down with the new label, and as PR, I have to be on top of things. But, I will call her. Okay?"

"Will do. Love you too, kiddo. Keep taking your vitamins though, chicky. You sound awfully tired. Better cut that young-boy back to twice a week."

"Been working hard, is all," Adrienne lied again. "Don't worry about me, I'll be fine. Now, go get Toni a good bottle of wine, and call me in a few days to let me know how our girl is doing. Even if I don't answer, leave a message."

CHAPTER 5

Jerome looked at the blue-gray light filtering in from the window and peered at the clock. Somehow, over the past months, his body was still regulated to awaken an hour before the alarm went off, even though he was sure that his wife was still holding siege. Against his better judgment, he'd climbed into bed when he'd come in the night before, and had taken Karen's lack of outright protest as a sign of a temporary truce. He'd hoped that she was just messing with his mind, and that her request for a divorce had been pure theater. The throb in his groin forced him to consider the possibility.

Maybe this morning there could be a cease-fire. And she looked so peaceful, so good as the rays of dawn crept over her exposed cream-colored shoulder. He breathed in her natural feminine scent, barely touching a wisp of her silky auburn hair with the tip of his nose. Just once, he wished she would awaken and open her wide gray eyes to him with expectation and need, instead with steel-gray-anger.

Maybe...

Wincing as he shifted his weight, it felt as though every muscle in his body hurt from the tension that had erected a salute to morning. Maybe she'd even relent just knowing that he was going to pull a sixth workday with a Saturday time-and-a-half premium for her and the kids.

"Baby," he whispered, "you awake?"

"Don't even think about it," she said in a clear, but husky voice that told him she'd been awake before he was. "Where were you last night?"

That was a good sign. A woman who wanted a divorce probably wouldn't care where her husband had been. That rationale seemed to make sense at the moment. Moving closer, he fit himself against her like a paired spoon. "I told you I was working," he murmured in earnest into her hair, feeling only her soft gown separate him from her nude form as he threaded his arm around her waist. "C'mon, Karen. Let's not fight this morning. I've missed you, baby. Let me show you how much." His breathing had become stilted when she didn't answer or pull away immediately, allowing him to savor hope as the slow friction between her backside and the center of his pain drew a groan from deep within him.

But, just as suddenly as she had seemed to relax, her body stiffened, causing him to remove his hand from her waist, driving him to the other side of the bed. "Seven months of this agony, because you don't trust me?" he whispered "When's it gonna end, K?"

She squeezed her knees together tightly to ward off the heated and unwanted effect he was having on her body. The icy valley between her thighs had begun to thaw, painfully becoming engorged with want. She would not let this happen, and she staved off a shudder as her gown caressed her distended nipples to the rhythm of her breathing. She was no fool. Just like her mother had always told her, men only wanted one thing, and she would never be a fool like that woman had been. No, she was stronger than the stupid woman she called Mother, and would never allow a man to traipse in and out of her life at will, directing her every move, especially when he'd never given her what she'd wanted--a beautiful house like her sister's. Then again, even her mother had managed to extract a pound of financial flesh from all of her efforts to manipulate the men in her life over the years. But, what did she have? Only four little children. She had to teach him a lesson, and it was working. Yesterday, she'd cried divorce, and now look at him. Back at home where he was supposed to be, trying to get some.

Anger doused the kindling embers between her

legs, a glacier began to form over the once molten surface. Jerome Henderson had never turned out to be what she'd expected. He'd never provided for her the way she'd been provided for by her warring parents. That was unforgivable. What was worse, the fool had expected her to love him despite it all, condemning her to a tiny home, the scant periphery of affluence that she could only touch through her friends, her sister, and their possessions. And he wanted her to give him pleasure? Never. Not until she got out of life what she'd wanted—an invitation to return to Mount Airy's black elite society.

Karen let out her breath slowly as she felt him waiting... hoping... for her answer. Choosing Jerome to trap into marriage had been a bad decision, she thought woefully, bringing her knees up to her chest to help chase away the fleeting pang of guilt. Her girlfriends had been right. He wasn't worth the effort. He hadn't gone up the ranks within the Air Force as she'd dreamed... had never even tried hard to be the best. All he was, was a high-yellow, half-Indian, red-bone. He had the looks to get into the social circles she coveted, but not the money, family background, or education. And, as his wife, she was painfully aware that that had condemned her and her children to his fate of having her nose pressed to the glass without access. Humiliation and rage scorched her reason. How dare he reach out to touch her! She was better than him, had always been, and he'd forced her to live beneath her station for long enough.   Karen drew a sharp breath and shut her eyes tight, forcing the ache in her body to recede its torment. She would be stronger than him, she reminded herself. A man needed sex more than a woman did. Right now, it was her only weapon.

"When I decide to end it," she finally snapped without turning to face him. "I suggest you go take a cold shower, fix your own damn lunch, and go to work. If you want breakfast, go to a diner. I don't have to get up for another hour until the kids start bugging me. And, since you can't keep your hands off of me, sleep on the couch when you come home this time. My bedroom door will be locked. I'm not going through this crap every other morning."

She'd kept her eyes shut as she'd spoken, hoping that her words would be acidic enough to make him leave the room. She needed space, fresh air to breathe, and privacy. Her body hurt too badly to ignore its nagging resentment of her decision. Seven months of her cold war were causing casualities upon her own sanity. If she could just get him to go, before her body changed her mind, then she could touch herself in ways that she'd needed him to so much. If only he'd just follow his usual pattern— escape in a wordless rage that sweltered under the heat of the unsaid.   "In fact," she added with urgency, "why don't you just get out now, so I can go back to sleep? You know I'm not giving you any."

The fact that she'd let him get worked up before

saying no, hadn't been lost on him. Renewed anger propelled him from the bed, and he grabbed his work-clothes from the drawer, then stormed out of the room. He hated women's games! He'd tell his supervisor that he could work another sixteen again today. Yeah. Then, he'd call Scoop's brother for that beeper. Maybe he'd even look in the telephone book and find a lawyer. Screw Karen!

Not caring that the bathroom door had nearly come off the hinges when he'd slammed it, or that their four-year-old, Christopher, had stirred, he threw the bolt, and turned on the hot water in the shower full blast—adding only a bit of cold water to keep from scalding himself.

Alone, under the blanket of the steaming spray, he mentally blotted out the sounds of the house and street coming alive. He let his mind soar away from the house to a sacred place in the past where there was only profound joy bonded with pleasure... Antoinette... Just like every morning, he simply closed his eyes and let the water fuse with the slick soap in his hand to become his woman.

CHAPTER 6

"Hey, Daddy... baby-girl here. Pick up. Got your message. Anybody home?"

Matt Reeves chuckled as he grabbed the telephone from the receiver and turned off the answering machine. "Adrienne! How's my Hollywood daughter?"

"What'chu guys doing screening calls?" Adrienne laughed into the line. "Dag! My pre-paid phone card is running out waiting for you."

"Hey, jus' 'cause we're senior citizens, doesn't mean we're always available," he laughed casually, sitting down slowly on the bed, and avoiding May's glare. "So, what's up?"

"You tell me?" Adrienne said in a cautious tone. "Are we free to talk?"

"Yeah," he lied. "May helped Toni move yesterday." He had intentionally structured his answer to address both his youngest daughter's question and May's hovering presence.

"You didn't go?"

He could hear the shock in his daughter's voice, and he looked at his hands as he formulated an answer. "Wasn't necessary," he replied, trying to sound calm. "You know your sister... Miss Efficiency. They were just going to decorate and clean up. She had moving men, anyway."

"Yeah, but, Daddy," Adrienne protested, "she probably needed moral support. She was leaving her husband!"

"I know. I know. But, she needed to do that for years. Anyway, how's all that West Coast sunshine? Met any new rappers, or musicians? You still doing public relations for that group?"

"Dad, the weather is fine. I still have the same job. But how is my sister?"

"Oh... she's fine. A little blue, but that was to be expected. She'll get over it."

"Toni doesn't have the flu, Dad. She will not just get over it."

"Yeah. I know." His voice had become gravelly, and tension wound itself around his heart. "But she's a survivor."

"You can't talk, can you? Just answer yes or no."

"No. Call your sister. She could stand to hear your voice, right about now."

"She needed to hear yours yesterday, Dad. And

I've already tried to call her, but her machine is on. I'm worried about her."

"We'll go by either later today or tomorrow," he hedged, not looking at May as he made the promise.

"You go by there. Alone. Then call me. I only have a few minutes left on this calling card, and I want Toni to call me so we can talk for a long time. I miss her."

"Me too, baby. I'll check on her for you, and will let her know that you called. She understands that you're busy."

"But, I'm not too busy for my sister, Dad. We just keep different hours. I don't want to wake the baby, and she has household things to deal with... I mean, I get in at four in the morning, sometimes. She's probably up and gone by seven or so on the job hunt. How's her search coming, anyway?" Adrienne already knew the answer to the question, but wanted to be sure that Cookie hadn't been wrong.

"She quit, baby. Doesn't really have anything lined up yet. She ain't been right since they laid her off, and she came home with Brian. Been hopping from job to job for a couple of years, and this last one, she just quit."

"What!" Adrienne let his words sink in. Sure, Cookie had told her, but the fact that her father had known and hadn't told her about this last change was an outrage!

"We didn't tell you because we didn't want you to worry."

"Since when? How long have you known?"

"A few months, I dunno, maybe a few weeks—since the papers came." Matt allowed his line of vision to travel to May's tight expression, then pulled it away.

"Toni... without a job for an indefinite period of time with no back up, no plan? Jesus... She's not all right, Daddy. Cookie said that her money was all jacked up, but I didn't really think—"

"I know. We'll handle it here. Just be well and come home for the next holiday. You missed the last few, and we miss you. I'll send you a ticket."

"Yes, we will," May interjected, "and tell Adrienne that we need to all sit down and figure out what she's going to do with her life, also. She cannot keep up this pillar-to-post artist lifestyle."

"What did she say?" Adrienne yelled into the receiver. "Keep your wife out of our family business! You, T, and Pearline are the only ones who need to say a word about what I do!"

"You heard it wrong. May agreed that we all need to get together, that's all, and that we'd send you a ticket," he said as calmly as possible. "Daddy loves you, now call me with your flight information so I can book it, and we'll talk when you come home."

"I'm not coming home—there is no more home. I'll call Toni myself. I love you, and I'm sorry, Daddy. Bye."

"Bye, baby. I'll tell May you love her, too," he

whispered addressing the dead line as a ruse for May. "Bye."

He watched his new wife take a very cautious seat in the bedroom chair, and wondered if his former wife's ghost had forced her to sit down in it. May's spine seemed so rigid that he was sure it would snap if she even tried to bend to take off her shoes.

"So," she said curtly, "all children have been heard from, and all we have to do is get them into shape."

"Let it rest, May."

"Let it rest?" Indignant, she shot out of the chair and folded her arms over her petite bosom.

"Let it rest," he said again, drawing out each word for emphasis. "Rome wasn't built in a day."

"We are not rebuilding Rome. We're getting them on the right track. And we have both invested heavily in the process."

"Yes, we have, because they're our children."

"Then, we have a right to an opinion."

"Toni is grown, May. Adrienne is a free spirit, and grown too, just like your kids are grown. I don't meddle in their affairs, and that's why we have kept the peace."

"Meddle!"

"Fight me on this, May, and they'll shut you out, forever." He looked at her hard, and tried to will her to understand with his mind. "That's just the way this family operates."

"I am so sick of hearing how this family operates!" she shrieked. "Pearline got an attitude with me yesterday during the move because I told the truth. The girl is overweight. Toni hasn't been taking care of herself, and I don't want to see her lose her self-esteem. She's too smart, and too pretty to just give up on life. I love her, too, and just because I'm her stepmother, she won't let me in. Toni and Adrienne act like they can barely tolerate me. And now you're siding with them!"

Tears of hurt and rage formed in May's eyes, and he let his breath out slowly, patting the side of the bed for her to join him. "They'll let you in when they're ready. Until such time, every time you push, they pull. Let me be the one to talk to Toni."

"You've never been divorced, Matt. I have. I know what that girl needs, you don't. Her hair is a mess; she hasn't had a perm in what looks like months. Her nails are unkempt, her clothes are getting too tight for her, she doesn't have a spare dime in her pocket, or a plan for how to find a new job. I've been there. The only person in the world who helped me—"

"Was your mother."

"Right," May said more quietly, her eyes brimming. "I don't want to see her go through that, and have some man take advantage of her just because she looks like she has no pride in herself. Men can tell when a woman has no self-esteem, believe me. They prey on it."

Again, Matt chose his words carefully and reached out for his wife's hand, refusing to ask her the unformed questions about her past that crept into his mind. "Let me say those things to her. I'm her father. She'll understand it better coming from me."

"Why wouldn't she understand it coming from me? I gave Antoinette her own place to live, have been more than generous with enough money to make sure that she and Lauren were comfortable in that new environment. We're both women. I'm older, and have more experience, and I care. I have done no less for your daughters than I have for my own children in the past. I'm not a stingy person, Matt."

"I know."

"So what is the problem, Matt?"

"It's not about the money, May."

"Do the girls resent me for marrying you? Is that it?"

"No. Their mother has been gone for a long time. They even used to try to get me to have a lady-friend."

"Okay. That's healthy. So, what's their problem? What's Antoinette's problem—why won't she let me in? She talks to me on the surface... answers my direct questions, but I can feel it. I'm nowhere near her heart and I'm still an outsider."

May's voice trailed off as she sat down beside him. The two big pools of water that she'd been fighting to keep from falling flowed down her cheeks. Matt's gaze edged away from hers, and he squeezed her hand tight while digging in his brain for the right words. His line of vision settling on the door frame of what used to be his wife's closet.

"Because," he whispered after a long pause, "you just aren't her mother... yet."

CHAPTER 7

Constant ringing besieged her senses as she tried to lift her head from the pillow. Almost knocking the clock radio off the nightstand next to the bed, Antoinette rolled over with a groan and slapped the off button. It took a few moments for her mind to catch up to the fact that the distant chime was not coming from the clock. Bright sunlight made her squint as it poured through the window directly onto her face, just as May had promised it would even against the wall. But, the smell of greasy cheese steak paper and cold fries made her body recoil into a fetal position under the piles of covers heaped on the bed. "Just a few more minutes, God, before they come again. Pleeeeeaaaaase," she whispered, trying to unknot herself before exiting the soft, warm womb that the bed created.

Suddenly, as if her prayers had been answered, the ringing stopped and her body relaxed slowly. Each muscle in her legs, arms, back, shoulders, and neck felt like a thick, heavy rope of tangled umbilical cord. Dull pain crept through her limbs, slowing her exit from the covers as she made her way to a sitting position in the freezing world beyond them. The sound of her front door locks being manipulated, then subsequent heavy footsteps, changed her posture from hunched over to bolt upright. How dare they!

"Hey, suga lump."

She didn't answer her father's call immediately. A sense of violation swept through her and merged quickly with anger.

"Hey, girl. It's me."

"I'll be out in a minute, Daddy." Antoinette took her time, pulling on her robe, brushing her hair back, and finding her slippers. What if she'd had company? Male company? Everybody assumed!

She didn't turn around as her father's lean brown form filled her bedroom doorway. Instead of facing him she watched him from her dresser mirror and sorted through the furniture for something quick to put on.

"I can't believe you're still in bed. It's eight o'clock in the morning, and you've got a lot to do before our baby gets back."

"I went to bed about five this morning, Dad," she intoned flatly without turning around to acknowledge his enthusiastic grin. "There's not much left to do. All the stuff in the kitchen has been put up. The furniture is placed, the condo is clean. May had that done before we got here. I hung the few paintings with the help of the girls, and Mom's china has been put away. And you know your sister took care of Lauren's room. Aunt Pearl got that together better than I ever could have."

Her father surveyed her room, gave an affirming grunt, then left the doorway to begin a room by room military inspection of the new dwelling. Calling from every room as he walked in and out of each spit-shined and polished entrance, she was thankful that he had gone from her immediate space before rage made her say what couldn't be taken back. Ever.

"Looks, good. Looks good, honey. You ladies have out-done yourselves. May was right. Pictures are all hung, food put away, cleaning supplies stowed. Looks like you've been here for five years. Aw, now didn't Pearl do a nice job on Lauren's room? Bet my baby is going to be so happy with her pretty new pink room, better than when she was in Jersey."

"Yes, Daddy." Antoinette couldn't bring herself to say much more as she slipped on a pair of panties and jeans while he was in the next room, then pulled a sweater over her head.

"Y'all didn't leave too much for an old man to do."

93

She ignored the wistful tone in her father's voice. She wasn't going to be baited into a joint home improvement project that would take all day long. Not this morning.

"Like I said, I stayed up till dawn putting everything that the girl's didn't put away in its place. I wanted to sleep in, go to the market, and think." Antoinette flopped down on the side of her bed and felt for her sneakers under it. She didn't look up when she saw her father's feet return to the entrance of the bedroom doorway.

"Well, May is already at the market. She said she went through your cabinets and developed a shopping list for you. That'll save you some energy, money, and worry. May is thoughtful like that."

This time, for the first time since he'd invaded her space, Antoinette looked up. "She what?"

"Went to the market. I thought that me and you could run on over to Home Depot and get a few things that you—"

"She went to the market? For my kitchen! Without asking me?" Antoinette was on her feet with sneakers untied and threatening to make her trip if she took a step.

"See," her father began nervously, inspecting the paint job on the door trim, "y'all women is so touchy about territory. That's exactly why May said it wouldn't work for the two of you to be under the same roof. It's different than if your Mom was livin' 'cause you'd know who was Queen B from the jump, so it wouldn't create problems. Things have changed, and we have to go on. Couldn't have two queen bee's in there trying to sting each other to death. Like I said, things change."

Antoinette was breathing hard as she placed her hands on her hips. "Yes, they have. Dramatically."

"Now let May do the shopping, to help you out. You gotta learn how to accept help from somebody sometimes. So accept her help with a little grace, and you and me can make a short run. Like the old days, we can go to the hardware store and spend some time together."

He wasn't fighting fair. The reference to the way he used to take her with him to the hardware store, or to the lumber yard, and then for ice cream so that they could fix up a portion of the house and surprise her mother with a new improvement that she'd wanted—while her mother was at the supermarket—it just wasn't fair. Antoinette dropped her hands from her hips and bent to lace her sneakers. She focused her gaze intently at the top of each shoe and took an inordinate amount of time to tie each one.

Her father began again, after a brief hesitation that always preceded the collecting of his thoughts. This time with more enthusiasm. "But nowadays, girl, the hardware store is fantastic. You been in Home Depot yet? It's like a mall! Let's just walk around and see if there's anything you need. Maybe something'll come to mind that we forgot?" He eyed her with a schoolboy grin that belied his age as she looked up, attempting to charm her and soften her position as he made his case. "You'll be with me till she's finished, and everybody will be happy. You don't have nothing else to do, do you?"

Antoinette didn't answer immediately. What did she have to do? Really? Wash some clothes. Take a long, hot bath, maybe? Rent a video? Look through the classified ads for a job from last week's paper? Rehash the previous day's events with her soldiers-of-man-woman-wars? Plus, she understood that this was just her father's way of curing the incurable loneliness he still felt. Despite his protests, she could tell that the void her mother had left hadn't been totally filled. That reality swayed her decision.

With her voice much softer in tone this time, she looked at her father's hopeful expression. "I have to check on Lauren," she said after a while, knowing that she'd already lost.

"The baby'll be fine. Your cousin Vanessa's got her over there laughing and playing with all her bunch of teenagers. She's probably on somebody's hip as we speak. Let's get some sunshine, give May some room to maneuver, then you can sleep in on Sunday. Church service ain't till eleven tomorrow."

Church? She hadn't even considered it this weekend. How was she going to endure seeing all of her mother's old girlfriends, or worse, seeing who was no longer there, and having to explain that she'd come home jobless and divorced? She could just imagine their opening statements... Oh, we didn't know you and Brian were moving back home. Any weekend, but this first weekend. She needed to commune with God one-on-one for a while before dealing with the gossip circuit nonsense.

"At least let me wash my face, and brush my teeth," she finally sighed, steering clear of any commitment to go to church with her father, "and maybe put on some make-up."

"That's my suga lump," he beamed brightly. "You've gotta fix up your face. Your Mom never went out of the house without her make-up. Ain't right. Plus, never know who you might bump into at Home Depot."

She stared at her father. "What? Daddy, please."

"Look, lotsa men be in there on the weekend. Can tell they's good brothers because they in there to work on a home. 'Specially the ones that's in there early... trifling ones don't get there, or get there late after they done woke up from a Friday night drunk. See what I mean?" he said pointing toward his temple. "The old man's mind is still sharp."

All she could do was shake her head. Her father was going to take her cruising for men in Home Depot!

"Dad, if we need a lock, some drain cleaner, or need to get some keys made, whatever, that's the only reason I'm going. But, do not, I repeat, do not, embarrass me in Home Depot. Okay?"

"Embarrass you?" Her father was almost indignant, but even he had to laugh at himself.

"Yes. Embarrass me, and you know what I mean. I don't want you walking up to some man in the store and—"

"—Girl, you let me work it. I know what to do. Hang around the plumbing, or electricals—they's craftsmen."

"Oh, my God..." Her gaze rolled up toward the ceiling before she shut her eyes tight.

"Listen, you done got a little heavy... put on some pounds... 'specially in the hips. But, good, hardworking, blue-collar brothers like that. The corporate ones, don't. So, since you still so hell-bent-and- fury-bound on not losing the weight, we just have to change brother-types, that's all."

She was stunned. More like mortally wounded. The one person in the world who'd always adored her, thought the unthinkable about her, things that she'd wondered about herself—feared about herself.

"I've tried to lose the weight, but it wasn't about the weight, Dad!" Her voice cracked as the words rushed past her lips without censure.

"I know. I know," he said quickly, trying to smooth over the new impediment to his progress. "I'll wait for you in the car."

"No. I'm not going."

"Aw, girl, see how stubborn you are. C'mon, I didn't mean nothin' about the weight. A decent brother wouldn't mind it at all. You got a nice head of thick hair, if you style it up right and go get yourself a perm... decent fitting clothes. All you need is a manicure. Always had pretty hands since you was a baby. You still have, and always will have a pretty face-medium brown—not too light, not too dark. Pretty." He folded his arms and leaned against the door, his face full of parental pride as he assessed his creation. "Just need to take off a few pounds. No real harm done. That's what I told May."

"No harm done?" He'd slapped her with his words. "A pretty face?" Tears blurred her vision as she looked at her father square in the eyes. "Let's get this straight once and for all. My husband began having affairs within six months of us being married—while Mom was in the hospital. I didn't gain weight until after she died, and after I found out about the women!" Her voice had escalated and her father's face went stone rigid. "I have tried every diet known to man to shake these extra forty-five pounds, but it keeps coming back. Then, after Lauren, it was futile. We had trouble because of my job—and every time I brought one of those stupid plaques home, or got a promotion ahead of Brian, evidence of some woman would show up... and the funny hours would begin, or he'd come up with a new business eureka that would wipe out our savings. It had nothing to do with my weight!"

"Okay. I stand corrected." Her father walked over and gave her a tender hug. "It's just that me and May want you to get yourself together. I have to agree with her that you too young and too pretty to be lettin' yourself go like this. You'll be old before your time, then it will be too late. That's why May insisted on going to the market, to get some low-fat food in here, to make sure ain't no greasy fried, heavy junk. You know how you cook, Toni. The hard-working variety of men like that. You a good cook like your mother was."

If she wasn't so angry she would have thrown herself on the bed and sobbed. Tensing against her father's hug, she pulled away from him, wiped her eyes with the back of her hand, and walked to the far side of the room leaving the bed between them.

"Look, if this isn't my space for the duration, I'll move right now. I want May out of my business. Today. Permanently. You are not to ever put a key in my door again without calling, knocking, and getting my permission first. I would rather take the last of my severance money and get an apartment, or live in the projects, than to live here under these conditions. Any day."

"What conditions? You getting yourself all worked up for nothing, T-girl. Now get dressed so we can go."

Antoinette defied him to move closer to her with a stare, this time ignoring the tears that coursed down her face. "I could have had company when you walked up here, Daddy. Why not? You don't know everything that goes on in my life!"

Looking around the room sheepishly for evidence of male companionship, her father hung his head. "You right. It's just that I thought—"

"That I'm unattractive, ugly, and can't get a man. That I'm pitiful!" Her voice had gone shrill.

"Naw, naw, see, you've got it all wrong." Shame washed over his face as his voice trailed off.

Her tears had turned to sobs, and salty mucous mingled with her spit as she spoke. "I'm thirty-seven years old, Dad. I have made and managed my own money, followed all the rules, kept a clean house, made all the social functions, gone to church, taken care of my child, given my husband nookie on demand, went to school, had a nice home, went to the supermarket every Saturday for my own damned family, by myself, for myself, with my own money for years! Now, I come home, for a month or two, to pull myself together after having lost everything I ever worked hard for, dreamed of, prayed to Almighty God to save, and I have to deal with this shit? Never!"

"Toni, calm down, baby, and watch your language. No need to go to cussing. It ain't lady-like. We all know you've been through a lot... and you've been a good daughter... the kind of daughter that parents pray for. Maybe May's right, and you should consider talking to somebody."

"I'm trying to talk to you! And don't mention her name when you talk to me—about us!"

The worried expression on her father's face created a new catalyst. Now he thought she was crazy. Veins stood in her neck and her temple pulsed with a blinding headache.

"Like I said," he stammered, "you've always been a good daughter—"

"A good daughter?" She threw her head back and laughed, but stopped her father in his tracks as he attempted to cross the room. "No. Good daughters don't get fat. Good daughters don't give their fathers sickly grandchildren. Good daughters don't get divorced. And good daughters don't come back home. I'm not going to no damned Home Depot today for you to show me off to the wolves. Forget it."

Hearing the locks turn, they both paused and stared at each other.

"It's just May."

"Get that woman out of my space. Now." Her voice had become a low, venomous whisper.

"Go into the bathroom, clean up your face, and don't ever let me hear you speak of May that way again."

Her father's whispered authority matched her own, and his glare paled her as she brushed past him to the bathroom. Her whole body shook as she washed her face and brushed her teeth, then buried her face in the fresh new hand towel that Valerie had hung. Fury consumed her as she listened to her father try to mollify and remove May from the premises under protest. Why did things have to change? If May could just give her a moment to regain her sea legs. Just give her a little distance, instead of trying to take over her life. It was as though May's control-oriented ministrations suggested that she had made a mess of her life, and now needed an adult to step in and intervene. That's not what she needed. She hadn't been the one to mess up her life.

Suddenly, her father's gentle coaxing of May seemed to fill the entire bathroom. "He's still guilty," she whispered into the towel. "Dear God, man, you didn't kill mom. It wasn't your fault. Being a doormat now won't change any of it."

Then, it became crystal clear in her mind as her body relaxed with the revelation. The entire family had been decimated, nobody was the same, and her father's new demeanor was all a part of transformation. Guilt had moved into their lives like a demon, possessing everything, everyone. It was time for an exorcism.

Seizing her power, Antoinette lifted her head from the towel, hung it neatly on the rack, and opened the door. She found May in the kitchen embroiled in a one-sided argument with her father. Although both stopped speaking when she approached, this time, she would not be moved.

"May," she said as evenly as possible, "I want to thank you for your help, all of your effort, and for caring enough in your own way to develop a solution."

Her father beamed with pride as his shoulders dropped with obvious relief. May nearly purred with contentment as she turned to face Antoinette.

"Why, Toni, I think you mean that, darling. I'm glad to see that a good night's sleep has brought clarity to your mind."

Antoinette watched the tension return to her father's body. He had obviously lived with his child long enough to know when a trigger had been detonated.

"Yes. Clarity. After a good cry."

"Crying is healthy. So is therapy."

Antoinette circled the older couple and came to rest at the counter edge.

"So is honesty," she added, never losing eye contact with May. This time she would not allow anger to eclipse the meaning of her words. It was imperative that they all come to an understanding about where she was at this juncture.

"I agree," May said warily, setting a six pack of low-fat yogurt on the far end of the counter. "It's good for the soul."

"And, we should let Antoinette have some space. After all, she's a young, single woman. She has a whole free day and night to herself, and might just have plans."

Her father's attempt to remove May without further incident was a bargain for time. It was an uneasy compromise. Like Middle East peace negotiations, he smiled at each warring side, offered a tentative solution, and walked toward the door halting to turn around when May didn't follow him.

Both women looked at each other, then at the man who had addressed them.

"May, while I appreciate being here, I don't want you or Daddy to ever again come into my living space with a key—uninvited. Understood?"

"Well, I—"

"Let me finish," Antoinette said calmly, yet firmly, holding up her hand. "And, while I appreciate everything that you've done for me and Lauren, if there are going to be strings attached, I don't want it."

May's hand flew over her mouth as she grabbed the edge of the counter with the other.

Antoinette held her ground, and she issued a warning glare to her father to stay out of it. "If you and I are going to have a relationship, it will be woman to woman, based upon respect—not some co-dependency where you get to tell me what to do, and I have to kow-tow to your generosity and never oppose you. I've been my own woman far too long for that, May. You caught me while I was tired, yesterday... and there were too many people around to speak on it. If you want me to leave, that's fine. I'll go. Today. Rent the condo to somebody else. But if I stay, you stay out of my business, my cabinets, and my space without invitation. You wouldn't treat a tenant that you didn't know like this. Your domain is at you and Dad's house. Not here."

"Don't you think you're being a little hard on May, baby? She's just—"

"Stay out of it, Dad! She knows exactly what I mean, and we'll be the better for it in the long run. Otherwise, we'll never get along—under your roof, or under this one."

May's facial expressions had gone from shock, to rage, and was now threatening to crumble into tears. Her father went to his new wife, and he wrapped his arms around her, kissing her forehead. Antoinette stood alone. In one morning she'd not only remembered that she had no mother, but now she was witnessing the loss of her father. He no longer adored her. He thought that she was flawed, and a new woman swayed his reason as they stood in unison against her.

"Maybe May's right," he said after a long time. "Though I never believed in it for black folk, maybe you just too angry at the world, and we're gettin' caught in the cross fire." Her father's eyes seemed to beg for an end to the struggle as he looked from one woman to the other—torn. "Maybe you can give her that number you found, May. That young black doctor your girlfriend gave you."

Impassive from fatigue, Antoinette sighed and leaned her head back against the cabinets. "I will go speak to someone, one day. Maybe. But, not when you two are paying for it, finding the person, and again, getting into my business. I had good dental and medical benefits, once. I have a degree, a stellar work history, and the capability to get medical coverage again. I am also not opposed to therapy, when needed. But I am opposed to being controlled. Crazy is doing the same things over and over and expecting different results. That's what I have been doing with you two, not speaking my mind, but hoping that you would sense my needs."

"We've been trying to be sensitive to you," May said on the verge of sobs, "but you haven't been sensitive to us! Right, Matt?" May's eyes searched her husband's face for affirmation that didn't come.

"May, there is no expenditure that you've made, that I've asked for. Though, I appreciate it. And I will pay it back. I have never not paid my bills, until this job crisis, which came at the same time as a marital crisis."

"The girl does work hard, May, and is honest."

Wheeling on her husband, May's tone became icy. "And I don't? I'm not!"

"Nobody is saying that, honey, you know that. I'm just saying that she's not trying to scam you, or get anything from you. Toni would cut off her nose to spite her face in a minute for pride—that's what's crazy. Look at how she left Brian, and didn't take him to the hoop."

May looked at her husband a long time before allowing her gaze to settle on Antoinette. "Fine. Since I'm not appreciated, she can fend for herself."

"Fine," Antoinette retorted as her father stood between the two queen bee's locked in a territorial death struggle. This was her hive, even though May had built it. Today, she would not give ground.

"Nobody took care of me when I went through this—my father was gone, and my mother didn't have it to give," May said in a huff. "My brother had his own household, and my mother only had her love to offer. The court didn't protect me. In those days—the judges laughed at a black woman coming to them for justice. She'll see, and you don't know how bad it can get before it gets better, Matt."

The two women stared at each other for what felt like a very long time. It was as though they were the only ones in the room, and her father had vanished. Wounded souls connected and a brittle understanding passed between them. They had both been through it, and she gained a sliver of appreciation for May's position. But pride kept them at arms length from each other.

"I know you had to change Mom's house. I would have done the same," Antoinette whispered. It was the only ground she was willing to give. "But, this has to be my space. Alone."

"What are y'all talking about, house re-decorations for? I thought the problem was coming in here with a key? How'd y'all get onto that dead subject?"

Her father's questions jarred them both.

"Nothing, honey," May said evenly, "she's made her position clear. I understand her, and she understands me. Mutual respect has been rendered. Let's go."

"Well, it's about time," the man between them muttered, still seeming disoriented as he reached for a pack of cigarettes in his breast pocket, "been three years of drama between y'all. Women. Who can figure 'em?"

CHAPTER 8

Jazz blared through the apartment, and the bottle of Zinfandel that Cookie had brought over earlier had truly become a godsend. Cookie was wild, but at least she was realistic and had some of the right answers. One could say she wasn't all bad, Antoinette chuckled to herself, as she twisted a crystal stem-glass between her fingers, appreciating the candlelight that caught in the facets of her mother's treasure. The war update reports had all gone out, she'd left another message on Francis' answering machine, and now she was free to cherish the midnight, which she could finally claim as her own. But, she still owed Val a personal visit: a good kitchen conference with her most trusted friend.

"Talk to me Grover..." she murmured with her eyes closed and her head tilted back. The smooth saxophone melody filled the bathroom as she slid deeper into the steaming bubbles. Heaven could be created on earth. The old dolls were wrong. A Saturday night bath for a tired, sore body. A cold glass of wine for an aching spirit, candles, scented bubble bath, Italian bread and brie, courtesy of a treat to herself. All the music she loved, courtesy of Tracey—when she wanted—with no sound of Barney or a child's constant demands. Thank God for her cousin, Ness—Saint Vanessa. No phone was ringing. Her bill collectors hadn't located her yet. Tomorrow would be Sunday, and she'd taken the phone off the hook for good measure. Anyway, it was against the law to call on the Sabbath, at least it used to be. May and Dad had been dealt with. Pearl had left her a refrigerator full of soul food, so she didn't even have to worry about cooking for a week—despite May's protests about the caloric count. Hell, it was comfort food, and that's what May couldn't seem to grasp. She needed a little comfort before tackling reality, or rebuilding her life.

However, right now, it was just her and her book: a hot, sensuous thriller filled with hope, love, and romance—courtesy Val. Her crew was on-point, and obviously loved her beyond measure, the same way she loved them and would do for them in a heartbeat. Antoinette held that thought. She was truly blessed. What else could she dare ask God for? A job. True. But, she'd let that request go for the night. She'd worry about all of that tomorrow when she'd look in the Sunday paper. At the moment, she'd claimed a little peace.

Antoinette brushed her lips with the cold glass and set the open book down on Lauren's potty-seat, then refilled her glass to the brim. She giggled as she peered at the half empty bottle, feeling the calming effect of the wine. "Remember what Cookie said. 'Enjoy, girlfriend.'" Taking a deep slurp, she shook the aromatic bubbles from her fingers and grabbed her novel again, flipping back the page where she'd left off and devouring every word between healthy sips of wine.

Who needed a man? A husband? A lover? She had all the friends and companionship in the world. Life was nearly perfect.

Turning the page with a damp finger, she let the words transport her to another place—the Caribbean—oh, yeah. As she read on, she allowed the heroine's rapture to become her own. To be taken, passionately, on the beach. Damn, this was a good book. The man was too fine. Val hadn't been lying when she said it'd be a scorcher. "Hmmph, hmmphm, hmmph, chile! I can see why you hooked up with Buddy, if he has any of this island fire in him."

Antoinette sat up and poured a new glass of pinkish liquid, never letting her vision stray from the page as she managed the wine with one hand. She took a deep breath through her nose with a luxurious sip. Lord, that man was making love to this woman the way it should be done! Have mercy.

As the lovemaking in the novel crescendoed, so did the ache that had crept between her legs. The heat rising from the bath became a constant nag that begged for attention. Bringing the side of the glass to her cheek, she reveled in the contrast of textures. The glass was cool, smooth—her face warm and moist. Just like she was on the beach. Just like she remembered Jerome... cool water ice in his mouth on a hot summer day connecting the chill to her neck, making it slip down her spine and burn her alive all at the same time. Sitting on a blanket in the park, listening to the crickets and the far-off noise of the streets, waiting for the sun to go down, sipping on cherry-lemon water ice, hotter than July, Isley Brothers crooning about that same Summer Breeze. Hoping the park patrols wouldn't catch you, wouldn't tell you it was time to leave. Looking over shoulders to see if the coast was clear. Stealing a sweet lemon-cherry-flavored kiss that melted down the dam between her legs, and allowed his hand to travel up her tied-dyed skirt. Tube top feeling like confinement, easy to roll over newly budded breasts. Just like in the book, under the stars with no one in sight. Making love anywhere one could find the time, anywhere one could sneak off alone, making time stop, sweatin' for the next time, summer. A brother had to rap then, not in discordant harmonies of anger, but smooth, mellow tones of love... had to be able to put need into words, to articulate in baritone, to coax his way toward what was out of reach. She'd loved his voice…

Not being able to finish what nature had started… steaming up car windows in August parked around the corner from the house. Trying to plot a scheme for a way to give it all you've got, only able to give love a half life under a broken street light. Glimpsing the dashboard clock from the corner of your eye, not wanting your Momma to send your Dad to come find you. Slipping into the house breathless, just kissed, and hoping for more. Addicted to the feeling for touch, male hands, and unable to turn back the hands of time.

"I would have married you, J," she whispered, no longer looking at the book, but now staring off into the candlelight. "If you hadn't been so crazy… hadn't just lost your fool mind when you went down to Dover Airforce Base. My father wasn't enough to get in between you and me. Not what we had."

She hated to feel this way, to feel the monster of unexpected arousal slither into her awareness—never knowing when it would awaken and rear its ugly head. Sometimes it would attack her in the morning. Sometimes in the middle of the night, robbing her of much needed sleep. Sometimes it would make itself secretly known in the grocery store when she was zoned out and trying to decide on what coupon to use. Erratic, sporadic, but demanding memories. It was delicious, but torture, especially when there wasn't any way to really quench the urge that now called to her from beneath the water's surface.

Every pore in her body felt the pull of its call. Her nipples stung as the edge of the water lapped against them. She should have never opened this book, much less gone down memory lane! At least Val could read this mess and roll over to Buddy, she mused, which was probably why they had five kids—cause Val was always reading this stuff. Yet, the pages had her in their grip, the same way that fine Caribbean man stroked the woman in his arms. Lordy, Miss Claudy, he was taking care of that woman, the same way Jerome always took care of her.

Antoinette slid the cool glass down the side of her neck as she flipped the page with her thumb. A shiver ran down her throat and coiled like an angry serpent within her belly. Swallowing another gulp of wine, she let the edge of the stem glass brush a stinging nipple. The shudder that coursed through her almost made her shut the book. It had been eighteen months.... Reading on more slowly, she tried to distance herself from the insistence of her lower body, but gave into the urge to stop the sting-ing at the tip of each breast.

The smooth glass surface became a tongue that slowly traveled over each erect peak—the same way that she could visualize the Caribbean man's atten-tion to her soul sister on the beach. The coolness of it, however, made each angry pebble seem to burn hotter, urging her fingers to stroke them. But, that would mean setting down her glass and her book to do so, and she wasn't ready to remove herself from the mental haven of the Islands. Nor was she willing to admit that she had passed the point of no return—the point in which relief was impossible without an orgasm. She was okay. It was just a book, and she was in control. It was just a really good book that sort of titillated her—but she didn't have to go there.

Antoinette read on, devouring the story as she breathed in the intoxicating perfume that rose in a steady steam from the surface of the tub. Soon she became aware of a difference in texture between the wetness of the water, and the slick moisture that her body contributed to the bath. Her thighs opened to allow in the rush of hot current and she found her hips making slight pulsing movements upward as though merely wishing hard could return the thrust. It had been so long.

Barely able to focus on the words on the page, Antoinette's eyes had closed to half slits. Giving attention to only one pouting nipple had made the other sting in protest to being ignored until she moved the now warm glass against it in a quickened rhythm. The heat of the water lapped at the swollen valley between her thighs as her hips undulated slightly faster. Touching the other nipple had sent a hard tremor of answered anticipation through her that urged her hips to move more quickly in response. And, each gentle wave licked the delicate folds of her opening, causing a subtle spasm to overtake the pouting bud that protruded in want of direct attention. Yet, the rim of the entrance below it quavered with a pulsing message of insistence, too.

Now, each upward thrust against the water's edge only teased and cajoled, and did not fulfill. The ache, near unbearable, Antoinette found her lips parting to give way to a shallow breath and involuntary moan. She immediately closed her thighs tight, attempting to squeeze away the acute call between them for a man. That aspect of her life was over for now, she reminded herself. At least until she got her life together.

As the lovers on the pages concluded, spent, she closed the book and set it down on the makeshift potty-seat table next to her. There was no way that her mind could withstand another chapter. Not tonight. Not when she was this aroused, with so few options. Touching herself wasn't the answer; she tried to argue in her own mind. Because all that did was leave her depressed after she orgasmed. There'd be no arms but her own to hold her afterward, and no one to kiss her eyelids and to whisper for her to go to sleep. She was tired of the loneliness that invaded her twenty seconds after she came. So, to avoid it, she simply wouldn't go there. No. What she had to do was to be strong enough not to need it. What she had to do was forget about it, and busy herself with constructively rebuilding her life. For the last two months she'd been able to force those feelings away, and had been able to ignore her body and not touch herself, hadn't she? Wasn't she cured yet?

She had finally gotten to the point where she could watch a romantic flick without crying too hard and could stave off horniness with a change in mental direction. Wasn't she beginning to get cured of this weakness? True, the first six months were tough, then the next six months were even tougher, and the last six months seemed even worse. But, while she'd been focused on the move, she had been able to come to a place of focus, if not peace. Right?

A shiver ran through her as she remembered how aroused she was then, and now, against her will. Images of herself in the throes of passion with her own pillow came into her mind. Memories of how she'd lie in bed at night touching away the loneliness made her cringe with shame and renewed desire, just as the awareness of how much she needed to end her own agony made her briefly close her eyes. Pouring the last of the wine into her glass, she finished it in three deep sips, gingerly positioning the crystal next to the book. Almost exhausted from the sexual tension itself, not to mention the internal debate, she closed her eyes again and laid her head back and let her knees fall against opposite sides of the tub. The movement of the water rushing into her swollen space again sent another shudder through her body, along with a perilous thought.

What would Jerome Henderson be like now, twenty years later? He had been much better than the man she'd just read about—in their day...

The monster had definitely taken over, and her sanity was within its clutches. She didn't care. Fantasy was legal, even if adultery wasn't. One hand slid beneath the surface of the water, finding the soft folds that needed an answer to the question, while the other stroked her breasts. The pouting nub that had been ignored issued a Siren's call and her fingers flicked against it lightly before delving deeper then changing rhythm to a persistent short thrust as they entered her.

Spasms of pleasure gave way to relief, and relief gave way to tears. Life was not supposed to be this way. She shouldn't have to do this—it just wasn't fair. Anger and shame fused, as her husband's smug expression removed Jerome's face from her mind. He'd told her that it would be this way. He'd reminded her that she would be alone like all the others, and hard-up. He'd reminded her before she'd left that half the black men in America were in prison, the other half were either married, or gay. He'd told her that she wouldn't beat the odds—not with her wide ass and bad attitude. Why couldn't she have just acquiesced, and not cut off her nose to spite her face? Believing in fairy-tale romances, passion, till-death-do-us-part. Plain foolish!

Tears ran from the corners of her eyes, and dripped off the edge of her jaw into the water. Her body was relaxed but her mind had been torqued by indignation. "Why, God, does he get to have a lover? Why does he get to have ninety-eight percent of his time to himself? Why does he get to have a career, when mine got taken away before it had even begun—because I had to care for my child? Why? Why does he get to restart his life, have someone who is probably giving him head as we speak? Why?"

She didn't open her eyes as she argued with God. What was the point? She let out a bitter chuckle and tried to sit up against the pull of the wine's effect. Slipping once, she managed to right herself to finally stand, but then thought better of it and sat down on the edge of the tub.

Peering down at the roll that had collected around her waistline, she sighed. Somehow, now didn't seem like a time to pray. Even though she was slightly tipsy, she was clear about the correct time to address The Father. It didn't seem like naked, in the bathroom, after she'd just taken care of her situation by masturbating, would be a good time to chat with On High. She hoped that He didn't watch that.

But, at least she didn't actually run anybody's husband, she told herself, trying to make mental amends. At least she didn't go pick up some stray man in a bar. And, at least she didn't stay after they'd told her that she'd gotten a mild STD from her ex—the bastard. At least she'd gotten tested for AIDS every six months after that, and God had been merciful enough to give her a clean bill of health.

So, celibacy was an option. A smart option. And, taking care of one's own needs by oneself was necessary at times, she told herself as she argued internally with God. Then, she reminded Her Maker that she didn't return the favor to her shaky husband by running around on him while they lived in the same house! "Ha! So there, God," she fussed, nearly slipping on the porcelain surface. "I even slept in the same bed and kept my vows—even though wasn't nothin' goin' on. So, at least I still have my dignity." She laughed again hard, new tears and wine blurring her vision, her body swaying as she tried to stand to get out of the tub.

The feminists had it all wrong, she thought, moving with difficulty as she stepped from her bath. Antoinette sucked her teeth at the imaginary tribunal of famous women forming in her mind. The ones that protested the loudest didn't have kids, were wealthy, and were white. The sisters that protested had achieved the rarefied air of star status and were also from an elite core. She wondered who fought for women like herself—the ones who needed two incomes to make it, and just plain wanted the luxury of having the option to stay home with their children? She almost laughed at the bitter irony of The Women's Movement. Poor women got to have two full-time jobs by the time the zealots were done. They got to bring home the bacon, work sixty hours a week in some dead-end job, and also had the twenty-four hour, seven day a week responsibility of wife and mother. And, if they balked about it, they got left—or encouraged to leave the non-politically correct male they lived with. But, nobody ever said what to do then. Celibacy and poverty somehow didn't feel like freedom. At least in her Mom's day, one of those jobs was respected. It all seemed like a sordid trick.

The thick air of the bathroom, with the over-powering scent of candle tallow and bubblebath fumes, were making her stomach churn along with the wine. New tears dropped on her thighs as she gazed at the cellulite they contained, and she could only let the tears continue to fall as she looked at the small thatch of dripping hair between them with disgust. "But, why did you send me back out into the world like this? I even have gray hair trying to grow in my stuff!"

With a great deal of concentration, she forced herself out of the tub, and pulled on her robe without bothering to dry herself. She knew that she needed to lie down, had to pee, and wanted to vomit—but why waste Cookie's good wine? Antoinette dowsed the candle, dropped it in the sink, and headed for the bedroom. They'd all been right, especially her father. She'd let herself go. Everyone said she was stubborn to a flaw, and now she was paying for it dearly, deeply, and very person-ally. This was definitely hell. Only moments ago she'd thought she was in Heaven. What a cruel joke.

CHAPTER 9

"Hey, girl." Antoinette shivered on the landing as she glanced into Val's living room, briefly registering the pandemonium of children who were still up at quarter to one in the morning. "I know it's late, and I should have called first. Is Buddy home?"

"Come on in here, girl, before you catch your death of cold. You know Buddy's always working." Holding Antoinette by the arm, Valerie issued a series of commands to the unruly tribe to let their 'aunt' pass quickly into the kitchen. Without addressing Antoinette's obviously inebriated condition, Val turned on the burner under the kettle and began rummaging for herbal tea and raw sugar.

"Rough night, huh?" Val finally murmured as she brought a steaming cup before Antoinette and set it down.

"Yeah." She couldn't even look up to face her friend. Where was her own home, her own noisy bunch of children and hard-working husband? Large tears hit the kitchen table, forming a splatter pattern of salty water around the cup that sat before her.

"It's gonna be all right," Val soothed, "Tell me what happened, now?"

"I drank a whole bottle of wine that Cookie gave me, by myself," Antoinette laughed sadly as she looked up. "But I guess you could tell that when I stood weaving in the doorway."

Valerie laughed and shook her head, but was kind enough not to comment.

"Then," Antoinette went on, slurring her words and rummaging in her coat pocket, "I read this mess you gave me," she exclaimed, producing the book and tossing it to Valerie.

Both exchanged a knowing glance and chuckled in unison.

"Hot, ain't it?"

"I do not need to be reading this mess in my current nun condition, girl," Antoinette countered. "Now, I really feel it."

Valerie sipped her tea steadily and looked over the top of her cup as she did so. "I thought it might bring you back to life, hon. That's the only reason I gave it to you."

"Yeah, but now I'm all horny and messed up behind it," Antoinette chuckled quietly as she leaned in toward Val while two big tears slid down her cheeks. "What am I going to do? Call Brian?" Her own comment was sobering.

"People change, sometimes, Toni... when under duress."

"Forget it. I've been without a man for some crazy amount of time, like eighteen months, and trust me when I say, Brian hasn't done the same."

"Do any of them go that long? Be realistic," Val said softly, monitoring her voice to keep the kids out of their business. "You knew he had an affair, so what? I told you that you didn't have to leave him because of that, alone, and, you can still be with him if you—"

"—Are you crazy?" Antoinette swayed in her chair as she spoke, then steadied herself to a more upright position. "It happened more than once, you know that. How could I ever trust him again? Plus, the affairs were only a symptom of the problem. He didn't like me, Val."

Val stood and hollered into the living room for her kids to go upstairs. After a series of death threats to her brood, they slowly straggled up the stairs giving Antoinette a series of disgruntled "Good-nights."

"Look," Val said in a more normal tone once she sat down again, "do any of them really like us? Do we ever really like them? What are you talking about? Anyway, Tracey's husband and my husband love the ground you walk on. Men like you, if that's all you want, or are worried about. Besides, both of 'em act like you're some goddess, anyway. So, what's like got to do with it?" She laughed more harshly than obviously intended. "You must be drunk, girl."

Antoinette tried to force the haze of wine from her brain so that she could absorb what Val had just said.

"I wanted what you all have—a friend, a companion, someone to have a bunch of kids with."

"Whose house are you talking about? Not mine, and definitely not Tracey's," Valerie scoffed. "We don't even talk to our husbands, beyond the perfunctory. Buddy nearly fell off the kitchen chair when I told him a few days ago that your papers came and you were actually moving back to Philly, alone. What's like got to do with it? We share the same space with these people called husbands, for lack of a better word. Scoop just found out about what had been going on with y'all when Tracey had to get a prison pass from him to help you move. Let's be real, here," Val countered, seeming to become suddenly annoyed. "You had it all going on, girl. You don't want this."

"I need some coffee. The herbal tea isn't making it. I feel like I need to throw up."

"All out, girlie," Val replied with annoyance. "Have to wait till Buddy gets home, whenever that is, to shake down his pockets."

"Listen," Antoinette whispered, leaning toward Val to ensure that little ears didn't overhear any part of their conversation; video games on the second floor notwithstanding. "Tracey's husband, Scoop, looks at anything with a skirt, and he hits her sometimes. We've all tried to get her to see it, but she won't budge, so all we've been able to do is be supportive when the big fights occur. That's a very different story. But, Buddy, loves the ground you walk on and is just an all around marshmallow, nice guy. How did you two do it? Keep it going like that—"

"His fat ass looks like a black Pillsbury dough boy."

"So. He's yours, and he loves you. Plus, he's never cheated on you. Not once. I've gotta believe that there are men who are honest, who cherish their wives and families, or, why did I leave Brian? What was that all for? You've got one of those. Doesn't that count for something? A good marriage, a life partner, a friend?"

Valerie looked around her kitchen quickly, grimacing internally at the sight of the matchbox-size row home she'd never wanted to live in. Her gaze settled on Antoinette and hardened. "You have no idea."

Again Antoinette shook her head for clarity. What was supposed to be a kitchen conference healing session was turning into something she couldn't put her finger on. The mood, the whole vibration, had become weird and strained. What was wrong with Valerie, her most trusted confidant, tonight?

"I know you've got to be tired, girl," Antoinette

murmured, awkwardly gathering her coat around her. "I shouldn't have just barged in on you at no-o'clock in the morning. You're kids were still up, Buddy's out working hard. You've got to be exhaust-ed. I'll be fine. Just wanted to get that book out of my house."

"So now you can't stay and talk to me because I'm being real? Or, is it that I'm not telling you what you want to hear, for once? Or, is it that you've looked around here and it's finally registered that you don't want this?"

"What are you talking about?" The wine was working with gravity, keeping Antoinette in the chair longer than she'd planned.

"Look around, T. You just said it yourself. My house is a mess, my kids are up at un-Godly hours, and Buddy has to work like a fiend to keep this piece of shit roof over our heads. You know this isn't your type of groove, Antoinette. Be honest. You're home slummin' till you get yourself together, and frankly my patience is running thin with the pity-party. You only have one child, you know."

"I never said anything wrong about Buddy, or his ability to provide, or, said anything about the kind of man I would choose, or about your home, Val. That's not what I meant. All I was saying is that you guys have something I never did—warmth in your home. That's all I was trying to say, girl."

Valerie sat back in her chair slowly and let the tension recede from her shoulders. "You're right.

Buddy's no catch. Look at this place, with all these kids in here. I hate West Philly. Always have."

"You are not listening to me," Antoinette nearly yelled, then checked her volume as she tried again unsuccessfully to stand, having to attempt the task twice before she was able to get to her feet. Leaning on the table for support, she peered at Valerie, her knees feeling like they might buckle as she tried to move her body to an upright position. "It has nothing to do with what he does, or doesn't have. It has everything to do with the fact that he's your friend."

"I wish you would just go back to Brian, and stop all of this esoteric rhetoric, and then, none of us would have to worry," Valerie blurted out and stood quickly. "You have options!"

"What?" The words didn't register, and Antoinette swayed again as she pushed herself to a full standing position.

Antoinette stared at Valerie for a long time, finally forcing her friend to cast her gaze down to the cracked linoleum floor. The stench of old cooking oil filled her nostrils and turned her heart rancid with resentment toward Val's comments. There was nothing to say. She had to be drunk, had to have misunderstood what Val said. "I'm going home to throw up, girl. I don't want to add anything else for you to have to clean up."

"You've always had options Antoinette," Val said in a rush, but obviously trying to keep her voice low enough to shield the children above from her words.

"You didn't have to get married. You were able to finish school and get a job in your profession. You picked out where you wanted to live, and didn't have to settle on where your finances could take you. And, you chose between Jerome Henderson and Brian Wellington. Then, when you got separated, you had a string of lovers before this celibacy routine. Your choice."

Almost totally sober from Valerie's tidal wave of emotions, Antoinette steadied herself by holding onto the back of a kitchen chair. "Sure, I traded insult for injury by dating fine, professional men during the first few months that Brian left the house. It was payback, vengeance... something to make him know that I had options, too. Pride, Valerie, and very poor choices. And, in that shallow process of retribution, I almost lost my soul. That's when I gave up all the running, all the trying to match Brian indignity for indignity, especially after he told me the one thing that is so unfair, but so true."

Antoinette tried to focus her vision enough to look Valerie in her eyes. "I had been out with a handsome date, and had my Lauren stashed at a baby sitter's, and oh yes, I very flagrantly promenaded this guy in public, where I knew word would get back to my estranged spouse who was playing the same sick little games. And, Brian showed up at my door, and looked at me like I was dirt, and he told me that no matter what, this was still a man's world.

He said that I was still somebody's mother, and in the morning, he would be Mr. Wellington, and I would be a whore. It was as though I could hear my own dead mother's voice ringing in my ears."

Valerie's expression had softened, and she lowered her gaze. "Girl, I didn't mean—"

"That man told me no decent guy would ever respect or want to marry a sister that had been in the streets like I had, then he left. And, Val, I sat down on the sofa angry as a hornet, but crying like a baby, because to some degree, there is still a double standard of conduct, unfair though it is. But, I thought that you, my home girl, of all people—the one who said not to take that mess from Brian and to go out on dates, and to show him who's boss—all of you said it, would understand? I haven't changed, Valerie. During that time I didn't maraud anyone's household. I was bitter, and angry, and jealous, and gave into spite, and hurt myself—me. Now, you think I'm somebody else?"

Valerie's words repeated in her head, beating each syllable of each phrase into her skull. Each fragment of the charges leveled against Antoinette made her mind recede further and further into a dark corner within it. Standing before Valerie, still half-tipsy and sobering by the minute, she watched the layers of denial peel away from a friendship that she'd cherished. All of their private talks became suspect... each award that she'd won, every highlight and low-light of what she'd shared with Valerie made her want sob. Her friend. Tears formed in Antoinette's eyes and fell without censure.

"I didn't mean…" Valerie's voice trailed off. "But you've always had it all. Don't you see that?"

Things that Cookie had told her, but that she'd refused to listen to, fused with the gong of reality going off in Antoinette's brain. Things that Jerome Henderson once alluded to, but was kind enough not to pursue when they were young. Things that her sister had told her with impudence, hurtful words that Brian had said in rage, truths that she'd warded off to defend her girl… things that she had known about Valerie, but had ignored, all because she'd loved her so much as a friend. Reasons that she'd eclipsed and tucked away safely. The reason why their conversations had become less intimate over the years, and why other newer friends had only gotten snippets of the guarded parts of her life. She'd compartmentalized Valerie, kept her memory safe, just like all the memories in the box were safe, still, and captured in the innocent photos of youth.

"I don't believe we are having this conversation," Antoinette whispered. She'd said those same words to Brian when she'd found out about his first affair. When Val didn't answer, and only hung her head, it was like an eerie deja vu. She'd lost another person in her life.

Somehow this betrayal of friendship seemed as vivid, and there was no way to escape its truth. Her best friend was jealous of her. Her best friend

133

resented her past success. Her best friend coveted the material possessions she'd once had. Her best friend envied even that poor choice of a string of lovers she'd just described, simply because they were professional men. Her best friend was a fraud, showing the world an all natural earth mother who ate only organic foods and wore locks, but beneath all of that façade was a bourgeois sister who wished she'd listened to her parents and had married a doctor. Antoinette gagged and covered her mouth, rushing toward the sink as a dry heave caught the pain in her throat.

"You know what it's like to have your husband not touch you for months, right?" Valerie whispered, focusing her emotions toward the peeling floor. "And to have to get yourself off, when he finally does give you some that ain't worth a damn?"

"Yeah," Antoinette said quietly, moving toward the table, sitting down with Valerie, and reaching her hand across the expanse of it to hold Valerie's. "I've laid in the wet spot that wasn't worth it for nearly half my marriage. But, don't tell me you and Buddy... Val... Don't let that eat away what we had as sister-friends, please promise me."

"I wanted what you all had," Valerie whispered back, clenching Antoinette's hand within her own. "Brian was fine, educated, sexy, made oodles of money, had put you in a nice home. My mother and father threw you up in my face every chance they got. Do you know what that's like? They all thought I should have a home like yours."

"House," Antoinette corrected. "And he knew he was fine. I bought that house, not him, and he gave me pure hell inside of it. Did your parents know that? Do you know that?"

"Yeah, but you got a chance to finish grad school, and do you thing..."

"Val," Antoinette whispered, "I had a gun to my head. I had to work to support my sister through school after Mom died. It wasn't an option. What has that got to do with me and you? You and Trace had your kids earlier, I didn't. Couldn't. It was just the way things worked out."

"I shouldn't have gone there, T. I'm sorry. It's just that I hate being stuck here, you know? There's no way out that's better. So, this is it. The sum total of all I'll ever be. I can't afford to go to work. The daycare bill alone would be more than my salary. You had the option, and you blew it when you left Brian for something that all men do."

Pulling Val up and into an embrace, Antoinette hugged her friend. They'd all been through so much together, and so much individually. The lines of demarcation had become blurred, and it was too easy to hurt those closest with friendly fire. "Buddy never ran on you, and you know it. He loves you and the kids. Right?"

"Look at Cookie, though," Val sniffed, "she's had married men—run with them for years. I even asked her why once, and she told me that because after six months of trying to find the right guy, of being celibate, she was so horny that she couldn't help it. And, Cookie comes from a good family, girl, regardless of their financial circumstances. They're church people, who sit in those four-hour services. Better than yours, mine, or any of ours! Desperation can drive—"

"Stop it," Antoinette warned quietly, squeezing Valerie's hand tighter as she became totally sober. "No poacher has ever crossed your threshold, has she? Nor did Cookie—because we're all friends. Code of honor amongst The Crew. Damn girl. Is that why you two stay at each other's throats? Is that what you now think about me?"

"No, but I can't stand the way she operates—I'm married," Valerie whispered, "and so were you—to men who have never fulfilled any of our dreams."

"Were they supposed to?"

Valerie hesitated and looked at Antoinette. Confusion laced her expression with pain. "Weren't they?"

"I thought we were supposed to also try, and at some point work together for the common goals?"

"That is so much bullshit," Valerie muttered in disgust, tearing herself from Antoinette's embrace and forcing both women to again stand.

"It's real," Antoinette countered, growing defensive. "I'm not talking about a knight on a white charger, I'm talking about an adult equal who puts in as much as you do. In our parent's day, everybody worked hard—and more importantly, respected each other's contribution. Now, everybody is out to do everyone else before they get done, without a thought of joint effort. What the hell's wrong with the world?"

"Now you sound like Cookie," Valerie sighed, removing herself from Antoinette's hold on her elbow. "Look at this place. It was too small when we bought it. I've got kids clothes in boxes and bags. There isn't a new piece of furniture in here, and there isn't a real piece of art on the walls. I've got crayon and dirty finger-print murals going up the steps..."

"And, it's yours," Antoinette countered again as she closed the gulf between them. "Tracey's still in a cramped apartment up on Cedar Avenue, and lugging laundry down the street to the coin-op, not just down her own basement steps—okay. I'm being held in May's internment camp condo—more like Allenwood prison, with her and Dad turning my locks and barging in at will. It's pretty, but there are rules, and the space ain't mine. Plus, I don't have anybody to watch my daughter when I have to go and find a job. I can't impose on Ness all the time. You, at least, have the option of being home with your kids. Tracey can't hold a job long enough before Scoop starts some mess and she gets fired, or has to leave. Buddy never did that to you. He's even encouraged you to do your art. I wish I'd had that with Brian. It's all relative. More importantly, we're supposed to be friends. Who's got what isn't supposed to even factor in."

Valerie sighed heavily. Without looking up at Antoinette who now hovered by the doorway, she took a sip from her lukewarm cup of tea, and set it down very precisely. "I need time and a place to create, and he doesn't make enough for me to put all the kids who aren't in school, in daycare. I need supplies, studio space."

"I know," Antoinette murmured, too weary to speak any louder. "But it's not because he doesn't want to. And, at least you still want your husband to touch you. I don't. It wasn't just the women, it was the timing of the affairs and the things he said that hurt so much when he got caught. Buddy has never said some of those ugly, down-to-the-bone-never-stop-bleeding things to you. And, at least Buddy keeps stable jobs, and isn't on the streets all day claiming to work at some beeper store on Fifty-Second Street with his brother, like Scoop does to Tracey. Truth be told, I don't think she knows how much money Scoop makes there—or from where. Not since the Navy yard closed down, has she known about his finances. That's scary—and it's all relative, girlfriend."

Seeming to pause from the severity of Antoinette's comments, Valerie extended her hand again to touch Antoinette's, perhaps to grab hold of something solid, yet, ephemeral—their friendship. "I know. Guess you caught me throwing my own pity party tonight, because Buddy's working another long shift, and I was sick-to-death of being here with these little monsters, dealing with everything by myself. Maybe I was the one who needed the bottle of wine and a good hot book?" she added sadly, "It's better than anything Buddy has done for me lately."

"You all just need some time to be together, alone," Antoinette whispered. "Why don't you let me take 'em for a weekend, so you two can—"

"Thanks, girl, but I can't remember a weekend that Buddy chose not to work. Making money at his little side jobs is more important than spending time with me. Trust me, Toni. You can't fix everything that's broke. Plus, you're just getting settled in, and before long, you and Cookie will be having the time of your lives."

All Antoinette could do was shake her head. The woman wanted more material things then resented the man for working like a dog to provide them. She wanted a break for herself, but refused baby-sitting help from a friend. She judged Cookie hard, without ever seeing any of Cookie's pain, and hadn't a clue about how Cookie had grown up. Valerie knew fear but couldn't sense it in others. Antoinette let her breath out on a long, slow, sigh.

"Remember that time when Cookie gave Tracey some money, and Scoop went off because he thought some man had given it to her?" Antoinette said quietly, pausing for effect and waiting for

Valerie to look up at her.

"Yeah. I remember."

"You know what Cookie did?" She added more slowly, gazing directly at Valerie to help her point sink in. "She came over with her latest man, and made her date give Scoop the money—claiming that it was for a beeper he didn't need. Then both men laughed and acted like Tracey was some spend-thrift, dip—all so that Scoop would take the money, save face, and not beat her up. Cookie went through all that cat and mouse drama to get money in Tracey's hands in a way that would allow her stupid husband to save face, and so that our girl's gas did-n't get shut off. Cookie never told a soul, other than me and Brian. She only told us because she wanted us to add to the kitty, to put money in the fundrais-ing pot for Tracey. And, to his credit, Brian never told a soul, either. So, even though I'm angry that Brian hurt me, even he's a decent man about some things, in his own way."

"I don't understand the point to this story, Toni?" Valerie whispered, her eyes searching Antoinette's face with the openness of a child's wonder.

"Don't judge so hard, Val, and don't make assumptions. All that glitters ain't gold. I've seen and know what I'm talking about. That's the point."

Declaring the end to the conversation with a light kiss on her friend's forehead, Antoinette made her way to the front door and stepped out into the cold air without turning back. Everything was in flux, even old friendships and alliances... spinning, churning, lurching out of control worst than any vertigo a mere bottle of wine could have ever created.

CHAPTER 10

"Hey, Pop." Jerome stood on his father's front steps and waited to be invited in. As the older man scowled at him through the screen, he surveyed the doorway that used to always be open to him. The cracked bricks and withering white paint around the sill seemed to hold the badly sloping porch onto the house by a mere thread. Yet this portal was once his foundation. A place where he didn't have to knock to gain entry, or need a passport.

"What'chu doin' here so early? Don't tell me you went to church looking like that?" the old man huffed, holding open the screen door and standing aside to gesture with his body for Jerome to enter.

"Just wanted to see you, Pop. Thought maybe we could talk?" Jerome hesitated on the porch, hoping for a warmer invitation in that never came.

"I don't have no money," his father said abruptly, allowing the screen door to slam between them.

"Don't need no money, just some advice," Jerome returned evenly. "Or, maybe I can come back later?"

"Well, since you here, and done woke me up, might as well get a load off your mind. C'mon in," his father sighed indignantly. "Tell me what's wrong—this time."

Jerome followed the old man before him into the dimly lit space, and waited for his father to claim a chair first. Each time he visited, the house seemed smaller and darker, as though it were closing in on itself. He wondered, if one day, he'd come and only find a tiny black box where home used to be.

Positioning himself on the sofa across from his father, he stared at the dated *Ebony* and *Jet* magazines that graced the coffee table. Why had he even come? Then, again, where else was he going to go? After he and Buddy had closed the bar for the second night in a row, this time keeping their conversation to money-making plans, he could only expect his friend to harbor him for a few hours of sobering sleep. This was the only home he knew.

"So," his father snorted, "you in some kinda trouble?"

"I don't know?" Jerome began slowly. "Me and Karen haven't been getting along, and, it's getting pretty bad."

"Yeah, well," his father snapped, turning on the television and snatching the *TV Guide* from an alu-

143

minum-framed television tray, "marriage's gots its ups and downs. That's life, boy."

"But..." Jerome began again slowly, choosing each word with excruciating care, "But, it's real bad, Pop. I mean, we ain't been together in months and it's at the point where all we do is argue. The kids feel it, I hate going home, and—"

"—So? Like I said, marriage's gots its ups and downs, and I don't git into people's domestics." Mr. Henderson, Sr., looked at his son hard, and sucked his teeth, adjusting his dental plate in the process. "You got all them kids over there that you made, if she tired of givin' it up for a while, let her be. Take your ass to work, and give her the money, and be done with it. That's all a black man gits outta this life, once you make them children. It ain't about what you want—or need. An', a man can go git what he needs, witout bringing nothin' else home. Jus' don' disrespect her, is all—by havin' her see it in her face."

"What?" Almost speechless, Jerome stood and paced to the small window that led out to the porch.

"You ain't no choir boy, known that since you messed up in the military and quit behind tail. Coulda gone far, in this day an' age, but you didn't wanna listen. You grown now so I'ma speak to you man to man, and put it to you plain. I brought my money home, and took care of my responsibilities— you and your sister."

His head throbbed as he listened to his father's

words. The defeat in the old man's countenance, and the way he seemed to cast off his disappointment with blame, made his stomach turn. Guilt and anger tore at him as his mother's face etched its way back into his skull. His father had been the one to work himself into lifelessness... along the same road he was traveling on alone now. He also remembered all the nights his mother had served dinners to them alone—sitting quietly staring out the window with her sewing kit on a TV tray, and fabric in her lap.

"I never cheated on my wife, Pop, and don't want to start."

"Never cheated on mine neither. I worked. Less trouble that way." His father turned up the volume on the television and changed the channel.

He hated TV.

"Then, why'd you come here whining about her—if you so happy? What'chu want from me? My blessin' to go run, or somethin'?" his father grumbled after a while.

"No. Just some advice about how to stay somewhere that's driving me insane. About how to make what's gone wrong, go right."

"Well, I done told you. You have one choice; go home and take it. You made your bed, now lie in it. You've already messed up your life when you left the Air Force. Coulda made somethin' of yourself, boy—but you didn't. So, don't come cryin' to me now that you're a man, about not gettin' outta life what you wanted. You married that girl, and she's yours for keeps. Jus' don't disrespect her, and pay your bills."

Jerome turned and looked at his father hard. Their eyes met with unspoken mutual contempt. "I didn't come here this morning to have the Air Force thrown in my face."

His father's glare roved over him with bitter disapproval. "Where you been in them clothes—out all night? You tryin' to use me as an alibi?"

"No," Jerome whispered, heading for the door. "Just a sounding board."

"If you want my advice—take your ass home."

He didn't turn around, but had stopped at his father's words. "I thought that's where I had come this morning."

"Not any more."

Cold air slapped his face and stung his eyes as he hopped into his Bronco and tore away from the curb. The park. He had to go to the park. He had to find a serene place, his favorite spot on top of the hill in Valley Green. A spot unclaimed by the sounds of traffic, or a moving throng of people. He needed to escape and think about what his father had said, not just about today, but about the past. He would sit by the Native American statue, and ask the Great Chief, 'Why?' And, when no one was around, he could let go of the pain that he repeatedly swallowed down as he drove.

Disoriented and furious, he hit Johnson Street hill like a speed demon—going in the direction toward the Kelly Drive. Sun-glare scorched his window, blinding him as his car bounced and came down again crossing Wayne Avenue. It was too bright. There was too much light as a scant flicker of recognition made him turn too late as she passed in his peripheral vision. Then in an instant, Antoinette was gone.

CHAPTER 11

Gospel swayed her soul and she let her body move with the harmony of the music. She closed her eyes and leaned her head back on her Aunt Pearline's sofa. The smell of Sunday cooking and the sound of Pearline's off-key humming filled her with peace. "Yes, I love the Lord," she murmured with the hymn, blending her voice in with Pearline's far away stanzas. This was all the church she needed. Sanctuary. Refuge. A home away from the home that was gone. A home to carry in her heart forever. A place where visions didn't haunt the living.

"Girl, now that's church," Pearline exclaimed as the spiritual came to an end, and the radio minister clamored for the round of amens that followed it.

"This is church," Antoinette sighed, opening her

eyes and smiling at her Aunt. "I couldn't take a dry Episcopal service this morning with Dad and May. I needed to hear good preaching and good gospel. Something to lift me up. The Baptist side of me."

Pearline smiled and wiped her hands on her apron as she stood in the kitchen archway. "Well, chile, you know your great granddaddy's people, my father's folk, was always High-Anglicans from the Islands. Then they went to the Episcopal when they came over here, I suppose. But, in your mother's blood and mine, is always a little Baptist. And we definitely give praise through song. Have Mercy! Always gotta find me some good gospel, or it ain't Sunday," she added with a little chuckle before disappearing into the kitchen.

She followed her Aunt into her magic room, the place where Pearline performed alchemy and transformed ordinary groceries into mouth-watering delicacies from a time gone by. She knew this was the place where all of the mysteries of The Universe were explained, where all problems were discussed, and world summits convened. The kitchen. Pearline's kitchen. A black woman's kitchen. An elder's place of unconditional glory. There was nothing like it. "Help was on the way..." She swayed to the music and murmured with the radio hymn as she walked.

Antoinette took a position on a rickety metal chair and waited. She was the protégé, Aunt Pearline was the mentor, a wise master of the world's ways. Pearline would stir bubbling cauldrons, while she would sit wide-eyed with wonder. Pearline would offer up lessons in parable form, and she would try to absorb as much as she could. Pearline would give her theory, and she would attempt to transform it into applied science. When she could take the stone from Pearline's hand... when she was old enough, wise enough, had lived long enough, it would be her turn to stir the pots, feed the masses with a loaf of knowledge. After all, she'd had a daughter, and was already a master-of-mysteries in training.

"So, chile-of-mine," Pearline said after checking her pot of greens with ham-hocks, her candied yams, and the slowly simmering pot of black-eyed peas, then looking into the oven to dote on her baked chicken, "what brings you way up to my house on a bright, sunny, Sunday afternoon? The Drive is still bad, and you shouldn't be riskin' yo' life tryin' to come see no ole lady. Anyhow, you're lucky you caught me here. Gots funerals to cook for. Col' weather's been hard on folk, plus Women's Day is coming up, third Sunday re-passe. You know, most times, I'm not in till at least four on a Sunday. You lucky I went to early service and came right home."

Antoinette let her gaze travel to the rows of pies, cakes, and cobblers that had been set out on the small dinette table to cool. The scent was intoxicating. "Well, I was just praying that you'd be here, so I guess, for once, God heard my prayers." Her comment, with God's name imbedded in it, was designed to let Pearline know that the conversation was serious. Serious enough to warrant her aunt's heavy concentration while she hummed and moved about her pots.

"Uhmmm humm. Well. Lissen, chile, God always hears your prayers, and by the looks of things, you've been blessed. Ain't homeless, and got food for your belly."

Pearline was going to be tough this afternoon. Antoinette smiled as the elderly woman turned around toward the stove and clicked her tongue over the greens that weren't progressing to her aunt's liking. If she didn't speak up, Pearline wasn't going to ask. It was always their way.

"Aunt Pearline," she said shyly, "how do you know when something is a blessing, or a curse?"

She watched as the master formulated an answer. It was in the rhythm of her aunt's pause. Pearline didn't turn around, but simply took up the end of the radio hymn, "Amazing Grace," and threaded it through her wooden spoon and dropped the notes into each pot before turning around to face her—spoon in one hand, eyes cast upward toward the kitchen ceiling, past the limitations of brick and plaster toward her Jesus. Yes, Antoinette breathed in silently. She could tell that Pearline was hooked. A question designed for a master by an advancing protégé, seasoned with a parable in the best kind of riddle that Pearline seemed to love. One that tested both faith and wisdom... Maybe she was coming of age.

"A blessing can never be a curse, but what seems like a curse going in, may sometimes be a blessing." Pearline looked at her squarely. "Like, it was never a blessing to marry, then have to get divorced. I know that broke your heart, chile. Broke mine too." Pearline's voice was quiet, heavy laden, and she left her spoon in the sink and crossed the room, taking up Antoinette's chin in her hands. "But, baby, you got somethin' beautiful out of that, didn't cha? A child. A beautiful little girl, who your mother never got to see on this side—but she watches over you and that chile from the spirit world. You gotta believe that."

"I do," she said, soaking in the warmth and love that oozed from her Aunt's thick palms. "But, why did it have to happen? Why did I have to come home to a home that wasn't here any more? Everything in Philly, and in the family, has changed."

Pearline patted her face and moved back to the stove, turning off the gas under the black-eyed peas. "Sometimes you have to let them set a while, let the heat come up from the burner without a flame before the spices go through them good."

Antoinette chuckled; they were back to riddles. "But what if you've taken the fire off too soon?"

Opening the oven, Pearline never turned around. "Sometimes you get a bad batch, one with a lot of pebbles, and you have to try to pick 'em out while the pot's still hot, or have to start again. Or, when you don't know what you doin' in the kitchen—before you learn—you start off with too much seasoning, instead of adding a little as you go.... then you keep messin' with it, and messin' with it, and it never gits right. They never taste the same once you stop a batch then start it again. Got to be evenly yoked from the start. Gotta know whatchu doing before you start."

Her mind was on fire. She couldn't take it this morning. She had to know. And she had to tell her aunt about her dream the night before. But, she had to also wait, to time it just right. "What does unevenly yoked mean, Aunt Pearl? I never understood that."

"Go to the rock....." Pearline hummed, taking some green apples from a paper bag on the floor and fishing for another glass cobbler pan.

Antoinette let her body slump in the chair. If Pearline was going to make a cobbler while she got an answer, then it was going to be a long session. Maybe the question was too hard for even the master, she thought, when Pearline shoved a stainless steel bowl and a paring knife before her. Without being told to, she began peeling the apples.

"When you believe in the same things, love the same way, then you's even," Pearline said in a matter-of-fact tone, dusting her wooden cutting-board with flour. "Not jus' religion. No. Like, how you

153

spend money. You think it should go into the house to make a home, and the other person thinks of buying pretty things. That's trouble. Uneven. When one person does little kindnesses, just because they love, and the other takes it for granted. One is hurt, the other is satisfied. When one person stays true, and the other don't... that's uneven. Chile, you been to a good school. You know the difference between even and uneven, now don'tcha?"

Pearline glanced at her from the top of her half-glasses, then went back to her pastry crust. Antoinette stared at the large can of Crisco shortening that flanked her Aunt and pondered the question and the answer.

"But, it says in the vows, 'through thick and through thin... sickness and in health... for better or worse'—"

"And it don't say nothin' 'bout for doormat to wipe your feet on!" Pearline had stopped all motion to make her point as she leveled a firm gaze at Antoinette. "Now, baby, I'ma only say this one time, so get it good. Everybody's entitled to make a mistake. And if they truly have remorse in their heart, and they try to change, you gotta forgive 'em, work through it. Gotsta have forgiveness in your heart. We's all human, an he who is without sin—let them cast the first stone. Amen." Pearline's voice had become serious. "If the man had made an attempt, went with you to talk to somebody, then, I'd say you was being hasty. But, this problem happened over and over again. It was breakin' your soul, chile—jus' bleedin' you dry. On the other hand, I know women who once somethin' has happened, throw it up till the end of time, become mean an keep theyselves away from the man... stop caring, and never ask why trouble started. Then what can the man do? See, folk have to be flexible, but not downtrodden."

Pearline had never blinked as she spoke.

"Ask yourself, chile, did you talk to him? Did you pray on it? Did you try to find out what you had done, understand why he did what he did, and did you stay till you just couldn't go on?"

"Yes." Antoinette's voice was barely a whisper. "But, when I went to the minister, he said that I had taken a vow to obey. That woman was created to be man's 'help-meet' and therefore man is in charge. It was up to me to stay, no matter what."

"Pullleeese." Pearline was indignant and she threw another handful of flour on her wooden board as though exorcising a demon. Billows of white dust hung in the air as she punched and kneaded her pastry crust. "A minister is just a man—not God. Gots good ministers and ones who shoulda never graced a pulpit. Gotsta consider the source. That's why I only go to one source," she said, pointing up for emphasis. "That's my source a'wisdom. Anyway, if they would tell it right, a woman was made from Adam's rib. Not his head to lead him, his foot to be walked on, or his tail-bone to kiss. Humph. Jesus, help me this morning! They confusin' my chile!"

It was all she could do not to chuckle. Now, this was The Word. The Gospel, according to Pearline. Antoinette waited for the balance of her aunt's sermon in abject awe.

"Lemme tell you about the days before Eve, who they blamed everything on. Humph," Pearline said with a smile as she worked. "The Lord made all the fishes, and animals, and everything else. He was glad. Then He made man to rule over all a'that. See?" She said pointing a flour-dusted finger at Antoinette. "But, Adam was lonely," she chuckled, grabbing the glass dish and spreading out the fresh-made pastry. "Now, I can only imagine Adam's prayer—seeing everything else was multiplying and being fruitful. Musta worked him up into a mighty lather, havin' to witness all that by hisself." Pearline stopped and looked at her hard with a wide grin. "Musta said, 'Lord, please, please, Father, I can't take it. I'm losing my natchel mind! Please, send me a woman.'"

They both laughed as Pearline went on, acting out the events by raising her hands up.

"Well, I imagine Our Father looked down and saw his new boy in a bad way. And you know how men are, can't think when they in a bad way. Fishes was probably messin' up the streams, cows was damaging the fields, leaves all over the ground. Everything was probably a man's mess."

"Oh, can you imagine a world without a woman?" Antoinette laughed as she thought back on the days when she had to work late and had to leave Brian home to tend Lauren. "It had to be painful for God to peep down and see that!"

"Yeah, baby. Bet the Lord finally shook his head and said, 'Let me improve upon my creation, let me out-do myself and make a woman—something that can cook, clean, love, take care of my land, but with something man ain't got—grace and humility and a little common sense. She can take low, even when she ain't wrong. She can clean-up what she ain't messed up. So lemme add to her good sense, and lemme sprinkle her with tenderness and motherwit, so all my animals won't be kill't—'cause man's got a bad temper and no patience. An' I'll make her smart enough to handle this mess of a man.'"

Antoinette laughed with Pearline as she began peeling apples again, trying to catch up to her Aunt's steady progress. "But she tangled with the Devil, and that got them put out of Eden," Antoinette countered, waiting for a sure rebuttal.

"So, I've heard," Pearline said with a snort. "An', a man told that story too. When I go on to glory, they gonna have to show me that one, 'cause I know a woman ain't stupid. She got second sight, mother-wit, and common sense. What, over an apple? Humph." Pearline shook her head no as she worked. "What woman you know would get put out of Paradise for negotiatin' wit the Devil? Humph. Don't make sense. Ain't a woman's way."

"Never sounded right to me," Antoinette chuckled, egging her Aunt on.

"You know that ain't a woman's way, a good-sense woman, no how—to mess up a man's job, when he ain't got no other job to feed 'em. She might argue, fuss, but she ain't messin wit his job. 'Sides," Pearline laughed, "if she was all that bad, wouldn't Adam have left her?"

Pearline set the crust-filled pan next to Antoinette and grabbed another paring knife to speed the progress of peeling.

"Nope," Pearline continued undaunted, "if she was a kind of woman to make a man lose his job in Eden, then she woulda got left—or put out by herself. Either that, or she was so good to that boy, that she made him walk away from Paradise with a smile on his face, 'cause he was already in Heaven.'"

The women exchanged a glance and let out a storm of laughter. Pearline shook her head and dabbed the corners of her eyes with an old rumpled piece of tissue that she'd fished out of her sleeve.

"Glad to see you laughin', chile. Laughter is good for the soul," she added with a wink as she stood and checked on her chicken, removing it from the oven to baste it.

"Wish I coulda found somebody to walk through hell-fire with me," Antoinette murmured in a wistful tone. The immediate mirth had slipped from her voice, and she fixed her gaze on the pan as she filled it with apples. "I thought I'd found the right one, and I would have gone through the fire with him. I did. Early on, when our money was funny. As he got a better job, and my jobs got better... it was okay. Growing together, through daily struggles... How do you know who is going to work out?"

When her aunt collected the Pyrex dish from her, and took it back to the side counter, Antoinette waited for more wisdom to pour forth from the well-spring of knowledge that stood before her.

"Needs cinnamon, brown sugar, plenty of butter.... little splash of fresh lemon. Yes, indeed, this one is going to be a good one."

Pearline was back to parables.

"Needs time to bake... not too hot, or the crust will burn."

"But how do you know when... when you're picking the right one?"

Pearline began humming again.

"How long does it take?"

"You interested again?" Pearline smiled. "Been a while, chile, and that ain't healthy. You ain't no old widow woman, like me. Plus, you got a baby. Better while they young, than when they older."

Floored, Antoinette stood and went to the refrigerator and rummaged for a soda.

After a long, motionless pause, Pearline walked over and sat down at the dinette table. "You ain't answered me, chile." Pearline's gaze was steady. "You interested again? You do know what I'm talking about, don't cha?"

It was impossible to look her aunt directly in the eyes. Humiliation burned her face, and she took refuge in the landscape beyond the windowsill.

"Only if it's the right one, and I don't know how to tell that any more. The world is different, today, Aunt Pearline."

She felt a warm palm cover her hands, and it brought her attention from beyond the window's edge to look at her aunt's face. Antoinette's vision blurred as she focused on the lines of age that her aunt wore like badges of honor. She'd disappointed everyone. Her father, her mother's memory, even her new source of vexation, May. She'd broken her vow to God, and now she was lusting after an old flame—who was married. There were no words that she could ever give her Aunt to explain her confusion.

"The world ain't changed since creation, chile." Pearline squeezed Antoinette's clasped hands between her own. "Lissen. What's natchel ain't nothin' to be ashamed of. But, you vulnerable right now. You got to pace yourself, and whoever's got you thinking this way again, might be a prince, or might be The Serpent. Wanna make sure you still in Paradise the next day. Understand?"

Antoinette forced a smile. "That's what I can't tell—when do you know?"

"Well," Pearline said calmly, pulling away her hands and standing to move toward the spice rack. "You young folk think the world is different jus' cause you got the order of it mixed up. See, y'all start with passion, then want love to bloom, then want that person to be a good friend—your best friend, then y'all want respect. Gots the seasons of love all turned upside-down. First ya gotta have respect for that man, and he has to have it for you, cause when all else is done, if you got respect, then even if you do part, you gots your dignity. From respect, you move to being a friend. You walk out of this world with a solid, by the rock friend, then you've been blessed. No more, no less. Somebody who will stand by you when you ain't pretty no mo'. When you get ol' like me. Somebody who wants to read the paper in the chair next to you at night. Who'll keep ya company when you cook, and knows what kind of apples you buy 'cause they seen you do it so much. That kind of friend is one that lasts through sickness and health, for richer and poorer. You can both laugh together with only a pot of rice and beans to fill your belly." Pearline took out her tissue from her sleeve and dabbed her eyes. "I know what I mean by a friend. Don't get to my age, chile, and not know."

Antoinette's heart lurched with remembrance of her Uncle who no longer sat in the chair she now occupied, the chair that held enough memory to make her Aunt Pearline stand, rather than ever sit in it again.

"That is a friend," Antoinette said quietly. "I never had one of those. Well, I did once."

"That's my point, girl. None of you young ladies make the man respect you first, then be your friend before you love him. That's the problem. Y'all jump right to love, then give him your body, then want his respect and friendship the next day. Crazy. Man's a creature of habit. You git in the habit of not respecting yourself, fighting over him like starvin' children over a crumb of pie from the table, he can't respect that—or see you as no friend. Why buy the cow if the milk is free? Y'all think we ol' ladies is talking about finances. If everything was based on finances, the race woulda stopped the next day out of slavery. Sometime a black man ain't got no finances in this country, but he can have ambition and character. An' if he got character, and the will to try, then you can respect him."

"Yes. I learned that the hard way."

"Take your daddy and momma," Pearline said, adjusting her frame a little straighter to emphasize the quiet dignity that had never left her. "She had the family background, a little education, an' people who lived well. Your daddy didn't have none a'that. Our side is plain folk, but good folk. She saw that in him, and respected the man for the man he was. And she became his friend, and he was hers. God rest her soul. She was more than a sister-in-law, she was also my friend. My best friend. Can't nobody take place of a friend like that."

"No. They can't." Antoinette let the two big tears that had formed in her eyes fall. "I wanted what they had." In truth, she also thought of her friend Valerie, and wished that they could have what her mother and Pearline had shared, true love between friends—untainted by jealousies. How did the old people do it, the ones who'd come before her time, she wondered?

"You right to have wanted that, 'cause yo' daddy and momma was true soul-mates. And, a friend like that, you love forever and a day," Pearline said, her eyes moistening as she reached for her tissue again. "That's not puppy love, it's a deep, abiding love. It can be carried in your heart till the end of time. Others come and go, your life gets lived, and in time, you can find a place for everybody else—but the lost claims that middle spot. They own it," she said pointing to her heart and clasping the tissue in her hand. "That's why you will always be my chile, for me to take the place of the mother that fell before she could tell you 'bout life when you needed to know it most. Praise God," she said whirling around to add her spices to the cobbler.

Antoinette let her Aunt's words seep into her soul like the warm butter that she brushed across the crust of her creation.

"That's why God took woman from the rib, chile... right next to his heart. Cause if a man loved a woman with all his heart, made her happy by cherishing her, filled her up with abiding love—a love that lived in her, even when he was not around, then, there wouldn't be nothin' he couldn't ask her to do.

Then she would be only too happy to please him, and it wouldn't be no issue of obey. Obey? Not like in the army, taking orders from a fool, but doing everything in your power to please the one who brings so much joy to your life, chile. That's what they was talking about. Even. Passion, jus' follows the course of nature. Don't let it come first. Get everything else in order, then I promise you, the experience will be Divine."

"Your life?"

"Not just your life, in general," her Aunt said with a side-ways smirk. "The love-making. You young folk don't know how to do that either."

Antoinette's jaw went slack before she could catch herself.

Pearline let out a hearty laugh. "Lord, have Mercy!" she cried out, looking upward, "Helen, my dear sister-in-law, didn't you teach this chile nothin' before you left us?" Pearline shook her head as she fussed over the top crust, still not looking at Antoinette.

"Honey, making a baby, or doing that funny mess y'all young folk read about, ain't makin' love. That's pure animal, and it might feel good, but it ain't as good as it could be."

She wasn't sure of how to respond. Antoinette looked down at her soda can and pondered the riddle. It was a delicate subject—one she wasn't prepared for—especially with Aunt Pearline. But, she needed clarity without transgressing respect for her aunt, or her aunt's authority. It was Sunday, for chrissake! Obviously, she had advanced a level in master's training. God help her.

"But..." Antoinette stammered, and let her voice trail off. What was there to say to a master at this point?

"But," Pearline said as she picked up her dangling word, "the difference is, when you respect the person who lays their hands on you, and he treats you like you some kinda gift from Above to be revered, when he looks into your eyes, no words are necessary, because he's been your friend and knows your mind. When he loves you more than life itself, and you hold him in your heart as though he's the very thing that makes your heart beat, when he touches you, you will know nothing greater, nothing more special, nothing more worth the risk. That's how you know."

Pearline wiped her hands and picked up the pan and moved toward the stove, removing the chicken for a last inspection before inserting the cobbler in its place. "Anything else is just feelin' your nature, and man feels his about twenty times a day. That ain't the lasting kind of lovin.' Now, if you had that with your husband, go home and work it out. If you didn't, you went in wrong from the door, and the way you start out, is the way you finish up. Sort of like playing the lottery—sometimes you win, sometimes you don't. In everybody's best interest to start over if you can't find the respect and friendship.

Ain't good for the children to see disrespect of the mother, or the father."

Pearline slammed the oven door, and Antoinette knew that the subject had been closed. The master had spoken. However, too many riddles still remained under the layers of sweet parables.

"But, what if you were the fool, Aunt Pearline? What if you had that, once, and made a choice to go with someone out of passion, and out of their place in the world, family pressures, and a little bit of friendship? But you had had what you were talking about... a long time ago?"

Pearline sighed and leaned against the sink. "That depends," she said, chewing the insides of her mouth with a frown. "Depends on if that situation is still available."

"What if it isn't, but you haven't been able to get it out of your mind?"

"Then you pray on it. If it was for you, then, it will come to you again. If it wasn't, then let sleepin' dogs lie—'cause you could wind up with fleas, or bit real bad."

"I think Mom sent him to me."

There was dead silence between them. Only the radio gospel and the light rattle from the steaming pot of greens. Her Aunt studied her face, and closed her eyes. "When did your mother come?"

"Last night in a dream."

"Was it night or day—in the dream?"

"Night. But she was smiling and surrounded by

this beautiful white light. And as I opened the door, she was standing in front of a man, who I couldn't see."

"Oh, chile, that was just anxiety. We all have them kindsa dreams from time to time—when lovin' ain't been in our lives for a while." Pearline chuckled, waved her hand and dismissed the subject again, but her carriage had visibly relaxed.

Embarrassment singed her. "No, Aunt Pearl... it wasn't that kind of dream."

"If you say so," Pearline said with a shrug, obviously trying not to let the smile on her face broaden. "Well, then it was probably just your Mom a little restless to see how you was doin' in your new place instead of under her roof, is all. But it was for the best—you couldn'ta lived under May's roof no how."

"No, Aunt Pearline." Antoinette was steadfast. "I was standing in water in the dream, Mom told me she'd always liked him—then, I woke up. That's why I knew I had to come see you, because I think it was him... the same one in the dream. Then, as I was coming up Johnson Street hill from the drive, the sun hit my window, and again, I couldn't see his face really till he passed because of the same kind of light... but, I think it was him."

"Good gracious. Helen," Pearline said looking up and grinning, "you can't go 'round blindin' the chile while she driving!. It ain't like you. Be mo' delicate wit yo' messages, sister-in-law. Now, my brother got to have somebody till he die—and you done scared this chile into my kitchen, gettin' in my way on a cookin' Sunday."

Pearline gave her a wide grin as she walked over and placed a hand on each shoulder. "Feel better? I done spoke on it. So, my sister-in-law will behave herself from now on. She's your Momma, and won't hurt you, or May. Sometimes the spirit world—"

"But, I think I actually saw him, Aunt Pearline." Antoinette held her Aunt's gaze and stopped her words. "She said in the dream that she'd always liked him. Then she smiled. I woke up, finished cleaning, and he showed up on Johnson Street. Twenty years later..." her voice trailed off into a whisper as a sob caught in her throat. "He's married, and has children. I know God couldn't have sent him. And I can't believe my mother would send him, unless she's in hell. Why would she do that? Why would I even have to catch a sight of that temptation?"

"Could be your mind playin' tricks on ya—that's Ol' Slew Foot." Pearline's grip tightened on her shoulders as she gathered her up in wide arms. "On the other hand, if you did see right, even though things don't happen when you want them, He's always on time."

"But, how will I know? What if I'm just wishing so hard..."

"Gotta wait for a sign. One thing's for sure, though, your mother ain't in hell, baby, even though, right now, you is. Pray, and make him respect you. First. An' don't cross no lines until he get's hisself together, and comes to ya right. This is between him and his Jesus. You stay out of it so you can sleep at night."

"I haven't slept well in a long time."

"That bad, huh?" Her aunt chuckled, and hugged her tighter. "It'a be all right, baby."

Antoinette held onto her aunt for what seemed like an eternity. "What would I do without you, Aunt Pearl?"

"One day you gonna have to do without your old Aunt Pearl. Then you gonna be somebody's aunt, or wise momma, and you have to tell them the same things me and your momma told you. Even if I'm gone, I'll be an angel lookin' out for you. An' if it's who I'm thinkin' of, an angel sent him, special delivery, I believe."

She gave her aunt a look of disbelief.

"Well, best to be prepared if he do come callin'. Take two of my cobblers, a peach and an apple, and put foil on 'em before you put 'em in a bag. Least you can do is give dat boy some good home cookin,' since he'll prob'ly be put out before long."

Her aunt tried to hide a chuckle but failed, and waved her words away before she could respond.

"Accept what you're given with Grace, and don't say a mumblin' word, especially to your girlfriends. This needs to be between you and your Jesus till everything's on solid rock. Trust me, baby. If who I think it is do come back to ya, envy is sure to follow. Yup, that boy had character—jus' like your daddy does."

"But—"

"Take the pies, chile," Pearline fussed with a chuckle, "and get out of my hair while I'm in the kitchen. Besides, Jerome always loved my cobblers, anyways. Like I said, ain't nothin' changed since creation. An' he used to look at cha' like you was one of my best cobblers. Like he could sop you up. So, give my baby, Miss Lauren, a kiss and go 'head home now. All we can do is pray on it—that he's still operatin' with character, and won't put you in no position of disgrace before he gets hisself organized. Gotta talk to my sister, your mother. She can't be goin' around match-makin' like this, might get her put out of Heaven. Then again, she was always stubborn about what she wanted, like you. Impatient. Grievin' a loss takes time, jus' like comin' back out in the Spring takes time. Jus' don' be rushin' God's hand, and you'll be fine."

Antoinette simply stared at her aunt as the older woman's grin widened with a wink. She marveled at how the old dolls knew things, without a name being mentioned, or a situation ever being fully discussed. It was definitely a lost art form. The pure magic of it all. No wonder in their day, a man didn't stand a chance.

Thoughts of her sister Adrienne oddly co-mingled with her aunt's broad smile, and it fused with her mother's in her mind, along with those of all of their older female friends. Not only did these women stay married for a lifetime, but they kept friendships and siblings close to their hearts for a lifetime as well. Antoinette returned her aunt's patient smile as she finally absorbed the real purpose of her visit to Pearline's. Truly there were many fences to mend, and maybe God had sent her to church in her aunt's kitchen. Maybe she just came to get confirmation that if she got out of God's way, He would indeed make it all right.

"It's okay, Aunt Pearl. Me and Lauren can't eat a whole one alone," Antoinette said quietly, trying to refuse the cobbler to no avail. "It's just the two of us now. I don't need one... my hips tell that truth. Even Dad said so."

Her aunt just waved her hand in disgust as she continued wrapping a pan with aluminum foil. "That was May, not your father, consider the source. Like I said, if a man's for you, you don't need to worry about all them particulars. If you want to do it for you, then you will, but it ain't nobody's bizness but yours. Hips, no hips—none of that has a thing to do with how lovable a person is. Stop talkin' foolish chile, and come git this food outta my kitchen."

"But, I have to go pick up Lauren from Vanessa's, anyway, and let you get back to cooking."

Her Aunt remained undaunted as she took out a brown supermarket bag and began wrapping a second cobbler with foil. "Wha'did I give you before?

171

Peach or apple?"

"Peach," Antoinette intoned without emotion, suddenly exhausted. "I don't—"

"—Then take an apple one, and a peach, too. Then put it in the freezer till you need it. They'll keep. Never know what you need, till it comes. Bring me back my pans, too, when you're done."

All she could do was sigh and accept the heavy parcel.

"Remember what I said, honey," Pearline whispered, giving her a peck on the cheek. "You pass that kiss on to my baby, Lauren, and tell her to mind her manners or Aunt Pearline is gonna pinch her fat little legs."

"She's going through what feels like a second phase of the terrible two's. Aunt Pearline, that child is a trip!"

"Go easy on my baby, she comes by stubborness honest. Runs in the family," Pearline chuckled, "Yes, indeedy, Jesus."

"I'll try my best," Antoinette laughed, shaking her head and giving in. "Oh, yeah, Adrienne said to give you a kiss, and—"

"—She's coming home for Easter!" her Aunt squealed, clapping her hands and finishing Antoinette's sentence. "Praise God, had to be extra patient with that one, you know. But she's comin' around, and comin' home. Lordy! That's my other chile."

"Yeah, Adrienne is all grown up now, Aunt

Pearline. I can't baby her no more."

Her Aunt kissed her cheek and issued a knowing glance. "Hurts when they grow up... don't it? Kinda miss them needing you so much. So, be patient with your Daddy and May too. 'Specially May... she's got some pretty big glass slippers to fill. I'd rather come behind a divorce, than a ghost, a good ghost, an angel that everybody loved. May just needs time and TLC. Sometimes people's just scared."

Antoinette returned her aunt's kiss and considered her words. "Yeah, I know she's got a good heart, but she get's on my nerves with her bossiness sometimes."

Pearline laughed. "Don't you say a mumbling word, chile! Gits on mine too. Was gonna give her a piece of my mind the other day. Had to pray on it."

Antoinette chuckled and pulled on her coat. "Yeah, I gotta do a lot of praying."

"Don't we all, chile? Won't hurt you none. We all gotsta pray. But, while you at it, make sure you save a hunk of cobbler to give Jerome—a taste of my best too—when he comes by," she added with a wink. "Jus' don't rush God's hand."

CHAPTER 12

He was grateful that the silent treatment had greeted him instead of a full-blown argument, and that he'd been able to fill the vacated bed instead of the sofa for a few hours. His rest had been broken for months, and today more than ever, he'd needed a nap. Just a moment alone, to close the world off. Time to think.

Out of force of habit, he listened for the sound of children. All seemed normal. Their voices collided against his brain and he relaxed again. Just the regular squabbling over the television. He'd half expected them all to be gone, his children swept away to his mother-in-law's house, and perhaps to be kept there forever this time. That was always the pending threat. But, nothing major had changed. By late afternoon, Karen was probably getting dinner started. It was Sunday, after all. It was part of the routine.

The hearty scent of food being prepared rose from the kitchen below and brought him into full consciousness. Karen. He needed to tell her something. Something plausible. Something that would salvage the balance of the day. Something that would save his marriage, and stop his wife from talking about divorce. Anything. His father was right. He'd failed in finding a solid career in the military, and now he was failing at being a husband. He should have gone home after work—instead of to the bar on Saturday night with Buddy and to his friend's sofa at three o'clock in the morning. He had to stay home, and make it work. There was nowhere else to go and nothing else to do. He was a lifer.

Lurching himself to a sitting position, he looked down at his grimy jeans. Damn. She'd have his hide for getting into bed with work clothes on. But, what had been his alternative? He hadn't been home. From Buddy's, he had headed straight to his father's house. Besides, when he'd left Saturday morning, he wasn't sure of the conditions of the perimeter before he'd crashed—whether he'd have to get up and be ready for a battle, or if he'd be able to sleep for a few hours to replenish his mental artillery. This was no way to live—always on edge in the temporary DMZ, the demilitarized zone.

Jerome sat on the side of the bed and held his head in his hands. The casinos.

"Well, are you going to move so I can wash the sheets?"

He looked up at Karen and shook his head, no. Instant panic froze his intention to get up. What if he'd talked in his sleep? Or worse? "I'll do it. It was my fault that I came in so tired. I don't need to cause you extra laundry." Suddenly he felt like he was fifteen.

Karen narrowed her gaze on him. "I'd prefer to do the laundry—unless there's a reason I shouldn't?"

Jerome stood slowly and prepared for her military inspection. If he'd left something from a dream, then at least he was there alone. To hell with her suspicions; she'd kept him at bay longer than was human.

"No, baby," he said sarcastically, trying without much success to temper his voice. "Check my clothes too. Look at my hands," he said as he extended them out flat, "Who do you think would let a man put his hands on her like this? Look at my face, I haven't shaved or taken a goddamned shower in twenty-four hours!"

"Where were you?"

"At my father's"

"I mean, last night?"

"At the bar, after I got off my shift. Then I crashed at Buddy's to keep from killing myself on The Drive."

"What bar?"

"The Third World Lounge, out West. Call

Buddy. We were trying to figure out how to legally make more money for our households. Call my father. I went by there when I left Buddy's sofa."

"I will."

He didn't answer, but looked at her with a steady grit. He hated the suspicion, the need to always justify and quantify his actions.

"Why were you out in West Philly, at some damned bar?" she hissed, glowering up at him with her arms folded across her chest. "Why couldn't you just bring your ass home?"

"Because you told me you still wanted a divorce and I was coming home to sleep on the damned couch again, and I wanted to get good and drunk before I had to deal with either of those realities." Through the haze of sleep deprivation and anger, his father's words rang in his head. But despite what he'd been told, rage held back reason for a moment.

They stood facing each other in a deadlock. When Karen brushed passed him and snatched the sheets from the bed, he steadied his voice.

"I want us to go somewhere. Alone. That's why I've been working overtime, to get some extra cash so I could take you down to the casinos."

She stopped and looked at him hard. "You want to take me out?"

"Yes," he said quietly, holding her gaze within his. "Something has to change, and I figure it's me." Jerome looked away as his mother's face came into his mind's eye. He let out his breath slowly before he spoke again. He did not want to become his father. "Look, you're stuck in the house all day with the kids... the money is always funny... we need some time away," he finally said in a quiet voice. "Something's gotta give, before this thing goes too far. I don't even know what started it."

Her demeanor seemed to soften as she gathered up the sheets more slowly.

"Okay. When?"

He studied her hard, and although her voice had gone soft, her expression hadn't. Trust left him as he watched her. He'd seen this game before, and could only hope that she'd stop playing with his head once they were away from the house.

"Next weekend, maybe. If you get a sitter—"

"I thought you were taking me out, but once again, I have to make all the plans—"

"I'll call Miss Hattie, down the street, to see if her niece can—"

"I don't want them people in my house, or in our business."

He could feel anger closing his throat, but fought through it. "Let me call Miss Hattie. She's the closest one, and we know her niece. Suppose we want to stay down longer, maybe overnight? It's been a long time since we did that. It's been a long time since we've done anything together."

Something flickered in Karen's eyes that he couldn't understand. It was some sort of recognition, maybe it was hope?

"What happened last night—or, this morning?" She'd asked her question while coming in close enough to smell him. "Something happened, or you wouldn't be coming in here all guilty and trying to be nice."

The hope he'd seen reflecting in her eyes had obviously been his own. As she stared at him, he knew instantly that it was fear and more mistrust that he'd seen within hers.

"Last night, I found out what a fool I've been, and how important my family is to me. I listened to Buddy talk about all the plans he and Val had, and how he was gonna build her a studio." He searched for the words. "Because, you can't recapture the past and act like a teenager all of your life. That's over. I came home."

Her radar scanned him, and he closed his eyes as she surveyed his clothes.

"So who, or what, made you come to this grand conclusion?" She'd asked a hard question, but her voice was just above a murmur and filled with trepidation. It was not the harsh blow he'd expected.

"I was on my way home, then decided to page Buddy to meet me at the bar. Buddy had offered me a way to make some extra money the night before—doing apartment jobs, when I get off shift. I thought about it all day, and as I was driving home, something made me call him. We had a few, then went back to his spot, talking about how we could hook up, had a few more rounds at his kitchen table, and I was just so tired, I crashed. He takes care of his family. I'm just trying to do the same. Then, I went to Pop's first thing this morning—to talk, and he told me no less. To go home."

He watched her body relax, and as it did, his mind recoiled from his heart with guilt. He'd lied, by omission, but out of necessity. He couldn't explain what hearing of Antoinette's return from Scoop had done to him a couple of days prior, or how glimpsing her out of the corner of his eye made him retrace his past and wish away his present, or how precariously he'd balanced his emotions at the traffic light until she'd vanished up the hill. How could he explain that seeing her was like seeing a phantom, and how that had ripped out the last anchor that held his heart inside of his chest? How could he explain that seeing Antoinette had made him let go of the last of his dreams, because those dreams were supposed to be lived with her? But that was such a foolish thought. And, although he hadn't made love to another woman, he'd thought about it enough to make sleeping alone any longer impossible. Yes, something happened Friday night—something had happened at his father's home... and something happened on Johnson Street hill. He had died, and all he had left to give Karen was his soul-less shell.

Jerome swallowed hard as salty liquid burned his vocal chords. "Please, Karen," he said in a hoarse whisper, as he brought his hands to her shoulders, instinctively waiting for her to flinch away. When she didn't, he leaned his head against her forehead and closed his eyes. "I'm only human. I don't know what went wrong, or when it started going wrong. Let's get out of Philly, before it's too late."

Moments collected and gathered within his spinal column until her voice let the tension drain from his body.

"Call whoever you want to baby-sit, and we can go next weekend. What hotel?"

"I don't care," he murmured against her hair. "Anywhere you want. I just want to get us out of Philadelphia."

"I'm tired of living like this, Jay."

"Yeah, baby. So am I."

CHAPTER 13

A full week of serious job hunting, running errands to settle-in, finalizing day care arrangements so she could interview without hearing May's mouth, and now, her girlfriends wanted her to go to a serious networking conference and she couldn't even do that!

Antoinette paced the floor with rage as she clutched the telephone receiver in her hand, wondering why her personal freedom was always in jeopardy for even the simplest desire.

"I know, I know, Cookie!" Antoinette bellowed into the receiver. "All of us had this planned for a month before I left Jersey, and he's not here. Got it? He's not here, and his daughter has been whining for him for the last two hours. I don't know if I can go."

"Calm down," Cookie snapped into her ear, "Look, you know how Brian rolls. He probably thought you were planning to go out and have some fun, so he's slow-walking you, girl. Shot blocking. Now, you have to switch to plan B. Why don't you see if Ness or Val can watch Lauren, they're always home?"

Antoinette counted to ten before she responded, this was not the time to air the strange discussion between herself and Val, especially not with Cookie, and especially not about the subject that had caused the tension.

"Val has enough children to watch," she said with firm delivery to close that option, "and besides, I just left my baby last weekend with my cousin. I can't be using up all my favors like that. What if an interview comes up, or something? The only reason I agreed to go with you and Tracey was because it was going to be Brian's weekend, and Trace can usually never get out. Hell, she might have had to run away from home to go. Who knows? Leaving your child with the other parent, is not like leaving her. She's been through enough trauma. You should understand this by now, Cook—"

"What I understand is, we've all put up our money to split the hotel room three ways. What I understand is that, you haven't really done anything for yourself, or gone anywhere since you separated and divorced—maybe even before that, if memory serves me correctly. And what I do know is that, this

Women's Conference, will have some serious opportunities for both you and Trace, which is how I sold it to Scoop. There will be some serious heavyweight sisters in attendance who, with your talents, can put you on the map. He's all about his woman making money, even if his trifling butt doesn't. He trusts me when it comes to money. So, if she can go, you can go. So, call your cousin, take Lauren back to her house, and get on the road with us. Worry about babysitters for interviews later."

Cookie's words slammed against her brain and something inside Antoinette snapped like a valve under too much pressure, or a twig caught temporarily between two rocks before it gives way to a thunderous current. She walked into the bedroom and shut the door. "I need a job, Cookie. You're right. To hell with this! This is business. My child's future hangs on it. Do you know what happened with the job leads I went on this week? Nothing!"

"What?" Cookie's voice went quiet. Mild shock hung in the air as neither woman spoke for a moment.

"I'm down to my last couple of thousand. Sounds like a lot, but when you factor in the rent here at six hundred a month; due to May's gracious reduction from twelve-hundred. The gas, electric, telephone, old credit card bills, and car insurance... I've got two months, maybe three, then I'm on parental-welfare. Do you hear me, girl? Unemployment isn't an option, because I quit; I checked Monday. The house only broke even when it was finally sold. All that aside, I'll be there tonight. I am going to wait for Brian, because I don't want to start telling his daughter that he couldn't make time to pick her up. Then, I'm going to read him, grab my road gear, then I'm gone. Save a glass of wine for me, and line up the prospects."

"But, your used struggle-buggy won't make it up to the Poconos alone. That's why I was going to take my Volvo. I mean, you don't even have snow tires. The ice on the roads is a bitc—"

"—Cookie, weren't you the one who said I have to take charge of my life? That I have to suit up, go in, and take Philly back by storm? Weren't you the one, girl?" Antoinette's voice faltered "I'm tired of this crap. Okay? I want things to go right, for just once, for just a little while."

"And we don't want you to be driving in this condition, pissed-off, near tears, and ready to kill yourself on the road trying to get to a maybe-job-lead. Girl, if you can't make it, we'll understand."

The sudden concern in Cookie's voice grated her. Now, she was the object of her toughest friend's pity! None of her reactions were fitting old patterns, and at this moment, she wasn't in the frame of mind to go through a telephone psychiatric evaluation.

"I. Will. Be. There. Period," she said, stretching out each syllable in each word.

"What happened with the job leads Francis faxed you this week, baby? Have you talked to her?"

Antoinette leaned against the door of her bedroom and listened to her daughter's squeals of delight as the theme song from the Disney *Aladdin* video blared through the condo. Kicking at her packed overnight bag, she went to the bathroom and again closed the door behind her. The sound of Disney was making her insane.

"I just spoke to Francis briefly. She was really busy and sounded tired this week. I didn't even go into the whole move drama. Anyway, the first one was at Drexel University," she said with a weary sigh, "but, the lead was only a formality. An internal candidate had already been chosen before they even began the search process."

Cookie sucked her teeth. "I hate that shit."

"Yeah, then Penn played with my mind some more. I went to two interviews, and both Directors looked at me like I couldn't possibly have had the nerve to apply for an Associate Director's position."

"What? You've got more credentials and work experiences than the people who interviewed you!"

"Tell me about it. But, Cookie, those weren't the worst ones." Antoinette smoothed the front of her blue powersuit and sat down on the toilet and let her head hang.

"Oh, baby..."

"Yeah, Cook, I went in for this public relations job at The Community Reading Program. For God's sake, they're right here in West Philly. A little low-salary, rinky-dink, non-profit organization.

But, after these two Laura-Ashley-wearin'-wanna-be- 'liberal-white-feminists,' looked me over, and virtually questioned the authenticity of my resume, they called me back the next day with a thanks-but-no-thanks. It-was-a-pleasure-to-talk-to-such-a-talented-black-woman pile of bull. They said they'd refer me to another program that was hiring. So, Cookie, tell me what's a has-been, record-holding, high-paid-hit-woman-of-sales supposed to do now?"

"Work for yourself."

"As a freelancer? Pulleeeze, Cookie, it takes money to start a business, and time. I don't have either. So you know what I did? I took a job for eight bucks an hour, on a twenty-hour work week, teaching in a basement up on Fifty-sixth and Chestnut Street. May will love that. She'll evict me. That's six-hundred and forty a month!"

"You what!"

Antoinette laughed as Cookie nearly burst a blood vessel in her ear. Yeah, she thought, becoming even more morose. Cookie was right, maybe she shouldn't drive. She was practically hysterical. She let out the pain with deep, resounding chuckles. But, this time it was hard to stop laughing at the situation. The sound of her own voice frightened her as she dabbed at her makeup while tears plopped on her navy blue pleated skirt.

"It's a drug rehab joint, Cook," she coughed through the laughter and tears. "Cool. I can do a drug program, since it's an allied health field. I probably need to do psycho-tropic drugs myself at this point. Who could blame me?" Although Cookie didn't answer or laugh with her, Antoinette threw her head back and laughed harder. "Check it out, I'm supposed to teach women who have been abused, on drugs, God knows whatever, how to get a job to take care of themselves and their kids. We haven't been able to impact our dearest friend Tracey for years. Now, I'm supposed to be an expert with women I don't even know? Can you believe it? I ask you, girl, can you believe it? On six-hundred and forty a month? That was my car payment and insurance when I used to pull down almost six figures! It's all gone, Cookie, from paying off debt, and deck extensions, and bills in a house that I don't even own now!"

When Cookie still didn't respond, she stood and snatched a piece of toilet paper from the roll and went to the mirror to touch up her foundation. That's all she needed was for Brian to walk in and see her crying. That would only add insult to the deep gash of injury. No. Not tonight.

"Listen," Cookie said as softly as Antoinette had ever heard her speak, "you come up here tonight, and we'll open some doors. We'll work on Tracey. Trust me. But, drive safely, and if you're too tired, come tomorrow. The conference runs all weekend. No pressure."

"Okay," she said, her voice regaining its original

composure, "I'll be there, hell or high water."

"We love you, lady. Now put on your military blues, and get ready to hit your target in the Poconos."

"Got 'em on now."

"Your face beat?"

"Beat lovely."

"Hair bouncin' an behavin'?"

"Thoroughly."

"Nails neat, no talons—French manicure, right?"

"Business clear, with a white-stick trim."

"Bag packed?"

"All systems go, captain," she mimicked, giving Cookie a military hail as she faced herself in the mirror.

"You remember how to do this? How to work a room?"

"I'm the flush, you're the steel trap. No prisoners."

"Good, girl. Synchronize watches. Now, let's go kill something."

"Thanks, Cookie. I love you."

"I love you too, girl. Drive safely."

"Bye."

"Later, chicky."

Antoinette tapped the off button and stared at herself in the mirror for a long while. Her old life was falling away, but nothing new, nothing good, solid, or reliable had replaced it. She looked at her gold watch and adjusted her double strand of faux pearls with annoyance. Seven-thirty. Damn Brian Wellington till the day he died; she was going out tonight.

She took a deep breath and prepared her senses for the thrilling conclusion of the video where a blue genie made everything work out all right. Where was her genie when she needed one?

"Mommy, Mommy, I'ma take it to Daddy's? We see it again!"

Antoinette plopped down next to her daughter and pulled her in tight. "Yup, suga-lump. You can take it to Daddy's and see it as many times as you want." She ignored the new wrinkles being ground into her suit, as well as the tiny Hunchback of Notre Dame sneakers that were precariously swinging near the edge of her one pair of in-tact hose. Should have gone for alimony, she thought briefly, as her mind glazed over and she watched the animated characters on the set. At this point, it didn't matter. None of it mattered. Her child was happy and oblivious. They'd been through combined tears of longing for Daddy, and nightmares.

She'd slept with a frightened toddler all week long in the new condo. She had wallowed in the guilt already, the same guilt that every women experiences when she has to make the final decision for the best—be she right or wrong, if it brings pain to her child in any way, she feels guilty. And that same paralyzing guilt about not staying and taking a bad marriage for her child renewed itself each time she'd changed the bed from Lauren's accidents at night, while she'd steadfastly refused to go back to the diapers that she couldn't afford. It just didn't matter. Nor did the Poconos, really, at this point. Brian had won, really. What had she gained from all of this? Was she happier, freer, more sure of herself, more in control? She doubted it.

Now, on the third round of Aladdin, she was just too tired to fight any more.

When the doorbell chimed, Lauren tore away from her side, snagging her stockings as she raced for the door.

"Daddy! Daddy! Mommy, open da door!"

Antoinette looked at the wall clock. Eight-thirty, and two and a half hours later than expected, the great Brian Wellington had decided to grace her. She stood slowly, smoothing her suit front as her daughter continued to wiggle in front of the door while turning the knob. By rote she buzzed the exterior door security without checking to see who was in the lobby. It didn't matter. If someone came up to her unit and killed her, at least that would have been a merciful conclusion.

"Move, honey, so Mommy can open the door," she said flatly, flipping the locks after a moment as calmly as she could. When she flung the door open, it took her mind a moment to process her sister's form.

"Adrienne!" she squealed, gathering her sister in her arms, while rapidly trying to console Lauren.

"Daddy's still coming, we just got an extra surprise!"

"Hey, girl!" Adrienne squealed back, returning the hug. "You never know what wind I might blow in on! How's my niece?" Adrienne laughed, trying to grab the wriggling youngster. "So, what's up, y'all?"

"C'mon in," Antoinette sighed, as they walked into the condo and Adrienne dropped her coat on the chair, "It's a long story. Brian was supposed to have been here to keep Lauren for the weekend. He's a little late... about two and a half hours late."

The two sisters exchanged a look that was designed to convey meaning around the wide-eyed Lauren. Holding any further commentary in check, Antoinette went towards the kitchen to instinctively begin making herbal tea for Adrienne.

"You got a surprise, Aunt A?" Lauren giggled as she followed the women.

"Aren't I enough of a surprise, chicken-licken?" Adrienne quipped, issuing a wink at Antoinette.

"No, I mean a real surprise," Lauren countered buoyantly, craning her neck upward to her tall, glamorous aunt.

"Kids are honest, A, what can I tell you?" Antoinette chuckled as she tried to shoo Lauren out of her path. "Let your Aunt get in the door good, honey. Besides, people don't always have to give you something when they come for a visit. It's just nice to have them come home."

"All right," Lauren sighed, becoming crestfallen,

"I just thought..."

"Well, you never know," Adrienne chuckled, winking at Antoinette. "I might just have something special in my bag for my niece," Adrienne added with a stunning smile, fishing in her purse for a trinket. "Have you been a good girl?"

"Yup! Tell her, Mommy. I been good."

"Then, this is for you," Adrienne laughed, handing the child a plastic Mickey Mouse watch. "Now scoot, so I can talk to your Mommy."

It was all the patience that Antoinette could muster to wait for Lauren to greedily snatch up the bauble and to show it to her before running to finish watching her video. Once alone with Adrienne, relief swam over her, and she leaned against the counter for support.

"I didn't know you were coming into town, girl. How did you get here so fast? I thought you'd be home for Easter? But—"

"That was the original plan," Adrienne said coolly, making a grand gesture with her hand. She took the steaming cup from the microwave before sipping it slowly. "But, I have this friend who works for the airlines, so, you know, you know. I got a free ticket. Voilà. Anyway, there's this hot new group out of Miami that I wanted to check out, and they're doing a gig here in Philly this weekend. So, I thought I'd come check on you, catch up, then go to the show, especially since I haven't been able to reach you by phone. You've been seriously out of touch.

So, what's up?"

"Been job hunting, and trying to move in and get used to the new place. Other than that, there's nothing really to tell." Antoinette looked at her watch and let her gaze travel over the sister's skin-tight black cat suit and punk-funk silver accessories. "So, you were just gonna pop in for a moment, and weren't planning on staying the weekend, I take it?"

"Naw, girl. Got thangs to do, places to go, people to see. Daddy doesn't even know I'm here, yet. Although, I might pop up to see Pearline before I jet. Anyway, how you been?"

"Well," Antoinette hesitated, "I've been better. In fact, I was waiting on Brian so I could go to a weekend job conference that I had been planning on. Actually, I thought you were him."

"Don't let me stop you, chile. I can crash here while you do your thing. Girl, you'd better stop planning your life around people," Adrienne flipped. "Especially him."

The comment annoyed her as she watched the svelte young woman casually sip her tea while leaning against the refrigerator, oblivious to the amount of the mother-logistics required to merely go out. "It's not that easy," Antoinette said dryly.

Adrienne made another grand sweep with her free hand. "You have to think it, then believe it, and allow The Universe to manifest it. Just manifest, honey. You're not free because you have not decided to manifest freedom."

Glancing at her watch again, Antoinette forced herself to remain calm. "Listen, if you're gonna be in town for at least a day, would you mind watching Lauren until Brian gets here? It's not like him to stand her up entirely. But, for me, he is perpetually late. I was supposed to leave with the girls hours ago. And—"

"Girl, look," Adrienne said quickly, cutting her off and growing defensive, "I would, if I could, but, like I said, I have a show, people to connect with. The timing is bad. I just wanted to see how you were—"

"Then jet," Antoinette mumbled with disgust, cutting off her sister's sentence. She wanted to add much more to the statement, but decided not to. What would be the point, anyway? Arguing with Adrienne about giving and responsibility was strictly a hands-off discussion. They'd warred over the subject for years, and tonight she didn't have the energy. Besides, she couldn't take one of her sister's rhetorical, cosmic discussions about paths and choices. Not at the moment. Not when all she could see before her was a selfish young woman, who had a me-first agenda. If it wasn't convenient for Adrienne then it wasn't going to happen. Why did she even go there, foolishly trying to get something that Adrienne had made clear years ago she wasn't going to give?

"I don't know what the big deal is," Adrienne offered after a thought-filled sip of tea. "Why don't you just take her to one of your married girlfriends who are home anyway? They don't have anything to do."

Antoinette allowed the comment to grow roots in her anger and she drew a slow, solid breath for patience before speaking. "Tracey's going with us for the first time in her life. Okay? Ness just had Lauren last weekend, and my friend, Valerie, has her own wild bunch over there with her own marital problems. Pearline is getting tired and has paid her dues. May is out of the question—she doesn't do baby-sitting for the same reason—she's paid her dues. My other single girlfriends are all at the conference. If Brian doesn't come, I'm stuck, and Cookie and Trace are stuck with my portion of the hotel bill. That's the only reason I asked."

"Sis, I'd love to help you out, but... I really have solid plans. Besides, if I hadn't shown up at your door, you would have had to come up with an alternative. Right? So, let's not even go there with the unproductive guilt thing. You got anything to munch on? I'm starved."

Antoinette didn't look at her sister as she moved toward the cabinets and produced a bag of chips. "I have some chicken in the fridge, and some greens, and rice. Oh yeah, and some of Pearline's cobbler," she added in monotone, giving Adrienne the potato chips. "Towels are in the linen cabinet, and there's an extra key on the credenza. Just put it through the slot when you leave."

"Cool," Adrienne smiled, ignoring Antoinette's tone of voice. "But, you know I don't eat that heavy, greasy stuff. You got any salad makings, or yogurt?"

"Yeah," Antoinette remarked in a tight voice, pushing past Adrienne to go sit on the sofa with her daughter. "May bought it."

"Well, that was cool of her," Adrienne yelled back as she hunted and rummaged in Antoinette's refrigerator without looking up.

"Just kewel," Antoinette whispered back, taking exception with the new, phony, West Coast Valley-girl accent that her sister now donned. "Like, wanna see May's place?" she added in a thick mimic of her sister's voice, "since I'm not going anywhere?"

"I show you, Aunt Adrienne," Lauren piped up, injecting herself into the conversation with bravado. "You sleep in my room wif me."

"Yeah, little bird," Adrienne quipped, ignoring Antoinette's sullen demeanor as the two made their way through the condo. "I'll sleep with you, since your Mommy has an unnecessary attitude."

"Don' worry, Aunt A," the youngster giggled, "Mommy's always sad."

Antoinette felt herself get dizzy with rage as the youngster dragged her sister by the hand room by room. How dare Adrienne blow into town like a big grand diva, supposedly to check on her welfare, but then in the next breath be too busy to help! Memories swirled around in Antoinette's head as she vividly recounted all the times she'd helped her sister, and now, the one time she needed help, her sister was too busy with her own agenda? Just great! Adrienne had more gall than anyone she knew—even May.

It was supposed to be okay that her sister wanted to eat her food—when she didn't even have an income, then crash at her spot, make the invariable mess that came with an Adrienne whirlwind visitation—and leave it for her to clean up. All on the one weekend that she had tried to carve out for herself since Lauren was born four and a half years ago? No, not this time.

Antoinette stood slowly and began thinking of what she was going to say as she wrung her sister's neck. She thought of ways she could have a knock-down, drag out, good old fashioned fair—one without a lamp or table hitting Lauren. The hell with Adrienne! She'd kill her. And to hell with any promise she'd made their mother about taking care of the baby in the family!

The doorbell stopped her steady advance across the living room, and she glanced at the clock again. Nine-fifteen, and Brian was just ringing her damned bell? She didn't know who to kill first. Him, for being the regular asshole he'd always been, or her Adrienne, for being the self-absorbed nymph that she'd always been. Lauren barreling through the room brought some semblance of clarity to her mind—enough to make her change direction, head towards the front of the condo, and hit the entrance buzzer.

Counting the minutes until the elevator in the hall sounded, she didn't even look at Brian as she flung the door open. Her alternative to slapping him was to turn on her heels and walk toward the living room as the child filled his arms. "I'll get her bag," she said dryly over the tiny child giggles that greeted him as he swept Lauren into his arms. She also didn't bother to mention Adrienne's presence, or acknowledge that she was in the room.

"How's my baby girl?" he asked in a chipper voice, tossing the child and loping into the foyer. "Missed my baby-doll. Hey, A! Didn't know you were in town?"

"She's not," Antoinette mumbled without looking at either of them, and feeling like she would retch as he lavished attention on the object of their mutual affection. "We thought we were going to miss you, tonight. We expected you at six. Lauren's been asking about you since it got dark at five. We were all just about to leave." Her voice was more acidic than she'd wanted it to be.

"What's that supposed to mean?" Brian asked calmly, appearing unmoved by Antoinette's annoyance.

"Hey, Bri," Adrienne inserted. "Was gonna catch a show, and Sis had plans."

"Oh, you're just here for a quick in and out?" Brian quipped affably, still pretending to ignore Antoinette as she shot a stay-out-of-it-Sis glare between him and Adrienne.

"You know me, brother," Adrienne purred, issuing a well-rehearsed grin designed to make men melt. "Gotta stick and move."

"I hear you. So, how's L.A.? I know you're killin' 'em out on the Coast."

Antoinette hated small talk, their kind of small talk, the timing of their small talk, which was making her later than she already was. She stood there between them grinding her teeth, waiting for them to give the smallest hint of consideration that she was a person, with a life, and had somewhere to go.

She surveyed Brian's immaculate camel-hair coat that hung at the right length over his spit-shinned and polished wing-tip Florsheim shoes. The way his navy blue suit and button down white shirt was perfectly complimented by a muted paisley tie. She wanted to kill him. Domestic violence was not out of the question. She'd cut off his vital body parts. The only thing that saved him, or Adrienne, for that matter, was the child. She looked at Lauren's happy, up-turned face and let her nails dig into her palms.

"It means," Antoinette said smoothly, "that I had an engagement to attend tonight. Therefore, if you were going to be here any later than you already are, then you would have had to pick up Lauren from Vanessa or Valerie's house." She cast a death-ray warning glare at her sister to not respond before she went on. "I would have left a note on the door, or called your voice-mail." She had made sure that she'd articulated every syllable of every word so that he could understand. So that Adrienne definitely understood. "I'll get her bag."

The fact that he was stunned annoyed her. He looked at his gold watch then at her. But the irony almost made her laugh. They were a male and female pair of bookends—evenly matched, armed to the teeth, dressed to the nines, and obviously ready for battle. That had always been their problem. Nobody could give an inch. The standoff made her tired.

"Well," he said checking his watch again, and looking her up and down, "I had a late appointment with a client, and assumed you would be home since you aren't officially working yet. I'm sure a couple of hours isn't going to hurt you," he added, this time allowing his gaze to roam around the condo then land back on her. "A little formal for a date."

Adrienne's eyes got wide and a smirk graced her lips as she quickly got out of the center of the potential fight by retreating into the kitchen. "Let me go make some more tea. See ya, Bri," she yelled from her remote spectator's position. "Take care of my baby."

"Yeah, A, have a safe flight back to L.A.," he said calling behind her. Then bending down to Lauren, he gave the child another squeeze. "Go give your Aunt a kiss so we can get ready to roll, pumpkin-lumpkin."

"Daddy, my video. See," Lauren squealed, rushing over to the television set as the credits rolled, then dashing towards the kitchen to give Adrienne a kiss.

"Yeah, pumpkin. We'll take it. Hurry up so your Mom can go out."

Antoinette smiled. It was the way he'd said "go out" that made her feel slightly vindicated. For the first time in a long while, she could tell that he actually felt threatened by a potential suitor. It was insane, but she liked it. Before this moment, he'd never seemed to view her as being capable of attracting anyone, especially not him. He'd treated her botched entry into, and immediate retreat from, the separated-and-now-dating world as some disease to be tolerated. But he'd remained unimpressed, and blasé about it all. The only time he'd become truly enraged was when she'd had the gall to date an old college rival of his. Perhaps that's why she did it?

Antoinette allowed the renewed feeling of inner power to bolster her. Yes, she did have choices. Yes, she was going to lose weight, and feel good about herself, in her own time. Yes, she was going to find a job. Yes, she could be a single mother and still have a solid home. Yes, she could drop the baggage of worrying about her sister, and what Brian thought of her in one, fell swoop. She'd paid off her debt to her mother's memory by seeing that her sister made it to adulthood with an education, and she was actually divorced now. That meant she wasn't separated and hoping he'd return, any longer.

Her smile of mischief broadened as her composure returned and peace entered her spirit. She was free of them both, and she enjoyed their confusion. Yes, Mommy was going out.

In an odd way, she felt sorry for him as she watched him struggle with what to do next. Maybe it was his expansive ego that had allowed him to believe he was above competition and watching that aspect of him become unsure made her sure? Whatever. Something had shifted. Maybe it was her new environment that had him a little off-kilter? The outfit wouldn't have done it—it was her standard work uniform, and it was a tad rumpled from Lauren at that. Maybe it was the fact that he thought she might be hanging out with Adrienne after her conference? Or, maybe he thought that Adrienne had some wealthy music-scene guy in the offing for her? She almost laughed. It was all so silly, so petty, but it gave her a slight edge of confidence. Yet, victory though it was, it was a small and hollow one.

"Well," Brian repeated after a moment of hesitation, "we'll be back Sunday afternoon. Maybe I should call first to be sure that you're home—or that it's kosher to bring our child back home."

She'd have to tell the girls this one. Her night was improving.

"Yes," she said evenly. "I'm going away, and you should call to be sure I'm home first." Drama had her in a stranglehold. She walked over to the television set, popped out Lauren's video, and handed it to Brian. "Let me get my bag, and I'll walk out with you." She wasn't about to say anything to Adrienne. Not even good-bye.

She didn't wait to see his reaction as she turned and went into her bedroom to pick up her bag. When she returned, she had to hide another smile. His face had gone ashen as they bundled up Lauren, she gathered her coat, and they moved toward the door in unison. She was going out. He had witnessed it. Good.

"See you all later," Adrienne called over the kitchen pass-through.

Antoinette didn't respond.

CHAPTER 14

Jerome tapped his fingers nervously on the dashboard of the Bronco as he snaked his way through the traffic approaching the last toll booth before they hit Atlantic City. Nothing could go wrong tonight. Everything hinged on perfection. All week long he'd kept the uneasy truce. No arguments. Karen had even let him sleep in their bed, although he'd known better than to reach for her. It was a truce, but the situation was far from stabilized.

Maybe after hitting the slots, trying a few hands of black jack, and she played The Wheel of Fortune, or maybe some roulette—maybe after she'd had a few vodka martinis and he'd had a few beers to chase the Cutty—maybe everything would be all right?

"E.T.A., fifteen minutes," he said searching for conversation.

"Finally, " she sighed, snuggling into the seat. "I hate having to drive in the snow."

He loved driving in the snow. He let it pass.

Oldies blared from the radio and grated his nerves. He hated oldies. Jazz was his thing. But not tonight. Just peace, some laughs. The only thing he wanted from that era was some old-fashioned loving. If Smokey Robinson would make her smile, and get her to lower her drawbridge, then fine.

"Are you hungry?" Jerome asked just above a murmur.

"No, not really. We can check in, drop our bags at the front desk bell hop, hit the casino first—then figure out where to go later."

Her voice was mellow and she seemed relaxed. He let his breath out slowly and all the tension that went with it. "I'm just your chauffeur tonight. You tell me what you want to do, and it's done." The only thing that disturbed him was that she wanted to go to the casino before even going up to the room. Then, again, he could dig it. They hadn't been together in so long that it would probably be best to have some fun, get reacquainted, and ease into any possibilities that sharing a room might hold.

She smiled and turned up the radio a little more, humming with the tune. As he looked at her, he couldn't help but wonder what insanity had come over his mind when he thought about giving up on their marriage? Karen was a pretty woman. A good mother. A good person...

He could do this. Yeah, he could do this.

Antoinette turned off the lights on her used eighty-three Nova and wrapped her arms around herself. Two and a half hours up to the Poconos with no heat. Jesus! The radio had long since died, but she had gotten a bargain. When she thought of the plush, company provided sales sedans she used to drive... then her own choice of a BMW...

She shifted in her seat, grabbed her overnight bag from the passenger side, and popped out of the car. Placing her feet down carefully to avoid slipping on the icy walkway, she crept along the path like an elderly lady afraid of breaking a limb. Forced to look down often, she noticed that her pumps were crusted with salt, and her snagged hose had sprung a wider run. But she was there. She'd made it. Victoriously, wonderfully, all on her own. She'd made it. Antoinette looked up at the moon and the still mountain sky filled with stars that sparkled down kindness upon her. Pearline had been right. She was truly blessed.

"You want to unpack while I go get some ice?" Jerome hesitated within the entry of the hotel room as Karen shut the door behind them.

"Yeah. Sure," she said pleasantly. "What'd you bring?"

"A bottle of vodka, Absolut, and some cranberry juice for you, a small Cutty, for me, and a six pack of brew. Did you want something else? I can get some Vermouth, so we can make martinis?"

"No. That's cool. I'm just going to take out and hang up what I'm going to wear tomorrow since we're only staying overnight. I've had all the martinis I need already. They ply you at the tables, don't they?"

"Yeah, trying to get you looped so you'll stay there spending money all night," he said in a mellow tone. "The room is pretty nice," he added casually, searching for a way to extend their benign topics of conversation.

"It's okay. It's not Vegas or anything, though."

"Yeah, well, it'll be a while before we can afford that."

"I wonder what it'll look like in the year two-thousand fifty?"

He looked at her for a moment and didn't speak.

"Okay, I'm sorry," she said quietly. "We're here to have a good time. It was force of habit, I guess."

He tried not to allow her comment about his finances get to him, and let it pass. So what that her sister's husband could afford to regularly take his wife and kids to Vegas. Things were going too well to start that mess. He stared at her for a moment longer as she moved over to their suitcases, noticing the way that she picked up hers, then put it on the side of the bed that was closest to the phone. When she grabbed the telephone receiver without looking at him, he pushed his hands in his pockets and leaned against the wall. He knew the drill. Her territory in the room had been marked. Why the hell did she insist on two beds? Was this some sort of female code that meant he couldn't be sure, couldn't take for granted how the night would end? It was working.

"The kids'll be all right... we've only been gone a few hours."

Karen didn't respond, but tucked the receiver in the crook of her neck and shoulder as she punched in the credit card number.

He prayed the kids would be all right. Glimpsing the ice bucket as he watched her dial, he struggled for something to say that would let her know that he cared about them too. It was just that tonight....

"I'll be back in a minute," he said quietly, hoping to get her attention. When she still didn't respond, he pushed away from the wall, grabbed the ice bucket, flipped the interior bolt to hold the door open, and headed for the ice machine down the hall. Why did everything have to be such a struggle?

Standing at the machine, he watched the cubes

fall and fill the container. Why couldn't the slots have paid off for her like that? he wondered, as he collected the bucket and made his way back to the room. At least if she'd won big, had been lucky, it might have improved his odds tonight.

"Everything okay at home?" he asked tentatively, re-entering the room with the ice bucket under his arm. Please, he prayed silently, no hassles.

He hated the way she suddenly put away her money when he'd entered the room. What was that about? He didn't want her money, or to count her winnings. Peace, he told himself. Let it go. At least she had won something. "Kids cool?" he asked again, still trying to get her to give him her full attention. "Want something to drink?"

But, why, in God's name, was the television on?

"Yeah," she said, moving to the small table and taking a seat.

"Yeah, the kids are fine. Or, yeah, you want a drink?" He forced a smile to let her know that he wasn't trying to start a sarcastic test of wills.

"Both," she chuckled offering him a smile with her comment. "Fix me one? But, don't make it too strong. Then, again, maybe you should," she said expanding her smile. "We are trying awfully hard to have fun."

"Yup. No problem," he replied without enthusiasm, his hopes sliding away from him despite her smile. Why did they have to try "awfully hard" to have fun? What was that all about? Snatching a beer from the plastic six pack holder as he brought her a tumbler of vodka and cranberry juice on ice, he wondered if her comment also meant that she'd have to try awfully hard to make love to him? Without looking in her direction, he poured himself an ice-less tumbler of Cutty Sark and sat down at the table across from her, then took a deep swig from his glass.

The television was stabbing at his brain. He loosened his tie, then stood up again to take off his suit jacket and to kick off his leather loafers. Standing next to his chair, he hesitated for a moment, trying to think of a way to reach her.

"Wanna listen to some oldies?" It was an attempt, but he'd have to wait. Feel her out.

"They've got cable. Maybe we could watch some music videos?" Karen looked at his face then down at her glass. "Okay, why don't you see if they have a good radio station down here?

He was not going to be the one to turn off the set. This was her province, her territory. Jerome walked over to the bed opposite her chair and sat down hard. Flipping on the radio, he tried to tune into several local options that would give her unin-terrupted oldies. "How about this one?" he nearly yelled over the clashing din of both sound sources. "Remember Marvin Gaye, babe?" he said with another forced smile, watching her mood intently. He gave the bed a little bounce and issued her a wink. When she ignored the reference to the way they used to make love, he stood up and moved back to the table.

"I guess it'll work," she said in a blasé tone, flipping off the television with the remote.

Once the clamor of the television receded, he sat down at the table. Okay, progress, but oddly, it felt like too much time had already passed. Somehow, they were still dancing to the same old music.

"You did pretty good on The Wheel?"

"Yeah," she said with an unexpected honest smile. "How'd you do at black jack?"

"Not bad," he noted, taking a sip of beer. "See, girl, this was all we needed. A little time away."

Jerome raised his tumbler of dark liquid in her direction, and Karen tipped her glass of vodka and cranberry juice toward him.

"I guess so. It is nice to be away. But, you made this drink too strong." Her answer had been non-committal, but considerably pleasant. "But, maybe that's a good thing," she chuckled. "It has been a while."

His heart slammed against his chest. Maybe. It was hard to tell. But, why did she need to be drunk to be with him? The question laid at the pit of his stomach.

"I'll remake your drink. I can add some more ice. Did you see that old lady on the slots?" He was trying too hard. He knew it. Had to chill.

"It's okay. I'll let it melt," she said quietly, then looked up from her glass. "Yeah, the old ladies are a trip down here. Jay, one kept putting in a quarter and getting mad because when she'd hit triple-sevens, the machine wouldn't pay off. Finally, it got on my nerves so bad, I told her that she had to play the maximum in order to win. Then, she had the nerve to get mad at me for telling her!"

Jerome chuckled and took another sip from his glass, then raised it to her again. "You told her right. You gotta give it all you've got, or it doesn't pay off. You gotta play the maximum."

Although she didn't answer him, he watched her lower her eyes as a blush highlighted her cheeks.

"God, you look pretty tonight." When she still didn't answer, he covered her hand with his own. "I'm glad we did this."

"Me too, I suppose," she said quietly, removing her hand from under his to take a sip from her glass.

He was too close to ultimate peace and a little affection to give up now. Pressing toward his goal a bit harder, he stood, switched on a soft lamp, and turned off the glaring overhead lights in the room. He watched her from the corner of his eye as he moved toward the bed nearest to her. "Wanna listen to the music from here?" he said in a low voice, patting the side of the bed as he sat down to wait for her.

She hesitated for a moment, picked up her glass and stood to walk over to him. "Why not?" she said in a casual tone, then smiled nervously. "I suppose we were going to get there sooner or later."

He hated the resignation in her. However, he'd been with Karen long enough to understand her brand of playing hard-to-get. Before, it used to intrigue him, was even a little exciting—the never knowing. But as he stared at her as she slowly approached him, it seemed as though she were being made to march to the gallows. After the months between them, it bothered him. A little eagerness would have been nice. Then, again, he wondered if it wasn't just a new game. What if it had become that bad, that unpleasant, for her? Damn. After all these years? Jerome reached for her glass, but she opted to set it down on the night table instead. He knew that he had to give her room to let her decide, to let her set the pace. There was so much that he wanted to say, but their history and time held his words in check.

"This is nice," she said, her voice now very soft, but still tinged with wariness as she sat down beside him.

However, he noticed that her body had relaxed and she didn't seem to be avoiding his close proximity. Against all of his instincts to wait, he touched her face with the tips of his fingers. Desire almost made his hand tremble as he came in contact with the soft skin beneath his fingers. More confident when she didn't pull away, he grazed her lips with a light kiss and sat back a little. "Yes. This is nice," he murmured, battling with himself to stay in control and not rush her. He had to slow down. No false moves, no bad timing. He stared at her and waited for the green light.

She hadn't moved toward him, but she also hadn't moved away from him. Moisture was building in his palms. How did this happen with a woman that had been his wife for a decade and a half? he wondered, as he moved closer and kissed her more firmly. They'd made four babies together. There was a time when they couldn't get enough of each other. Now, it was like being on a first date with a stranger. But when she accepted his mouth fully, all of his questions became murky, swirling in his mind on a dark sea of Cutty and beer.

His need to be with her took over his fears as he lowered his hand to cup her breast. Her response was immediate and driving. Seven months of separation vanished as her palm warmed his throat and slid down to his chest. Her tongue became more ardent and he returned her kiss hard, remembering and searching for what had been lost. He could feel her tremble and arch toward him as he nipped the swell of her breast through her blouse, and he began to push her back onto the bed. Covering her with his body, he moved against her and slid his hand up her skirt. The feel of her slick readiness evacuated the air from his lungs in a hard rush as a moan traveled up from his gut. Dear God, it had been so long. He'd do anything to keep her this way, keep her this soft, and happy, and open to his touch. Deferred passion obliterated his fears to explore her body in the way he once had so long ago. This time would be different. This time they had a chance.

As gently as he could, he cradled her body and found the center of her stomach with his mouth, then began kissing down her belly through her clothes toward the sweet haven that waited for him between her legs. When she didn't respond, he removed his hand, and stopped his advance of kisses to begin unbuttoning her blouse. His gut registered a warning signal, something was going wrong. He kissed her neck, and she didn't move. She was suddenly too tense; she had gone from hot to cold. What happened?

"Did you bring anything?"

"Huh?" He could barely speak. Her words were being swept up in an undercurrent of repressed need as he nestled his face in her hair.

"What do you need, baby?" Seven and a half months of agony... no arguments, not now. "Just tell me," he breathed as he nipped at her neck.

"Did you bring something?" she repeated more formally.

He stopped, rolled over, sat up, and looked at her.

"I thought you were on the pill?" he stammered. Confusion tore at his brain, and he reached for his glass and took a deep swig of the hard liquor.

"I am," she said flatly, standing and pacing to the other bed. "But if this is going to happen tonight, you need to wear something. I know you were thinking of somebody else. I could feel it. You never act like this with me—or, try that foul oral shit," she added with a bitter whisper. "It's always the same, and you do this to me every time... think of them, and not me. I'm not one of your whores; I'm your wife!"

She sat down very precisely, folded her arms over her half-unbuttoned blouse, and tucked a wisp of her auburn hair behind her ear. He stared at her tiny heart-shaped face, and let his gaze travel over her full, recently kissed mouth. She was so beautiful on the outside, but something on the inside was scarred. Her bosom heaved with short, shallow breaths, and her light, hazel-gray eyes shone with the glimmer of tears. Absolute confusion must have registered on his face, because all he could do was hold his glass in mid-air. Why after fifteen years of marriage would he need a condom? Why was trying something they'd shared a long time ago now a crime? What was wrong with changing their tired, worn-out routine! But, more importantly, how had she allowed a phantom to create a barrier between their bodies, which had been pressed together only moments ago...

"Don't play dumb, Jerome," she said in a harsh whisper, then looked away from him. "I need to be protected. Okay? I don't know where you've been for the last seven months... you could have picked up anything from anywhere. Last week, you claimed to be at Buddy's overnight, but, how do I know that?

217

I wasn't about to call his wife to ask her to confirm it, or to ask his lying ass. So, I need protection."

"I haven't been anywhere!" He measured his voice and stood up. Anger gained a chokehold on him as she looked back at him and defied him with her eyes. "You need to stop talking to your girlfriends so much. They're polluting your mind, just because they have problems—"

"They're the only friends I've got," she snapped. "And we've got problems—had problems from the beginning. I knew this was a bad idea."

It was back again. His one transgression before they were married. The thing that always slipped under the sheets between them. "Then, why were we able to make love without protection for the last fifteen, huh, Karen? Why now? What happened when I was in the service is an old story," he fumed, "one that's time to drop."

"I didn't use protection because I wanted children. You finally got your boy, okay. I'm done with babies, so why take the unnecessary risk?"

He was stunned. Modulation left his voice and he found himself locked in the old pattern of rage. "Yeah, but Christopher is four! You didn't want me to wear one after he was born—so, why now? Why are you ruining the evening with this old bull shit?"

"I haven't been with you that much since he's been born—or, haven't you noticed? Besides, you did it to me once, decided to have one last fling before we got married," she said evenly, "and I was pregnant! I couldn't do anything about it, then, because I needed you to marry me. I wasn't stupid—you had the upper hand. Then. So, now at my age, I'm supposed to think after seven months, you've been a Boy Scout? And you've been out till all hours of the day and night. I wasn't exactly thrilled about the possibility of your whereabouts during every pregnancy—not just the first one. And you talk in your sleep, dammit. So—"

"I talk in my sleep! Woman, are you crazy!" He found himself walking in a circle in the middle of the floor. "After seven damned months, you're lucky I don't need a straight jacket! I tell you when you worry, Karen," he said heaving for air as he hollered, "You start worrying when I stop talking in my sleep! Yeah," he bellowed, continuing to pace, "I've got a lot of mental girlfriends—Vanessa Williams, Halle Berry, Toni Braxton, should I go on?"

"Antoinette Reeves," she spat, turning her chin upwards as she said the name.

Stunned and embattled with the concept, he stuttered a quick response before collecting his indignation into a full-blown rail. "Who's fault is that, huh, Karen? And, after seven months, you've got 'em too! Denzel Washington, for instance. You've made me hate every movie that sucker is in because you and your friends giggle and talk about the brother like he's the only man in America. I have never done that to you. Me and my boys don't trip like that over no movie stars in front of you. It's

219

called respect, Karen! This whole conversation is bull shit!"

She watched him carefully and tried not to smile as he leaned against the wall and closed his eyes. He'd passed the test. Her girls had been right— she'd taken his ass to the brink, and now he was grateful for the whiff she'd given him. She almost chuckled to herself as she watched Jerome struggle with the possibility that he wasn't getting any tonight. Her best friend's words echoed in her mind... "You gotta train the fool, darlin'." Oh, yeah, her husband needed it bad. Damn, so did she. Now the only problem was how to back off of her position and save face while keeping some leverage over him for the next time. A man always required a pending threat to keep him in line. Any woman knew that. But, damn, it had been a real long time, and he looked too good, felt so good on top of her.

"Whatever you say," she murmured calmly, "But, let's be real, Jerome, and get this over with. We both know you don't think about me when you're with me. I've lived with that from day one. The only reason I'm here, is to save what's left of this marriage... to give it one last—"

"I have not been anywhere," he said carefully, holding his anger in check. What could he say? He'd thought of Antoinette too many nights, and was guilty as charged. But the other crime that she had incarcerated him with, had been committed over a decade and a half ago. Hell, he had done his hard time already! "Can't you just let it go, K? Since that time, I haven't done a thing. Truth. And I'm tired of the litany about it. Okay? Besides, if I'm so bad, then why in God's name do you want to live with this criminal—if that's all you think I am?"

He'd addressed her with seething rage and his voice had become nearly a rumble. How much longer could she twist the knife on this old wound, he wondered? No, he thought, slowly appraising her petite, curvaceous body, maybe it just wasn't worth it.

"Yeah, right. Whatever you say. Look me in the eyes and tell me you don't think about her—ever," she muttered, still staring at him, contempt haunting her eyes. "I can always feel her. Okay—you need some; I need some. That's cool. Plus, we've already paid for the room, so why not try to enjoy it? But let's not pretend that we're having more than sex."

Her attitude stripped a foundation gear in his pride. "Don't you want more than just sex tonight?" Jerome looked at the woman across the room from him—hard. She wanted to save the marriage and this was how she was acting?

The way he stared at her stopped her heart. It was definitely time to ease up; she could tell. Something was different about this argument... this week. He wasn't going to be badgered into a corner, and the expression on his face told her that she was teetering precariously on the edge of no return. But, he wouldn't leave—not with all the kids. Would he? They were and had always been her investment protection. Nah. He'd come crawling back after she'd asked him for a divorce, right?

Shaking the terrifying thought, she decided to dig in her heels. He would not win this siege. Ever. Drawing a deep breath to renew her confidence, she took a solid stance, leveled her gaze at him, and fired a last shot targeting his ego. It was the only way to back him down and to retain her power. She had to hurt him, and wound him deeply.

However, she was no fool. She'd pull out her best negligee and give him a little glimpse of hope while she did it—regardless of what her friends had said. Maybe she'd even do him good—just to let him know where home was, and just to keep him from getting any really crazy ideas.

"At one point I did want more than just sex," she murmured wistfully, expelling a well-timed sigh as she popped off the bed and opened her suitcase, "but aren't we too old to believe in fairy tales? Forget it. Just go get something, and I'll be ready when you come back. I even bought a negligee," she added, casting the new silk nightgown across the edge of the bed so he could see it. "I wanted this to work for the children. I don't want to talk about it anymore. You've practically blown the groove anyway—just like you always do, Jerome. But, I need some too, I suppose. So, let's squash the argument."

For a moment, he was speechless. It took a few

seconds for his mind to digest and swallow her bitter admission. His wife was going to just screw him—because that's what she needed. No more. No less. The new reality just didn't set right with him. Immediately, a new and more toxic thought arrested him. Where might she have been? He needed distance, space, time to sort the whole nightmare out. He needed to take flight, to let the dust settle. This was unreal!

"If it'll make you feel better," he finally muttered, regaining his composure. "I'll go down to the gift shop in the lobby." He looked at the turquoise silk at the edge of the bed with disgust. A month ago, maybe as little as a week ago, he would have been turned on by it. Now, all he could think of was where had she been... to ask him to wear a condom? What sordid logic had her friends come up with?

"Thanks," she muttered without emotion, as she gathered up the gown and slowly moved toward the bathroom.

"Don't mention it."

It was all he could say as he paced across the room and downed the last of his drink. Refilling his glass at the TV table, he stopped and stared at her in disbelief as she stood at the bathroom door clutching the gown. Anger and humiliation went down better with the entire new tumbler that he'd just poured. He steadied himself and looked at the bottom of the empty glass, and refilled it again. The effect was numbing and erection killing, just like her words had been. But tonight, being drunk was a better option than thinking about what she'd just said to him. Anything was better than that.

"Are you going to just stand there getting wasted, or what?"

"No. I was just tryin' to have a few before I went downstairs," he laughed harshly. "Just tryin' to enjoy the evening. Just tryin' to give it my best shot."

A tense moment of silence engulfed them as he finished his drink. He thought about pouring another, but changed his mind. He needed space; had to get out of the room and away from her.

"Listen," she said sadly, "maybe you don't have to go get anything. It was just that... I thought..."

The sudden change in her tone made him look up at her. Her eyes held a devastating mixture of fear, resentment, and yes, hope. The combination was lethal, and as he watched her unfold her arms, and appear to accept his presence, new rage filled him. He hated games, and this had become a blood feud, one that violated trust, intimacy, and the deepest needs of partners. He'd never forgive her this transgression. The thought of what she'd said to him, how she'd damaged his pride, provoked him to find her inner ghosts and haunt her with them.

"No," he said evenly, after a moment of consideration, "If we're going to enjoy ourselves, maybe I'd better get something to protect both of us. No sense in either of us taking a chance again on unprotected sex, right?" He watched her eyes glisten with tears of hurt rage. Good, he thought to himself, now maybe she knew how it felt—to be slapped in the face with evil words. It was too late, she'd detonated the timer on the bomb. Maybe he would just go downstairs and play some more Blackjack and never come back to the room.

"You drink too much anyway. Always did, Jerome."

"Always needed to, babe."

He refused to look at her as he picked up the hotel key and made his way into the hall. The sounds of laughter and televisions made his vision blur. All he had to do was get to the elevator, find the freakin' gift shop, buy a three pack, come back to the room, and get laid. Yeah, a three pack of foils— why bother with a six? Or, better yet, he could find a hot table and win some money. That would be better than coming back to the insult his so-called wife had hurled at him. He laughed to keep himself from crying as he tripped on the plush pile carpet in the hallway and caught his balance. When the elevator doors opened he walked in, closed his eyes, and felt for the lobby button. There was too much light.

"Rough night, huh, Buddy?"

Jerome didn't open his eyes to the sound of the male voice that accosted his senses. "Yeah, you could say that."

"How much did ya loose?"

"Everything, man."

Leslie Esdaile

"Gotta pace yourself, or you'll get robbed blind down here. How much did you play?"

"I played the maximum."

CHAPTER 15

"Girl, we didn't think you were going to make it!"
"You okay? You must be freezing!"

Antoinette hugged Tracey, laughing with delight as she encountered her. "Fran! You made it up from Hotlanta, GA? I didn't know you would be here! I've missed you guys so much! Wow, this is fantastic, just like old times. Look at all of these beautiful sisters! Did Olivia come?" Smiling at Francis, she held onto her a little longer, becoming anxious as her friend's body weight felt so different, and much too fragile during their embrace. "How's my baby, Miss Camille? I bet she's getting tall, and has always been beautiful like her Mommy." No longer scanning the room for Cookie, Antoinette solidly fixed her gaze on Francis.

Francis grinned and held her back, "She's eight

going on eighty... but the real question is, how are you, Doll?"

"Dealing with the aftermath, girl," Antoinette laughed easily, "and trying to keep from killing my wild sister." She wanted to leap out of her skin as a hundred inappropriate questions fought for autonomy in her brain. What had happened to Fran? Her friend's eyes were slightly sunken in the sockets, and her once-radiant sandy-brown hair that always boasted a hint of natural blonde, now looked dull and lifeless despite the razor sharp salon style that was Francis' trademark. Even her light-weight mustard- colored wool suit with moray monochrome silk blouse, brilliant gold buttons, and fierce matching suede shoes didn't seem to perk up her appearance. It was in her eyes.

"Is she still in L.A.?" Francis crooned. Not waiting for an answer, she spun around toward the crowded room, "Isn't this fabulous?"

Antoinette only nodded in agreement, still speechless from her observance of Francis. The combination of the fights to get to the gala, juxtaposed against her friend's gray pallor, and Tracey's ruthless-red-everything-look was overwhelming. This kind of soiree was where Francis normally sparkled. Tonight, she didn't. "Where's Cook?"

"Girl, you know she's working the room like a barracuda. See, over there, she's been in the lady's ear who catered this dinner all night. She told us to go mingle, because she was working without a person to flush the target to her tonight. And you know, Miss Thang, Olivia, is right on her heels." Francis' voice held a tinge of annoyance. "I could have been her flush. I mean, after all, I'm one of the best sales execs around."

Antoinette kissed Francis' cheek and smiled. "You are the best, lady, but you know how Cookie can be. We're all the best!" She tried to appear buoyant, and she hugged Tracey and Francis again to try to cover her growing distress.

"Oh, lady, its so good to see you smiling for a change." Quickly redirecting the subject, she cast her gaze at Francis briefly, then around the room and allowed her line of vision to settle on Tracey. "Look at this spread. They have smoked salmon for days... oysters, and canapés, fresh veggies, vegetarian quiche... fresh raspberries... Trace, you picked a great conference as your coming out party. So did I!"

Tracey laughed and gave her arm a squeeze. "The service is superb, and wait till you see the workshops they have scheduled tomorrow. Perfect. Done very well," Tracey beamed, "and you know I know how it should be done."

"Of any of us," Francis commented with a tired smile, "Tracey would know. She is the ultimate class-police... has been to more charm schools and modeling schools than any of us could shake a stick at."

"Oh, yeah, girl, if you say it's righteous, done in

haute couture, then it is righteous!" Antoinette forced a laugh as her gaze swept the interior of the spacious carriage house and landed on the huge walk-in fire place. "I would love to be able to do something like this one day." Her gaze moved about the lush Indian print rugs, to the Native American Medicine Wheel that hung above the mantle, and settled again on the variety of indigenous artwork that graced an exposed brick wall that was adjacent to a spiral staircase. "I could definitely live like this," she added with emphasis to appease the always conversational Tracey--anything to keep their light banter moving until she could get to Francis alone. "Valerie should have been here to see this art. I could live like this..."

"Couldn't we all?" Francis chuckled. "But, right now, you're dry, and that calls for some champagne for this celebration." Motioning toward a tuxedo-wearing server, Francis swept a champagne flute off the tray and handed it to Antoinette. "We're so glad you made it."

"Don't you want one?" Antoinette murmured in Francis' direction when she noticed her friend's shaky delivery of the glass.

"No, hon, I'm already tired. The travel from Atlanta, and getting Camille over to my mother's... all of that with a hectic work week behind me was enough to sap my energy. One drink and I'll curl up by the fireplace like a lazy cat. By the way, how'd those job leads work out?"

"I'm in a holding pattern, but I'm sure one of them will turn into something," she lied, more concerned about Francis' health than any job leads. Although Antoinette didn't buy the explanation about merely being fatigued from the woman who used to go non-stop and who could drink them all under the table. She'd let it go. She knew above all else, Francis was a private person. And, Tracey was like a news anchor: in everybody's business—all news. She'd inquire later. But something was definitely wrong.

"The ambiance of this place is spectacular. There's a loft up there," Tracey mewed as she pointed toward the spiral staircase. "It even has a Jacuzzi in the room. The architecture calls to me and says, entertain."

They all laughed. Tracey was such a trip. But, they all revelled in their friend's rare chance to escape and to be her old self. Antoinette wanted to kiss her face and squeeze her tight. Instinctively she knew this was a giant step for Trace—to do something she'd wanted to do—and there was probably a high price her friend would have to pay for it in the coming weeks.

"Trace, one day you're gonna have your entertainment capital. Fran, you'll have your cottage in the country. And I'll have my own restaurant."

"Yeah, and Cookie will have her Fortune 100 consulting dynasty," Tracey laughed, sipping her champagne. "I'll take my fortune through a second, wealth-inspired marriage, thank you. It'll be easier that way. That's the one thing wrong with this conference. No men. All this time and elegance going to sheer waste. Such a pity."

Francis and Antoinette looked at one another, laughed, and shook their heads. It was a new and welcomed insight into their friend's mental space. Tracey was obviously just biding her time. Even they'd pegged her wrong. But, it was all talk, that much they knew from experience.

"I can see us now," Antoinette giggled, the champagne starting to have an effect.

"You have to visualize, ladies," Cookie chuckled as she joined in with them from behind. "Now, let me and Antoinette get busy."

Cookie hugged Antoinette briefly and a silent exchange made them squeeze each other again. "I have been working OT for you, girl," she said against Antoinette's hairline. "There's someone I'd like you to meet." Pulling away, she issued a sly smile, moving Antoinette by her waist from the group. "Don't blow it. She's one of my biggest clients. She'll test you, and she's a trip, but she also has a good heart. She's good people."

"As long as she's good people, Cook. I guess I can stand the precursory once-over-lightly." Dropping her voice to a low murmur, she asked about what had been haunting her. "What's wrong with Fran?"

"Good," Cookie whispered, giving Antoinette a

last squeeze of support as they crossed the room, while blatantly refusing to answer the second question with a discrete shake of her head that translated into, not now. "This time, you're the trap, I'm the flush—so there's no conflict of interest. Got it? Like old times, girl. Just like old times," she said, giving her a little tug of confidence, and bringing her before a Grande Dame. "This, Ms. LaMann, is the best sales rep and public relations magnet on the East Coast—

Antoinette Wellington, of the Connecticut Wellingtons."

Jerome sat on the side of the bed and reached for his cigarettes. It didn't matter what Karen thought at this point, and he'd needed a cigarette since they'd gotten into the Bronco.

"Do you have to smoke that in here? This is a no smoking room, Jerome, and you know how much I hate the smell of cigarettes."

He didn't bother to look at her. He hated the acrid sound of her voice now more than ever. Choosing not to respond, he lit the end of his Marlboro.

"At least you could open a window, or go in the bathroom!"

Her voice was shrill and he cringed at the sound

of it. He watched her dispassionately from the corner of his eye as she snatched up her new robe and went into the bathroom. A hard click of the button lock sent a shiver of renewed rage down his spine, and the water running in the shower made him close his eyes. She was washing him off of her. It was bad enough that they'd touched like strangers, joined without connecting. But for her to wash him off of her, right after, like that... To release into a void instead of into a woman who still loved what they had created, a family—maybe even one that just liked him a little—was worse than if he'd paid for it. At least he would have been mentally prepared, knowing in advance what the terms were. He probably shouldn't have even tried. He definitely shouldn't have touched her when he was that angry at her—when they were that angry at each other.

He considered the end of the lit butt and stared at the red ember before he brought the filter to his lips to take another drag. What the hell was wrong? What had changed in a blink of an eye? Sure, she'd moved under him. Her body had responded. His functioned properly. He'd waited for her to finish first, any man knew that. What the hell was it? Could she have really held that much anger for fifteen years? Or, was it a slow smolder like the end of his cigarette, something that had just gone up in smoke over time? He listened to the soft pelt of water running in the shower, and wondered where the soft murmur that he'd expected to come from her had gone? Where was the bond? Why didn't he feel like telling her he loved her when he was done, and why hadn't she searched his face for those words to come from him? They were married, for Christ's sake! He'd honored his commitment inside the marriage. He'd done hard time with her! Paid his dues.

Jerome pulled hard on the Marlboro, causing the nicotine to send a shock wave through his system. One, lousy, bachelor fling before he married a woman that he wasn't ready to marry in the first place... "Damn," he muttered. "Damn." Anger renewed itself and stormed all of his mental barricades at once. She had no right to lay claim to that transgression, not when he'd had to choke down every need, want, and desire of his own to take care of her after she'd trapped him! His father had told him that hell hath no fury like... but, there were four children to consider. Children that he loved and wanted—every last one of them. Children that even in her anger, she wanted to save. But, how much longer could he live in hell?

Common sense took leave of his mind and went AWOL. Counseling was out of the question. Jerome dragged hard on his cigarette again and this time he let the smoke slowly retreat from his lungs through his nose. He went over the past like a homeless garbage picker. He'd tried before this, but even suggesting a minister had nearly made her slap him. He'd asked her repeatedly, and it only created more fights about white people, or church people being in her business. Even a black counselor hadn't been good enough, according to her. But this was their business.

He stood slowly and crossed the room, and turned the handle of the bathroom door. "Karen. Open up," he said quietly to the locked door. "I need to talk to you."

When she didn't answer, his mind mounted a preemptive strike. If not a counselor, then a lawyer.

◑◐

"Cynthia has told me so much about you," the older woman crooned as she looked over Antoinette's slightly rumpled navy-blue networking uniform.

Smiling in civil return, Antoinette surveyed the inimitable Ruby LaMann. Her perfectly coifed silver hair hung at the appropriate length to show off her one carat diamond stud earrings. The only break in her attire hue was her brilliant, multi-colored silk scarf that set off her monochrome accessories, which in turn matched a stunning, winter white designer suit. Feeling totally out of her league, Antoinette brightened her smile and took a deep breath. "Well, Cookie—Cynthia, and I go back a long way. And, I am good at what I do." She wanted to kick herself, and knew that Cookie would have been mortified to hear her around-the-way nickname used in a business setting. She was definitely out of practice.

The return smile that Antoinette received was kind, but somewhat patronizing. She hated the way the diva before her continued to look her over, allowing her gaze to settle briefly on every imperfection in her presence and in her attire. If only this had been five years ago.

"I'm sure you are, darling," Ms. LaMann said after a well-timed pause, and in an all too pleasant tone. Extending her hand, the woman's gaze left Antoinette's face and settled on another near-by group of guests. "The best to you in all of your endeavors."

Panic shot through Antoinette's brain. She was being dismissed. Not tonight.

"Yes, Ms. LaMann," she said curtly, "and as a well-established caterer, I hope you will be able to take advantage of the recent changes in Philadelphia's health care systems."

The matron stopped her retreat and smiled. "We would love to take advantage of that lucrative market. Health care, after all, is a booming industry in the nineties."

"So people have read. But the intricacies for the uninitiated are quite complex." Antoinette kept the smile pasted on her face. She was not going down without a fight. Definitely not tonight.

Feeling an unusual surge of energy, she kept

Cookie in her peripheral vision. The tension on her friend's face was easily measurable as Cookie stood off to Ms. LaMann's left, yet now well within earshot of their conversation. Taking her time, Antoinette reached into her purse and pulled out a small slip of paper and her Mont Blanc pen. "I'll give you this bit of consulting for free, Ms. LaMann," she said in an authoritative tone, scribbling notes as she spoke without looking up. "I was a major account executive for some of the biggest health care agencies in the Delaware Valley. I know these people. Well. And I have a lot of favors still out there. They are not hiring, and are downsizing, but are also looking to outsource many of their functions. That means consulting work, and large contracts for other related services. Let them know I sent you, and you'll get an audience."

Antoinette allowed her tone to become slightly bored. "Right now," she added, finally dignifying her target with eye contact, "they are all going through major reorganization, getting ready for the impact that the State's Healthy Start program will have on the way that they do business, Ms. LaMann. They need minority contractors to meet State guidelines, and the hotels can't do it. They need promotion by, and for, their target market. Minorities. Let me know when you're ready for a marketing plan to go after catering for the big eight."

Cookie smiled and Antoinette felt absolute

power pump through her veins.

"Ruby. Call me, Ruby," the older woman crooned as she stood transfixed before Antoinette. "Here's my card, and do let me put my home number on the back of it."

Antoinette nodded as she accepted the card, glanced at Cookie's wide grin, and walked away toward another group of dignitaries. "Call me when you're ready," she tossed over her shoulder, "You have my number."

That's right, damn it. She was a master player, and sales was her game.

She was back!

CHAPTER 16

The ride home had been cloaked in violent silence. Karen didn't wait for him to even turn off the motor when they pulled up to the house. She simply jumped out of the car and headed up the steps, managed the locks, and slammed the door behind her. At two o'clock in the morning, he was too weary to care.

Jerome collected their bags slowly, and walked with a pall-bearer's stride to the door, dropping his suitcase on the enclosed porch and bringing Karen's bag inside. He looked at Miss Hattie's sleepy nineteen year-old niece who yawned at him from the sofa. Only the dim light from the television set lit the room. Karen was nowhere in sight.

"I thought you guys were staying till tomorrow afternoon?" Shawnetta said with a stretch. "Everything's okay. Kids have been asleep since about ten."

He looked around the living room, and noted that this girl-child had even straightened up. Good home training from Miss Hattie, no doubt, and Karen didn't even want the girl in the house. Damn. The child kept a neater house than his own wife, he thought, the rage inside of him broiling as he fingered his keys.

Jerome reached in his pocket and pulled out his wallet, finding a fifty. "Change of plans, Shawnetta. It didn't have nothing to do with you, though. Place looks nice. Thanks," he mumbled in a far-away tone, handing her the bill. "Let me walk you down the street. It's late. Lotta creeps out at night."

The young girl accepted the bill and shot off the edge of the sofa. "Oh, no, Mr. Henderson. This is way too much. I just watched 'em for a few hours, plus, my grandma would never let me—"

"Girl, let's get you home," he said cutting her off. "You did me a favor tonight."

Still shaking her head no as she put on her sneakers, Shawnetta laid the bill on the coffee table and began re-fluffing the pillows and folding the throw. "All I did was clean-up a little. Dag-gone, it wasn't worth no fifty."

"Yes it was," he said quietly, handing her the bill again and grabbing her coat from the hall hook. "You helped me clean out my house, more than you'll ever know."

"And where are you going? Back out to the bar?

Well, the damned bars are closed!" Karen stood at the top of the steps and glared at him. "You are not walking out of here without telling me where you're going!"

"I'ma walk this child past a crack house and down to her grandmother's. Then I'm coming home. Is that all right with you?"

He hated fighting in public, with witnesses. The way Shawnetta's eyes darted between the two combatants and shined with anxiety in the sky-blue light from the set. It was just like when he'd tried to take Karen to his boss' Christmas party, and all hell broke loose. In public. His grip tightened on his keys. How many times had he not said what needed to be said? This time, he would deal with her directly when he got back.

"You don't have to walk me home, Mr. Henderson," Shawnetta said in a tiny voice, her body receding into the shadows of the enclosed porch. "I'm just down the street."

Jerome ignored her and opened the door for her. When they reached the pavement, he escorted her from the curbside. But, as they approached the drug house, his body shifted between the house and the girl. Shawnetta smiled nervously and moved a little closer to him until they passed the run-down property. He kept his keys knotted in his fist as he made eye contact with the gang of mangy customers who were waiting for the door to open.

"Thanks, Mr. Henderson. I hate them people."

"Don't ever deal with a man who won't walk you home at night. Make him respect you and your grandmomma's house." He'd kept his gaze straight ahead as he spoke to her, but he could see her staring at him from the corner of his eye.

"Nobody walks you home these days," she said in a quiet voice. "They just don't do that."

"That's 'cause y'all don't expect us to do it—if your boyfriend doesn't, drop him. Y'all have more control than you think."

Shawnetta paused and looked at him for a moment before she bound up the steps and opened her door, yelling a quick, "Thanks, g'night!" behind her.

Once the girl was inside, he took out his cigarettes and lit the end of one against the wind.

"Jerome. Wait a minute, boy! Hold-on, an lemme gits my robe on."

His line of vision shot up to Miss Hattie's second floor window as he took a drag.

"Let her keep it, Ma'am."

"Boy, you jus' hold on. I'm old, an' cain't move as fast as you young folk. I be down in a minute."

The cold air felt good on his face as he took another slow drag. Jerome walked over to Miss Hattie's steps and sat down. He knew the deal. She wanted to know what her granddaughter had given him worth fifty dollars. It was to be expected. Miss Hattie was old-school, which meant that he'd have to defend the girl's honor—as well as his own.

"C'mon in an git outta this cold, boy," the old woman said as she opened her screen door. "On the porch is mo' betta den in da streets."

He crushed out his cigarette and threw it in the direction of the drug house, far enough from Miss Hattie's house that she wouldn't have to sweep it up. With both hands on his knees, he pushed himself upright and stood, feeling every muscle in his back lock and fight against sudden gravity.

"Ma'am," he began slowly, once she'd shut the door, "things got kinda tense down in AC, and Shawnetta had cleaned up the house so good... just wanted to thank her."

Miss Hattie smiled and patted his cheek. "Ain't worried 'bout yo' cred'bility none, Jerome. No expl'-nation necessary. Knowed you since you was a little boy and you raked my leaves. More worried 'bout a hard workin' man that cain't stay out a night with his wife. Troubles' finding they way to yo' door, boy. Ever'body done spoke on it. We got eyes. Ain't nobody 'round here blind."

Her words fell on him like wet cement, suffocating him, and clogging his pores. "I got three daughters, and a boy," he said looking out of her bay-window towards the drug house. "I need to be here to keep them from that," he said with a nod toward the milling crowd on the porch two houses down. "They're like vampires. Sleep all day, suck the life out of a community by night, and kids got to play around crack vials. Where's the men, Miss Hattie?

Where's the men?"

"Somes left," she said quietly, staring at him with a sad smile. "But, sometimes, a man's gotta do what a man's gotta do. Jus' take care of them chirren."

Her face blurred and he looked away as hot moisture filled his eyes. "Been trying to, Miss Hattie. Like my Pop did for us, you know? But, I don't know what to do..."

"Look at me, boy," she said with tenderness in her voice. It had the kind of balm in it that he hadn't heard since his own grandmother had died. "You got the face of a young man, but the eyes of an old one. Don't you lose your faith, jus' do right by the chirren. Stay in they life, love 'em, an' let 'em know they's got a Daddy." Miss Hattie sighed and patted his cheek, holding it before she withdrew her hand. "Even iron wears out, chile, sooner or later. Somethin' gotta give, or you be finding yourself down there one day," she said in a hoarse whisper filled with emotion, nodding toward the drug house. "Lost my baby girl to that, 'cause she jus' plain wore out. We don' need to lose you too, Jerome Henderson. You's a good boy, don' cha never fergit that Miss Hattie toldya so. No matter what cha decide. Hear?"

"I ain't made of iron, Miss Hattie. She's breaking my back." It was all he could do to speak, and he looked away from the ancient one who'd dropped pearls of wisdom at his feet. His life was public knowledge, and his elderly neighbor just confirmed it.

"Lord have Mercy," she said moving to the door. "I'ma pray fer ya steady, boy. Cause you done been to the rock. That girl must be missin' her mind. Gotsta trust on The Rock now, boy. That's all ya kin do," she said kissing his cheek as she opened the door.

He slipped past her, but couldn't turn around or say good-bye. The cold wind stung the water that had run down his face. His gait was slow as pain shot through his lower back. Yet, something in her presence behind him, held him, as he gazed at his street, his block, his house. For the first time in too long, he remembered what it was like to have a Clan Mother, an elder advisor. His mother would have approved of Miss Hattie. He felt it in his bones.

"Put the straight in yo' back, boy," she said in a firm voice from the doorway, "an' don' cha never let nobody break it. We'll miss you 'round here, but we'll watch out for 'em."

Her words propelled him forward, past the crack house, up his steps, through the door, and up the stairs to his bedroom. He wasn't made of iron.

"I know you don't think you're gonna sleep in here tonight--not after starting that shit in AC? You whispered for Toni as you drifted off to sleep." Karen swung herself out of the bed and stood in front of him with her arms folded.

"I apologize for that. It was unintentional," he whispered, truly sorry deep in his heart that he'd brought Antoinette with him to Atlantic City. She deserved to stay in his mind, and not to be trashed in the middle of a domestic dispute. And, at the same time, in this moment as he stared at his wife, he felt sorry for Karen, sorry that he'd never been able to totally make room in his soul for her to replace his past.

"You're sorry? Is that all you can say for yourself. And after you been down Miss Hattie's with your girlfriend, too? You must be crazy!"

"The child is nineteen. She's a decent girl, Karen. Miss Hattie raised her right. It ain't like that." His voice held no emotion. "I'm leaving like you asked me to three days ago."

"Good. Take your ass down on the couch and out of my face. I should have known that you hadn't changed."

"No," he said, quietly. "I'm leaving this house. I'm done, Karen. I'm tired." He stepped around her and began slowly taking clothes from the closet. "You got your divorce."

"What? Have you lost your damned mind!"

"Yes." His voice was still monotone.

"Then get out of my house!" she shrieked, snatching his clothes from the hangers so hard that he had to duck as the wire ones bent and ricocheted past his face. "I'm having my uncle draw up the papers. I don't need you. I already have a lawyer!"

He looked at his clothes on the floor and left the room. He could hear her footsteps behind him as he made his way down the stairs to the kitchen. Rummaging in the shed, he found the box of garbage bags.

"You ain't taking shit out of here." Her voice was a low threat. "This is my house."

"I don't want anything," he said too tired to fight, and not looking at her as he pulled several bags from the box. "The house was, and will always be, for you and the kids. I'll sign it over to you. You can have every stick of furniture in here. I bought it for you and the kids. Anyway, it's Cherokee custom for the man to leave everything behind. Maybe that's why my pop stayed, 'cause he was married under Mom's laws and couldn't part with things? Maybe that's why my mother died young, 'cause the bad vibrations in the house killed her. Who knows? Either way, you can have it all."

"What?"

"Been doin' a lot of thinking, K. Even iron wears out."

She had moved into the kitchen entrance and stood blocking his passage to freedom. But her face looked stricken. He saw the same flash of fear flicker behind her eyes that he'd seen earlier. Only, this time, it didn't move him. Too much water had gone under the bridge. Even iron wears out, he repeated to himself. He wasn't iron.

"You're gonna pay, fool." Her gaze narrowed on him, and her voice began to escalate again. "I know you don't think you're gonna just walk out of here and not take care of us? I'll take you to Support Court so fast—"

"—Haven't I always taken care of you and the kids?" Blood beat a tempo in his ears. "Answer me, damn it!" His gaze tore around the kitchen and she backed up a step. "Look around here, K! I work sixteen hours a day."

"And this was the best you could do?"

Something fragile inside of him snapped. "I'll never make what your brother-in-law makes. Ever. I never had the chance to, but I take care of my kids. I work hard and pay every bill you can make!"

She paced dangerously close to him, and circled him as she spoke. "How dare you blame me for getting pregnant. You didn't think before you got what you wanted either," she hissed in a low voice. "Just like you finally got it tonight in AC. So, don't blame me if you didn't do a damned thing with your life."

He straightened his back and moved toward the door. "You're wrong. I never got what I wanted from you. Especially not tonight. No. Don't even go there, Karen. I never blamed you for having our first kid. Remember? Who was happy about her? Who showed her off to the world? Who took her everywhere? Who, K? Tell me now, woman! I love every one of my children." Her body recoiled from his as he hovered only inches from her face.

"And tell me," he railed on, taking heavy breaths of sudden fury, "that I didn't encourage you to do what you wanted to do? Who watched them when you went back to school, or changed jobs fifty times while you were trying to find yourself? Who makes fuckin' breakfast for them, takes them to school plays? Who, damn it! Answer me, woman! Who sat with the older ones at two-o'clock in the morning when you nursed the littlest ones? Who changed diapers, also does the laundry so he can find a clean pair of work duds to go to work in? Tell me!" he yelled, as she fled from him and pinned herself against the cabinets. "Who fixes his own damned dinner when he comes in from work, and eats alone—except maybe on Sunday!"

Jerome flung the garbage bags down on the floor. "Your Momma? Where was she, Karen? At the casinos. Where was your sister? Out of town. Who? Then who listened to your litany about not being happy, and wanting this or that—then who went out to try to buy it for you?" His vision swept the room then settled on her stunned expression. "You can have it all, baby, and no judge has to tell me to take care of my kids."

Winded, he fished in his wallet and pulled out his medical card, an Employee Assistance Program card, and his money then slapped it on the counter. "Here. Take it all. As long as I'm working, you all have good medical and dental. Call a lawyer on that EAP list, it's free. On me. And, when I get my next check, I'm comin' with your money, and to pick up my babies for a visit. Expect me, Karen. Every other weekend. If you try an' take 'em from me, or hide 'em somewhere, I'll hunt you down to the end of the earth. Don't ever take me there."

Standing at the cabinets she stared at him, and he could see that hot tears had formed in her eyes. "When did I ever get to do what I wanted?" she wailed, folding her arms around herself and pacing to the doorway. "Tell me that, since you have all the answers, Jay."

"You have a degree. I don't. You have a Momma to listen to your side. I don't. You have a fully furnished house with thirty-thousand dollars of blood, sweat, and tears of equity in it, good credit, and an extra car. I don't now. You have a place to lay your head, and babies that can crawl in bed with you when you need to blot out the world. I don't. You can have a career. I have a job as a workhorse. You've got a fighting chance. I don't. You'll be the poor victimized woman of a no-good-black-man. I'll be the no-good-black-mother-fucker who left a nice wife and four babies. Forever, K. A statistic— as people shake their heads and talk about it on Oprah. You just got your freedom, K. I don't know what that is. I never did."

Tears streamed down her face and her gaze pulled away from his. "Are you gonna tell the kids? Or, do you want me to?"

"After I pack, I'll tell them."

"Tell them what? How are you going to explain this to them?

"I don't know, but I'll tell you two things. I

never cheated on you while we were married, and I never made you feel like dirt when I touched you. Woulda walked through the fire for you, girl, if you hada given me half a chance."

"Is that what you call this? Walking through the fire? Because I wanted you to change?"

"Change is a two-way street." He felt the life drain from his body, down through the soles of his shoes. His voice became quiet. There was no point in yelling any more. It didn't matter. "The problem is, you never knew what you wanted. All you knew was what you thought I should do. Well, now you can find out what it is out here. You can go meet the man, and find out how they look at you like you ain't shit, but then you gotta take whatever the white man says you got to. You can see what it feels like to have a brain, and a piece of heart, and have them treat you like you just one of their fork lifts, or trucks... just disposable equipment... old equipment—that's easily replaced by younger, stronger, newer brawn when the young boys come on a job. Do you know what that's like?"

Karen looked at the floor and didn't respond.

"I pray that I can make enough so that you won't have to ever find out, for the kids' sake, 'cause it'll take somethin' outta you, girl."

"I've worked before," she said defensively, but all of the bite had gone out of her voice.

"But, you always had the option not to, K," he sighed, gathering up the bags that he'd dropped from his hands. "All that glitters ain't gold, baby." He stepped around her and made his way into the hallway towards the stairs and stopped without turning around. "I'm going to take my clothes, my albums, a few pictures, my tools, and my old stereo in the basement and pack up the Bronco. If anything around here breaks, call me, and I'll come fix it."

"Where're you going to go?"

"My Dad's, if he'll have me," he said, climbing the stairs. "My sister's, if she's got room. Ain't got no money left till next check, but I'll be back for my kids when I get some more."

The sight of his oldest daughter stopped him in his tracks. He stood paralyzed on the landing as he watched her dissolve into sobs.

"I knew it. I just knew it!" Patsy shrieked, running to him and almost making him lose his balance.

He clutched her to his chest and smoothed her hair. God help him.

"Things have been wrong for a long time..." he stammered as her wails escalated. "C'mon, c'mon, Patsy, you're my big girl. You gotta be here to look out for Kitty, Darlene, and Christopher."

His heart shattered as he felt his first child, his love child, the love of his life sway and go limp in his arms. Half carrying, half walking her to his bedroom a sob caught his breath. "Daddy'll never leave you, baby. I'm coming back for you, soon as I get settled."

"Why can't we go with you?" Her blood-shot gaze searched his face. "Why do you have to be the one to leave, Daddy? Why you? She can go, but not you!"

All he could do was pull the child against him and rock her to their sobs. When three more small bodies collided against his, he tried to open his arms wide enough to gather them all. But he couldn't seem to keep his arms around them. Children slipped from his grasp as he pulled at their pajamas and tried to hold them by their hair. His arms weren't big enough. God, make his arms big enough. How could he protect his baby girls from dope fiends, child molesters, and drive-by snipers? How could he ever look in his son's face and call himself a man; a man who didn't leave their mother, a man who'd kept them safe, a father who'd stayed? How could he tell him, at four years old, to take his place, so that his exhausted father could stand down? How could he make sure that they all got what he never had? An education. A fighting chance. How could he make enough money to move them to a nicer house, a better neighborhood, where crack vials didn't get swept up by double-dutch ropes?

"Tell us Patsy was lying, Daddy," Kitty wailed, joining their tight circle. "You're not leaving us, Daddy? Nooooo!"

Christopher's muffled sobs mingled into

Darlene's as the two youngest children clung to his waist and sucked their thumbs.

"We'll do more to help Mommy not get mad," his oldest pleaded. "I'll clean up my room. I'll watch the rest. We'll all help. Just don't go, please..."

"Is this what you wanted?" Karen asked in a whisper at the bedroom door.

The three smallest buried their heads in his abdomen, and thick rivers of snot choked his words. "No. Never. They're just babies."

When Patsy flinched away from him, she took his heart across the room with her. Standing between both him and Karen, she straightened her spine, and wiped at her nose and eyes roughly. Her gaze narrowed on Karen as she spoke. The profile of her semi-adult face held him in a trance. She looked so much like the proud reminder of his mother...

"Darlene. Kitty. Chris. Come into the bathroom with me and wash your faces. Let Dad pack. He made us a promise to come back, and he doesn't lie." She whirled around to face him and her bottom lip trembled as two big tears splashed her cheeks. "You have never lied to us, Daddy. I know you'll come back, but I know you can't live here. I'll take care of them. You can go, and even if nobody else does, I believe in you—she never did."

He covered his face with his hands and let what was left of his soul pour into them. His baby. A fourteen and a half year old baby had more courage than he did. Even she could see. Tiny hands petted his shoulders and kissed his rough palms that blocked his face. Angels' wings kissed his neck, and angelic voices, too grown voices, soothed him as they murmured in unison, "Don't cry, Daddy. Please don't cry anymore ."

"I never meant..." his sobs threatened every word, but his angels repeated their hymn to him—stanzas with the same refrain—telling him not to cry. That it would be all right. That they would be all right. That they believed in him. That they loved him, and not to forget to come for them. Their voices rose on the dawn, swirling above him in the air full of conviction, and ringing out with majesty. Children. Angels. Beings that could see beyond the surface, ones who had looked into his soul and had seen him. Those who had woken him up from the sofa every day, who had heard all of the arguments, and the neighbors' whispers, those who were the unseen but had seen it all. The blessed who still saw a little good in his wretched soul. Ones who still had hope, and faith, and charity in their innocent hearts. And their cherub hands pulled him to his feet as their chorus begged him to be a man.

CHAPTER 17

The sun was high and bright. Sunday, blessed Sunday. Although her body was tired from the drive, and from staying up two whole nights with the girls, she practically skipped up the steps to May's condo. It had been a virtual slumber party, a spiritual healing, even Francis seemed to perk up, albeit there had been no real chance to find out what had made her initially look so bad. But, with the laughter and the reassurance from Cookie, she'd been able to accept that Francis, like the rest of them, was probably only going through some temporary changes. She'd let the subject drop for the weekend, pending Francis' promise to call her to really talk like they'd used to. Even Tracey was different, no longer looking wide-eyed and afraid of her surroundings.

And maybe, just maybe, she'd come away from the conference with a couple of job contacts. God was good!

Antoinette flung the door open wide and by rote punched in the deactivating alarm code, despite the fact that Adrienne hadn't turned it on. Oh, yeah, her sister had been here. She only gave the memory brief residence in her mind as she kicked the Saturday mail aside, and stooped down to pick up the keys that had been left through the mail slot. Not this morning. No bills, no fights. It was The Lord's day, and her day. She would deal with bill collectors on Monday. She would deal with this dreaded new job at the rehab unit on Monday. Today, she would savor a fraction of peace. She ran into the living room, dropped her bag, and found Pearline's gospel station--Gospel Highway. She flung her arms open wide and spun around in the room, singing wildly and swaying in the sunlit space, ignoring the mess Adrienne had left.

"Hold, on! Just hold on, cause help, help is on the way!" She belted out the spiritual with everything in her. "Help. Yes I need your help, is on the way... you told me to just hold on..."

Giggling and singing, she danced over to her answering machine and let out a whoop when she saw it had registered seventeen messages. "I was out," she sang, adding her own words to the song, "but, help is on the way!"

As the first beep toned, she waited with impatience, her eyes closed and still swaying to the radio.

"Hey, suga-lump, it's Daddy and May. Just checking on you. Did Adrienne catch up with you yet?" the machine blared before it beeped again and cued the next message.

"Hey, Sis. Hailin' from LA to let you know I got back all right. Your keys are in the doorway. Girl, it's eighty-five degrees out here. You oughta come for a visit. The weather's great, and the men are fine. Don't bother to call back, save your money. Love ya. Chao!"

"Mrs. Wellington, this is Strawbr--" Antoinette sped past the bill collector, and then four more. Not today, she told herself.

"Baby, it's May. Your father and I have been trying to reach you all day. Call us, hear, sweetie."

"Not on your life," Antoinette giggled. "Not today. Joy, joy in my soul," she wailed with the new song that had come on."

"Antoinette, this is Brian. I need you to contact me ASAP."

All the joy bled from Antoinette's body as it tensed to her ex-husband's words. The baby, she breathed in... "I have to catch an early flight, and need to bring Lauren back this morning."

"Ha!" she shouted and stood up. "Go to hell, I'm still on my date with myself!" she laughed and spun around. "Where do I go, where do I go..." she sang. "He better go to The Rock. I ain't his rock. Where will he go, Lord...." she laughed and twirled around as Francis' voice drew her back to the machine.

"Sorry those leads didn't work out this week, girl. I'll have some more mid-week. I'm coming home again for Easter, we'll catch up real good then. I have a lot to tell you. I loved our time together this weekend."

Francis' voice didn't sound right, and something about its resonance stilled her. Antoinette made a mental note to call Francis back first, and she sat down on the side of the bed. Her girlfriend's tone was too serious, and her voice sounded too distant for their having just been together. But, then again, Francis always sounded business-like on the phone. That's why she'd missed her warm face so, which only gave up formality in close-knit, safe circles. Yes, she would call Francis at her mother's house before she flew back to Atlanta.

The next beep on the answering machine startled her. "Trace, Fran, and Cookie, here, hailing from a cellular. Status check from the road on the way down the mountain. You did good, chicky."

Antoinette laughed hard as she waited for the rest of their message.

"Yeah, hon, you worked a mojo!" Cookie screamed into the unison of voices. "But get off my phone, y'all runnin' up my bill on mess. We just spent two days de-programming with the girl."

Giggles and hearty laughs surrounded her from the answering machine as their three-party message clicked off.

"Girl, call me. All hell is breaking loose and it's heading your way. Can't talk now. Bye."

Antoinette cocked her head to the side and pondered Valerie's cryptic message. "All hell's breaking loose?" Her shoulder's slumped. Each time Val's voice filled the speaker again, the message was the same, but her voice seemed more strained on every subsequent call.

"Call me as soon as you get in. This is Val. It's important. Okay."

"Okay. Okay," Antoinette sighed, switching off the answering machine and picking up the phone. "Well, thank you anyway, Lord, for a little peace."

∞

"I don't know what to tell you, man? Are you sure?" Buddy took one of Jerome's cigarettes from him and leaned against his Bronco. "Your Pop put you out after one night? What happened?"

Jerome stared at the ground. "He let me sleep in my old bed, and put my car in the garage. Told me not to unpack it. Didn't say much all day. I slept all day, watched some TV, we ate a couple of cheese steaks. I went back to bed. This morning, he said I needed to go the hell back home, and couldn't run from what I didn't like. Threw the Air Force in my face, about how I decided not to re-up when Karen got pregnant." Shame kept his gaze focused on the icy pavement. "Told me I wasn't no man, wasn't his son, if I couldn't let this blow over and go home. He won't let it rest—so I'm out."

"Damn," Buddy whispered. He took two quick drags as he shook his head. "Damn. What about your sister?"

Jerome considered his friend's question for a moment. There was no real way to explain not wanting to go to his sister's house, or the fact that it had nothing to do with his strained relationship with her husband, or even their semi-impoverished circumstances. How could he explain not wanting to see her because she had their mother's eyes—eyes that could haunt him forever if they even contained the slightest glimmer of disappointment or judgment? What he'd already seen in his father's eyes had been enough.

"Got a full house, and a crazy preacher husband. You know that joint will be too live," he replied quietly, summoning the strength to make his point. "Plus, she ain't tryin' to cross my Pop and get him on her case. Like I said, I'm out."

Buddy put a hand on his shoulder. "Look, man, I'd let you stay on my couch again for a few days... but Val's been havin' a hissy-fit ever since Toni stopped by a little tipsy last week. Says she doesn't want us to end up like everybody else, or to catch the divorce syndrome—or, some ole nonsense... and is nervous about people's morals all of a sudden."

"What?" Jerome stared at his friend for a

moment, then shook his head. He lit another cigarette and let his full body weight fall against the Bronco's grill. "That's just perfect. Hung, without a trial or a jury."

"Just like O.J., man," Buddy said with a laugh. "Y'all's kickin' up a lotta dust in everybody's household, man. No offense."

"What's that supposed to mean?" Jerome took another deep drag and let the smoke come out through his nose.

"Means," Buddy said, his smile disappearing, "that my wife is accusing me of aiding and abetting your crime of leaving home, that my credibility as a potential accomplice who might decide to leave, too, is also on the line. Val said she ain't harboring no fugitives—even if Antoinette is her girl. All of a sudden she's scared to death that we might break up."

"Me leavin' Karen ain't got nothin' to do with your household, or Toni. Damn, man. I haven't even as much as talked to the girl in somethin' like fifteen or twenty years. How'd Toni get into this?" Outrage coursed through him as he stood away from the vehicle and flung his cigarette on the ground. "I'm homeless, brother. I turned my pockets out for Karen at the casinos, and gave her and the babysitter the last of my green till my check comes a couple of weeks from now. Even then, I can't afford the security deposit on an apartment. All I own is packed in a freakin' car—after working all my life," he yelled, sweeping his hands in front of his loaded-down Bronco. "This is supposed to be the sum total of a man's life? Buddy, we go back, man. All the way back. We've been boys since we played stick ball." Disbelief made him search Buddy's face until his friend looked away.

"You gotta pay the cost to be the boss, man. That's the way it goes after you get a wife and kids. I told you that before you lost your damned mind. Didn't I? A long time ago." Buddy whirled on him and pointed his finger at his chest. "You dumb son-of-a..." Buddy faltered. "You can't win. Ain't no Cherokee posse comin' out of the hills to save your stubborn, black ass. Grow up, man. Get real... All them babies... I love you, man," he choked as his eyes filled. "That's why I told your stupid ass to stay— to suck it up, just like I have to everyday, and to stay. Goddamn you man. If you hada only listened to me, you wouldn't have had to go out like this with no where to go! Look at you man," he yelled, kicking the side of Jerome's Bronco. "You had it all going on. Me and you, blood. Now even my wife is all over my back, accusing me of a bun-cha stuff I only dreamed of doing. She's ready to read her girl the riot act, and get a militia of wives to string her up. She called Scoop and found out they all went to a conference, now, Scoop won't even let Tracey go near poor T after this weekend—thinking the girl might spread 'the bad wife disease' to her— and all you did was lick your chops about her in a bar and prob'ly wet dream about her. This is crazy. You kickin' up too much dust! You can't stay here! Go home, man. Go the hell home."

"I can't," Jerome said quietly, moving to the driver's side of his car.

"Then where you gonna go, to Toni's?"

Jerome stopped and looked at Buddy hard. "Never. I'll sleep in the damned street before I bring this to her door. I'd never let her see me like this. And, this ain't about her. She don't have a thing to do with it, and you need to get Val and Scoop straight about that, if you don't do nothin' else—I ain't seen the girl. Promise me."

"Aw, man," Buddy sighed, scratching his head. "I know. I know. She ain't the type. She's always been a thoroughbred. Wouldn't scrape your street urchin' ass up in this condition, no how. Let me think, man. Let me think. You can't go on no grate in February. Damn, man, you gotta store your gear so you can at least go to work Monday, and now your ass better work. For real, for real. 'Specially when the judge catch up to you."

Jerome didn't move as Buddy paced about. The cold air cut his face like a knife and he shut his eyes against the glare of the sun. What had he been thinking? Because some old lady had told him he was at the rock, and wasn't made of iron, and he'd gone into his house and made a political statement. Stupid! This was the rock. His kids were at risk, had been traumatized, all because he hadn't been laid right in Atlantic City? Pitiful. His own father had called him a punk to his face, and his sister didn't want to get in the middle of it. Now a good woman's reputation was on the line. Again his back felt like cinder blocks had been loaded into every disc. But he waited for Buddy's plan. Home was no longer an option. It didn't exist.

"Maybe... can't make no guarantees, man. But maybe old man Miles will have mercy on you, and let you sleep in one of the basements if you work for him for free till your check comes. Damn, man."

ꙮ

"Oh, hell no! Y'all ain't bringin' no domestic mess to my door," old man Miles protested. "I runs a clean shop, tend the boiler, and fix rich folks buildins. Thas all I do. This ain't no shelter for the homeless. Ain't the Salvation Army--or, Father Divine's! I'm retired, and my name is Bennit, cause I ain't in-it. Hear?"

"Aw, come on, Mr. Miles," Buddy pleaded. "My boy just got put out, ain't got no family, works like a damned slave, will work for you with no cut. He just needs a couple of weeks till his check comes."

Buddy looked nervously between Jerome and Mr. Miles, then at the floor.

"These ain't my buildins, boy. You think they won't put me out too? I live here, thas all. Right here in the basement under white folks' good graces. Now, y'all comin' around here wit some mess." Mr. Miles glared at Jerome. "See, boy, a woman runs the house. You supposed to pay the bills, and pray that she give you some regular tail. Didn't your friend tell you that? He's married, ain't he?"

"Yeah, he did," Jerome sighed. "So did my father."

"Yo Pappy tol' you right!" he exclaimed, slapping a meaty palm on his metal desk.

"Look, old dude," Buddy said losing patience, "can't my boy just store his stuff in one of them empty cages till his check comes? If he keeps it in his car, the pipers will take the last of what he got left in the world. His ball-and-chain got the rest. Have a little mercy. Or, the cops'll think he robbed somebody, 'specially in this neighborhood where they lock up the locals to protect the students—even you know that much ain't changed in a hundred-fifty years. C'mon, Mr. Miles. The cops'll only see a brother on the street with a lotta stuff in his car, and an innocent man will get the mess kicked out of him in the back of a paddy-wagon. Damn. He gotta go to work to feed them kids he left, and keep a roof over their head."

"Where you work, boy?" Mr. Miles looked at him hard.

"I'm in the union. Do construction. Right now we're working on some airport hanger sites. In the Spring we'll be doin' roads."

"Yeah," the old man said, sounding unconvinced. "You ever been in jail?"

"No," Jerome said flatly. "And I don't do drugs."

"Ever been in the military?"

"Yeah."

"What branch? You get an honorable discharge?"

"Yes. Air Force, sir," Jerome straightened his posture and exchanged a glance with Buddy.

"Remind me to tell you 'bout the Airmen of Tusgeegee," the old man said with a sly smile. "Was a mechanic. Never flew, though."

"I never got my wings either, sir. Had to leave before that happened... to get married and take care of my baby girl."

"Might notta got 'em anyway, boy. Can't blame yo wife fer dat. In my day, they stopped a black man before he even got started. Thangs ain't changed that much in the military—or in the last hundred-fifty years," he said issuing a quick glare at Buddy, "don't care what the talk shows say. Humph!"

"I don't blame her, sir. Wasn't 'bout that, or, no other woman either. Things just got messed up."

"Yeah, yeah, that's what they all say. Yo Daddy, he fight in the big one too?

"WWII, sir. South Pacific, then Italy."

"How many kids you takin' care of?"

"Four, sir."

"Plus," Buddy added in, gaining excitement, "he left her the house. My boy is honest, Mr. Miles.

For, real. For, real. Good with his hands, even licensed. He's with the union—"

"So, I've heard. You repeatin' yo'self, Buddy. But, I done tol' y'all, I don't make it a habit to git involved in domestic disarrays. I mines my own bees wax."

Jerome held his breath as more cinder blocks loaded onto his spinal column.

"You drink, boy?"

"Sometimes." Jerome studied the old man's hard-to-read expression. He wasn't sure of how he should have answered the question. What if he was a bible-beating Baptist? God, help him.

A wide grin captured his sudden benefactor's face after a moment. "Well, then, lemme pour you a drink, son. Cause I'ma work you like the pure fool you is."

CHAPTER 18

"Hey, girl. Whatssup?" Antoinette kicked off her loafers and flopped on the bed waiting for Val to finish screaming at her brood in the background.

"Whew! They always get under you when the phone rings. It's like the phone is a magnet. Soon as you want to have a minute to yourself... Girl, are you sitting down?"

"I'm prone," Antoinette chuckled, then grew more serious as the battery of recent messages filtered into her memory bank. "Have you talked to Francis? I haven't been able to catch her at her Mom's house yet before she goes—"

"—I haven't talked to Fran in a couple of months," Val whispered. "But, have you seen him?"

"Seen who?" The comment made her sit up and pay serious attention to any hidden changes going on in Valerie's voice.

"You know what happened, don't you?"

"C'mon... Val. I've been at the conference all weekend with Fran, Trace, and Cookie. I haven't even called my parents yet. What blew up in Philly during the last forty-eight hours?"

"That's right. I forgot."

Her friend's botched attempt at espionage grated her. How could Valerie have forgotten that she was at the conference? She'd called Val briefly before she'd gone. She hated being tested. They were friends, and no tests should have been needed.

"So," Antoinette said after a minute, "do you want to take it from the top?"

There was an uneasy silence, and she could hear Valerie shooing kids away from her phone post. Antoinette closed her eyes, imagining her friend wearing a black spy trench-coat with dark sunglasses and talking into her watch. With all the fuss that Valerie was making about the kids giving her some privacy, she knew this had to be hot. A code blue information emergency.

"Did he try to come over your house?" Val finally whispered into the telephone.

"Scoop? Looking for Trace, or something?" Antoinette stood up. "That no-good, low—"

"—No, no, no, not Scoop. He wouldn't try to get one of us to take his sorry side if something went down."

"Buddy? Is everything all right with you and

Buddy? Not y'all. Dear God, Val—"

"—Buddy is definitely on my list, but—"

The call waiting on Antoinette's line clicked and broke off Val's comment.

"—Hang on a minute, girl, " Antoinette rushed in, "my child is with her father, and Brian said something about going away. I have to take second line calls. But hold on, okay?"

She didn't wait for Val to respond as she tapped the button to take the second call.

"Well, it's about time. Your father and I were worried sick about you."

Antoinette sighed, and swung her legs over the side of the bed. Her phone had been lit up like an AT&T switchboard all weekend, and apparently her case load had started another round. "Hi, May," she said in a tired voice. "I'm sorry. I was at a conference all weekend, and—"

"—A conference?" May snapped. "Why didn't you let us know?"

Antoinette let out another exhausted breath. "It was an oversight. Plus, I didn't know till the last minute if I was going or not."

"Well, you have to plan these things in advance. I told Adrienne the same thing when she breezed by here on her way to Pearline's. One would think that in your financial circumstances, a vacation would be the last thing you would try to spend your money on."

"May, it was planned for over a month. It was a

job conference, and me and the girls split the expenses three-ways." Antoinette could feel her blood pressure rising.

"I see. Well, I do hope that it was a productive experience?"

"Yes, May, it was." Antoinette summoned all the civility that she could scrounge within her. "I might have a good proposal writing job lead, anywa—"

"—You do? That's good. Where?"

"Oh, my goodness, Val!"

"Who?"

"My other line. May, can I call you back in a little bit?"

"Your father and I need to talk to you."

"May, my friend is having problems, and I need to get back to her. She's on the other line, Okay? I promise, I'll call you back."

"Fine. We'll be over in ten minutes."

The phone abruptly clicked in Antoinette's ear and she swore under her breath.

"Val, you still there? I'm sorry girl. It was May."

She could hear that Valerie's line was still open, the kids in the background were still raising Cain, but her friend had not responded.

"Val?"

"I'm still here," Valerie said in an annoyed tone. "You done?"

"It was only May, she wanted to run a federal security clearance on my whereabouts. I am really sorry for keeping you on hold like that. Now, back to you and Buddy. What happened, honey?" Her tone went soft and she prayed with all of her soul that the one stable couple in the group would be okay. All those children....

"Then, I guess you haven't seen him?" Val's voice was distant.

"No. I just got in, listened to my messages, then called you back—you're the first call I made after I tried to catch Francis."

"Oh," Val sighed. "then I guess you really haven't heard?"

The second line clicked again before she could respond.

"Girl, this phone is crazy. Can you hold on one more time? Please? I promise to be quick."

"See if it's about the baby," Val sighed. "I'll hold."

Again, Antoinette tapped the button and took another call.

"Hey, cuz, so where have you been?"

Antoinette relaxed and laughed easily as Vanessa's voice filled the line. "The way people are hunting me down, you woulda thought I went to Siberia. Girl, I was at a job conference all weekend—but, look, I've got Val on the other line and—"

"—Don't worry about Lauren, she's fine, and I'll watch—"

"—What? Lauren's with you? She's supposed to be with Brian!" Rage curdled the coffee and danish in her stomach that had been her breakfast. Antoinette stood, slipped on her loafers, and moved toward the living room to get her coat. "What time did he leave her with you? I bet he didn't even leave you her asthma medicine, did he?" When the cord stopped her progression, she edged back into the room. "Let me switch to the cordless."

"Stop stressin', hon. He left everything with me. I'm glad you had a good weekend. 'Bout time."

"Let me get the cordless," Antoinette commanded. This was war.

She dropped the bedroom phone, ran into the kitchen, switched the line open and ran back into the bedroom to hang up the other line, then made a bee-line for the living room.

"Start at the beginning. Where's my baby?"

Her cousin laughed. "She's watching TV with the big girls. We went to church, then they ate—"

"—He dropped her off this morning?"

"Last night."

"What!" Blood shot to her temple and the effect was dizzying.

"Calm down, calm down—"

"—Calm down! As long as I was stuck in that financial death trap of a house in Jersey, that son-of-a-bitch could come pick up his child. Now, because he thinks that I might have a life, his ass comes late, drops his child off on my cousin, and is playing mind games. I will read his black—"

"—Stop cussin' and fussin' on Sunday," her

cousin laughed. "The baby doesn't know the difference. All she knows is that her Daddy took her to Chuckie Cheese, then she got to be a hair baby doll for her big cousins all weekend. You should see how nicely they braided her hair, with little beads—"

"—Beads! Beads? Do you know how long it takes to re-comb that mess? I have to go to work, Monday. I don't have time in the mornings—"

"—You got a job! That's great, cuz."

Antoinette flopped down on the sofa and let the air out of her lungs in a rush. She could hear shooting and screaming on the television in the background of Vanessa's household. "Had a little piece of a job lead when I got to Philly. What are they watching? Where's Lauren?"

"Oh, I dunno? *Predator,* or *Friday the Thirteenth,* I think? I don't know what those kids watch."

Antoinette went still. Her four-year-old was either watching an alien rip out the innards of military men in some remote jungle, or a crazed entity that cut up pre-teenagers when they fell asleep! After she had been so careful to screen Lauren from violence, had sequestered her to Channel 12, Barney, Disney tapes, and the Discovery Channel when she'd had cable.

"You know I don't let her watch that junk, Vanessa," she said firmly, walking over to get her coat. "She'll be traumatized, have nightmares—"

"—Yeah, sometimes the kids get scared, that's why I put her in the bed last night between me and

Ted."

This time when Antoinette went still, her vision blurred.

"She slept in the bed with you and Ted...? When did he come back?"

"Oh, girl that's a long story. His drunk ass came back the middle of last week draggin' all his shit in a garbage bag. Said he was really gonna leave his wife this time, and you know I put him on hold all week. By the weekend, I didn't want to give his horny behind none, so I just plopped Lauren in the bed between us. Today, he's pissy, been hollering and screaming all day—but talkin' marriage. So, Brian droppin' Lauren by really worked out—"

"—I'll be right over to get her."

"Take your time, cuz," Vanessa said in a chipper tone. "I've got two heads to do this afternoon. Gotta make my side snaps. My case worker don't need to know 'bout what I do to get by. So, take your time. I'm home all day."

"I'll be right over," Antoinette said evenly. "Twenty minutes, tops. Thanks for everything," she added, clicking off the phone and throwing it on the coffee table.

Emotions bounced off of one another and simultaneously slammed into both the left and right side of her brain. This was her cousin, they'd grown up like sisters. She loved Vanessa dearly, and would never want to offend her. But this was her baby, being exposed to things she never wanted her to see-

-tossed between a drunk, verbally abusive, horny man and a half-crazy woman.

Brian, the nerve! Dropping his child off for all the wrong reasons—to get back at her. A month of a clingy, scared, confused baby with new nightmares to contend with, and two million ready-to-choke-on beads in her hair! Jesus help her before she lost her mind! If she had only known. Everything had seemed so calm last weekend. No miscellaneous male baggage, just her cousin and her kids and Lauren. She had just lost a babysitter. Never again.

The phone rang, and she gasped with instant memory. "Val! Oh Lord, I'm sorry girl!"

"Yeah. Maybe I should call you later, if you have time?"

"No, no, no, girl... It's just that Brian left Lauren over Vanessa's... long story... talk to me, baby. I'm sorry, about—"

The doorbell chime and her locks being turned stopped Antoinette's tumble of apologetic words. "Oh, damn! It's May and Dad. I do have to run," she whispered. "Look, let me take care of this fire-drill, pick up Lauren, and I'll call you back after I de-program her from Vanessa's drama. Okay?" Her chest was heaving and her eyes darted around the condo as her father and May stepped into her living room.

"So, what is this job that suddenly materialized?"

Antoinette looked at May hard, and considered her words before she began. She knew the routine.

May was going to play bad cop, asking all of the questions, and her father would take mental notes and smile as the good cop. If she could answer their questions fast enough, maybe she could finally go rescue her child. She didn't want to even go into the fact that they'd come in again using a key instead of just the doorbell. An argument of that magnitude would take too much time.

"It's only to fill in, around twenty-hours a week teaching. I start Monday. But I went to the conference to find something more permanent—with better pay and benefits."

"This Monday?"

"Yes, May. This Monday. That's why I have to go pick up Lauren, get her ready to go to the Parent Child Center on Forty-Second street—around the corner, and get myself ready to teach."

"That's good, baby. You makin' Daddy proud—you teachin' and all. And that's a good day care center, too. Glad we was able to help you get past the troubles. Any word on Brian's support payments, like when they gonna start coming directly from his check instead of this word-is-his-bond-arrangement y'all have... so you can git on your feet?"

"I have to call my lawyer and check the status, but until City Hall can get its act together, he's been fairly good about giving it to me himself. I totally forgot to ask him about it when he picked up Lauren. I'll leave him a message on his voice-mail. This week has been so hectic. I'm sorry." Fatigue worked against her like a sump-pump, draining her energy as she watched the older couple form their opinions without words.

"Are you sure you want to keep her in a place that expensive, baby? You think it's worth it?"

Antoinette mentally dismissed her father's comment. She knew that May had probably checked out the place before she'd even arrived in Philly.

"That is an excellent center, and you were lucky to have gotten Lauren in there. They have a really long waiting list, don't they, Matt?"

Antoinette didn't change her expression as her suspicions were confirmed. "I submitted an application months ago when I knew I'd be moving back," she said in a dry voice, "I don't want to go through finding another daycare center, unless I have to. I'll catch up with Brian Monday, but there's nothing to worry about because a couple of weeks ago he told me he'd already sent in her deposit and everything was fine."

She hated this. It infuriated her the way they assumed that she couldn't plan her life, think through to solutions. She had planned every aspect of her life pretty well to this point. She'd gotten through an undergraduate and master's program at Cornell—on the Dean's List. She'd bought a home, invested in stocks and bonds, chose what companies to work for, and decided school systems and neighborhoods before she bought the house. She'd handled the family money, and kept herself out of bankruptcy. She had planned everything, all except the variable of getting divorced. An Act of God, not covered by life's insurance policies and requiring an extra rider, just like she'd once had to constantly explain to her client base.

"Good thinking, baby," her father said nervously as the two women stared at each other without speaking for a moment.

Her father... Antoinette's thoughts drifted with his tense smile in the strained silence. So different. When her mother was alive, he'd seemed so sure, so confident, no undercurrent. He'd ruled his home with a kind, but iron fist. When he spoke, the walls trembled. Her mother had only been a sort of quasi-lawyer, able to plead your teenage case before the ultimate judge. Sometimes her mother won, sometimes she lost, and many nights Antoinette was sure that the woman had to take her case to the pillow. But the next day, you might be blessed with a Governor's pardon. But to see this, a man of his legacy, not even able to get his new wife to shut up with his heat seeking missile glances. To see May's outright disrespect. Tragic. Her eyes met her father's. No wonder her sister couldn't come home. Adrienne hadn't been married to know the way the Willow must bend sometimes to keep the peace...

"Everything is going to be great, Daddy," she said brightly, flexing her best mask muscle, more to help him preserve his dignity than her own. "Don't worry. I'm now teaching for a great agency, helping

281

women. I'm sure I'll love the job, and it pays pretty well. Plus, the hours are only half a week's work. That gives me time to get a little pocket change and to find a good corporate post. It won't be long. In the interim, I can write proposals for people, like the great woman I met at the conference."

"Oh, baby," he sighed, standing and walking over to give her a hug. "I'm proud of you. Teachin' is an honorable profession. Stable, too. They'll make you a principal before you know it. That's my girl."

"It's not that kind of teaching job, Dad." She knew before she said it that he wouldn't understand, so she didn't elaborate after the initial comment.

He held her and rocked her much harder than the minor news called for. Antoinette smoothed the tension from his shoulders and let her hand settle on his face as their eyes met. "Now, I'll give you and May something when my first check comes. I have to pick up Lauren and get ready for Monday. Don't worry, if I need anything, I know who my Daddy is."

The old man smiled and wiped his eyes quickly and pulled away from her. "See, May. Everything's fine. The child went to a conference to network with her college buddies, and even found herself an extra job. So, let's put whup to our horse and let her git ready for work tomorrow."

It wasn't exactly his normal thunder and lightening proclamation from on-high, but he had spoken, and there wasn't too much left for May to inspect. Although she could tell from May's glances around the condo that the messy conditions resulting from Adrienne's drive-by visit were surely noted, and going to be blamed on her. Oh well.

May stood and glanced around again, and headed toward the door with her chin held extremely high. "I'm glad you are finally pulling yourself together," she flipped over her shoulder as Antoinette opened the door. "C'mon, Matt, I have a lot of errands to run for the rest of the day."

☙☙

Antoinette opened the door to her cousin's house without knocking. The scene before her made her close her eyes briefly and let out her breath slowly. Teenagers were sprawled across every surface and rap music blared from different radios all over the house. The television was on, and she could see Ted's half clothed carcass lumbering in her direction from the kitchen.

"Yo, cuz, back here with a head," Vanessa called out.

She never answered her cousin's hail, or Ted's grunt of acknowledgment as her gaze tore around the room for her baby. Ready to bound up the stairs to find her child, she stopped mid-step as Lauren made her way down the steep, carpet-worn flight

from the bathroom. She held her breath and positioned herself to catch Lauren if her unlaced sneak-er caught in the buckled rug. Her vision scanned things in the environment that she'd missed before, never worried about before: a hot curling iron plugged into a worn extension cord, dangling precariously from the edge of the living room coffee table; several open cans of beer on the dining room table—courtesy, Ted, searing cups of hot chocolate down low on a side table within little-kid-range, a hot steam-iron set up on a rickety board in the kitchen, a hyper dog and bugs a-go-go. She watched in repressed terror as her child negotiated past her worst fears and into her arms.

"Mommy!"

Antoinette swept her daughter up into a tight hug and held her as though jungle ravaging monsters had been after her. "Mommy's here, baby, get your coat."

❧

Antoinette stared down at the little curled-up lump that sucked a thumb and whimpered in her sleep beside her. "Oh, Vanessa," she sighed quietly, throwing the Sunday paper off her lap onto the floor by the bed, while putting her red pen behind her ear. She stroked the fine wisps of Lauren's hair away from her flushed face and bent over to kiss the vel-

vet cheek that pulsed from intermittent sucks. "Nobody's gonna hurt my baby," she whispered, trying to imagine what monster, or bad man, had entered her child's dream world. "Mommy's right here."

Bone weary from the weekend, all the explanations, phone calls, a rescue mission, and looking for a job, she gave up the futile task of concentrating on job ads, and grabbed a stack of bills from the night stand. "Okay, gentlemen," she said with disgust, "let's see how we can rob Peter to pay Paul."

Each minimum balance on every menacing notice that she opened seemed to want to extort more than the next. She sighed as she took out her check book and stamps from the night-stand drawer, doing high finance by the high-low method; if it was a high total balance, she paid a low amount, if it was a low balance, she paid as much as she could squeeze out. Renewed anger coursed through her every time she had to go through the process. These weren't her bills alone! They were joint bills. Bills that had been made in a joint marriage. Bills that covered joint expenditures, joint purchases, necessities for a joint life-style. Bills from the past that followed her to the present.

Antoinette filled each envelope and stamped for each one, slapping on the postage and muttering a curse. Just because her name was on all of the household credit, and Brian had skillfully only put his individual purchases on any credit he'd had... Damn. Cookie was right. She was a fool. Maybe she should have fought him in a War of The Roses over every penny. "Nah," she sighed, dropping the stack on the floor with the pile of resumes she'd just sealed. It wasn't worth it. Pearline had told her that some things, like freedom and peace of mind, were worth more than money. At the moment, however, she wondered what prayers covered financial realities.

She had only another month before many of the bills would go to litigation if she didn't make some sort of arrangements, and no high paying job-lead bites. Ruby LaMann was probably a dream.

When she opened the last bill, the phone bill, she almost screamed. "Four hundred dollars?" she breathed in, trying not to disturb Lauren. "They have got to be kidding..." Renewed panic surged through her like a current as her eyes scanned every line of the half inch thick invoice. Calls to her sister. Calls to Francis to check on her, to get moral support, and find a job. Calls to May and her father to get a place to live. Calls to area day care centers. Return calls to job leads that ended in nothing. Calls to her female moving team of worried friends. Return calls to Vanessa.... All from Jersey to Philadelphia. Long distance. Prime time. Day time. Night time. Any time she needed to keep herself from losing her mind; just a part of the price of getting her life together... Damn. It was like paying for phone therapy, and May had wanted her to go to a shrink with no medical and dental? Ludicrous.

Antoinette leaned her head back and closed her eyes. In a matter of a month, she would be lucky to have local phone service. This was the third time she'd have to try to make payment arrangements with the phone company--arrangements that would have to be broken. Just like her broken promises to Visa, Mastercard, Sears, Strawbridges... What was happening to her? Before, she was always good for one thing, and that was her word. Now, her word wasn't worth the air it floated on. Her promises and commitments were being broken all over the place. It seemed like ever since she broke the big commitment she'd made in church, every other commitment had shattered too. Pearline always said, "You don't have nothin' if you don't have your good name." She let out a sigh, because if that was true, she didn't have anything at this point.

Perhaps that was the way it went, she shrugged, looking down at the last bill and writing out a check for fifty dollars. She made a mental note to call her sister in L.A. one last time, and Francis in Atlanta that night, before the line went dead. What the hell. Didn't they have a Definitely Divorced Plan, instead of a Friends and Family Plan?

She shifted herself to sit on the side of the bed and gathered up Lauren's limp body in her arms. "C'mon, pumpkin. Mommy's gotta go to work tomorrow," she whispered to the rag-like body in her grasp. As she edged the child into her own bed, she said a silent prayer, and hoped her baby would sleep through the night. Clicking on the clown lamp on the dresser, she kissed Lauren's forehead three times for good luck, and gently shut the door behind her.

Her attention went to her closet as she went back to her room. What in the world was she going to wear? Instinctively, she didn't look at the clothes that hung under plastic to the left side. Those were pre-pregnancy suits, dresses, and outfits... Things that she swore to God Almighty that she'd get back into again one day. Those items, just like her shoes from that time of Paradise Lost, would be hers to claim again one day. One day when she was fit, trim, and pretty again. One day, when her spare tire got a flat and disappeared. One day, she breathed in, sucking in her stomach as she searched. "C'mon, Lord, have a little mercy," she sighed.

Her roving gaze stopped on a tweed jacket, and she snatched it out with triumph. "Okay, Momma, now we're cookin' with natural gas!" A skirt. She needed a plain skirt. Hunting and pecking through her suits, she found a black skirt that was a different blend of wool, but would work in a pinch with her black and brown herring-bone tweed. Okay. Progress. Now, a blouse... The skirt had a waist-band that was a little too tight, and all of her blous-es from yester-year needed to be tucked in. Finally settling on the one she'd just worn to the conference, she gave up. "Pearls... loafers... a strong bra for these boulders," she grumbled, "and hose." Damn!

She didn't have a pair of stockings without a run!

Like a garbage picker, she scavenged through her dirty clothes hamper and found a pair of plain stockings from her interviews the previous week—the ones with a fat run in the foot. "Necessity is the mother of invention," she mumbled to herself as she found her bottle of clear nail polish, and swabbed on a healthy glob, blowing on it as she walked into the bathroom. Convinced that it had dried, she dropped them in the sink, pulled the stopper shut, and ran the hot water. Her eyes darted around and landed on Lauren's Sesame Street bubble bath. "Good as Woolite," she sighed, sucking her teeth with annoyance. Damn. Why was it so hard to do what had come so easily B.C.—before child?

"Man o' man," she muttered as she cleaned her hose, it seemed as though it cost a fortune to go to work. After having to pay a deposit and the soon-to-come bill of over a hundred-and-fifty a week for extended day care—a bill her ex didn't have to pay, plus the cost of gas for the car, and of course the little things she'd need to just go in and look presentable. Brian never had to deal with this. He got to heal in a nice bachelor pad, with his body, job, and clothes intact.

"Val!" she breathed in, dropping her hose. "Oh, girl!"

Antoinette paced to the kitchen, turned on the iron, and set up her ironing board as she dialed the phone. Then she'd have to try to call Francis again, call her sister back to finish the near-argument they'd had before she'd left for the conference, and check on Tracey. As each ring blared in her ear, she looked at the clock. Ten-thirty. Exhaustion claimed her, and each conversation was destined to be an hour, if not more. Not to mention, she still had to read over her new client case files again to update the paperwork, pack Lauren's lunch box, throw a load of her laundry in.

"Hey, girl," she said in a monotone when Valerie picked up the line, too tired to care whether or not her friend was pissed-off. At least she'd kept her word to call Val back.

"Well, thank you for finally getting back to me. I'm glad that my life didn't depend on it."

Antoinette counted to ten. It didn't help.

"You know what, Val... I'm sorry if you have a case of the ass, and that I'm not Johnny on the Spot. But, I have had an enormous amount of stuff to contend with today. Believe me, I paid a dear price for having the gall to go away for two days, and I'm still not finished. Okay? So, stop it. Now. Let's talk, for real, for real."

"If you have company, that's all you had to say. You don't have to get nasty with me."

"Company? Are you crazy? Val, you've been watching too much daytime TV, girl. I'm washing out runned-up stockings, ironing my gear for tomorrow, and—"

"—Oh, and because you have a job now, all I do

is watch daytime TV, and don't work!"

Antoinette checked the setting on the iron and went to fetch her blouse with the phone still in the crook of her neck. She refused to respond, or say what was on her mind. Not tonight. Not before her first probably harrowing day on the job. No. Val could go to hell with her paranoid crap. She'd let the silence slap Val out of her frenzy, then they'd talk calmly. She would make her other calls, pack her briefcase, get ready for the next day, then set her clock and go to bed. Simple. Don't say a mumblin' word, she told herself.

"Well?" Val hissed. "Is that what you think?"

Antoinette began ironing her blouse and sighed. "No. Never did. Working at home is a twenty-four hour, three hundred and sixty five day grind without a vacation, low pay, no pension, rare gratitude, and shaky benefits, at best. You're not talking to Cookie, but, my schedule has changed, and I have twice as much on my plate as I did before. Been there, okay?" Antoinette paused and looked at her blouse, returning it to a hanger as she reached for her tweed jacket. "I'm sorry about not listening earlier. I really couldn't. People were flying in and out of here, calls were beeping in, my kid was somewhere crazy. Girl, this wasn't about not caring, it was a timing issue. So, let's not fight about what you really want to tell Buddy. What happened today?"

"I told him that this was my house, and that I wasn't helping him help his friend leave his wife.

Not in my house. Not even for you, girl.."

"What?"

"Never mind."

Antoinette pressed the wrinkles out of the jacket sleeve and admired her work before she went to the other sleeve. "Look, Buddy is probably just pissed-off because he feels like he works hard, and he didn't have any say in the decision. You know, the testosterone thing. It has to be their idea. What could the harm be, Val? You gotta let his friend come over for a day or two, crash on the sofa, they do their caveman bonding thing, and Buddy gets to save face. Then, by day three, when his own friend gets on his nerves, you're vindicated. You look like the supportive wife, he's kept some blood oath that he made at age nine on the basketball court, and, you girl, are a good woman. " Antoinette chuckled and hung up her jacket, then placed her skirt on the ironing board and tested the iron. "You know how this goes."

"I figured you would say that."

Something in Val's tone stopped her, and she sat the iron up and leaned against the wall. "I know that I'm divorced, and therefore, I'm certainly no authority, but this is a basic case, Val. C'mon, you know what I'm saying is true. Buddy is a good guy. He's as even-tempered as can be. He only flares up when he's been embarrassed. Other than that, he works hard, brings his money home, and really doesn't ask for much. Girl, chill out, let his friend crash, and he'll be gone before next weekend. Plus, the side benefit is, Buddy will be oh, so grateful. I'll even watch the kids while he shows you how grateful his is," Antoinette laughed. "Damn, I wish I had that option."

"I'm glad you think so highly of my husband."

What was wrong with Val? They used to joke around like that all the time. They used to solve the mysteries of the married universe as a Cagney and Lacey team. Something was definitely wrong. It was as though what had been unearthed between them in Val's kitchen couldn't be hidden away again. Since then, the intimacy between them had been fractured. It was like trying to repair fine crystal—there would always be pieces missing, and a fine crack showing, even if one carefully reconstructed it. Antoinette paused and gathered up as many shards as she could, cradling them for fear of losing more of what they'd had before she spoke.

"Yeah, Val, I do think highly of Buddy," she said with sincerity. "He's a decent human being, and I think pretty much above suspicion or reproach. This isn't like you. What the hell is going on?"

"I told Tracey you would say that. Once you found out, you'd be trying to get us in the middle of your mess. But, I'm a wife, Toni. So is Trace. We don't have fancy business degrees to back us up, or only one child that a financially comfortable man can take care of. She has three, I have five. There's an order of magnitude-"

"-Wait a minute. Are you saying that you both think I'm after your husbands?" The air left Antoinette's body. She couldn't speak or think.

"No, gurl. Not at all. But, what's going on has influence."

"But, what is going on that you think I'm influencing? Being broke, and overweight, and running around like a chicken with my head cut off? You're right, Val. I ain't following."

"I'm saying that our husbands are his friends. And as his friends, they'll be sitting around, drinking with him, and talking about how much they hate us and their lives. Probably talking about how they should just up and leave their wives for some long-lost-love that should have been left dead and buried. And all our lives, kids, and homes will be caught in the crossfire. That's why me and Trace don't want anything to do—"

"—Who is this friend that's causing my closest girls to lose their damned minds?" She held her breath and clenched the phone in her hand. Please, God, no.

"-Don't play dumb, Toni. Since he came by our house and slept on my sofa, a lot of dust has been kickin' up, and a lot of bull has been kickin' off—ever since you came back to Philly. And to think, we helped you move in, like inviting the plague to take up residence next door! You both had to have this planned, and we were too stupid to see. Why didn't you keep your mess in Jersey? Or were the tolls too inconvenient?"

The venom that came through her friend's voice brought tears to her eyes. She covered her hand with her mouth to stifle a wail of pain. Her best friends. Her girls. Her support network. Her camp. Her reputation. A sob replaced the words that she struggled to say.

"I'm sorry, girl. But I can't be a party to this." Val's comment had the ring of a final death-knell.

There were no words. Only quiet tears. Instant recognition stung her mind. The only friend that this could have been was, Jerome Henderson. The one known to stay. The one known to pay, to take care of his family. The one who'd stayed at one job for over a decade. The stable guy with a union label and nice home in Mount Airy, like they all wanted. Her heart folded and gave in. She knew that this kind of break-up would shake both Valerie and Tracey to the foundation. Their worst fears had been realized—that it could happen to anyone, and no home was safe.

The new reality now splintered and fractured their friendships of a lifetime. This was the male friend that they'd held up for their husbands to emulate, the one whose name was pitched in their faces during the arguments. The one she was supposed to marry, but had blown the chance of a life-time on an unknown, non-Philadelphian risk factor. Now, she was considered a home-wrecker—just because she came home to a home that wasn't there any longer...

"T, you still there?"

"No," she said softly, placing the iron on her skirt and moving it back-and-forth in a daze. "Neither is Jerome. Nobody is where they used to be. I have to go. I have to go to work in the morning."

CHAPTER 19

"Mommy, don't want to goooo!" Lauren wailed, clinging to Antoinette's skirt as she tried to get their coats on.

Dislodging the child from her hem-line, she pushed tiny struggling arms into a snowsuit jacket, and forced a hat on her daughter's head. "They'll be lots of children there," Antoinette soothed, tying the hood down on her daughter's resistant head, "plus, a lot of toys," she added, wiping tears from the chubby cheeks that faced her, "and stories..."

"Stay with you," Lauren whimpered, "just Mommy."

Antoinette stooped down and held the child away from her. "Did you know that Mommy feels like crying too this morning?"

Lauren gazed at her with her thumb in her

mouth and sniffled.

"Mommy is going to miss you too, but Mommy has to go to work so that we can buy pizza, and ice cream, and do lots of fun things. When Aunt Francis helps Mommy get a better job, we'll do better things, okay?" Antoinette searched her heart for the words to make a four-and-a-half-year-old understand. Hell, she didn't understand what had gone wrong in America. So wrong that a mother was forced to drag her asthmatic child out in the February cold at seven-fifteen in the morning—only to be left until six o'clock in the evening. How had things gotten so insane that it cost more than most mortgages to have a child safely cared for until that mother returned. So out of whack that even if there were two parents in the same house, working, money would still be an issue? Antoinette sighed, "Can you give Mommy a hug, honey?"

Lauren rushed into her arms and gave her neck a big squeeze.

"You have to be Mommy's big girl, cause mommies get sad sometimes too."

Lauren wriggled from her grasp, stared at her, and touched her cheek. "Mommy, don't cry. I'ma big girl."

A broad smile found its way to Antoinette's face. Her baby had understood some of what she'd just said. Perhaps the child didn't know why, or how, or any of the logistics, but a connection had been made, a new awareness about this all-powerful entity called

Mommy had transpired. Pride glowed in her chest. Her baby had taken another step.

"C'mon, honey, let's get your brand new lunch box. Can you carry it for Mommy? And Mommy will pack up your inhaler for the teacher. We don't need to take your nebulizer to school, because you aren't going to get sick there, right? Not with all the fun toys and stories—you don't want to miss everything, right?"

"No, I hate when I can't breeaf." Lauren scurried over to the kitchen counter and swept up the colorful plastic lunch container with glee. "Toys an' stories, Mommy? Like Aunt Nessa's house?"

Antoinette stood at the door and smiled. Her baby, so innocent, had been unscathed. Relief poured over her slowly as she watched her child bound towards her. "Yes, sweetie. Toys and games, lots of new fun kids to play with. You wait and see!" Antoinette exclaimed brightly, holding Lauren's arm and juggling her briefcase as she set the alarm, "just you wait and see."

"Mrs. Wellington?"

"Yes," Antoinette said with a big smile as she stoop-walked with Lauren towards the day care center entrance.

"I'm the director of this center, Marilyn Steet.

This must be Lauren?"

Antoinette beamed at the heavy-set German-looking woman who faced her. "Say hello, Lauren." She chuckled nervously as her daughter hid her face within the folds of her winter coat. "She's just a little shy... first day don't-wanna-leave-Mommy blues." Antoinette's gaze traveled to the other mothers who were beginning to swarm the door with anxious youngsters. It looked like a happy place, but she wondered silently if they'd had to go through the tears to get their children to let go of their coat hems too?

"Well, we have a little problem," the director said without emotion. "Lauren cannot start today."

Antoinette's motions froze, as did those of a few of the other mothers who were within hearing range. The undiluted shock must have registered on her face, and inadvertently in reflex, Antoinette checked her watch. It was seven-thirty, and she had only a half-hour to begin her first day on the job. This could not be happening.

"I don't understand?" she whispered, trying to preserve what was left of her dignity as other mothers passed her and slipped their children into the warm refuge of the church-school. But she knew before the woman spoke, it was about money. It was in the woman's tone. The righteousness had oozed from her lips as a look of disdain penetrated Antoinette's plain wool coat.

"We were supposed to receive the initial payment for tuition before the child is admitted. It is our policy to ensure that a security deposit is received prior to admittance."

"I know Brian sent a check. Can we discuss this in your office?"

"His check bounced, Mrs. Wellington."

Humiliation turned her feet to stone. She couldn't move, much less breathe as the frosty air cut her lungs. "What?" Her voice had been less than a whisper.

"Mommy, it's cold. I wanna play in dere!"

She extended her arm and pressed Lauren's face into her coat, trying to both hush the child and shield her tiny lungs from the cold—and to keep her baby from hearing what a child should never hear.

"What we need to discuss can be made brief, Mrs. Wellington. I don't think it's a good idea to get the child's hopes up for the day, then have to remove her after we've had our discussion. It will just humiliate you both, if she creates a scene."

Mothers continued to brush past them, giving her and her daughter inquisitive glances of pity. She was an outcast, a mother with unpaid freight that couldn't be dropped off at the loading dock. She hated the way the woman glowered at her, accused her with her ongoing stare... put her business in the street... stripped her naked in public... labeled her child, before her child had even gotten a chance. Her gaze shot around the perimeter at the well-dressed, but harried, mothers who had driven up in

Volvos, SAABs, BMWs, and Mini-vans. She glimpsed their contrast to the women who came leisurely up the walk in slacks, penny-loafers, and walking coats dragging children on sleds—and, obviously not on their way to work. Her vision scanned the sign that had happy faces painted on it in various shades of the rainbow, finally settling on the director's Pro-Choice button. A feminist. A career woman, like herself, who probably mouthed her same political views... somebody who ought to know a woman's situation. Antoinette was livid. It was first degree fraud!

"As I told you," Antoinette said in a tight voice, "we had been going through a divorce." She ignored a mother who stopped and turned around. "There must be an issue that I am unaware of, but it will be corrected. May I use your telephone?"

The director let out a huff of annoyance. "Mrs. Wellington, we are a non-profit entity. If you can get at least half of her tuition to us this morning, we will allow for this one irregularity. Come into my office and make the call—as long as it's local."

Antoinette pasted on a false smile as she stared down at her shivering child. "C'mon, baby, you go play while Mommy takes care of a few things, and I'll come to kiss you before I go."

Lauren had transformed herself to immovable granite around her legs, and she pried the child away from her with unspoken firmness, willing the child with her mind not to balk, not to cause a scene, and to placidly obey so that mother could go to war. Her mind raged, Stand back, baby, and take cover. Your mother's gotta kick some ass, and it won't be pretty. So, go stand the hell where I told you to, and don't give me any lip! I'll come back for you when it's safe. She had seen this look on her own mother's face before. Things became clear and merged in an instant; everything at home had not always been Wonderland.

The words formed mentally—festering inside her brain, inside her heart, crushing her soul. Antoinette knew that this warning had been told to so many black children by so many black mothers that surely it was locked within each child's cellular memory. A firm tug, and laser beam eye contact, ignited it with their combined extra-sensory perception. Lauren's slow release and confused upturned-face confirmed it. The child had sensed danger, but had also sensed the need to leave her mother's side for her own good. Instinct seemed to be the only thing that propelled her dazed baby before her, down a long hall—alone, looking back only once before she slipped behind a door while still clutching her lunchbox like a teddy bear of security.

She'd deal with Brian Wellington, then address the haughty bitch that strode in front of her.

Antoinette stepped into the director's office with her head held high and rummaged in her purse for a calling card... Damn! Her long distance was sure to be out, and Brian was in Boston. She could not afford to panic, show fear, or waver. Her hand went to the phone and she called her father. After two rings, he picked up.

"Dad," she said quietly, then turned her back to the woman who sat down with a smug expression. "I have a little situation at Lauren's day care center."

"My grandbaby's okay, isn't she?"

God, why wouldn't this woman give her a moment to conduct her family business in private!

"Yes. Lauren's fine. I have to be to work in less than fifteen minutes... and Brian's check bounced. I just wrote out my bills last night and dropped the letters in the box on my way here. I want to be sure that I can give them seven-hundred dollars and have it clear—until I can reach Brian. My other alternative would be to leave Lauren with you for the day, and catch up with Brian tonight, then have him wire a payment—so that the center will admit Lauren."

Her heart and her pride fused and melted into the puddle of icy slush that her shoes had tracked into the director's office. Her father's silence widened it, making it threaten to consume her.

"I'll have to ask May," he finally uttered. "I'm retired, she's the one who still works. Baby, I just don't have that much laying around until my check comes."

Antoinette heard a commotion in the background of her father's house. She could hear May's shrill voice and her heart sank.

"Baby, May has to go to work, that's where I was

on my way to taking her now. She hates to drive in the snow, and it's too cold for her to be waitin' for the bus. Maybe Pearline can watch Lauren?"

"Pearline is over a half-an-hour away up in Mount Airy, especially in rush hour traffic. Then, by the time I got back, I wouldn't have a job. This is my first day." She could feel her cheeks flush with shame and rage and hot tears as she faced away from the director and stared at the wall. "Can't you watch her? This once? You're just five blocks away..."

"I don't know nothin' about watchin' no child all day... and wit her medicine and all..." Her father's voice faltered and suddenly became muffled, "Hold on, May, let me think," he said, obviously trying to conduct two conversations at once by putting his hand over the receiver at points to block Antoinette from hearing all that was said. "What about Ness, or your girlfriends, Tracey, or Val? They don't work."

"Vanessa is as far away as Pearline, traffic-wise, up in Overbrook." Her mind tore at the options. "Tracey works too, and Val isn't home," she lied.

"Why don't you track Brian's ass down, then, and get him to wire the school the money he owes them. You have a court order. He's supposed to pay for that baby's daycare tuition, since he didn't have to pay for nothin' else. Show the lady the paper-work—"

"I can't do that," she whispered through her teeth, steadily watching the minutes on the wall clock slip away from her. "I have to leave Lauren somewhere until all of this gets straightened out."

"Listen, your father and I cannot begin to deal with your lack of planning, or Brian's, first thing in the morning." May's voice cut into her ear and almost made it bleed. "Antoinette," she said with no-nonsense harshness, obviously having snatched the phone from her father, "you all have to get your priorities together! Now, your father will bring my check over to the school, and you get your business straight with Brian tonight."

"Thank you, May," Antoinette whispered and closed her eyes briefly. "Thank you."

When the phone clicked in her ear, Antoinette turned around slowly and faced Marilyn Steet. "My father, Lauren's grandfather, will be by within the hour to drop off the full payment."

Appearing unimpressed, the director continued to riffle through her mail and paperwork without looking at Antoinette. Fury burned the saliva away from Antoinette's mouth until it went dry.

"Well," Ms. Steet said in a bored tone, "I'm glad that's settled. And I take it that you will be working the annual winter flea market held two Saturdays from now?" The woman stared at her and smiled.

The bitch had her.

"I wasn't aware of the center's activity?" Antoinette hedged, not wanting to come anywhere near the place that had just made her open her mouth, show her teeth, and lift her skirt on a public auction block.

"You are aware that in addition to tuition payments, there is a parent co-operative agreement, which translates into two-hundred and fifty dollars per semester. If parents elect not to donate twenty-five hours of volunteer time. Also, our late pick-up fees are a dollar a minute, so don't be late tonight when you pick up Lauren. These additional payments are required in cash. Given your situation, I would think you'd be interested in understanding your full responsibility as a parent within our school's community."

Antoinette's gaze narrowed, and she fought to keep her talons retracted. "I'll be here for her—on time. And, yes, I would be pleased to work the flea-market Saturday after next."

"Good," the woman said, standing and thrusting a handful of brightly colored flyers at Antoinette. "Have a nice day."

Accepting the flyers, Antoinette shoved them into her briefcase and headed for fresh air in the hallway. But something crazy, half-cocked, aimed, loaded, and fired in her brain.

"Do you have any children?" Antoinette asked in a too-smooth tone while hovering in the door frame.

"Why, no..." the director stammered.

"I didn't think so," Antoinette replied, "you just extort for them."

As she pulled up to the basement on Fifty-sixth Street, Antoinette looked down at her watch. Eight twenty-five. Damn!

Teenage girls huddled in the doorway, smoking cigarettes, talking and laughing. Fingering her janitor-size ring of keys, she hopped out of her car, grabbed her briefcase, and held her head up. Yes. She was late. But she was the teacher. Antoinette approached what she assumed to be her class, with caution.

"Good morning, ladies," she mumbled as they cleared a way for her to open the door.

"'Bout time. Damn," one of the girls grumbled, sending a titter through the group.

"We was gonna leave and tell 'em our teach didn't show. It's fifteen degrees," a bolder one fussed, entering the dark room behind her.

Antoinette didn't respond. She couldn't as she turned on the flickering fluorescent light which held a strobing gasp within her. She let her gaze sweep the unimaginable. Her eyes met broken down chairs and trash that hadn't been removed in over a week. There was no black board, only a rickety wooden table, a metal military desk, and roaches that scattered at the intrusion. Stacks of cased Pampers for her to distribute blocked her entry to a smaller back office—her office. A metal file cabinet hung open with papers jammed in it. The stench of Pine Sol hung in the air so heavy that it made her eyes water. She didn't breathe.

As her reluctant students took their seats, she searched for a hanger that was not to be found, giving up she dropped her coat, pocketbook, and briefcase on what she assumed to be her chair. Defeat claimed her as she looked at the disgruntled group before her. Ten young women, each in varying stages of hostility faced her. She was supposed to tame this cold, angry, probably hungry group of lions with a curriculum and no teaching tools—all for eight dollars an hour?

"Okay," she finally said, grappling for her composure. "My name is Mrs. Wellington, and this is the job training portion of your—"

"Yeah, yeah, yeah. We know the drill. We come here for twenty-hours a week, get our certificate, and you get your check. Been there, seen it, done it, lady."

A round of hoots and high-fives passed around the dim room. Antoinette eyed what she instinctively knew had to be the ring-leader. "What's your name?" she said evenly, staring at the young woman who looked like a walking sign-post for every designer known to the free world.

"Why? You gonna report me for speakin' da truth? You got the case files on us, right?"

The others giggled as her tormentor tossed her head and grinned. Antoinette stared at the pretty coffee-colored girl who challenged her authority. The girl beamed and smoothed her slicked-down, finger-waved hair, then brushed the excess sparkles off of her perfect three-inch long gold talons. Antoinette smiled, and another branch in her mind snapped. Her smile grew to laughter as the girl continued preening and adjusting a solid gold dolphin hoop earring that hung in her lobe next to a one-carat diamond stud.

Antoinette continued to laugh, and it was the group's turn to go still. Edging her way to the table, she took a seat on the side of it, opting not to sit in a roach infested chair. She snatched her briefcase from it and pulled out their files and flung them on the desk. No student moved, and all mirth had vanished from their faces.

"Cut me a fucking break," Antoinette exclaimed, still chuckling. "I don't give a damn about reporting your asses."

Appearing shocked beyond all measure, another student touched the files and withdrew her hand. She stared at Antoinette. "Den, why you here, Miss? Dats all dey do is write us up so dey ken git paid. Ain't dat what it's about?"

Confusion held them ransom before her, and Antoinette considered her words. The unvarnished truth and her word was all they had to bond them. It was now her only way in.

"This curriculum," she said, holding it over her head, "is bullshit. This program is bullshit. And none of you will ever get a damned job in America using this curriculum. They don't care, don't you see?" Her fervor grew as nervous glances passed between her students. "They make money on your stupidity." Antoinette slammed the curriculum down on the table, and the girls around it flinched back as though she had slapped them. "The system is getting paid to keep you in it! Damn. Look at y'all."

The sound of Chestnut Street traffic was the only noise that competed with Antoinette's voice. They stared at her, but without harshness. Their street-wise eyes held a new component. Fear.

"Y'all, smoke, right?" she finally said, moving back to the front of the room.

A few nodded as Antoinette snatched down the no-smoking sign in her classroom. "Pull 'em out, and light 'em up, ladies. We gonna learn something today that's not from the books." She dumped out a bent pencil holder and flung it to the center of the table. Waiting for them to light up, she again sat on the edge of the table. "I've been inside, y'all. I know how this system works—from health care, to welfare, to unemployment. I live on family section-eight myself."

A round of gasps met her, but their eyes never left her face.

"Yeah, y'all," Antoinette said shaking her head as she slipped into the easy neighborhood patois of street language. "I know what it is to not be your own woman. I know what it feels like to be held hostage by a man's money, for the sake of your baby. I know about funny money, and parents who think that money solves it all—when its really time and money that you need to pull yourself together. See," she said standing again and pacing, "I know how even your own child can feel like a noose around your neck... I know how badly you just need a little something just for yourself, and when you get it, how they judge you. I know how they look at you. I know what it feels like to know you're smart, but have them treat you like a beggar. Just went through that public rape this morning. So, let's cut the bull-shit in here and figure a way out for all of us."

"Damn, Ms. Wellington, you preachin' this mornin'," her original agitator said in a low voice, "ain't she y'all?"

"Sho' is," the group murmured in unison as they nodded.

Antoinette sighed and sat down again heavily. "What's your names? Not for the files, but so we can talk."

"Tianisha," the bold one said.

"Fayletta.... Delcetta... Rashina... T'quneal... Yolanda, Wynett, Kisha, Karim, Darlette! "

Voices rang out, and names heralded around the table as they tried to make her know their names, know that they existed, mattered, breathed, had faces, and hopes, and dreams....

"Good. I'm Toni, call me T. From West Philly," she almost sang.

"You from 'round the way, teach?"

"Yeah, Westside!"

"Get out? Teach is from West-side! We thought you was from Mount Airy, or somethin'. All the rest of 'em don't live nowhere near the city."

"You got kids?"

"Yeah, one. Her name is Lauren. She's four."

"Damn, you kinda old to only be havin' a four-year-old. The rest of your babies die, or somethin'?"

"Dag, if dey did, why you ask her like dat—maybe she don't wanna tell you 'bout losing her kids."

"I only had one," Antoinette countered, becoming strangely amused.

"Like I said, den, she kinda old for just one baby."

"Yeah, ain't that the truth," Antoinette laughed.

"Got a man?"

"Girl, pulleeese," Antoinette chuckled, "ain't got one now, but had to have one to make that baby. Y'all know that. You ain't stupid."

A round of hoots and laughs went through the room.

"What'chall good at? What do you do really well?" Antoinette watched their faces fall, and their eyes lower.

"We ain't good at nothin', Ms. T," the one who had identified herself as Delcetta said, "I'on't know."

"Hold it," Antoinette said indignantly, "You are good at something. Tianisha, you're the fly girl in here. Bet you keep your old man's drug money straight, don't you?"

Tianisha appraised her slowly, but smiled. "Damn right."

"Bet you know how much weight he brought in, how much inventory went out, who owes him money, and who he's gotta pay." Antoinette smiled and leaned toward the girl and gave her a nod. "Don't play dumb."

"Aw, Miss T... C'mon," Tianisha chuckled as her friends around her shoved her arm.

"That's bookkeeping, credit and collections, cost accounting. You ain't no punk, that's why you're good at what you do. You just don't do it formally, through a job, is all. But you do it. And you've scammed the system so hard, because you're smart. You know that a job paying five dollars an hour, with no benefits, isn't going to cover the expenses of three little kids. That's serious math skills. Girl, you working with the metric system, when you do his drug weight! Get a clue."

Tianisha beamed with pride. "I'm definitely good wit da money."

"The problem is," Antoinette said, growing serious, "your old man is in a high risk profession."

The room went quiet again.

"You need to buy some life insurance on him, and get a clean hustle that won't get swept away if The Man puts him in jail. Might want to get life insurance on your children, too. They live in a war zone, and drive-by is probably how they'll go."

"Daaaamn," one of the girls exclaimed. "She

said that so matter-of-fact... cold. Damn, teach."

"It is cold, ladies," Antoinette said without blinking her eyes. "Look, I'm not impressed. If your man does asbestos removal, he's in a high-risk profession—gonna die of cancer. If you put your kids in a war zone, chances are, they're gonna get shot. If you got extra cash around, then hold up on buying the next pair of earrings, and buy some damned life insurance so your Momma can bury y'all. Live fast, die young, and leave a good looking corpse. They make some real pretty baby caskets."

Shock held her group in thrall as she dismissed Tianisha's stricken expression.

"Okay... who can cook, or bake?" Antoinette asked, counting their hands mentally as they raised them. "I can burn in the kitchen, too. Y'all are the ones who keep the churches in business. You're caterers of some of the best pies, cakes, and fried chicken. Come on, tell the truth, I know about five dollar platters sold out the back door around the way."

Laughter seized the group again as the women made proclamations about who could make the best kind of whatever dish that was yelled out. Her spirit lifted as she watched them sit up a little straighter, hold their heads up with true pride, instead of the false pride of self-defense.

"Who sews?" Antoinette called into the fray.

"I do. I do!" Two students yelled.

"Tailors, seamstresses," Antoinette called back.

"I watch children on the side," another yelled.

"Day care center owner," Antoinette yelled with a grin, "a lucrative and booming business!"

"I do hair," one called.

"I braid hair, and do nails," another shouted.

Antoinette laughed and turned her face to the ceiling as they all began talking at once. They no longer waited for her prompts as they found things that they were good at, remembered why God had made them, and that above all else, why they deserved to live. The chaos was soul-reaching. Pure joy.

It was like watching a pebble get dropped into a still pond, then ripple after ripple spread out in concentric circles to reach far shores. In her heart, as she listened to the women, she began to know why she'd been set upon such an unbeaten path. It was all a part of the Master's plan. Every part of the pain and the joy of what she'd experienced had brought her here, because had she not gone to The Valley, then, surely, she would have had nothing catalytic to impart to this group.

As their eager voices rang out, it was as though God had sounded a chime in her brain. This is what was wrong with every single person she knew. No one, including her, liked themselves. They had forgotten why they were made, had lost touch with their special gifts. Valerie had forgotten the beauty of what she could create, and was looking at the cup as half empty instead of half full, when her greatest canvass was her family. Her sister was running from the things that had hurt her, replacing family words with loud, blaring music, instead of finding peace and creating harmony within her own heart...

Tracey was still trying to pay off an emotional debt, beating herself up, and allowing Scoop to beat her up, for never saving her family by becoming a star. And, her dad... He was still grieving the loss of her mother, taking low and not having a voice in his own home, probably wrestling with every moment he didn't appreciate her mother, and trying to take back every struggle they had. Thoughts bombarded her as the women's voices rose to chaotic proportions.

May was no different. She was still fighting the system that had made it hard for her when she went through her own divorce, and God knows, she was still fighting men—fearing that they might control her. So, she was always on the attack, like Cookie, striking before stricken and using her tongue as a lethal weapon. Then, Antoinette had to assess herself, as all the voices and laughter and positive vibrations surrounded her.

Valerie had been right. She did have choices. She wasn't a victim, and her cup was half full. May was right. It was time to pull herself together. She needed to guard her health, and lose weight—not for a man, but for herself! It all made so much sense, just as Pearline said it would one day. And, maybe that's why Pearline and her mother were the hub of the family, because they were women who'd found their centers, and were comfortable in their own skins. Perhaps that's why they could be such intimate friends, because they'd let go, and let God— had released all their personal demons, turned them over, and were whole.

It wasn't about finding someone outside of you to like yourself, first. It was the other way around. Antoinette realized in that moment that, again, Pearline had been correct. Her seasons were all turned topsy-turvy. How could women-friends, or men friends, or lovers connect, if each individual was not whole?

Antoinette's eyes filled with tears as the epiphany unfolded in the most unlikely place—a basement on Fifty-Sixth street. She hadn't liked herself, and most of the damage that was inflicted upon her was self-inflicted wounds. Toxic relationships that she'd held onto for fear of being abandoned. Not speaking up firmly, albeit from a positive place, when someone had broached her parameters. This was what had happened to her relationship with Jerome. When she went to college, he'd feared that she would leave him, and he began a path of self-destruction that frightened her—more than any of her father's warnings ever had. The dawning awareness almost paralyzed her as she tried to shake the thought, and the new information about his separation from her mind. One day, she vowed, she'd talk to him about it... just like she needed to put things to peaceful rest with Brian.

But, looking at the women around her, she knew she had to first get her own issues addressed, lest her girl-child pick up and repeat her same patterns.

"Look at you," she finally murmured to the group, love glowing within her, "sisters, women of worth."

Tears streamed down Tianisha's face, and she turned away from the group. Another student patted her back, another stood and one edged by the Pampers boxes to fetch some toilette tissue for her to blow her nose. Antoinette let her own tears flow and didn't wipe them away.

"Let's beat 'em, ladies," she said as they nodded fervently and sniffed. "Let's not go work for five dollars and hour, and get put off Welfare before you have a way to really cover living expenses, medical, dental, and educational expenses for your children and mine. Let's not believe the hype. We know we're not leeches. The system is broken, and they can't fix it. So, once again, as time immemorial has proven, they're gonna blame women. Black women. And put our babies at risk." Antoinette paused for effect to let her words sink in. Not one of her students moved, or seemed to breathe.

"A man ain't the answer," she went on, gaining confidence as some unknown source of power filled her. "Not because there ain't no good black men— but because, by design, they have the highest unemployment rate in the country, have the greatest possibility of going to jail if they try to hustle to make what a job can't provide. They have issues, too, just like we do. Yo' mommas and grandmomma's can't do it. They're old... done cleaned floors, cleaned toilets, or been under this system too. They don't have it. That's why you're here. The men can't do it, that's why they're crazy, and hit on you, and run around on you. Not that it makes it right—but that's the reality. Cold fact, ladies. We're living in a system that never intended for us to be here as free people, or to survive in it. But you, and your babies, have got to survive! So, you must get yourselves together."

"Then what can we do?" Tianisha sniffed. "I tried to work, but every time my kids got sick, and I had to take off, I got fired."

All eyes turned to Antoinette for answers that she hadn't even found for herself. But the trust in their gazes, the hope on their faces, their belief in her words found a chord of harmony that connected with something bigger than herself.

"I know. I saw all of your histories in those stupid case files. I knew immediately when your kids were born, I could see the work stoppages, when you dropped out of school and got on Welfare. I went on family welfare when I had mine, and I have a solid gold work record, two degrees, and I can talk the talk—when I have to. It didn't save me either."

"Do your man pay child support, Miss T?" a shy voice asked from the group.

"This morning, I was late because his check bounced at the day care center. I almost had to bring my child with me to work. Even with a job, if you have a child, you are dangerously close to the system every time you drop a load, that baby gets sick, has the chicken pox, sneezes—whatever. Your job is the one in jeopardy. That's why I can't teach what's in this book, the mess about how y'all supposed to take your braids out, cut your fingernails down, talk the King's English, smile pretty, and poof-you-got-a- job-forever-that-will-take care-of-you lie. Couldn't do it. Not today."

"See, that's what I'm talking about," Tianisha exclaimed, fury replacing her tears. "If somebody like you ain't got a chance, den, what we got? None of us even graduated high school."

The question gave Antoinette pause until her cousin Vanessa's face flickered in her mind. "Yeah, but, all of you have a skill. None of you are stupid. You could be business women. Hell, you're running side-hustles out of your house to survive now. You are already entrepreneurs! What they give you isn't enough to live on, that's why I'm not reporting anybody. It ain't my bizness what a woman gotta do to feed her babies. It's called mercy," Antoinette said, sucking her teeth in disgust. "They make me sick. Defining your life for a few measly hundred dollars. Freakin' modern-day slavery. The amount you get from Child Support, if you get it, is a joke—like Welfare."

"Business women?" Tianisha asked, leaning in as though to soak up her words.

"If you can make it on what they give you in Food Stamps feed your kids—for a month, if you can make a couple of hundred dollars stretch over Section Eight rent, pay the gas, electric, and telephone, pay for Septa tokens, if you can get what little a working black man makes—which is less than what Welfare would give you, and live off of that—damn, that's money management. You ain't managing money when you got excess, you handlin' thangs when you ain't got enough—but can make it stretch. You baaad, den, ladies." Antoinette laughed and snapped her fingers twice for effect.

The group relaxed and laughed with her, showering her with a round of high fives.

"Tell it, sister!" They yelled in unison.

"She all right!" one laughed, "an' she ain't stuck up!"

"C'mon, tell us how to start a biziness, Miss T. I'ma be here every day," another voice rang out.

"Yeah, she all dat, and a bag of chips," another chimed in.

"She ain't judgin'," another added.

"We'll be here every day," Tianisha grinned, "and if you late, we understand. We all been there, seen it, done it, girl! Ain't dat right, y'all?"

A sense of calm enveloped Antoinette as she smiled at the women in her class. This was her therapy, the kind that flashed back her life and its possible paths right before her eyes. New strength coursed through Antoinette as she suddenly realized that one person might be able to make a difference—just as the people who'd shaped and molded her had. She was not a victim, if she chose not to see herself that way. She did have choices! And as Antoinette counted the heads in the classroom, she could have transposed her face, her sister's face, or any of her girlfriend's faces upon those of her students.

There but for the Grace...

CHAPTER 20

The hall was dark... the only light seeped in around the edges of the door. Water seized her legs, and weighted them against further motion... the door was in sight, a way out... and she reached out her hand... but it opened before she could touch the knob. Then the light--brilliant, white light almost blinded her as a familiar voice called to her softly... her mother's voice. A tall male silhouette stood behind her mother, who smiled... "Oh, Toni, I've always liked this one."

She woke up sobbing for her mother and peered at the clock. Five a.m. The dream was back again. She tried to clear her mind, yet the sound of water was still resonant. Just like before, the urge to pee outweighed her fear of getting out of bed. Antoinette wrapped one arm around herself like a make-shift shield and reached for the night-stand lamp, turning it on with her gaze darting around the room. God only knew how much she missed her mother, even after all of this time. Maybe she was indeed swimming upstream like a stupid salmon, believing in all this self-love stuff? Maybe she just needed professional help?

What if the water in her dream was, perhaps, a sign—a manifestation of things being over her head and that she was drowning? Maybe her issues were deeper than any self-revelation could address, and perhaps Pearline's wisdom about letting God handle things was out-dated? Sure, her aunt had said to trust The Father, and when she'd come far enough along the path, God would send her a sign to keep hope alive... But, it sure did look barren on the horizon. Now, she was having dreams about her mother endorsing some man, again. Very Freudian. She was losing it.

Half stumbling, half running, she scooted into the bathroom and plopped down on the toilet. Releasing a night of iced tea and wine, she felt her body slump from the effort as the adrenaline in her veins started to dissipate. Damn, thirty-seven years old, half-drunk, on a work night, and almost peeing the bed. She laughed out loud, wiped herself, and reached for the spigot and soap to wash her hands. But, why was she still hearing water?

When she turned the valve, only a thin trickle came out of it. Quickly washing her hands, she popped on the bathroom light, and inspected the mess. The tub was fine—no leak, just a ring from what was now becoming her nightly bubble bath ritual. Her new self-help rite of self-love consisted of a book and half-filled wine bottle and glass. All of it was still on Lauren's potty where she'd left them after the baby went to sleep. She'd even forgotten to take the candles out of the sink this time. But other than the now damp candles, and the low water pressure, the sink was fine. She'd remove the old, wet candle from it and put it on the shelf later. Wincing as she made a mental note to remove the blackened wax from May's custom pink porcelain. She opened the linen closet and inspected the small washer-dryer unit that it housed. Dry as a bone. But she still heard water.

Gathering her robe around herself, she headed toward the only other water source in the condo, the kitchen. Moon-lit water made her stop mid-way into the living room. "Oh, shit! Give me a break, God." Hitting the ceiling light, she trudged across the wet oriental rug, gingerly tipping through the half-inch of water on the hardwood floors, finally making her way onto the linoleum surface of the kitchen floor. She looked down, then her gaze searched anxiously for an answer. Like a detective, her eyes narrowed on the ceiling, but there was no evidence of a leak coming down the walls. Thank God for that, at least. May's floors! Defeat claimed her soul. What was she going to tell her?

Inching toward the sink on tip-toes, she reached for the faucet and turned it on. The same slow trickle greeted her as renewed fear swept through her body. What the hell was she going to tell May? She had just borrowed money from the woman, now she'd damaged the condo somehow. Lord, have mercy.

She opened the cabinet under the sink to check the pipes. Dry. What else had a water source? There was no way in the world she was going to call May and her Dad at five-fifteen in the morning— during a work week! She was grateful that May had put the number for condo maintenance under a refrigerator magnet. Maybe she could call them, get it fixed, and have the floors redone so that May wouldn't have anything to be angry about? But at five-fifteen in the morning?

Antoinette took the wall phone from the jack and dialed the number anyway. Six, seven, eight rings. It was hopeless. Okay, she'd leave a message if the machine picked up. But a crotchety voice that connected with her senses startled her.

"Yeah-llo, maintenance," an elderly voice croaked into her ear.

"Oh, yes... I'm in unit number thirty-one, and there's water all over my floors."

"Where's it coming from, lady?" the disinterested voice asked with a yawn.

"I... I don't actually know. It's not a ceiling leak, I don't think, but the pressure is low and it's still spreading."

"Well," the voice said after a long pause, "if it's not coming into your unit from the building, it's a problem internal to your unit. I only fix problems for the building."

Her shoulders sagged and alarm pumped her blood till her ears rang. "But, Sir... I'll pay you. I just can't have these floors damaged or water seeping into a neighbor's apartment below." Antoinette felt her throat closing with salty moisture. "My baby will be up in a couple of hours. I just moved in here Friday before last, and I wanted everything to be right for her. Mister, I don't know what to do."

The voice paused again, and she could hear a disgusted breath being expelled. "Look, Miss, I ain't fixing no apartments at five-o-damned-clock in the morning."

She didn't answer for a moment, but summoned the energy to speak. "I understand," she whispered.

"You just moved in, 'bout a week or two ago? Got a baby, and all? How old's the chile?"

"Four," she said, feeling her voice give way. "She's four and a half."

"Don't you have no husband to fix it?"

"Not any more," she said quietly. "Sorry to have disturbed you so early, Sir. Thanks anyway."

"Oh, damn," the old man said, sounding truly perturbed, "I'll send a young boy up soon as I can. But you gotta pay him—cash. This ain't part of the building's responsibility, ya hear? And his fee is for y'all to negotiate, not me. Understand."

Antoinette cradled the phone next to her face and closed her eyes. God was being merciful, for once. "Yes. Oh, yes. Thank you so much, Sir. Thank you."

The old voice hesitated again, but his voice was much softer this time. "Yeah, whatever. Can tell you was a young sister. Don't do this for them others, you know what I mean? Plus, you was real respectful, and didn't cuss me out when I first said no. Gots good home trainin' and ain't the bougie type, I can tell. So, you remember Mister Miles, come the holidays. Well, they should be there in about an hour, or less—if'n I can get 'em on the beeper. Okay?"

"Mister Miles, thank you," she whispered as deep appreciation coursed through her. "I promise, I'll remember."

ꙮꙮ

The phone had felt like a bullet in his brain when it had rung next to his head. He was glad that old man Miles had picked it up in the bedroom. The days at his first gig, and then working like a slave for Miles at night, were killing him.

"You got a job," Mr. Miles hollered, scratching his belly as he entered the living room. "You burnin' daylight, boy."

"What the hell..." Jerome mumbled, as he tried to sit up on the makeshift cot. "Damn, I gotta be at work in about two hours. I thought I was just supposed to be doing night jobs?"

"Well," Mr. Miles grunted as he shuffled into the kitchenette area, "shit happens. Dis is an emergency, an don' fergit you here on my good graces anyways, boy. So don' sass me none, and git yo' lazy ass up an' fix dat woman's problem."

"Okay, but it can't be nothin' that takes a long time—'cause I gotta go to my regular gig," he croaked back at the old man. "Who is it?"

"I'on't know! All I know is dat it's in unit thirty-one. What I look like, Dionne Warwick on the psychic hotline? I knows my customers by dey unit numbers—an' I done tol' you, it's unit thirty-one."

"All right, all right," he mumbled through a yawn, pulling himself up to sit on the side of the cot, and suddenly remembering how in the past he'd gotten thrown out of the bedroom for even questioning the Visa bill. The last thing he wanted at this point was to get thrown out of a basement for something as stupid as arguing about making a unit run. But he still wanted the old man to take back the part about him being lazy. It was a matter of honor for the record.

"I just got in here at midnight from a long shift, worked until three for you—and now you want me to go back out at five something—but, I'm lazy, right?"

"You lazy if yo' ass don't git a move on, is all I'ma say. Dis lady say she'll pay cash. An, since it is sort of outta yo' way, you kin keep da cut. Now, dats all I'm willin' ta do!"

Jerome allowed his gaze to wander across the dark livingroom and settle on the clock. He looked around at the messy basement unit that had junk cast everywhere, and immediately thought of how his home used to look with toys strewn on the floor. If he were home, the kids would've been up in less than an hour anyway. His mind couldn't take the screaming and yelling and kiddy cartoons this morning—or Karen's silent treatment, if he was lucky. Then, again, it would more than likely have turned into another a serious rag-session that turned into a harangue—if he were still there. Now, a crotchety old man took her place, notwithstanding his new locale. Nothing ever changed.

He drowned out Mr. Mile's voice as he weighed his options. The choices were simplistic, either get up on two hours of sleep, half drunk, after a sixteen-hour, back-breaking shift in order to stay with Miles, or try to crawl back to Karen after work and catch some zee's while she stood over him, fussed, slammed drawers and cabinets to punish his hang-over and fatigue, all while the kids yelled happily at his return at the top of their lungs.

"How much, man? I seriously need the bread. Karen ran up my Visa last month 'cause she was pissed, and I just took her to Atlantic City. Plus, I promised to bring her some more money at the end of the week. I can't do it all in one check, and keep the lights on over there too. If it's serious green, I'll go."

"She ain't say how much. If you took your scroungy ass over there, you'd know. You da one who's broke, and cryin' 'bout money."

The choice was becoming easier as his mind replaced Mr. Miles with Karen's form at the bottom of his cot. Mentally picturing her there with one hand on her hip sealed his decision.

"How come you didn't call Buddy?"

"Tried him first, already! Buddy's got a sick baby, and a wife who gots a nasty attitude—givin' me da blues when I call, like I was some woman he was runnin.' See dats why I don' git involved in domestics."

"I got my tools in the Bronco," he managed through another yawn. He was outta there.

Slowly pulling on his boots, and gathering his jacket and his cap, he thought about the hundreds of arguments he'd dealt with on account of his friends. Jerome strode into the tiny bathroom to let out the previous night's beer, and then splashed cold water on his face to chase the ghosts of arguments away. Yet, he could still hear Karen's high-pitched screech and his own bellows through the sound of the running water...

"I'm lazy and I don't do shit for you?" he said out-loud to the mirror, considering his current fate within Mr. Miles' small bathroom.

He closed his eyes for a moment as his wife's response to the question became almost audible. He knew what she'd say.

He never waited for her response in the mirror. He was gone.

∞

Mopping furiously against the deluge, Antoinette stood in the kitchen in bare feet, trying not to get the pair of gray sweats she wore too wet. It was the only sensible thing she had been able to quickly scavenge from an unpacked garbage bag that had become the catchall for clothing that her dresser and closet couldn't hold. If she could just keep the water back long enough for them to find and turn off the main valve—wherever that was. Her hair kept slipping out of the rubber band and she stopped her efforts every few moments to tuck the wisps back into her ponytail.

How long were they going to take to get there?

She hoped they wouldn't be like Triple-A road service, where an hour meant two hours. She'd fall out for sure by the time they got to her unit—and, once again, be late for work, and she couldn't do that. Not just because of the money, but because of the women there who believed in her. Going to work every day was like going to church, and it filled up her soul. Where was maintenance?

When the doorbell chimed, she let out a breath of impatient relief. "Finally," she said in a huff, forgetting about her initial gratitude. This was a pain in the butt, and she put the mop down and tiptoed through water to the door.

Transfixed, it took a moment for her brain to register and connect to her vocal chords. God was cruel.

He couldn't speak. Without thinking, his hand went to his jaw and he rubbed the stubble of newgrowth on his face and looked down at his workboots. Why hadn't Buddy told him this was Antoinette's unit—in the same damned building? This was bull. His boy had let him get ambushed with all those years of history without firing a warning shot in advance. He looked like crap, felt like crap, and was now standing in front of the only woman that ever made him give a damn—about anything. Buddy! He'd kill him.

"Jerome? Jerome Henderson?" she said with a shy smile before looking down at her feet.

God, she was still pretty. And that smile hadn't changed in all the years, nor had her eyes. They were still deep, rich chocolate brown—innocent. Summoning his breath, he tried to speak, but nothing came out at first.

"Antoinette Reeves?" He knew he sounded like a fool.

"Well," she said quietly, "It's Wellington, now. I used to be Reeves."

A knife went through his heart. Buddy was not only dead wrong to let him roll up on a ghost like this, but Scoop had given him screwed-up info too. The girl was married. Damn. How was he supposed to come in, fix her water pipes, make small talk with her obviously well-to-do husband, then go home like a raggedy blue collar, stiff? It wasn't right. Friends didn't do this to friends.

"Well, come in, come in" she finally said, "I'm sorry, where are my manners?"

Jerome focused on his grimy work-boots, then looked around the immaculate environment.

"It's okay," she said, touching his jacket sleeve and reading his mind, "there's nothing you can do to May's floors that the water hasn't already done."

He looked around again, and stepped over the threshold, closing the door behind him. "May?"

"Oh, yeah," she sighed, leading him to the kitchen. "After Mom died, Dad got remarried. This is May's unit. Me and Lauren are just here now for a while, until I can get myself together. Divorce changes a lot of things, especially where you live."

His senses were overloaded. Lauren? A child. Toni had a child? That's right, Scoop had mentioned that. And she was back in Philly—divorced. He cast his gaze around the unit, seeing no evidence of male claim to it. The whole place was pink. No man would allow this. His shoulders relaxed, and he opted for a topic of conversation that he had the full facts about. "I was sorry to hear about your Mom,

T. I always liked her."

Toni turned around with a puzzled expression. "She always liked you too..." Her voice trailed off in an odd sort of way as she looked past him at the front door then shook her head. "Yeah, Mom always liked you," she said with more conviction.

"Well, let's see what's causing the trouble in here," he said as firmly as he could. He had to pull himself together.

When Toni nodded and turned away from him, heading toward the kitchen, he closed his eyes briefly and took a deep breath in through his nose. Lord, the woman was fine. Her hips had spread and filled out the form of her damp sweats, and he was sure that she wasn't wearing anything under them. God help him. She had gone from a curvaceous teenager to a full-grown, woman. Now her ample breasts swayed lightly without a bra under the thin cotton sweat-top, and her face was still flawless without makeup. He wondered what her thick, mahogany hair would feel like? Probably like pure velvet, just like her warm, cinnamon-colored skin always had.

"Well, doctor, can you fix it?" she asked with a smile, putting one hand on her hip as she motioned toward the river on her floor with the other.

That smile. He watched her voluptuous form move under the soft gray fabric, and his attention was drawn to her lush mouth as his heart answered her. "I hope so, Toni-girl. I'll do my best."

Toni-girl. Oh dear, God, why was she being tortured like this? Toni-girl. He remembered, and so did she. Why, on a Tuesday morning, was everything that her mother and father had ever taught her about right and wrong being put to the ultimate test? The man was married. The man had children. He was a lifer. Regardless of a temporary domestic separation. And she was standing there, half dressed, looking like a banshee—with her hair standing up on top of her head, a mop in her hands, bare feet, no make-up, no underwear, and sweats on. Why, Lord? Why couldn't she have bumped into him at a store, the mall, anywhere that she could have hidden the extra pounds and flaws under a winter coat? But to stand there, semi-naked, in front of the only man that had ever made her shiver like a school-girl, was cruel.

She wanted to disappear into the water that she'd wrung out of the mop, just float beneath the gray muck in the bucket. Vanish. Poof! God had a mean sense of humor. But, God knows, he was still fine. Tall, sort-of lanky, with those high cheekbones, and coarse jet-black hair, thick, black mustache, and that Cherokee-red finish to his skin that kissed his brown with an undertone of warm color. The way it set contrast to the five o-clock shadow of rough that once felt so good on her cheek... And those dark, penetrating eyes that spoke volumes. And his work had obviously filled him out with a chest like cinder blocks and the arms to go with it. Jesus, he'd

337

improved with age.

"It keeps coming from somewhere in the kitchen," she stammered, refusing to look at him any longer. Her dignity was in shambles, how could she look the man in the eyes? She could only imagine what he thought—that he was glad that she'd turned him down almost two decades ago, because look at her now. A wreck. She blinked back the moisture in her eyes, turned away and went toward the sink. "See, the pressure is low, but it keeps replacing itself on the floor." But, God, he was definitely still fine.

His heart was pacing inside his chest like a trapped cat. How long had she been divorced? How old was the child? What fool in his right mind would have given her up? Then a thought stopped him as he looked under the sink, what if the stupid SOB had hit his Toni-girl? He'd kill him. It would be the only thing to make a woman like Toni leave. Reason came to his mind slowly as he stood. She wasn't his Toni anymore. By what right could he claim her? He had a damned wife, four little kids—that only God knew how they were made, because it sure wasn't from excess love and affection. But he did know that Antoinette was not the kind of woman to take sloppy seconds, by going out with him while she still thought he was solidly married and at home. No. He'd never do that to her, or try to propose it. She deserved better—way better than him. Always did.

"You got an automatic ice-maker in the fridge?"

He had to do this job and get out.

She looked puzzled. "I don't know, Jay-bird.... What's that got to do with all this water on the floor."

His heart lurched. Why was she doing this, calling him by his old Air Force nickname, and all?

"Stand back, cause we'll see in a minute. It's not coming from outside of the building; your walls would have been ruined by now. If the bathroom is okay, and the only leak is in here, then, probably it's the connection to the ice-maker."

He opened the side-by-side freezer door and arctic water poured out.

"Oh, God! Look at this... all my groceries... Oh, Jay!"

"Just like I thought," he said, moving quickly to turn off the valve under the sink and ignoring the tremor that went through his body when she called his name. Lord, he had it bad for this woman. "All I have to do is to disconnect the ice-maker. Look, honey, most of the food is still frozen and can be saved. Give me the mop, and I'll get this together for you in about twenty-minutes. But you'll have to call the refrigerator people, or me messin' with it will void your warranty. Okay?"

She nodded and stood aside. He was glad to have a few moments to pull his head together, and to be able to work without conversation. Her voice was like a rush against his soul, every time she opened her mouth, every syllable that escaped from it. She made him remember something that he needed to forget in the next twenty minutes.

"How much do I owe you, Jay? I'm sorry that it was something so stupid."

He just stared at her, "Nothin'. You don't owe me anything. I just got paid."

As he expected she shook her head no, and went toward the bedroom and began rummaging in her purse. The sight of her had been worth a weeks salary or more. Yeah, he just got paid.

"I mean it, Toni-girl, I just got paid last Friday, and don't need a dime. Now, how can I charge my baby for something little like this?" He looked down at the floor and wished that he could have retrieved every word. He'd called her his baby. Force of habit. Force of will. Jerome let his breath out slowly, and he closed his eyes and leaned against the wall. His body was tired, and his head hurt.

"Jay," she said quietly, moving into the room and still focusing toward the floor when he opened his eyes, "I didn't know they were calling you, and wouldn't dream of interfering with your life. I'm sorry it's so early. I know you've gotta go home and—"

He cut her off with a wave of his hand. "Nothing to go home in a rush for, but an argument. Do you have any coffee? I'll take that as payment. No harm done. You didn't interfere. You just needed your refrigerator fixed."

Her smile flowed over him like the breaking

dawn. "I not only have some coffee in here, but I have some of Pearline's cobbler."

She wasn't fighting fair. "You got some of Aunt Pearline's cobbler? T, stop-it! Apple or peach?"

"Take your pick," she said with a satisfied wink, "and I can heat it up?"

"Peach." He looked down at the floor and the linoleum blurred. Damn. It had been so long. He'd not only lost Antoinette when they broke up, but her whole family of aunts and cousins and relatives that loved him like their own. "I'll pull your rug up, and hang it over the shower curtain. This way your floors won't warp from the water. You got any floor polish?" He needed distance.

"No, Jay," she protested, moving into the kitchen, "you've done enough, I can do that. Just wash yourself up, sit down, and coffee and cobbler will be ready in a minute."

"Won't take but a minute," he shot back, gathering up the soaked Oriental as he said it. He had to keep moving, do anything before he really made a fool of himself. The girl was just being nice, he told himself—for old time's sake. She was way above his caliber now. Scoop had been right. She was out of his league.

Half dragging the heavy roll through her bedroom, into the bathroom, he refused to look at the bed... or her robe... or the tousled sheets. Jesus, it had been a long time. Grunting from exertion, he heaved the large nine-by-twelve over the rim and prayed it would hold. The wet rug weighed a ton, about the same weight that was filling his groin. He had to stop thinking about it.

Standing on the toilet seat, he leaned on the tile and pulled the dripping rug length-wise down the pole, trying to avoid the half-empty wine bottle, glass, and book that sat on the potty-seat. She had a toddler. She had taken a bath—by herself. There was one candle in the sink. She was obviously lonely enough to read a book and drink all that wine by herself. She was available. "Help me, Father," he whispered into the tile, his voice echoing back the prayer. Jerome closed his eyes momentarily as the smell of warm cobbler drifted into the neat little bathroom. The woman could cook, kept a clean home, was pretty as a picture, and if memory served him right—could make love like a panther... Who was the fool that had let this woman go?

"Cobbler's ready, Jay."

He loved the way she called his name. Sing-song like. Not a screech. Not a bellow. But a sing-song. "Be there in a minute. Just gotta get this rug over the tub so it doesn't mess up the floor."

Jumping down from his perch, he walked quickly into the kitchen area and sat down. When she put a mug of coffee under his nose and a heaping plate of cobbler before him, he met her gaze. "Been a long time, girl." He couldn't help it. It was the truth.

"Yeah."

He could barely hear her voice when she'd spoken. That told him all he needed to know.

"What happened?" He didn't care if it wasn't his business. Half of the question was about her divorce, but the core of it was about them. What did happen between them, really? How'd she get away?

"Time. Me and Brian split up over time, money, other women. I still don't know."

Her face was so open, so serene. She'd just said it plain, and never accused the man. That was his T.

"Other women?" he said without looking at her, taking a shovel-full of cobbler, and chasing it with a slurp of coffee. He closed his eyes as the warm confection melted into the coffee, sank into his tongue, and slid sweetly down his throat. It was a poor substitute for the kiss he wanted, even though it was a cobbler by Pearline. "Man musta been outta his black mind. Fool," he said emphatically through bites. "A fool."

He'd repeated the word fool, once for himself, then once for whoever her husband had been. They were both fools, and had both been out of their minds to let this one slip away. He wanted to cringe when he thought about the way he'd acted down on the base—when he'd suspected her of cheating, got jealous, and listened to his friends. Jerome wolfed down his cobbler, allowing the pleasure of eating to supplant any other desires he had. Plus, how could he really look this woman in her eyes?

Yet, he could feel her gaze boring into him.

Eventually, he was forced to meet it. When he looked up, he noticed tears in her eyes, and immediately regretted the reflex comment about her husband being a fool.

"Thank you, Jay. That was sweet. But, we have to be honest. Look at me. Things have changed with time."

He set his fork down very slowly and gazed at her face. When she lowered her lashes and he saw the sheen on them, a force greater than his own drew his arm out—stretching it across the table until his palm cradled her cheek. "The only thing that has changed is that you've become more beautiful. The man who went elsewhere for your brand of loving was a fool, girl. Take it from a man's perspective. I ain't just being kind."

When she covered his hand with her own, and kissed the inside of his palm, he closed his eyes and dropped his head two inches over his plate. A shudder went through his body, as the contact from her warm, moist mouth lit a fire in the center of where her lips had touched. God wasn't playing fair this morning...

"Thank you... for saying that, when I look like hell." Her laugh was self-conscious and she pulled away her hand, leaving an inferno in the middle of his.

"No. I meant what I said, and if I wasn't quasi-married, I'd show you."

He stared at her for a long time. No words

passed between them. He had no right to say that to her, and prayed that she wouldn't be offended. It was just that everything was so strong... the pull to this woman... this life that was supposed to be with her, but wasn't.

Her dark lashes half covered her eyes as she looked at him from beneath lowered lids. "I'd let you... if you weren't married. Jay, you were always a good man. Go home, and don't mess up your life for me again. Hear? I heard about the temporary separation. It's easier to stay and work it out, if it's salvageable. Trust me."

"We both learned that one the hard way, didn't we?" he murmured, thinking about how much different his life might have been had they stayed together from the jump and worked it out.

"Yeah. We did, didn't we."

There was nothing to say. She'd admitted that she felt it too, and just as strongly as he did. It was in the way her eyes went to half-mast, and her breath hovered over her words just before she looked away. Just like when she was younger, and he'd want her, and she'd want him back. He ran his hands through his short fade haircut and stood. "Can't handle this, Toni. It's getting' thick in here. I want you too bad, and I got too many responsibilities... and you ain't the type to be on the side. Would never put you in that position. I gotta go."

She nodded and stood up with him, passing him as she moved toward the door. He watched her from behind... the way her round bottom and hips swayed. No. He had to go. As she managed the locks, reason accosted his brain, telling him to go home. But the trouble was, he was already home.

"Thanks for everything, Jay," she said in a near whisper as she turned around to face him.

God, why had she turned around? Her sad eyes haunted him, and he let his gaze travel down her throat to the edge of her sweat-shirt, and over her heavy, pendulous breasts. "I have to go home," he said again, almost to himself. "It's been a long time."

"I know," her voice murmured, stroking his soul. "Please. Go home, Jay.... before I change my mind."

✂✁

Seven o'clock in the morning and he was driving around the streets like a homeless piper. He couldn't go home. There was no such place anymore. His Pop's joint had never been home since his mother had died. His sister went to the early church—all day, every day, and wouldn't be there. None of his boys would be up yet—if they were, they were getting ready for work. Maybe Buddy would be home, since the baby was sick, and all. Then again, maybe not.

He found himself on Buddy's steps, ringing the bell and banging on the door like a madman, trying

to hold back the tears. This was messed up. He'd

kick Buddy's tail.

"Yo, Man," Buddy hollered from the other side of the door. "Chill out. Lemme git the key. Damn, Reds."

When Buddy finally flung open the door, a jumble of kids fell out behind him, curling themselves around Jerome's legs and waist like kittens. All he could do was pet their heads and look away. Emotion caught even a hello in his throat. What about the kids? His four, beautiful, innocent babies—and their father couldn't go home.

"Uncle Jerome! It's Uncle Jerome, Mom!"

"Swing me around, Uncle Jerome!"

"Can Kitty, and Pat come over after school today?"

"Y'all go in the house and put some shoes on," Buddy hollered, trying to dispel the gaggle of children. "Let the man come in out of the cold, now, y'all hear!"

Jerome didn't move, and Buddy stood in the doorway looking at him. Swatting the children away and handing off children to Valerie amid barks to leave their uncle alone, Buddy took another look at his expression and grabbed his jacket. "Be back in less than an hour, Val."

Jerome walked hard and fast toward his Bronco, with Buddy in fast pursuit as he scuffled along in slippers and tried to get his jacket on. But the two said nothing. Neither spoke until they had slid into the seats, and Jerome had turned on the car heat and shut off the radio.

He leaned his head against the steering wheel and his voice gave way under the strain. "Yo, man, that shit was fucked up!" Spit fused with mucous from his nose as he sputtered out his complaint. "You supposed to be my boy, and all. What kind of mind games you playin', man? With no goddamned warning!"

Buddy touched Jerome's shoulder and he shrugged it off in anger.

"Whatchu you talkin' 'bout, man? The kids okay? Karen? What, man? Just tell me."

"You tell me! How you gonna send me out at five a.m. to do a job at Toni's place? Tell me, man?" he yelled through blurred vision, focusing hard on his friend's face, "When we supposed to be boyz— when you know how I've felt about that woman all of my life! How could you let me roll in there and get ambushed, with my situation all jacked-up, huh? If I was ever gonna see her again, I'da wanted to show her my best—not this."

Buddy sat back and his eyes widened. "Naw, man," he claimed, shaking his head excitedly. "I wouldn't even play no mess like that. No. Scoop would pull some bull like that, maybe. But not me. I'm ya boy."

Jerome relaxed, and wiped his face with full palms. "She's still beautiful, man."

"You didn't?" Buddy whispered, almost in awe.

Jerome left his palms over his face as his head

fell back against the seat. His normal breathing rhythm recovered slowly as he began to speak. "No. Toni ain't like that, man—you know that." His voice wavered briefly as he struggled for control. "I wanted her so bad, man. She felt it too, I could tell. But I have to go home. I've got four kids."

Buddy placed a reassuring hand on his shoulder and shook him hard. "It'll be all right, man. Just give it all to Karen when y'all get back together. That'll get the monkey off your back. Livin' wit Miles is temporary."

"Toni is free... like I always wondered. She's available again, after all these years, and she remembered what we had. She did, man. She did. She called me, Jay-bird."

"Aw, maaaan..." Buddy whispered. "You sure."

"Know it like I know my name," Jerome murmured.

"Tell the truth, man... did you hit it?"

"No. Would I be sittin' here talkin' to you, if I did?"

"Then go home, change faces in your mind while you gittin' it, if you have to, then forget about it. You got four kids. Remember that. Responsibility, man. You been at Miles' for a week, done made your point, now go the hell home—and stop trippin'."

Jerome looked at his friend squarely in the eyes. He gathered his words before he spoke. "I can't give what I got to give to Karen. It was Toni's for the last twenty years... all through while she was in high school and for fifteen years after that to this day. Maybe that's why Karen don't want it from me. I can't blame her. But, I can't go home to what I've been living with. I want a divorce," he whispered.

"Man, stop talkin' crazy. You scarin' me. Don't do nothin' crazy. Did you talk to Toni 'bout leaving home? Are you outcha black mind, from seein' an old flame, once? Don't even go there, man... Hell, we all get tired of home from time to time. The kids and woman get on your nerves, from time to time, but you can't be leavin' all them children. Be realistic, man."

Reason fought its way back into the crevices of his brain. Jerome let his body slump in the seat. "Yeah. You right. It was just that when I saw her—"

"You was about to let the little head do the thinking for the big one," Buddy laughed and shook his head. Relief broke the tension in his face as he slapped Jerome's back. "Don't be scarin' me like this, all early in the damned mornin', man. C'mon, brother. You know the little head ain't logical in the mornin'. You was just feelin' the early mornin' rise and shine--that's all."

"Yeah, man," Jerome laughed back as he looked out the window, feeling new moisture well up in his eyes, "it was something like that."

"Go home, man, and take your whippin' from K like a man. When you drop the extra green on the kitchen table, she won't stay mad for long. She may even give you some, good brother. You mighta scared her into reality this time. She'll chill."

Jerome let his head fall back and he laughed from deep within his soul. "Ain't no money, Man. I'ma get my butt kicked."

"No money?" Buddy was incredulous. "Are you out'chure damned mind? You can't be out in the street all hours, leave on a fight for a week, and not bring your wife home some money above your normal pay. You's one crazy, half-Indian, licka drinkin' fool!"

"Yeah," Jerome offered in a sad chuckle, still wiping at the corners of his eyes. "I'm losing my mind."

CHAPTER 21

"Mr. Miles? Mr. Miles? I know it's still early in the morning, but I just wanted to leave you a thank you before I ran to work."

Antoinette glanced at her watch and the stack of flea-market flyers under her arm, while listening to the old man grumble in the distance. Furniture from somewhere in his apartment moved before she heard any footsteps. In ten minutes, she'd be late for work, but needed to get this task done immediately, and hang some flyers in the building—while Lauren was in school. It was her only way of bringing much-needed closure to any outstanding debts. At least she'd make good on this one.

As the door opened in the dim basement dwelling, she could see that she'd awakened her elderly savior from a very sound sleep.

"Oh, I'm sorry."

"No trouble." The old man yawned. "Whatcha need, Miss?"

"Oh, I'm the water job from number thirty-one. Remember, that crazy call you got?"

He frowned, scratched the gray stubble on his face, then smiled. "Oh, yous the po' damsel in distress. Yup, I remember. No mo' trouble I hope?"

Antoinette returned his kind smile. "No. Just a present from my Aunt Pearline. She makes the best cobbler on the East Coast. For you—just to keep my promise not to forget. I really appreciated your 'call to arms' this morning. I've just started a new job, and couldn't take a day off to babysit the pipes."

Mr. Miles chuckled and dropped his eyes. She could tell that he was flattered beyond measure as he accepted the dessert without looking at her.

"Aw, shucks, honey. D'is my job. You ain't have to go an' do that...."

"Yes, I did," she said smiling back at him. "You went above and beyond the call of duty, and I wanted to let you know."

"Don't see this no mo'," he said shaking his head. "Home trainin'. Knew it like I knew my name when ya called. Well, honey, yous got a friend in dis here buildin'. You need anything, inside or out, you jus' call old Milesy. Hear?"

Her smile widened as her soul lifted. She loved to make people happy, and his tender appreciation warmed her. "Don't you worry about that. This is from the heart. And you remember that you've got a friend in thirty-one too. If I can cook it," she smiled as she looked around his dingy environs, knowing that he lived alone, "you got it. Sundays are my day to burn up the pots. Expect something on Sunday. You like chicken?"

"Cain't turn down an offer like that," he chuckled as he walked her to the building exit, the wide tray of cobbler held tight in his grip. "Now you shoo on, and don'cha worry 'bout no ol' maintenance man. I be fine, an' even better tonight when I heat this up, and put a little somethin' in my coffee to go wit it."

൭൭

Jerome sat down slowly on the edge of the rickety metal cot that Mr. Miles had pulled out for him. He was wedged between the radiator and the stained plaid sofa that he was thankful that he didn't have to sleep on.

"An' don'tchu be leavin' no mess in my bathroom neither like you did this mornin'," his grumpy host called from the small kitchenette. "Only let'cha git away wit it on account of you was rushin' to go to one of my unit jobs. You lef' water everywhere. An' turn the TV set off when you done wit it, and rise an shine is early—six-thirty. Sheets an' a blanket is still over on da chair—which I expect washed 'fore you give 'em back. Ain't got no pilla fer ya, like I tol' ya before, wasn't 'spectin' to be entatainin'—and yo' friend lef' you a towel, plastic razor, an some toothpaste, plus a bar of soap. Don' be usin' my stuff, ya hear, boy? Done tol' you I ain't runnin' no mission."

"Yes, sir," Jerome groaned, not bothering to cover the spotted mattress with a sheet. His body hurt so bad, and his back had so many sore muscles in it, he just wanted to get horizontal. If the old man would just stop ragging him, he might be able to slip into a mild coma and be fortunate enough to die in his sleep.

"An', like I tol' ya when you firs' came, I keeps me a loaded thirty-eight under m' pillow. So, if you ain't honest, I'll kill ya quick."

"Sir," Jerome said without emotion, "killing me would be a pure act of mercy. Just do it neat, twice in the head to make sure I die. Don't leave me a cripple."

Mr. Miles let out a little grunt as he shuffled into the living room and stood over him. Jerome groaned again inwardly. He didn't have the energy to argue, prove his integrity, or to care that a surly old man might get jumpy at night if he went into the bathroom to take a piss. Damn. He was really homeless.

"You eat anything today, 'tween them jobs?"

"No, sir," he mumbled as the coma he'd prayed for began to eclipse his living nightmare. "Grabbed a little something this morning, is all."

"Humph," his host exclaimed, moving toward

the kitchen. "A man cain't be runnin' on E all day, do five apartments every night, den git up an' meet da man early in da mornin'. Simple. Y'all young folk don' be usin' common sense."

"Gotta save this twenty that my friend gave me, sir. Gotta put it in the Bronco for two weeks of gas. I'm more tired than hungry, anyway. I'll get a hoagie in the morning."

"Plain waste'a money! If you took yo' sorry ass to the supermarket and cooked up some rice an' beans, you'd save three of the five dollars you'd spend on no damned hoagie. Humph!"

Mr. Miles seemed indignant as he left his side and began to bang around in the kitchen. Jerome covered his eyes with his arm and tried to extinguish the sounds of pots and pans clanging. It reminded him too much of Karen.

"So, what'chu plannin' on doin', boy? Starve to death for two weeks, den try to die on my cot? Simple. Young folks is simple."

"I'll figure it out tomorrow, Sir." Please, he prayed, just make his tormentor have a little mercy and stop the noise.

"See," Mr. Miles continued with his litany, "thas the kin' a thinkin' dat ends y'all young black boys in prisin. Belly get tight, money be funny, den next thang y'all know, y'all done hit a Seven-Eleven, or y'all—in yo' stupid thinkin'—goes an' gits some drugs to fight da hunger, and be hooked," he said with a snap of his fingers, "jus' like dat. Da monsta gotcha. Simple. Y'all don' be usin' ya noggin.'"

"I'll be fine," Jerome said, losing patience, but having enough sense not to excite the old man with an irritable comment. Maybe years under Karen's roof had taught him something.

"Humph," he snorted again as he shuffled back into the room and dropped a tin platter on the box that was his make-shift coffee table. "Some pork and beans. Least dat'll fill a hole."

Jerome sat up slowly and peered at the greasy creation, but the rumble in his stomach removed any reservations that might have made him decline the offer. "Thanks, sir" he said with full gratitude, rising to accept the plate and consume it from the side of the cot.

The hot slurry hit the bottom of his acid-filled stomach with a thud, and he practically inhaled the nourishment, realizing with every bite just how hungry he was.

"Well, even white folks fed dey slaves. Damn, boy.... ya musta been really starvin'.'"

Mr. Miles' voice held what might have been a note of concern. Jerome heard it as he'd slurped down the last of the beans, and the tone had made him look up from the dish.

"When's the las' time ya ate, boy?"

"This morning—a cup of coffee and a piece of pie. Before that, yesterday night, sir," Jerome said standing up, and moving to the kitchen to wash out the plate. "I'll clean it up, so I don't leave a mess.

Leslie Esdaile

Don't want to cause you no trouble—you been nice enough to have me. Thank you, Sir."

"Now, see. Dat's a crime! Ain't nobody should starve to death like a dog in da street. Nobody. 'Specially a workin' man!"

Mr. Miles walked into the kitchen behind Jerome and stood in the doorway as he cleaned the tin pie plate and the big metal spoon he'd been given.

"Ya know, boy... I been watchin' you. Gots good home trainin'. Where's ya people, boy? Whyn't dey take you in? Ya seem like a nice young feller. You works harder den any of them lazy no-counts I try to git to work fer me, even cleans up after yo'self, has a nice car, good manners, a decent married friend... cain't figure it." he said, not really looking in Jerome's direction. "What happened to ya people, boy? Dey all dead, 'cept da wife 'n kids?"

"Yeah. And since I left the military, my Pop don't think I rate much." What else could he tell the old man? His mother had died a long time ago, just like his grandmother had. Ever since his sister hooked up with a evangelical minister, she hadn't been right, and his father might as well be dead. Yeah, he hadn't lied. His family was dead.

"Damn," the old man said, rubbing his scruffy chin. "Well, sometimes... sometimes we don't get a good poker hand, an' we gotta play wit da bes' one we got. But praying helps, boy. Got me through da Depression, Jim Crow, da big war... when my kids died 'fore me, den when my wife closed her eyes. Gotta pray."

Jerome let out a breath and moved back to his cot. He didn't need a sermon on top of everything else, but he couldn't let the comment go.

"Been prayin', sir. Didn't get me my wings. Didn't get my wife to ease up. Didn't get me no better job. Didn't keep my kids' hearts from breaking— even though I prayed to my Mom to watch over them. No harm intended, Mr. Miles, but prayer won't pay a security deposit, child support, or my Bronco note. Right now, The Lord and I ain't exactly on speaking terms, you might say."

Again Mr. Miles hovered over him as he stretched out prostrate on the cot. Jerome turned over and gave Mr. Miles his back to consult. Damn, he was living with somebody worse than Karen. At least she could be counted on for the silent treatment. Maybe going home was the only option. Right now, it seemed better than this.

"Don't be mockin' da Lord, now. Not in my house. Did ya pray fer a roof ov'r ya head today, boy?"

Jerome didn't answer immediately, but as the old man stood steadfast, he gave in and spoke. "Yes, Sir."

"Dats right! An' did ya pray fer a morsel ta eat?"

Jerome couldn't answer.

"Got amnesia now dat ya belly's full, huh? Well, did ya think an ol' crotchety man might have mercy on ya?"

Jerome refused to answer as the elderly man shuffled away and began banging in the kitchen again. He kept his arm over his eyes as he flopped on his back and feigned sleep. If only the old man would cut it out and go to bed.

"An' did ya think an angel might deliver ya some to-die-for-cobbler, by way of that same ol' man that had mercy?"

Jerome opened his eyes and sat up slowly.

"Dats right," the old man said with a wide smile, extending a plate in Jerome's direction. "Purty as a pic'chure, old fashioned girl whose apartment you fixed. She come down here, don' even know yo scrungy ass was here, boy... an' she brung ol' Milesy some'a her Aunt's cobbler—jus' because. She didn't want nothin', just wanted to thank an' ol' man. So, da way I figure it, ya musta been honest an' mannerly... musta let'cha home trainin' shine, cause she ain't no beggar—didn't have to say nothin,' but if ya was nasty to 'er, I woulda heard 'bout it—sho' nuff."

Jerome accepted the dessert, but still couldn't touch it. He could only sit there, mouth agape, staring at the old man.

"Thas right. Go 'head. Eat up. You did good fer her, so ya good turn became mine, and mines became yours. Dats how it work, boy. Ev'ry thang comes full circle," he said with a chuckle, crooking his finger around in the air in a wobbly motion. "Shoulda seen 'er..." Mr. Miles sighed. "Smiled like an angel's sunshine, and skipped outta my door like she had wings. Fine 'nough to make a old man git a flashback. Have mercy!" he exclaimed, slapping his knee. "Now, tell me," he asked with a grunt of total satisfaction as he plopped into the adjacent chair, "as ya fill yer mouth wit the most divine, dat none a'ya prayers came true. So stop mockin' da Lord in my house, and eat'cha damned cobbler, boy, den say thank ya, Jesus."

"Thank you, Jesus," Jerome murmured, still unable to take a bite. Instead, he closed his eyes and raised the plate up in the air before he violated it with a fork. With soul-felt reverence he began to savor the first bite, rolling it around on his tongue and closing his eyes each time he swallowed. "Damn, Pearline can burn..."

"How you know her Aunt's name was Pearline?" Mr. Miles didn't bother to hide his curiosity. "You know somethin' 'bout my new tenant dat I don't know, boy?"

"Uhmmm, Uhmmm...." Jerome said shaking his head, too caught up in abject rapture to respond.

"Well, she mentioned 'er Aunt's name was Pearline when she handed me dis cobbler. Ya got some hooo dooo, E.S.P. mess goin' on wit your half-Indian self? Humph," he exclaimed as he collected his plate and shuffled toward the bedroom.

"No, sir," Jerome quipped, taking another bite. "Been prayin', is all, sir. Good night," he mumbled, filling his mouth again.

"Damned, crazy, half-Indian bringing hooo dooo to my door," his host grunted defiantly. "Better git on betta terms wit yo' Jesus, boy, an' git some sleep. Marks my words," he added with a slam of his bedroom door.

Jerome smiled at the anticipation of being allowed to finish his dessert in peace—another taste of a Pearline original, at that. He definitely owed God an apology, as well as The Great Spirit to whom his mother and grandmother had always prayed. They'd always said that there were 'forces behind the scenes,' like the strong invisible air current that made the eagle soar. Damn, he was learning how to fly in a basement.

CHAPTER 22

Her mouth melted into his as she whispered his name. His hand became tangled in her dark, velvety hair, and the lush warmth of her body drank him in to the hilt. His other hand found leverage under her bottom and reveled in the voluptuous, smooth sphere that it met. "God, I missed you," he moaned, as she nipped at his neck and his mouth found her earlobe.

Thick hips pushed back in rhythm with his own, and his heaving motions were cushioned by her soft, pendulous bosom. Profound pleasure forced the air from his lungs, and he struggled to keep his line of vision fastened on her gorgeous brown eyes. He wanted to etch every moment of the way she made him feel into his memory—for there'd be no telling when she'd allow him to be with her like this again. His last memory of her this way had lasted him twenty years. And, when she called his name, he could feel the damn of pressure that had been building in his groin begin to give. Then, her voice became louder, and deeper, and older... and she began to fade in his arms, leaving him helplessly caught in the limbo of unspent frustration.

He cried out to her, half asleep half awake, feeling as though his chest would burst from grief as she slipped away and became, once again, the pillow—and Mr. Miles called him to announce morning.

Jerome sat up quickly on the edge of the metal cot and groaned. The nearly completed dream left him drawing shallow sips of air. This was not the place to be discovered with such a problem. However, the intensity of this particular erection was giving him a blinding headache. He'd have to work this one off, do some serious labor, just like he'd had to since he'd seen Antoinette and been stuck in old man Miles' basement. He cringed as the old man yelled again for him to wake up. "Okay!"

Moving fast to avoid unwanted morning commentary from Miles, Jerome headed toward the bathroom, took a quick cold shower, and got dressed.

Two weeks of twelve hour days at work, then another four or five hours for Mr. Miles, and a few hours to shiver to death on the rack that he sat on... he couldn't keep living like this!

Jerome scratched the stubble on his face and

laced up his work boots. Saturday's were always a busy day in the apartments, but he'd promised the kids he'd come and get them in a week, on his Saturday off—not thinking ahead when he'd left that this Friday wasn't his pay week. His mind had been all screwed up since the night he'd left two weeks earlier. Damn. Now, he'd have to wait an additional week for a freakin' check! At least he was able to take them to the movies last Friday when he had dropped some money on Karen. Since his pockets were tight, he knew she'd never let them go with him on an off-pay week. All he could do was call her and try to work out a way to get them on pay Fridays every other week.

Hell, the last time he'd gone over there, she'd handed him an envelope from her attorney with divorce papers in it. Then, like a fool, he'd briefly glanced at them, saw that she wanted the house and everything, and signed them. What was there to argue over. The only part of it that he'd read thoroughly was the part outlining his visitation rights.

Jerome tried to stretch the knots out of his back. He rolled his shoulders and slumped forward. Where could a man with seven dollars to his name take four children? He'd even cut back on his three-dollar-plus a day smokes, when the money could be used to hit his gas tank. Thank God Mr. Miles had fed him once a day.

Jerome reached over to the box-coffee table and retrieved his wallet. He opened it with disgust,

365

passing the paltry sum of bills and taking out the folded bright yellow flyer that had been left on one of building walls. He tried to let his mind absorb the concept. Maybe he could do it, but what if the kids wanted to buy something else? What if he had to tell them no, then see the disappointment on their faces when he couldn't come through for something so little? Some Daddy. Maybe he could just swing by and get the kids for a couple of hours, then take them home. Too bad it wasn't Spring yet, where time with them in the park could offer a free option.

"Damn!" Jerome stood up and paced. He needed a cigarette and a cup of coffee. Bad. Real bad.

"Whas all da comoshun? Too early to be startin' da day cussin', boy."

Jerome paced from the small windows with bars on them to the door and back again, repeating the motion over and over, banging his fist on the door each time he neared it.

"Boy, yo' gone loco? You been messin' wit dem drugs, or somethin'?" The old man moved into the room cautiously and stared at him.

"Gotta see my kids, Mr. Miles. I promised them! But I ain't got no money to even take them to a dog-gone church flea market," he shouted and threw the flyer on the floor. "What kinda father is that? And I already prayed on it. Hell, I'm even trying to take them to a damned church!"

Mr. Miles shook his head and sat down in the chair. "You pacing like a cat is makin' me tired, boy.

Sit yo'self down, and calm yo'nerves. Don' be bangin' on ma'door no mo'neither—makes rich folks edgy hearing a lot of commoshun. I'ma make some coffee. Want some?"

"Yeah," Jerome muttered, declining to sit. He went to the window and stared out of the bars, ignoring Mr. Miles as he muttered and rose and began making his usual syrup-thick brew. He was trapped in hell. Karen must have put a curse on him.

"See, the problem wit you young folk is, y'all want ev'rything yesterday. Ain't got no patience."

Jerome didn't answer.

"How many jobs you do this week boy?" The old man had called the question from the kitchen doorway, bringing two cups of instant coffee with canned evaporated milk to the box-table.

"I don't know," Jerome said, letting his breath out in a rush as he took the mug and slurped at the muddy mixture. "I lost count. Five, six, seven a night—every night—all week—just like last week, I suppose."

"Dats a lotta hard work, boy."

"You telling me." Jerome grunted, becoming impassive as the caffeine hit his system. Maybe he would just call the kids and make some excuse until he could go to them right.

"But, you still tryin' to go see yo'kids anyway—an even a blind man can see yous tired, boy."

"Yeah, well, a man's gotta do what a man's gotta

do," Jerome grumbled between slurps of too-strong coffee. "What can I say?"

"Dats what I'm talkin' 'bout. See, I's been checkin' on ya all dese two weeks. My work-load done decreased, cause you done caught all da slack. You been a big help to me, sorry it was on account of yo' misfortchin... but, da Lord do work in mysterious ways."

"Glad to have obliged you, Sir." Jerome felt his throat get tight. Only two more weeks, he told himself. Stay cool till next pay.

"Plus, all them rich ol' widow women's been callin' for extra work—nonsensical stuff dat don' really need fixin'... on account of dat nice young man I's got in my employ... I bill 'em the sky, and dey been payin', boy. Fifty here, seventy five there... throw in a coupla hundreds... So, my side money jobs done increased on account a you, boy. Don't know what'chu been doin' to 'em, but deys all askin' fer ya by name. Don' wanna see me nor Buddy," he laughed, slapping his leg. "Never see'd nothin' like dis in all my born days!"

"Look, Sir," Jerome said growing agitated by the clear insinuation, "I go in, say hello, thank you, yes Ma'am, no Ma'am, smile, pet their teenie dogs and talk to their spoiled-rotten cats, fix their curtain rods, fluff the pillows on their sofas, look at their drains—what the hell ever—get my hat, and leave. That's all."

"Yeahup, it's yo' home trainin' dat dey love... plus

a little male attenshun." Mr. Miles stood and grinned and began walking around the apartment with his wrist bent. "Dey say, 'Oh, send that nice young man, Jerome... he holds the door, has such manners, and cleans up after he does a repair," Mr. Miles mocked, as he made his voice go up a pitch. "Gotta send them my Jerome," he chuckled, "but not today, boy. You go gits yo' kids."

The smile that Mr. Miles had coaxed onto Jerome's face vanished at the mention of his children. Jerome paced back to the window and held onto the bars as he peered out.

"I can work today, Mr. Miles. I owe you for room and board, and a hot plate every night. Plus, where am I going to take them with seven bucks?"

He felt Mr. Miles' hand on his shoulder, but didn't turn around.

"Yo' promised 'em, didn'tcha?"

"Yeah," Jerome whispered, looking out at the disappearing snow.

"A man's word is his bond," the old man countered softly, "'specially to his kids."

"I ain't no man, in this condition, Mr. Miles. Don't want to see them like this. Don't want them to see me like this. My Pop told me it would go like this."

"Dey love you, boy. You young folks is so crazy. Dey care 'bout you, not yo' money. Go see dem kids, boy."

"I'll work today, and see them when I get paid

369

next week—Friday."

He listened to Mr. Miles as he huffed away. All he wanted was for the old man to give him his job list for the day. That's all. Not for some stingy old coot to get into his business.

"Go see yo' kids, son," Mr. Miles repeated more firmly.

"Tell me the jobs. I'll knock 'em out.... maybe even hit the bar with Buddy."

Jerome refused to turn around, or speak. He'd made his decision. He'd work.

"Yous stubborn as a Georgia mule!" the old man bellowed and slapped his shoulder. "Probably what got your ass put out."

The slap on his body and the sound of paper hitting the floor made him turn around.

"Count it. It's all dere," Mr. Miles said glowering at him from the middle of the room. "Eleven hundred—even, honest-earned, American dollars. I might be a lotsa thangs, but ain't no slave master. Been blessed wit all I need, an' hits my numbers wit regularity... Cain't see no boy lose his children's belief, not over somethin' as stupid as money. Dat ain't right. Seen it once in my own boy, b'fore I buried him. It ain't right."

Jerome stared at the old man. On emotional overload, his thought processes seized his nervous system. He couldn't move.

"Go 'head, boy. Pick it up. You earned it. Dis ain't no drug money! It's the part I held back for ya, knowing that a man gotta save somethin' fer hisself, too."

Jerome bent slowly and touched the outside of the envelope, clutching it gently as though it might break. "I don't know how to thank you, Sir..." he stammered as he stood.

"You gave me hard work, security in ma buildins' and in m'sleep... knew you'd be on da case 'fore da police, if'n da druggies tried somethin'... could trus' ya... m'tenants was all happy... gave an ol' man a little comp'ny an' a few good laughs... Ain't got a son dat lived to help me," his elderly host said in a quiet voice. "You been a big help, boy. I was gittin' tired," he added with dignity, straightening his posture and issuing Jerome a salute. "You gots m'repect, young man. An' money couldna bought dat."

"Mr. Miles... you saved my life." Jerome murmured and looked down at the envelope. He couldn't say anything else. This old man, a stranger, had done more for him than his own father had done since he'd become a man. The envelope represented more than money. It was hope, and faith, and trust, and caring. It was the very beginning restoration of his belief in himself.

A silent understanding passed between the men, and Mr. Miles smiled.

"Den, go do what a man's gotta do—an' always remember, dats what'chu is, son. A man."

∽

Antoinette stared into the steam coming up from the warming tray full of hot dogs. What a week! Albeit, this one was better than the first one she'd spent in Philly, it had been a drill. Now, still tired from working, job hunting, daily visits from her father, inquiries into her business from her friends, and voice-mail battles with Brian, she had to smile pretty and look like a perfect suburban mom who'd been relocated to University City's fortress against urban reality. But, at least she did have her students. She smiled as she lined up the hundreds of individually wrapped bags of popcorn that she'd made and packed all night. Mischief crept into her mind as well-dressed-casual parents began to stream into the gym. She wondered what Tianisha would say if she'd walked into this scene? A quiet chuckle found its way up from her belly. She'd even forget about being angry with Adrienne, just to tell her sister about this.

Calmness buoyed her spirit through the fatigue as she arranged the snacks on the table. For the first time in a long while she felt good knowing that, although her students were all still on Welfare, like she was, theoretically—owing May a replacement check when Brian's money finally came—she and her girls had won many personal victories during the past two weeks.

Antoinette beamed as she began unwrapping

brownies. She had sold her natural butt off, and this time it was a product that she cared about—people. Two of her students had been placed in a Baptist church in legitimate part-time jobs, all from making their famous once-bootleg dinners. She'd gotten one of Pearline's ministers to relent and buy the food—the women would split the profits with the church, fifty-fifty. They'd done so well that the pastor had finally hired them part-time to manage the after-school snack program, and they could even bring their kids to work. Antoinette sighed with satisfaction as she arranged the cookies in a pretty display, thinking of how one of her students had cried when she'd gotten her vendor's license.

She peered over to the table of exquisite African print, hand-crafted hair bands, book bags, barrettes, small wallets, and the other miscellaneous items that her two seamstresses had given to the flea market on consignment. Antoinette filled with a mother hen's pride as she made a mental note to sell every item— even if she had to buy them herself. She'd paired up her hairdressers with Nessa, and they were doin' some heads from Ness' house! Gettin' paid. But, that darned Tianisha... she chuckled to herself, stacking cans of soda on ice. Cookie had met her match.

It was all she could do not to laugh out loud again as she thought of how Cookie had cussed and fussed about taking the girl on as a bookkeeper and typist, and how she had worn the impenetrable

Cookie down. When her fly-girl, Tianisha, had sashayed into Cookie's home office, sucked her teeth, and fired up her computer like a pro—then took a phone call, and put the client in his place, screening for Cookie like she was a Presidential Aid, Cookie had screamed and slapped her five. Yeah, she was on a roll! And she was so proud. Even her boss' mouth had dropped open when they'd spot-checked her basement classroom. All of her students were present, accounted for, placed eleven weeks ahead of schedule, and deep into lively, positive discussion.

The agency had been so impressed that, they'd told her they were going to extend her contract another twenty-hours. Now, she had a forty-hour a week job—all because her girls had seen danger coming when the Executive Director decided to do a site spot check. They'd all been there, looking studious and demur, working hard at their entrepreneurial business lessons, and were shrewd enough to ask all the right questions in front of The Gestapo. They'd saved her, and she loved them.

"Mommy, Mommy, keep my doll?"

Antoinette smiled and took the toy from Lauren, then glanced around for a place to safely stow her daughter's favorite sleeping pill. "That's why I told you to leave her at home," she said gently. "You better remember her when we leave. Mommy's got a lot on her mind," she warned.

"Don't care, don't want her no more. She's ugly."

Antoinette stood up straight and held the doll out in front of her. Something gave her pause, and she glanced around the room. "I thought that Bessie was your favorite? She's beautiful," Antoinette said softly, lowering the doll to her daughter.

Two big tears formed in Lauren's eyes, and she pushed the doll away. "She's dirty. She's brown," she whimpered, shaking her head no.

Antoinette blinked like she had been slapped. People milling at the doorway and getting food tickets had begun to head toward her table. A line was forming. But, her baby had been wounded, mortally wounding Antoinette, too.

Reaching for her child with reassurance, she held Lauren's hands and stared into her eyes, trying to send four-hundred years of history to the child via mental telepathy. "Do you think Aunt Nessa is pretty? And, Aunt Adrienne?"

"U'huh," Lauren nodded, looking back nervously to the line of impatient customers that was beginning to swell.

"Do you think Mommy is pretty?" she asked, holding her breath.

"Umhummm," her daughter nodded and smiled shyly.

"What color is Aunt Nessa and Aunt Adrienne?" she asked the child as softly as possible, ignoring the people who were beginning to filter away with impatience.

"Brown, like me and you, Mommy," the child

whispered.

"Say it loud," Antoinette commanded.

"Brown like me and you," Lauren said a little louder, but still seeming cowed.

"And aren't we beautiful?"

Lauren smiled. "Yup."

"Then whoever told you your Bessie was ugly, was ugly inside... and jealous of how pretty brown babies really are. Now, you go tell them that your damned mother said so!" she commanded from low within her throat, unable to keep the tremble from her voice.

Her child's smile widened and her shoulders went back. Lauren snatched her doll and turned on her heels, running as fast as her little legs could carry her. Her voice boomed and echoed across the gym. "My Mommy said brown is pretty and you're ugly!"

"Damn, right," Antoinette muttered. She couldn't wait to tell her students this one on Monday.

"Are we having a problem, here?" Marilyn Steet said, looking at the full-blown line before Antoinette's table. "Perhaps you need some help?"

Antoinette stopped, with a customer's hotdog in her hand. "Yes. We do have a problem, Marilyn," she said in an escalating voice, using the hotdog as a pointer.

"Well, perhaps we should get some help here to keep our customers moving and served, and you and I can talk in my office," Marilyn said nervously, eyeing the crowd.

"No," Antoinette snapped, half throwing a hot-dog at a teenager, who had thrust a ticket at her. "Let's talk here, in front of everybody—like we did on that first Monday."

The center director smiled and tried to gather up a chuckle from her gut. "Now, Mrs. Wellington, I'm sure—"

"I'm sure that you have a diversity problem here." Antoinette's gaze swept the room. "You have children at this school from every country in the world. Professors' kids from Asia, India, Africa, Latin America, Europe... interracial kids, Professionals' children from seemingly-liberal households—which was the only reason I decided to allow Lauren to come here. I thought that the rainbow would out-weigh, what I now understand to be, pseudo-liberal politics. But, one of these little arrogant, snot-nosed, brats just told my beautiful, African-American, brown baby, that her brown doll was ugly and dirty. My child just came over here to hide her favorite toy! I have a problem with that," Antoinette raged, "and I wasn't about to let that slide, because that bull would land her on a therapists' couch fifteen years from now. So these decent people," she added with a sweep of her arm, "will have to wait."

The director's face went scarlet, and her eyes darted between Antoinette and the line of food patrons. "We will most certainly address your concerns, Mrs. Wellington, we deplore intolerance at our center," she said, sounding like a press secretary. "We'll discuss this during the teacher's staff meeting."

"I am an instructor," Antoinette said evenly, "and I think it's high time that you added a little sensitivity training to your curriculum. How about that for the balance of my co-op hours?" She noted how some of the other parents and teachers smiled knowingly then looked away.

It was oddly reassuring that they also agreed, and to sense that not everyone was like the director and a few isolated parents. They just needed a voice, someone to tell it like it was—real plain.

"Oh, yes. I definitely agree," Ms. Steet said after a moment, trying to edge away from her. "We could use your insight."

"I want to run a session on not only cultural diversity, but economic diversity," Antoinette said in a calm voice as she lifted her food boycott and began to serve ticket holders.

Marilyn Steet's face looked like the blood had drained from it. "We never thought that that was an issue."

"Oh, yes," Antoinette said as she turned to offer a parent a brownie. "But, don't worry, I have some student mothers who have children within this school's age range—that qualify for State daycare support funding. I'll make sure to invite them to apply, so that we can improve the diversity of our school's community." Antoinette had to stir the punch to keep from smiling. She had hated the way Ms. Steet had emphasized the words, 'our school's community,' before. She'd have to tell Pearline about this!

Caught up in her own thoughts, Antoinette kept the food assembly line going until Lauren's happy voice broke her musing.

"Can Darlene an' her brother come over sometime and play?"

Fatigue weighed on Antoinette's shoulders. "Baby, Mommy is busy," she said without looking at her child. "Ask me later when the people go."

"But they have to go home soon," Lauren pleaded.

Wiping her hands on her apron, Antoinette looked at the two children who waved tickets at her eagerly.

"Hi," a little girl beamed. "Can we play with your little girl? My big sisters' always say I turn rope double-handed. She's little, but I can teach her while my brother holds the ends."

"Yes!" Antoinette laughed as the burnished-brown child accepted a hot dog with one hand, brandishing an old fashioned double-dutch rope in the other. "You guys play double-dutch?" she exclaimed, leaning her head back for a full-bodied laugh. "Honey, I used to burn up the cement in my day. That's all we did!"

The child's sparkling eyes opened wide. "Miss,

you'kin jump?"

"Oh, baby," Antoinette chuckled, "let me find somebody to watch this table, and if you can turn, I can jump," she challenged with one hand on her hip. "But, go easy on an old doll. Not too fast."

The imp howled with delight and tore away from her table, yelling across the gym. "Patsy, Kitty, dis lady's gonna jump!"

Antoinette's gaze followed the girl, who was trailed by a small boy and her daughter, Lauren. She laughed again as a frenzied message was relayed to two pre-teenagers, who tore off in her direction. Wow, maybe nothing had changed. Somewhere in Philly, little girls still jumped rope. Maybe little boys still played stick-ball and street hoop. Her thoughts drifted to Nessa's steps in the summertime where barbecue potato chips got eaten and hair got corn-rowed, back to the streets that got roped-off for all day block parties, and double-dutch championships reigned supreme while drill teams marched. Oh, yeah. She would give these people a lesson in cultural diversity today. Right in their own gym!

"Miss, you kin really jump?" an out-of-breath teen giggled.

"At your age?" another slightly younger one inquired.

Antoinette wanted to kiss their faces, for the expressions that came from them were so open and honest, filled with awe and a bit of out-of-fashion respect. Their eyes held her, too, for unlike her teenage students, they still had the eyes of children who hadn't seen the full horror of the world. They were still kids, even though their bodies were changing into women's forms. And, like the days gone by, they were also giving the old doll a stand-down.

She laughed as she motioned to another mother who had a slow crowd at her table.

"Can you cover for me while I show these girls, I Been Told?"

"What?" the other mother asked with confusion as she neared Antoinette's booth.

"Get out, Patsy!" the second tallest gasped. "You know, I Been Told?" she said staring at Antoinette.

Removing her apron and handing it to the other mother as she came around the oblong table, Antoinette patted her foot and snapped her fingers with a beat to cue her rope turners to her speed. "I been told when a boy kiss a girl—take a trip around the world, hcy hey, shabadooba..." she sang with a bop, "Hawaiian-eye, kick one..."

"She knows it!" the eldest exclaimed. "Oh, my God! Gimme the rope. Gimme the rope, Darlene—so we can give her a professional turn. Over there," the eldest instructed as the younger children raced ahead of her to the other side of the gym. "Away from the tables and the little kids. C'mon! Y'all's so slow! Come. On!"

"Hey! Where're you guys running off to? I. Told. You. To. Stay. Put—until I got the rest of the tickets and hung the coats up," a male voice bellowed. "Over here. Now."

The authority that boomed a bass-line from behind her, stopped Antoinette's forward progression. For a split second, she had become twelve again herself, and had heard her father. She froze and didn't move as her mind rewound and played back years of instinctual obedience. The kids.... she gasped inwardly. She had to fix this... Oh, God, she and Lauren had gotten them into trouble... It was like watching a car accident.

In a slow motion skid past her, four children came to a sliding halt at what she was sure would be the feet of a towering Thor when she turned around. She almost didn't want to see it. Thunder had rung through the gymnasium, echoing like the screech before a collision. Parents seemed to hold their breath in anticipation of the kaboom. Every kid in the place seemed to take pause, then nervously check to see whether or not it was their Thor calling, or if it was their transgression that had awakened him—appearing definitely relieved that it wasn't.

When she whirled around, her gaze collided with Jerome Henderson's.

Dumb-struck, she weaved a bit, and blinked twice. This could not be happening. Not here, of all places—where the world could see her embarrassment.

He hadn't even looked up, and she watched as he inspected his troops, reprimanded them verbally for not following orders, and recounted the dangers of not minding him. God, he looked good... and damn, he had those kids in ship-shape. They didn't even challenge him. Old school. Definitely old school.

Antoinette breathed in as she watched the other near-by children goad and manipulate parents, or fall-out in intermittent tantrums. Not in Jay's army. Oh, hell no. Antoinette chuckled to herself, then mustered up her nerve to walk over to Jerome. For the kids' sake, she told herself. A mission of mercy to save the innocent.

"It wasn't their fault," she said shyly, catching him in mid-sentence.

He lifted his face from the eldest child's and the color drained from it.

"See, Dad. She wanted to jump rope with us, we weren't bothering her. Were we, Miss?" The eldest child plea-bargained as her eyes darted nervously between the two adults.

"She wasn't a bother at all," Antoinette smiled. "I started having double-dutch flash-backs, and told the kids I was an old pro," she chuckled. "Give 'em a break, this time, Dad."

It amused her how quickly Thor had lost his thunder. Maybe she was even a little flattered. The kids picked up on his change of emotional current immediately, however. She smiled as their child-radar snapped on. Telepathy. The second eldest moved in toward her father, obviously no longer interested in the game of jump rope, but the two little one's smiled back at her—the oldest hovered between them deciding.

"You still wanna jump, Miss?" the small girl who had first approached her asked. "Is it okay, Daddy?"

Jerome cleared his throat and thrust his hands into his jeans pockets. "Look, you all go play with each other, and uh, stop worrying this poor lady to death. She was just trying to be nice," he said nervously, looking at each child with a telepathic grit. "Go 'head, go find something to do. You all have tickets for everything in here, and you can jump rope any time."

Small shoulders slumped and grudgingly walked away, her daughter following the rag-tag army that had been disbanded.

"Dag," Lauren said with disgust as she trudged behind the group.

Antoinette covered her mouth to stifle a smile. "Dag, Jay... Whatchu do to your kids? Hang-em up by their thumbs?" she said once they were out of earshot. "I wish Lauren would mind me like that."

He chuckled and shook his head, still appearing to be a little overwhelmed. "I put my bluff in early. I'm getting old, T. Can't be tangling with no teenagers," he said smiling as he watched them without looking at her. "Especially the boy in the bunch. By the time he's a teen, I'll be taking Geritol."

"I've got a while to go, but the terrible two's

never ended. At four-and-a-half, Miss Lauren is still a trip!" she chuckled, her vision following her daughter's recalcitrant form. "You have a nice bunch of kids, Jay. They're beautiful," she murmured with genuine admiration. "You're a good Dad, too. I can tell," she smiled. "Are you hungry?"

"Thanks, T. I ate, but the kids can always eat."

"Well," she sighed, "I probably should get back to my table. Parent co-opt hours."

He gave her a puzzled expression, and smiled, but didn't move. "Yeah, maybe you'd better."

She hadn't moved either.

"If your brood is hungry later on... save your money, you can bring them by. I can fry up some chicken, and throw together some potato salad. I promised to cook for Mr. Miles anyway. Are you sure you ate?" She asked again as his stomach growled.

Jerome hesitated, and looked back in the children's direction. "I dunno, T. I only have them for a few hours. Their mother would worry, might cause static if they carried the story home, anyway. But, thanks for the offer."

Why had she said that? She could have kicked herself. Stupid! Of course the man would want to spend private, quality-time with his kids, if this was his visitation weekend. Plus, everything was so fresh, and break-ups were often just temporary breathers—not the ultimate split. He was probably sleeping on a comfortable couch somewhere, drinking and having a cave-man-fest, then he'd be back home. That was Jay. Stable. Damn, she was so stupid! The kids would only take her name home, stir the pot, when all she did was fry chicken!

"You're right, Jay," she smiled, trying hard to seem cool. "Well, you all have fun. I gotta serve up some more hot dogs. Take care of yourself and those great kids of yours," she said turning quickly and hurrying to her table. She would not look at anyone as she served food. She would keep her head tucked down and her voice real low. She would stare the metal off the trays.

What had he been thinking? The woman had smiled at him, practically scooped his kids up. They seemed to really like her, and she was gonna make her prize-winning fried chicken. He was out of his mind! No, he was "missin' his mind," as Miss Hattie would say. Damn, she looked good, too, with a little sassy one who was her spittin' image. And, how in the hell was he going to walk around a gym for two hours and not look at the woman? There was nothing in there worth holding his interest, but for the sake of his kids.

He knew he should have gone to work. His Pop always said hard work would keep him out of trouble. But damn, she looked good. Trouble was drilling a hole in his brain like a jackhammer.

Depression temporarily arrested all of Jerome's thoughts.

But, then again, she had smiled at him. Then

again, she'd also offered to feed him and the kids. Humiliation crept between his shoulder blades. It would be just like Toni to feed the hungry, and take in the homeless. It was pity, a humanitarian effort, but not personal interest. Why would a fine woman, with all the education in the world, probably a good job, and a great home, plus an ex-husband who made a mint, be interested in his raggedy ass? Mr. Miles was right—he was crazy.

"Kin I help you, sir?"

He stared at the young woman with neat braids in her hair for a moment. "Naw, sis, just looking."

"Well, you been lookin' a long time," she giggled. "C'mon. It's for a good cause."

"What cause?" Jerome said with a smile as he flipped over the price tags on the kente-print book bags.

"My cause... and the school's," she laughed, handing him a matching cloth-covered calendar. "You have a bunch of kids, Mister, and they all love this stuff. C'mon, brother. I'm in school, and I need to sell this stuff. I get to keep two thirds, and the center gets to keep a third. Dey only ten dollars each. Dag."

"What school is this, where you have to sell kente book-bags?" he chuckled, admiring the young woman's work. "Tell me straight-up, and you might get a sale. This stuff is nice," he said in earnest. "My girls would love it."

"Miss T's my teacher, ask her."

Jerome looked over at Antoinette and let his gaze linger. "I might have to do that," he said in a low voice.

"So, you like my teacher, huh?" the girl asked with a soft giggle, respecting his privacy, and definitely making her sale. "I know why you do, sir. She the best... care 'bout people, got me my vendor's license outta her own pocket, cause the agency wouldn't give 'er da money. Dats why I gotta sell this stuff, to cover the cost, and pay her back two-hundred dollars, plus a hundred for fabric. Was the first time anybody ever believed in me. She gots bills, stuff going wrong in her life, man wit checks bouncin—dey almost put her baby outta this day-care. But she gave me a bizness loan anyway. First loan I ever had. That's why I am going to sell this table out today. For teach."

He never took his eyes off of Antoinette as the young woman had spoken. "You definitely have a worthy cause, Miss," he said quietly. "How much inventory did you already sell today?"

"'Bout, two hundred dollars worth. Dese people in here got money, okay. But, you all right. I'll give you a discount, brother."

He ignored the enthusiasm in the young vendor's voice as he continued to watch Antoinette while she worked at the food table. "With no discount," he said, reaching into his jacket pocket for Mr. Miles' envelope, "what can I get off of your table for a hundred dollars?"

"Dag, Mister!" the teenager said as he handed her five twenty dollar bills. "You kin git a whole buncha stuff! I can't wait to tell my crew. We did it!" she yelled, shaking her head and taking the cash.

"Then give me things that three girls... no, make it four girls, would like, and stuff for a little boy. Divvy it up even for all the kids, 'cause you know otherwise they'll fight. But, bag one of the girls' things separately, and give it to Mrs. Wellington on Monday, or the deal's off."

Today, he would be patient.

CHAPTER 23

"Ya been tossin', an' turnin', an' walkin' da floors all night, boy. Whas yo' problem? Ev'rythang went all right wit dem kids yesterday, didn't it?"

Mr. Miles shuffled into the kitchen and grunted as he began his normal routine of making terrible coffee. Jerome didn't look at the old man as he'd spoken. After he'd dropped the kids back home, he'd worked Saturday night until he couldn't stand. His body hurt, and he didn't feel like unnecessary conversation—despite his benefactor's crochety brand of kindness. Agitated, he laced up his boots from the side of the cot and scratched his face. He needed a shave. A good, hot, straight-edge razor kind like a barber could give. But it was Sunday. Just like every thing else, his timing sucked.

"You ain't answered me, boy," his elderly tormentor grumbled as he set a mug of coffee on the box for him. "Yo'babies all right?"

"Ycah, they're fine, sir," Jerome muttered as he stood and paced to the window. "They had a ball yesterday."

"Den whas yo'problem? Da ol'battle axe at home pesterin' yo'nerves?"

"Naw, she was cool," Jerome grumbled, still looking out of the window. "She was probably happy to have a few hours to herself."

"Ya miss 'er, boy?"

"Hell no," Jerome said quickly without turning around.

"Den you didn't do nothin' foolish, like give 'er all yo' money?"

"Hell no. I gave her everything I had to give already, and I told her I'd give her half of my pay check next week—plus, I had a good place to take them, thc flca market, and they came home with bags in hand, so, that kept things cool. Didn't really see her, she just put the kids on the porch, asked me what time I'd have them back, and I dropped them off at the door when I brought 'em back. The extra money you put aside for me from my jobs is so I can get myself together. I need to get a place for the kids to visit me, maybe spend the night. I have to take care of something I need, for a change," he said with sudden conviction, as he began pacing from the window to the door and back again. "I gotta get myself together, Mr. Miles."

Leslie Esdaile

"Well, dats good, boy. Least yo'ain't loss yo'-mind. But, if'n ev'rythang is so fine, and you a man wit a master plan, money in yo'pocket, an' a good job... happy children, an' done lef' a woman who make you crazy—den why you pacing my floor, walkin' a hole in da wood... flippin' an' floppin' all night? Huh?"

Jerome went back to the window and tried to keep still. Okay, so if the pacing bothered the old man, he wouldn't pace. If that would stop the investigation this morning, he could stay put in one spot until he got his job list and got out of there. He just needed to move, motion, progression, anything other than being stuck in this cage.

"See, dere you go again. Goin' def an' dumb on me, boy. Gittin' you to talk sometime, is like pullin' wisdom teeth. Might as well tell me whas on yo' min', cause yo' ain't gonna las' like dis—you gonna wear yo'self out, an' me in the process."

He had to change the subject without hurting the old man's feelings. Although he owed him a great debt of gratitude, he needed his own space. He just couldn't take it any more. "Mr. Miles, I have to start making plans to get my own place, sooner or later."

"Oh, is that all it is? Well, these things take time, son. Gotta save up, make your move when you git on solid ground. Patience," he laughed. "Hmmmph. Young folk ain't got no patience."

The old man wasn't getting it. Patience? Six

more months here and he was going to lose his mind. Jerome let his breath out slowly. They'd discuss it later. "Apartment 1A has a leak coming down from the outer drain gutters, the lady said—"

"So, now I'm da one who's crazy?" Mr. Miles chuckled, and sipped his coffee slowly. "I'ma tell you what I think, boy."

Jerome sighed and picked up his lukewarm coffee and took a deep gulp. "C'mon, Mr. Miles. Not this morning, okay?" Irritation kindled in his gut. He had to get out of there.

"See, you all evil... testy... cain't sleep... walkin' da floors like a tiger in the zoo. Ever go to the zoo, boy?"

Jerome groaned and took his coffee to the window and peered out as he drank down the nasty brown brew. "I got four kids, Mr. Miles—no offense, but I've been to the zoo more than once. Make your point."

"See, yous always in a hurry, boy. You got da pitiful look of dem big cats in the Springtime. It's gettin' to be Spring, ina month or so."

He shook his head and closed his eyes, downing the cup. This old man was going to make him lose his home training. "Can you give me the job list so I can get to work sometime today?"

"Yeahup. Boy, you like dem big cats. Now, when dey was free, dey ate whatever dey kilt—ten point buck, prime rib... lotsa thangs. When yo'see 'em in the zoo... all dey do is sniff the dog food dey give 'em and look at the old tire dey leave dat po' creature to play wit. Dey sleeps all day, or pace. Only option dey got. Den, dey hair gits all mangy lookin'— scruffy, not majestik like dey s'posed to be."

Jerome rubbed the stubble on his chin and only grunted.

"Yeah, boy, tis the livin' truth. An' dey mean as a rattlesnake. Cain't do nothin' to ya through da bars, dey know dat, but dey give ya da evil eye, somethin' fierce. Can almos' see it in dey eyes, dey sayin' 'I'ma git you one day,'" the old man said with a chuckle pointing to his head. "Da mo' people stare at 'em, an' tease 'em, da mo' dey give 'em da grit—or, go to sleep."

"Mr. Miles, I just—"

"Now, come Spring, boy, dey looks change. Dey don' sleep. Dey pace. 'Specially da big males. Dey walk to an' fro, real agitated, but dey eyes got a beggin' quality to 'em, like dey sayin' 'Please, Lord, unlock dat female next do'... jis for a little while... all I need is a little while.' An' dats da look you got, boy. Like you hurtin' pretty bad, in dat way." Mr. Miles stood and walked toward the kitchen, chuckling as he shuffled along. "I got eyes, an' wasn't born yesterday, boy. Some female done opened yo' nose as wide as Broad Street, an' she real nearby too, cause you pacin' wit an awful hungry look in yo' eye, son... was growlin' all night in yo'sleep. I gots ears, too."

He had been hunted down, trapped, and the old man's tranquilizer truth had stunned him. Damn that old man for getting into his business. His personal business!

"Look," Jerome bellowed, "I need my own space. Okay. That's what's got me pacing! I been sleeping in a basement, working like a dog... I need my own apartment," he practically stuttered as sudden rage choked his words. "Can't a man have some damned peace on a Sunday morning—Christ Almighty!"

"See. You roarin' an' carryin' on, jus' like dem big cats. Dey kick up a mighty ruckus in da Spring time. Oughtta see 'em," the old man said with a sly smile, without appearing perturbed. "Well, I ain't no zoo keeper, an' look like Spring done sprung on you mighty hard, boy. Gotcha nature all in an uproar. Must be baaaad dis time?" he laughed with a wink. "Whew, doggie!"

"Listen," Jerome said, trying to steady his voice. "I need a place, the problem is, it could be months before I can afford a security deposit."

"Uhmmm," Mr. Miles said with a wide smile. "Months is a long time when da female scent hits da air—when you kin barely stand da minutes. I know, boy. Done tol' you, I wasn't born yesterday."

"Like I was saying, sir," Jerome said, not looking at the big grin on Mr. Miles' face, and ignoring the outrageous parallel he was trying to make. "A security deposit around here, say for a cheap two bedroom apartment, would maybe be five-hundred a month—at least. So, for first month, last month, and current month, that's fifteen hundred. Then to turn on gas, electric, and telephone... plus I gotta furnish it—"

"—Answer me this, boy. Why you gotta be in dis neighborhood? Dats a long ride up ta Mount Airy where yo' kids is. Why cain't you jus' go git you a room somewhere's mo' affordable, no how? Unless you got your nose pressed up to the bars of da cage next do.' She 'round here, ain't she?"

This old man was really getting on his nerves

"This doesn't have anything to do with a woman," Jerome hedged defensively. He really hadn't thought about it. Well, maybe he had a little, but no woman was going to force him to make any major decisions ever again. Especially not the very unavailable one around the corner and an elevator ride up in the same building. After a pause, he paced to the door, then back to the window. "I need a second bedroom so I can put the kids in bunk beds, and have a decent place for them to sleep—so they can stay with me for a whole weekend. Plus, I need a room for myself."

"Dat, you do, boy," the old man chuckled with a wink. "Well, if you so predetermin'd, den, you needs a plan."

"I know," Jerome muttered. "It'll be months..."

"Months is gonna make us both crazy," Mr. Miles sighed with smile. "You look like you need somethin' as soon as humanly possible."

"No, lie."

"She purty, ain't she?"

"Yeah," Jerome conceded.

"See, I ain't crazy. Now, lemme give ya some advice, since we bein' honest."

"Oh, so now you're gonna give me some advice, like you haven't been already," Jerome chuckled, still looking out of the window.

"Don' sass me, boy," Mr. Miles said peevishly, then chuckled. "Only reason I'ma have mercy on ya, is cause ya ain't in yo'right mine. But, you gotta use yo' brain. Da big head, boy, not da little one."

A deep chuckle came up from Jerome's insides and he squelched it with a swallow. "Yes, sir. But, I've heard about the birds and the bees."

"Well," Mr. Miles scoffed, whipping himself up into his usual tizzy. "By da looks of thangs, you got four kids—which means to my mine, dat you got a powerful predilickshun for da female species. An' dis ain't da era to be goin' into combat wit yo'guns blazin' an' no helmet."

Jerome couldn't help but laugh, and he let go of the chuckle that he'd already swallowed down twice. "Look, I haven't even taken her out anywhere, yet—not that she'd even go. She's not that kind of sister to just take up with a man with pending paperwork and a long story. So, I just want to get settled, maybe take her out once or twice. Let her know—"

"—Stop lyin' on Sunday mornin', boy!" Mr. Miles laughed. "You talkin' 'bout movin' out, gettin' a place where she kin lay her head, an' where you can breathe in 'er face. Now, les' be honest."

"No, for real—"

"For real, you got it bad. You talkin' dinner, prob'ly flowers, an' courtin' a woman. You making nestin' plans. Wanna show her you a good man, takes care of yo' kids and can take care a her too. Wanna git yo'self another ball an' chain, is what you anglin' fer, boy."

He paused and looked at the old man. Mr. Miles had him. "I asked her once, and she said no. That's how I wound up in the service."

"Lord have mercy! How long you been carryin' a torch, boy?"

"Twenty years," he said quietly looking down.

"Good golly, Miss Molly, boy! A torch like dat'll burn a hole through ya soul!" Mr. Miles stood and paced. "Den how'dchu wind up wit... aw, it don't matter, boy. You wasn't in yo' right mine. I hates domestic mess!"

"If I could just let her know..."

"Look," Mr. Miles said, pacing in acute agitation. "Dis what we gonna do. Firs', Ima ax dem ol' rich ladies, an' my minister, who got a duplex 'round here. See—"

"No, sir, I gotta do this on my own."

"Boy, stop talkin' stupid! Pride goeth before a fall. Now, since you done made a good impresshun, an you gonna be still workin' wit me—so's I kin keep my eye on ya, I'ma git somebody to have mercy, an' relent. Letcha move in wit no secuirty depos—"

"No way. I can't let you—"

"What'chu gonna do is lissen fer once, boy. Don' sass me now, while I'm thinkin.'" The old man glowered and folded his arms across his chest high to avoid his belly. "Now. Once we gits you in, you pay the first month. Yo' hide, and hard work'll be da security deposit."

Jerome sat down on the cot and stared up at Mr. Miles. What could he say, but thank you?

"Den, you go gets yo'utilities turnt on. Dis way leaves you wit some money in yo'pocket fer courtin'."

"But, sir, I have to still give you something for room and board... and I can't furnish—"

"See, pride. Done tol' you, ya already paid me." Mr. Miles shook his head and leaned against the wall. "Impatience too, 'cause I wasn't finished m'thought."

"Okay. I'm sorry. Go ahead, 'cause your mind is working better than mine at this point," Jerome conceded honestly. "I can't even think right now."

"Well, least yous finally truthful, boy. Dats what I like about 'cha. Okay," the old man grunted as he pushed away from the wall. "Now, you ain't purticular 'bout used furniture, is you?"

"No. Beggars can't be choosy. But even used furniture... after I cut on the utilities, pay out the first month, take care of my car note and Karen—"

"Is free a good 'nough price?"

Stunned, Jerome stood and began pacing.

"Not illegal, boy. Free. Lotsa rich folks throw stuff out, an' I git it before da trash men."

"I don't know..."

"It'a be nice stuff. Nice enough for a girl wit a pure heart. Plenty antiques too... Like, take the old lady up in fourteen. She got a mahogany dresser with cedar lining dats been in storage here for two years. She don' wan' her gran'ma's furniture, jus' cuz it's scuffed an' don't match her daycor—or fit in a particula' space. Tol' me to jus' throw it out. But, old Milesy," he chuckled, pointing at his temple, "know quality when he see it. Like what I seed in you, boy."

Jerome fastened his gaze to the man who was rebuilding his life and his hopes. Ironic that his angel of mercy would be disguised in a funky tee shirt that had grimy liquor stains and coffee on it.

"No lie. Beds is easy to git, long as you can haul 'em—but chu gotta build the frame. You good witcha hands, any way. An' I bet if I put a whisper in the right ear, dem old ladies dat love you so much be given me cleaned and folded sheets, towels, and pilla cases. Dey be sending plants, and pies yo' way—"

"No!" Jerome shouted, pacing toward the window. He could not afford to have Toni get wind of this. Ever. It would be like Welfare. She'd know that he had to beg for rags of linen. Never.

"Hmmmm," the old man said circling him and issuing a sly smile. "Struck a nerve..." he muttered, following behind Jerome who had turned away and headed toward the kitchen to wash out his coffee mug. "Will sleep on an old man's stained sheets, nasty ol' mattress... eat off a tin pie plate all week, but won't take custom sheets and towels from da rich. Don' want dey dishes... dey good heavy drapes..."

"You can't mention my name," Jerome said as panic made his motions jerky. He almost dropped the cup in the sink as the soap foamed over his hands.

"You usin' too much soap," Mr. Miles observed calmly.

"Sorry 'bout that," Jerome muttered.

"She in da next cage, ain't she? In dis buildin'?"

Jerome didn't respond as he brushed past Mr. Miles and grabbed his jacket. He needed air.

"Slow down, slow down, boy. Get ratshunal. Now, I can gits dese thangs for my long loss nephew. I can let it ride on ol' Milesy reputatshun, alone. Don' have to drag yo'name in it. In fact, I think dats what I'ma do, since you all panickin, an' what not."

Jerome relaxed and put on his jacket slowly.

"Now, you need this stuff, boy. An' she probably would 'preciate it. Cain't serve 'er wine an' roses on no tin plate," Mr. Miles said with conviction as he scratched the white, two-day-old-stubble on his cheek. "I'll gits you some crystal, china plates, an' maybe flatware."

Transfixed, Jerome stood there and stared at his

fairy Godfather.

"Caint' woo no thoroughbred like that."

"That's what Buddy always called her," Jerome said quietly.

"See, dats why ya boy cain't git out da house. He's an accompliss, an' you done got his ass locked up at home till the dus' settle."

"Yeah," Jerome chuckled. "That's probably why all this work has fallen on us."

"Think about it," Mr. Miles said with a smile. "She cain't lay her pretty head on no dirty mattress. No..." he said walking over to Jerome, and placing a supportive arm around his shoulders. "You got to gentle her, boy... if she a thoroughbred... and I think I know which one she might be. No... that one's special... Cain't just slap a harness on her, or whup her to mount her. She gotta be cooed to, gotta be called to with a soft click of yo' tongue," he whispered, issuing a soft ticking sound from the back of his dental plate. "Gotta put a little suga in yo' hand, an call her to ya, boy. An' at first, her ears gonna be up, her eyes dartin' all 'round, nostrils flared— smellin fer deceit an' danger... specially if she got a foal nearby... she might even rare up on ya once a twice—to test ya... jus' stay steady. Hold ya ground. Don' rush 'er, don' get impatient, boy. Dats da mark of a rank amature. Jus' keep callin' her low an' soft. She'll come," he laughed with a wink. "Den when she let cha know it's all right to ride her—climb up slow, an' don't ride her too hard. Trot her. Let her pace you. If you a good rider, she'll run like the wind fer ya when you get up dere—an won't nobody else be able to do nothin' wit her, or be her jockey. She'll die fightin' 'em. Thoroughbreds is loyal." Mr. Miles slapped his back and went toward the kitchen. "Be Spring before ya know it," he yelled through the archway. "Gotta get yo' stable in order—first class. Patience, son."

No one, no man, had ever talked to him like that in his life. No one had ever helped him so much, with so little of their own, or had offered him such credible words of wisdom. If his own father had just taken the time to hear what he hadn't been able to say... Jerome made a mental note to always be there for his son. If he didn't do anything else in the world, he would tell his son this secret.

CHAPTER 24

S he had asked the man, and his children, to dinner! Antoinette shook her head as she scraped
garbage from the Sunday dishes into the disposal.
At least Mr. Miles had seemed to want the platter of
chicken she'd fixed for him! No pride. She'd just
seen Jay's face, the way he handled himself, fell in
love with the children, and she'd been off to the
races. Insane. But the way their little faces had lit
up, and the way Lauren took to them so well, and
the way he'd looked at her, like she was a piece of
Pearline's cobbler...

"Stop it," she whispered to herself. She had
work to do. For starters, she had to get ready for
Monday, laundry to finish up, and a couple of calls
to make now that Lauren was in bed. She definitely had to catch up with Francis; it had been almost

two weeks since she'd seen her at the conference, and they'd kept missing each other. Adrienne could wait.

"Next weekend, Brian had better not be late picking up his child again," she threatened towards the sink as she watched the garbage shred and disappear in the disposal—or he'd be ground meat! Yeah, she told herself, stay busy keep moving.

Antoinette sprinkled some dishwasher detergent in the receptacle, and slammed the door, then flipped the switch. The steady drone of the gears engaging was a comfort, something like a heartbeat. She glanced at her briefcase as she moved into the living room and sat down on the couch. There was no need to review her student files, she knew them all by first name, and better than any forms could tell her. She wanted to call Val so bad, just to share this special news about seeing Jay today, but her confidant had made her position clear. Grief renewed itself, but with much less force. Things had changed. Even Tracey was unreachable, since Scoop answered the phone these days like a pit-bull. She'd already blown a twenty-dollar instant calling card between trying to reach her sister and Francis.

Adrienne wouldn't have understood the impact of her story about seeing Jerome anyway, and Francis' message on her machine even sounded tired and harried. Cookie had been ripping and tearing with clients since the conference, and even they hadn't talked. Pearline had a cold and sounded tired too;

she hadn't even gone to church. That left Antoinette to her own counsel.

Be still, she told herself. Let it go. Just sit down and read the paper for enjoyment, maybe. She flipped on the television set and surfed the stations with disinterest. For the first time in as long as she could remember, there was nothing to do. She'd even talked to Brian earlier in the week and had gotten the money problem straight, but not without having to get his mother to intervene.

It had taken her a full week of screaming arguments on the telephone to get him to finally cough up her childcare money for the current month so she could repay May. "Yeah," Antoinette chuckled. Okay, maybe it was a low blow when she'd pulled out the heavy guns and called his mom. But it was effective. The pure shame over having his mother involved in his child support arrangements had somehow worked in her and Lauren's favor, and had probably been what made Brian give up the following month's tuition as well. Then, like a crazy person, she spent her first paycheck on buying one of her students a vendor's license for the church fair. Sure, the two-hundred bucks had set her back, she reasoned, but it was well worth it in spirit. She just hoped that the bill collectors shared her same spirit of charitable giving, because they would have to wait until her student paid her back.. "It takes a whole village..." Antoinette murmured. "That's what they don't get."

Antoinette shut off the set and listened to the dishwasher. Music would only make her sad from the memories, and she just wanted to be numb. She couldn't even stay mad at Brian.

Sure, it had galled her that the check had bounced, and yes, she'd left several threatening messages, and hollered at him like a banshee—with May present for theatrical effect, but, after he'd told her about the IRS, what could she say? He'd been the one without a tax shelter and a solid income when he left the house first, so, the tax man cometh and the tax man taketh away. He had to pay them before they garnished his entire check, or possible made him lose his job from their inquiries—which would be problematic for everyone concerned. Ironic. They were divorced, but inextricably linked through Lauren—which meant their families and finances would be indefinitely interwoven. That's what people could never seem to understand about why divorce was so hard. Rarely was it a final burial.

Well, at least she'd definitely satisfied May by allowing her to be a part of the whole drama. Antoinette laughed, and laid her head back on the sofa and closed her eyes. May as a trip—like a Terrier, the way she'd defended her. On the plus side, it had taken the heat off, and it seemed to bring them a little closer together. Maybe The Lord did work in mysterious ways, she thought, still chuckling. People weren't all that evolved, and were probably fooling themselves to think that they were, she noted. Each of them had a likeness to some other creature. The past weeks had definitely shown her a primal side of everyone she knew—especially within herself. She wondered what animal incarnation she most resembled? Brian probably thought she was a saber-toothed-tiger. Okay, so she'd apologize later to Brian—much later. But, what did Jay see her as? Anything but an Orca, she prayed—especially when he seemed to be a cross between panther at times, eagle the other.

It had been a full work week, and a fuller weekend, but as weary as her body was she didn't feel sleepy. She had found that weird fourth dimension between physical fatigue and mental alertness. Or, maybe it had found her. One thing was for sure, she had to pull her act together to meet her students. They took every ounce of mental juice from her brain, and standing all day was no joke. Now her students were even pushing her to get her own business license.

Maybe she would take them on a field trip next week and go through her own start-up process with them in tow. Maybe she could even get the agency to spring for some ledgers so that she could demonstrate the process of starting and keeping business records. Yeah, that was a good and practical use of their time, hers too. Tianisha, her star, could lead the discussion—she'd love it, and she had the wherewithal to make the others absorb the concepts. The only problem was that, she didn't have a clue about what kind of business she could start with no bucks, and that would cover her level of expenses. In an odd way, she realized, they were in a better position—because they weren't in the incredible debt that she was in. Because they didn't have anything to start with, the climb up and out was different than hers—which required digging out from underneath the mountain before she could even begin to climb it.

The chime at her door made her go still. Jerome knew where she lived... the only problem was that Lauren was home. No, she told herself as she paced to the door, you cannot sleep with this man. Not with Lauren in the house—or for any reason! Don't even allow yourself to consider the possibility! Antoinette inwardly chided. He's still married, and only temporarily separated. Fussing with her sweater as she walked, she briefly glanced in the mirror and smoothed her hair back. Maybe he'd stopped by to see about the pipes? Just a follow up call, she wondered, giving in to the sheer excitement of an opportunity to look at him again. Hoping that she was wrong, and that her late visitor might want more than coffee and cobbler, she unlocked the door quickly, and let out a disappointed sigh when May and her father greeted her.

"Tell me what happened to the floors?" May said abruptly, entering the condo without a hello.

Her father bent and kissed her forehead. "Heard you had a little problem, suga. Why didn't you call

Daddy?"

Antoinette looked at her father then back to May. At least they'd waited without using the key to get in this time, she noted.

"You might as well tell us, because the maintenance people sent over a trouble report about the unit," May said with one hand on her hip and waving a piece of paper before her. "Thank God that Mr. Miles sent this to us, or we might have never known."

"I could have fixed anything that went wrong," her father said in a too-chipper voice, seeming to ignore May while trying to counteract her peevishness. "That's my job, to serve and protect."

"It was just a problem with the refrigerator. They sent a man to fix it, and I called the refrigerator repair man over to fix the ice maker. It's been handled. I didn't see a need to wake up your household at five-o'clock in the morning when it happened."

May cast her gaze around the condo, then left the father and daughter team to inspect her floors. "Did you polish the floors to protect the finish after you got the water up?" Sashaying over to the refrigerator, she flung open both doors to check for herself.

"Yes," Antoinette said evenly, not feeling like launching an argument. All she wanted was peace.

"Of course she did, May," Matt Reeves said with annoyance, inspecting the floors and trying to divert

May from Antoinette's refrigerator. "Look at the shine on 'em. They ain't hurt. The girl did a good job."

Antoinette ignored the evil-eye glare that May cast in her father's direction.

"Well, I'm glad you took care of it, and when are you going to stop making this cholesterol-ridden food? Fried chicken and potato salad, Antoinette? You don't need that," she chided with annoyance as she strode into the living room, and flipped over the edges of Antoinette's oriental rug. "Mr. Miles told us that you'd fixed it for him, so I can only guess that the rest of it is in here." Appearing satisfied that no damage had happened to the wood, she moved to the sofa and sat down, folding her hands in her lap.

"Most of the chicken and potato salad was for Lauren, and, Mr. Miles, the nice man who responded to the call and sent out one of his men at that crazy time in the morning." Antoinette stared at the woman who had once again tried to make her feel like an incompetent child. One day, she was gonna cuss May out, for sure!

"That's right, baby," her father said in a pleasant tone, moving to the door to signal to May that it was time to leave. "Gotta take care of those who take care of you. Your Momma raised you right, darlin.'"

He issued a private wink at Antoinette that made her smile, then walked back up the steps in May's direction to collect her from the sofa. Her father wasn't oblivious. Something was again

411

changing, and perhaps May had gone too far during her brief reign as queen?

"Oh, May," Antoinette almost sang, encouraged by the unspoken telepathy with her father, "you need to call before you come by. I could have told you this over the phone. I was expecting company."

When May's mouth flew open, her father belly-laughed in earnest. This time he didn't try to hide his amusement in the least.

"Well, if you would stop trying to keep—"

"Told you May, let it go," Matt chuckled. "The girl is grown. Mind your damned business and leave her be—don't she look all purty with her hair fixed in a sharp pony tail with her make-up on?" Refusing to let May get started, he ushered her by the elbow toward the door, with May fussing all the way. "Keep hope alive, like my man Jesse says!" her father laughed over May's protests while turning the locks with one hand, "and get some rest, suga. Love you. Bye!"

Antoinette had to laugh as she closed the door behind them, watching May pitch a hissey-fit all the way down the hall. Tonight she had won, and her father had stood up for her and taken back some of his household. Icing on the cake would have been if Jerome Henderson had come by—even if just for a little coffee and conversation. It had been so long since she'd been on a date, or in interesting male company.

"Give it up and go to bed, fool," she whispered

to herself in the quiet space, pushing herself away from the door, then dousing all the lights and activating the alarm. She chuckled in despair as she went into her bedroom and thought about how she'd prayed for peace.

Pearline had told her to be careful of what she prayed for, because she just might get it. Tonight she wondered if God would be offended if she prayed for a man like Jerome?

ভিঙ্

"Ooooh, Miss Toni, we heard all about it. Now you gotta tell us!" Tianisha cried out as she approached her classroom door. "C'mon, Teach, open da door!"

Confusion made Antoinette hesitate as the group buzzed with indecipherable winks, glances, and giggles, she turned the locks. Mondays always came too soon. Whipping winds and serious chill factor had made her hurry to find out what all the ruckus was about inside. She had barely gotten her coat off, as her students pulled her to the table and made her sit on the edge of it.

"Okay, Teach. Delcetta done tol' us, so give up the tapes!" Tianisha laughed with a wide grin.

"I don't know what—"

"Here," Delcetta laughed, thrusting a paper bag in her hand. "I couldn't tell you at the church thing, 'cause so many people and kids was around. Check it out," she urged, not being able to wait for Antoinette to open the bag. "You like it?"

Delcetta dumped the contents of the bag in Antoinette's lap and sat down.

"These are beautiful Delcetta, but you don't have to give me gifts, this is eating into your profit margin—"

"Tol' y'all Miss T don' want'chall in her bizness," T'quneal quipped with a wide grin. "She see us all week. Weekends oughta be hers—for her an' her new man."

"Wait a minute," Antoinette said carefully placing the braided cloth bracelets, hair ornaments, and school paraphernalia on the table. "You all need to take it from the top. I'm missing something."

"See," Tianisha laughed, slapping the table and putting her head down, "she gonna do us like we do her when we don' want to answer a question. Play dumb. Okay—we outta ya bizness."

"No. For real. For real," Antoinette said giggling against her own better judgment. "I don't know what—"

"See, she even gotta laugh herself," Yolanda giggled.

"I'm laughing because you all are making me laugh. Somebody please explain how Delcetta giving me some of her gift table stuff—"

"Well, I saw him, Miss Toni. I was there, workin' the table, remember? And he was fine, y'all!"

Antoinette blushed and looked down. Delcetta had obviously seen her talking to Jerome, probably longer than she should have. But damn, they had some serious ESP going if they'd read her thoughts.

"Yeah, well... He is sort of cute. But—"

"Cute ain't even the word! Y'all shoulda seen the way he looked at her," Delcetta exclaimed, riveting the attention of the group like an expert witness. "The brother had it bad. Dropped a hundred on my table for all the kids—hers too. Check it out. Just cause I told him she was my teacher, y'all!"

"What?" Antoinette whispered.

"Get out!" Tianisha screamed.

A round of high-five's swept around the table, along with hearty hoots.

"See, that's handlin' some thangs, Teach. Dats what I wanna learn dis morning, how to have two men taking care of one kid. You all dat, an' a bag of chips!" Tianisha laughed as she slapped Delcetta five again.

Antoinette was horrified. Her class was out of control. And everything she had tried to teach in the weeks before was being washed away by a specter of a man. "Hold it ladies! Hold it, ladies. It's not like that," she interjected. "He's just an old friend."

"You think we stupid, Miss Toni," Delcetta said as she smiled and folded her arms. "Do old friends just drop a C-note on the mention of somebody's name?"

"Well, no," Antoinette stammered. "But, I haven't seen him in like fifteen or twenty years..."

"Ooooooh, girl!' Tianisha whooped, shaking her head with admiration. "What did you do to that man to keep his nose open for twenty years?"

Antoinette chuckled. "The question is, what did he do to me."

The group broke out into pandemonium again, and she had to laugh.

"Okay, okay," she said. "Here's the scoop. I was fall-down-on-your-knees-and-smack-your-momma-crazy about that man."

"All right, y'all, she droppin' knowledge. Shut up, and let Teach tell it," Tianisha commanded, quelling the lingering howls of laughter. "Dis is gonna be good, y'all."

"Yeah, I was fifteen," Antoinette said in a distant voice, reliving the past out loud the way she had needed to for so long.

"Fifteen?" Delcetta gasped with astonishment, "Dag. You sound like one of us."

"I was," Antoinette said plainly. "My people could have thrown me out, and I would have walked to California for that man."

"Den, what happened?" Tianisha nearly whispered. "How old was he?"

"Eighteen, or nineteen," Antoinette sighed. "With the biggest afro... tall, fine... and that voice...y'all. Help me."

"She still got it bad," Fayletta giggled.

"Girl, you would too," Delcetta said, defending her. "He's a slim-goodie, and makes some purty kids. Seen 'em all. And sound like a late night, love hour DJ, y'all!"

"Stop, you hurtin' us, Del," Karim teased. "Let Teach tell the story."

"Okay. All right," Antoinette sighed. "We broke up."

"Wait. Uh, uh. There's a whole buncha story between part A and part B," Tianisha chuckled. "We got all day."

"Now, see," Antoinette laughed and stood up to walk around, "y'all are in my bizness."

"You can't hang half your drawers out, then say, 'scuze me, never mind. Uh, uh," Karim protested. "Please, Miss T, don't do us like dat!"

Antoinette sighed and walked back to the table edge and picked at the splintered wood. "Couldn't get enough of each other..."

"Wait. In your time... y'all got busy?" Tianisha's expression held unabashed shock

Antoinette laughed as she stared at the girl. All she could do was shake her head. "Even in my time of the horse and buggy, young people were making love."

A collective gasp went through her group.

"Did your mother know? I mean, you don't seem like..." Darlette's voice trailed off.

"But, you only got a four-year-old," Rashina queried as her brow knitted. "He leave you 'cause you had an abortion?"

Again, something grabbed hold of Antoinette and made her know that this crazy, insane, and deeply personal issue offered a teaching moment. She hesitated, feeling her way into its entrance, deciding which caverns she would explore, which stalactite she would pass. As the group leaned toward her and each woman-child held their breath, she found a tiny point of illumination in the dark.

"He respected me," she said as plainly as she could. "He never called me out of my name. And the first time he took me, he found a gentle way, a private way, and I never heard it in the street. He was also responsible, every time—so that neither of us had to ever worry about having a baby, or an abortion. He told me that we had time to start a family after we'd reached our dreams. He told me all of that while he held me in his arms. Respect, ladies. That's what he had. And, he was a real man—an officer and a gentleman from 'round the way, at eighteen."

Unshed tears made her stop speaking. Her class hadn't uttered a word, and she could see their eyes shining as they wiped at their own. In that moment, she knew she had entered the dark place that gets buried under layers of subsequent men, hang-ups, and life, the place that lies deep within the core of every woman's heart. The first time. The most important time. A time that could decide a lifetime, because it was the tender layer that must be solid for self respect to grow upon.

"And that's why I left my husband..." she said in a far away voice, finally understanding, "because he didn't respect me," she whispered. "And once you know true respect, you can never tolerate anything less." It all had become so clear.

"But, your Moms... she let y'all?" Tianisha looked confused. "You don't seem to come from people like, who would like... You know what I mean, Miss T?"

"Yeah, I do," Antoinette said, scavenging her mind, and pausing to find an answer to her student's very important question. She had to get this right. They were all mothers, and would have to know when their time came.

"You know, ladies..." she said drifting with her mother's voice in her mind, "she respected me too. And I respected her. Pearline was right. It all starts with respect."

"I'on't understand, Miss T," Delcetta said quietly, "but y'all did it, right?"

"Yeah... but, a lot of things came first," Antoinette admitted, recalling her youth. "Like, he came by and met my parents, and sat with my Mom in the kitchen. Would bring her ice cream, and abided by her house rules. I was the wild one who would always want to break curfew. But, if my mother said to be home by eleven, I was home by ten fifty-nine, if I was out with Jay. He was adamant about me respecting my mother and father's home."

Antoinette stood up and walked, as she threw her head back and closed her eyes. "Aw, ladies, I don't know if I can go through this, this morning."

"You had a really nice family, seem like," Tianisha said as she swallowed hard. "My Momma been callin' me a bitch since the day I was born."

Her student's voice rang in her ears, and pierced a maternal center that moved her into action. No counseling degree was necessary to tell her that a baby was in pain.

Almost running, she hastened over to Tianisha and held the young girl in her arms. "Oh, honey, no mother is supposed to call her child out of her name—like bitch, slut, or stupid, or filthy, or dumb." Antoinette rocked the sobbing teenager as though she were Lauren, crushing her face to her breast as the woman-child clung to her waist.

"This is the stuff that cuts to the bone and stays in your heart forever. Remember this pain when you raise your children and never call your kids out of name. If you don't learn nothin' else from me, please hear this—they lied when they said sticks and stones can break your bones but words will never hurt you."

"I know," her student whispered through thick mucous. "You can't take some things back once said."

"True dat," another student whispered from behind. "Didn't your Mom and Pop ever call you more than your name?"

"My mother, and my father, never did. We didn't have much money, ladies," Antoinette whispered, trying to make some sense out of all the chaos in their world, "but we had respect, and fun, and peace, and laughs, and dinners together, and kids wall-to-wall to party in the basement. My father never put his hands on us, even though he mightta been angry, or had to fuss. But, beat on us, for real? Call us bitches? Never. And that wonderful old man worked like a damned dog to keep a little roof over our heads. Maybe that's why I could never stay with a man who respected me less than my own father did. Don't you want to give that gift to your children? Don't you see that, if you let yourself be disrespected, then you are robbing your children of their rightful inheritance?"

Delcetta burst out into a sob as Karim rocked her. "My Daddy did it all to me... and all my Momma's boyfriends did too," she whispered as she wept quietly.

Yolanda and T'quneal rocked silently, as Fayletta covered her head with her arms and wailed openly. What was happening in her class? In her basement on Fifty-Sixth Street? Heaven help her. She'd tapped a vein and didn't know how to seal it.

"I never knew my daddy," Rashina said in a numb voice. "My mother drank herself to death and left eight of us. I learned about men in Foster Care."

"I never knew mine neither," Kisha whispered. "I learned in the street. Initiation style, and the whole gang talked 'bout me so bad, I quit goin' to school."

"What should we tell our kids, Miss T, when ain't nobody told us?" Darlette sniffed. "All I know is what I seen, an a lady like you don' wanna know what you kin see as a chile, Miss Toni. So don't even ask me. Hear?"

"I do hear you, Darlette," Antoinette murmured, still rocking Tianisha. "More importantly, I feel you in my soul, girls. Like you my own."

Darlette covered her face with her hands and wept. "You love us, Miss Toni, don'cha? 'Cause you crying real tears. My own mother never gave a damn... an' you down here, tellin' us da truth in a basement. Dats all I ever wanted was for somebody to hear me!"

"C'mon, let it out, baby. We going to church today—in the most humble abode we gather." Antoinette sniffed as she left Tianisha and made her way to Darlette who had begun to scream.

The others moved to Darlette's side in unison, and a tangle of arms wrapped around the stricken girl—patting her, rubbing her back, touching her hair... Hands that reached through and past their own pain... Hands that gave love and absorbed it... Hands that knew how to give and mother and make things... Women's hands lifted a soul that was drowning, to bring it safely ashore... Hands trying to fight the odds, with nothing but hope and faith and love... Hands reached out, threw a branch, and saved a life. Today, she was a witness.

As the emotions quelled and a roll of toilete tissue got passed around the table, the group let out a collective sigh. They all looked weary, drawn, and much, much older. Antoinette shook the tension out of her hands and arms, allowing her head to fall back.

"Well, we got in your bizness, Miss Toni, an' you sho' got in ours. Damn, Teach," Tianisha chuckled, breaking the tension as she blew her nose hard and theatrically.

Her levity rippled through their small pond, and was a much-needed relief after the storm of emotions they'd just been through.

Antoinette chuckled and let out a sigh. "I sure didn't expect this today, y'all."

"Me neither," Delcetta chuckled and wiped her eyes. "Whew."

"But, you still didn't answer about how your mother acted when she found out," Darlette pressed, wiping her nose and turning the tissue over and over. "Did she put you out?"

"Ain't you had enough, gurl?" Tianisha said indignantly. "The poor woman done tol' you her life story, an' you still ain't got enough. Damn!"

"No. It's all right, Tianisha," Antoinette rushed in, "She's got a point." Letting out a long breath, she steadied herself, before they'd all have to rock her this time. "It's hard to talk about my mother. She died, and she was my best friend."

"You don't have to," Delcetta said in a soothing

voice, "Miss Toni, you got good memories, prob'ly the kind dat make you cry when you think back. Things we all gots to remember, should be forgot. But not you. Don' make her go there, Darlette."

Tears formed and streamed down Antoinette's face, and Delcetta stood up and walked to her side.

"No. We gotta go there, baby. Sit down, and thank you. I'm fine. Now, y'all, I'm gonna cry, can't help it. But, I'ma tell you about an angel who is still with me today."

Delcetta went back to her seat, appearing unsure but following instructions. Again, the group seemed like it didn't breathe.

"She was my friend in stages. When I was little, she would kick my butt and love me rotten—just like my grandmothers did. But as I started becoming a young girl, she made me do chores, learn things. That was our agreement. If I got good grades, and did her list of chores, I could go out. Little by little she eased up. She was a mother-friend, not a girlfriend—and she conducted herself like a lady. So, there was never any confusion about what she was, or who she was."

Antoinette paused and looked at the group. "Do you know what I mean?"

They all nodded, and Tianisha spoke up first.

"Like, she wasn't trying to dress like you, or hang with your boyfriends and your girls... like, your mom was the way my grandmother was. She would talk to you, joke with you, but she wasn't trying to be like you."

"Yeah, like somma my teachers be acting like dey so down. Don't even look like a teacher. Can't respect dat," Wynette said with conviction, "Nope. Dat don't go."

"Right," Antoinette said, scanning their faces. "So, my mother didn't conduct her business—and at thirty-seven, I still don't know what that was to this day—in front of us. Those mysteries went to her grave with her, " Antoinette chuckled as the group appeared stunned by her age, thus elder states-woman-ship.

"For real?" Tianisha seemed genuinely shocked.

"For real, for real," Antoinette said firmly. "Some things a child doesn't need to see, I believe. Maybe that's old-school, but every one of you has been wounded by seeing things that you didn't need to. Right?"

When they all nodded she pressed on. "Okay, so I had come to respect her before we became friends. I didn't go in her dresser, or her purse, or call her what she'd never called me. And in return, when my period came on, she never went in my dresser, searched through my things, or snooped looking for what she didn't want to see."

"No way...." Kisha said, her eyes widening. "She didn't practically strip search you when you came home from being out?"

"No," Antoinette said, gaining confidence. "Not because she was blind, or stupid. She had laid a foundation and believed in it. Look," she said, standing and walking again, "my mother had already set the precedent for the types of boys she would allow in her home. The ones she liked, she fed, the ones she didn't—she'd be pleasant to, but my curfew went back by two hours, my workload went up, and all done with a smile. She was shrewd, discrete, knowing that as a hormonal teenager, if she just went off, I'd go off too—and probably do something stupid."

The group slapped a round of high-fives as they muttered their agreement in assent.

"So, she kept watch by opening her home to well-controlled parties," Antoinette chuckled. "How much can go on with six strapping uncles at the kitchen table, and your mother buzzing through every five minutes with more fried chicken?"

They all laughed.

"Yeah at that age, the boys wanted food as much as drawers—so she fed 'em. Investment protection. And then, she'd cull the wheat from the chaff with a blade so sharp that those young boys didn't know they'd been cut—just like she'd had a straight-edge," Antoinette laughed, mocking a slash across her throat with her fingers. "Gone. Next. And, I thought it was my decision, so I didn't rebel. The old doll was a smooth operator."

Her class whooped and hollered.

"Yeah, y'all," Antoinette laughed, "and after one had bit the dust, I'd tell her the whole story! She'd sit there sewing and acting like she wasn't listening, and she'd say, 'Yeah, baby, now that's a shame... I never liked him, anyway, truthfully,' and her problem was solved, by me."

Tianisha just shook her head and roared with laughter. "Damn, that is too smooth."

"No flare-ups, cussin' 'bout what was going to go on in her house. Oh, no," Antoinette chuckled as she walked. "If you did something wild, my mother would take off her glasses and look at you like you had lost your ever-livin' mind. You'd be so ashamed, 'cause she was so fair, that even your girls would talk about you."

"Dag," T'quneal shook her head. "Even had your girls up-tight."

"Right," Antoinette said, "'cause she would talk to them, loved them when their own mother's didn't, and let them have a place to be heard, and be protected, and fed, and made to feel like little queens. She adopted every one of them and screened every one of the boys who wanted to deal with her daughters—and by blood, there's only two of us. But, by soul... I couldn't count 'em."

"There's a lady up my street like that," Kisha said, "y'all know Miss Mabel, right?"

Heads bobbed in the affirmative and recognition flickered in their faces.

"There's a lot of angels out there, y'all," Antoinette whispered. "But, you gotta be still so that one can land on your shoulder. Gotta respect 'em when you see 'em, gotta listen, and soak up something to pass on to your babies. Drugs make you blind to it, alcohol makes you deaf to it, and living hard blocks your child's blessings. That's common sense, and the old dolls had it. If you walk the walk, then you can talk the talk to your kids. Children sense fraud a mile away, and if you let it all hang out, you can't say, 'do as I say, not as I do.' They'll laugh in your face, and tell you to go to hell. Isn't that what you did?"

Again heads bobbed in the affirmative.

"That's just what I did," Tianisha sighed. "Got out there, and got hurt real bad. She told me not to, but I didn't respect my mom. How could I? She did it all in front of me."

Antoinette nodded and let her breath out. "Yup, it keeps going back to respect. If you run a respectable household—I'm not talking about a phony one, real-deal respect for everyone in there, maybe your kids will respect you. And if they respect you, maybe you can tell them something when they need to hear it most, even if they stray. Then, maybe you can save them. That doesn't take money."

"But, when your mom found out... that was disrespectful, wasn't it? To her house?" Antoinette's student looked at her without blinking. It was not an accusatory gaze, but an intense, penetrating one that begged for an answer.

"I wasn't in her house, number one," Antoinette

said slowly to be sure they understood. "Number two, I followed all her rules, cleaned the house, did my homework, brought her home As and Bs—not babies, and came home when she said to. Understand?"

"You didn't put it in her face," Tianisha said plainly. "You were as smooth as she was, and she showed you how."

"The word is, being discrete," Antoinette laughed. "Y'all always talkin' about not wanting people in your bizness, but you put your own bizness in the streets!"

A thunderous wave of laughter rang through the group.

"I know," Antoinette laughed with them. "But, see, he didn't go bragging to the fellas, and I didn't say a mumbling word to my girlfriends... and we had it bad, cause we had to take care of business under serious time pressures, rules, and regulations. We had freedom, but not too much.... had to be creative. But, a current will always find its way to the sea. So, fighting against human nature is like spitting against the wind. You'll lose every time. A smart mother knows that."

"You didn't even tell your gurls? Dag, Miss Toni," Rashina whispered, shaking her head.

"Nope. The particulars were between him and me."

"So, how'd your Mom find out—did she confront you?" Delcetta's voice held a tone of awe.

"I really don't know how she found out, and she never directly confronted me, or accused me..." Antoinette's voice trailed off and she scratched her head. "All I know is, one day I had come in on cloud ninety-nine.... It had been all day long, ladies."

The group laughed so hard that several of the girls had fallen out of their chairs. Antoinette chuckled at the bittersweet memory and waited for them to collect themselves.

"Whad'she say when you strolled in feelin' good?" Faylette laughed, wiping her eyes from tears of pure mirth this time. "My mother blew my nookie-high and kicked my natural ass."

Antoinette laughed hard. "I know my mother wanted to. See, she only smoked her one Kent cigarette at night, but she pulled out one that day."

"I know she did," Wynette whooped, and she laid her head down on the table and laughed harder. "Oh, Lord!"

"But, I was on cloud ninety-nine, y'all, remember," Antoinette chuckled as she sat down. "I was grown. I was a woman. He was my man. He had a job... makin' a hundred dollars a week... I could take care of my black, grown, woman-self... and I flipped passed her like I knew it. Set her off, I know it had to—let Lauren do it to me... but she was coooool."

"C'mon, Miss Toni, whad'she do?" Tianisha could barely hold her head up as she roared with laughter.

"Oh, girl.... My mother went to the stack of bills, and got out a tablet. She said, in a very calm voice, 'I need you to help me take these bills to the post office, and ask Jerome to drive you, baby.' Then she had me write down the bills for every house account. The mortgage, gas, electric, telephone, food money—said she had to cash a check for later in the week. She tabulated a number that scared me. Then she looked over the top of her glasses and licked the envelopes, and told me that I had just seen the real cost of living my own life, and that until I could get a college degree, and Jay could too, we didn't need to start a household. She was real. Never said nothing about no babies. Then she smiled, and said, 'I always liked him, baby. I know you love him, but give yourselves time to get a foothold.' And she meant it. I felt like two cents, not a quarter--because she'd trusted me, never accused me, and for the first time in my life I saw how hard it was to give us things, and, after that— just what kind of noose I'd put around my man's neck, and my own, if we slipped up. All of a sudden, it was in black and white, and real clear. I knew I couldn't bring her a baby. Not like that."

"Damn," Tianisha whispered, "I wish we all had a Mom like that."

"That's why I miss her so, and don't mind sharing her with you, ladies. Between her, and my Aunt Pearline, I don't know where I would have ended up without them."

"Is that's why you always call us, ladies, Miss Toni? You really mean that, don'tchu?"

She stared at Faylette and smiled. "I do. You are ladies. Remember that. Because you have to show it to your kids."

"But, did you stop messin' with him? Howd'chu just stop?" Kisha was incredulous. "Go cold-turkey, when you loved him like that?"

"Are you kidding? We couldn't hardly stop," Antoinette laughed as she rolled her neck and waited for her students to stop giggling. "We got extra careful, is all. I think we must have used four different kinds of birth control each time. But, it made us think and made us more serious about the relationship. That's when he went into the service, to be able to get college money and to be able to marry me..." Antoinette trailed off as new tears brimmed and fell.

"I can't go down this next road, ladies," she said in a tight voice. "This one hurts too bad, and it's a fresh gash. I ruined a man's life and wasted twenty-years. 'Nough said. Let me tell y'all about that later."

If only God allowed second chances here on earth.

"C'mon, Miss Toni, it's all right. You told us enough," Tianisha said, rising and coming to her side.

Antoinette stared at the wall as her body went rigid when the girl rocked her and cooed. Little by little the wall within her came down, and she allowed Tianisha to really hug her. Every fiber of her remembered the day she'd said no, the day she'd yielded to her father's opinion... all the calls that she'd refused from Jerome, all the letters that she never answered... the day he'd taken refuge in another woman's arms... the day she'd lain in another man's arms, wishing it was her Jay, and the way that new man had treated her the day after... She'd married that man. Antoinette shut her eyes and let an internal sob claim her soul.

"We should break for lunch, clear the air, and go take a walk," Antoinette said softly, rubbing Tianisha's back. "C'mon, baby. This goes way down to the bone. Mistakes I've made, he's made, and promises neither of us kept. High body count."

"You oughtta do this for a livin' without no agency to check on you, Miss Toni," the girl said quietly, touching Antoinette's face with her fingertips. "You oughtta bring women together, and help them heal. You a healer, Miss T, like my grandma was. You heal people."

All she could do was hold this young girl and stare at her face. Seeming so hard on the outside, but so, so soft on the inside. This woman-child had been her angel today, and had given her the answer to all of the questions that had robbed her of sleep the night before. This young girl believed in her more than she'd believed in herself. Even forgave her for what she could never forgive herself—things she couldn't even voice. She'd called her teacher, when it was she that had just begun to learn as a student. Her mother and Pearline would have been proud to have this young girl under their wings—and God knows what she would have been or achieved, if only she'd had them there to watch over her. Again her soul ached for her sister, Adrienne, and their once ago bond. If only God granted second chances...

Admiration and awe filled Antoinette as she looked at the most unlikely source of comfort. Tianisha Williams. Down in a basement on Fifty-sixth Street.

CHAPTER 25

The new March sky took an ominous stance against the pregnant gray clouds that were threatening to give birth at any moment. At least his week of no-sleep had not been in vain, and the furniture had been kept safe from a sudden angry down-pour. Even if the lumber that he, Buddy, and Scoop hauled from the top of the Bronco got wet, it would be dry enough to paint before the kids got there the following weekend.

"This is nice, man. Real sweet. How'd you swing this? Last I heard you was livin' in a basement, dude." Scoop appraised the massive duplex that sat back from the street on Forty-second and Chester Avenue. "These spots around here still have a lot of the original fixtures... gorgeous, man. I was thinking about gettin' one of these one day myself."

Jerome gave Buddy a disgusted glance before he

decided to answer Scoop. Obviously his prior whereabouts had been disclosed, but at least neither of his boys knew about Mr. Miles' charity. "Took me a minute to pull my act together, you know. But, I needed a spot for my kid crew so they could visit overnight."

"You're really serious about this. Deep," Buddy said in a low tone, "never thought you'd go through with it."

Jerome ignored the comment and began cutting the ropes which held two-by-four pine studs on the vehicle. "I appreciate you all helping me today. I just gotta put these frames together, paint 'em, then I can throw the kids' mattresses on them."

"This spot looks real convenient, brother," Scoop said trailing off as he watched a young female student make her way into the Deli a half block from them. "They even have a joint that sells brew on the same street—plus, we gotta check out the Track n' Turf next door. But, I brought you a house-warming present till your money gets real right enough to hang out with us," Scoop beamed, "I could get used to this, man. How much it run you a month?"

"You gonna stand around watching tail, or you gonna help us haul?" Buddy asked with a grunt as he caught the end of Jerome's load.

"At least open the door, man," Jerome called over his shoulder, following Buddy up the steps to the porch. "C'mon, Scoop. I got the heavy end, and it's gonna rain any minute."

Scoop hustled around them and slipped the key in the lock. Going in first, he stood in the spacious foyer admiring the tiles, but blocking their entry.

"We'll give you a tour later," Jerome hollered, "C'mon, man! We got two flights. Get out the way, and watch the wood on the car."

Scoop moved aside and flattened himself to the Spanish tile wall, making space for Jerome and Buddy to pass.

"Okay, on three. Drop it low and catch the weight when I turn and step up, " Buddy huffed.

"You okay, man? Want to let it down and catch your breath?" Jerome asked, becoming concerned as Buddy weaved when he backed up the stairs.

Shrugging off the suggestion, Buddy pulled harder. "No, man," he huffed between breaths. "I'm cool... was just this turn. Five more, and we hit the landing." Buddy stopped briefly and took a gulp of air through his mouth. "Scoop. Open his door so we can go straight back to the kids' room."

"You got it man," Scoop yelled, taking the steps two at a time. "Why don't you put that end down and let me and Jerome take it in from here?" he insisted more quietly as he opened the door. "For real, man."

"Just open the damned door," Buddy winced, straining under the load. "I'm cool."

Jerome kept his eye on his friend as small beads of sweat began to form on Buddy's brow. On the next load, he would make sure to diplomatically ask Scoop to take it up with him. Damn. They were all getting old—he and his boys. There was a time when he could have probably taken the load in alone. Watching Buddy struggle was just like watching the time tick away on his own watch. One day he would be the one who had to take the light end of the load. There were already streaks of silver coming in at his temples—however a baseball cap could hide that. But at least he hadn't lost his hair to a horseshoe like Scoop had. The process was unnerving. When the day came that he finally stopped being able to get it up, they could just take him out to pasture like the old workhorse he was, and shoot him.

"Damn, man!" Buddy gasped with relief as he dropped the wood. "How many more loads we got?"

"Take a breather," Jerome grunted as he dropped his end with a thud. "Scoop ain't doin' nothin'. Go get a cold one, and watch the car. We only have two more. All the hardware is in the room already."

"Don't mind if I do," Buddy said, still breathing hard. "Yo, man, the place looks good. Did you paint it yourself, or did it come already gift wrapped?"

"Yeah," Scoop said with appreciation. "This is sweet, brother."

"Thought you were watching my wood, man?" Jerome chuckled, knowing that Scoop couldn't stay in one place for more than five minutes.

"I am. Chill, man. I keep checkin' on your load

every few from that big bay window in the living room. This is fly, bro. Damn, it must have wore you out paintin' with these twelve foot ceilings, man. But, it's sweet, brother. Where'd you get a sleigh bed and all dis art?" Scoop popped from room to room like an excited child. "You even got mini blinds up, and drapes and what not. Antique furniture, stereo... But your TV is sorry, brother. Let me hook you up wit my boy down the bar—somethin' to match this joint, with all the bells and whistles. We could rent some smokers... see da lovelies go to work..."

"Naw, man. I'ma be workin' so much, won't have time for no TV."

"You gotta git a VCR, at least, man. For the kids. You ain't gonna make it without one—not for no whole weekend," Buddy laughed and slapped him on the back. "Unless you got cable. Damn you pulled this together. I'm proud of you, man. Wish I could get out of Alcatraz and land like this."

Jerome looked around his new digs and nodded with satisfaction. A VCR could come later. He'd worked like a dog, since sleep had been next to impossible. "I put in a few hours every night," he said, minimizing the effort while he caught his breath. "Only had to do the two bedrooms, the living room, and kitchen. The hall was good. Basic white. I only put up the yellow and blue border in the kids' room for my girls really—but some blue for my boy. Bought some stuffed animals and games from the brothers who work the tables on Fifty-second Street. Got a couple of plants... No biggie."

"No biggie?" Scoop said with amazement in his voice, following Jerome through the hallway. "I'ma get you hooked up with a VCR, so we can go huntin', fishin' and a little skinny dippin,' and bring the catch back here. You know, you know, brother."

Buddy followed them down and out into the street. "You can't hunt no tail, but what's in your house, man. Don't get our boy involved in nothin', Scoop. For real."

"Oh, yeah, I forgot. You can be no accomplice, or den your butt will really be incarcerated—locked in the house on the weekends and after work with Val," Scoop hollered as he took the heavy end of the load before Jerome could lift it down. "You been scarce, man. And git out the way so we can get by."

Jerome chuckled as Buddy gave Scoop a warning glance. "Yeah, Buddy," he teased, "couldn't even get you to help me and Mr. Miles, man."

Buddy rushed up the stairs ahead of them and took the middle of the wood as they walked back to the second bedroom. "Look, ever since you started this mess with Karen, Val has been on a mission. Won't even talk to her girl, Toni."

"I'm sorry to hear that," Jerome said letting out his breath as he dropped the load. "Because I haven't even seen Toni, except to fix a water valve for her fridge. Then, I accidentally bumped into her when I had my kids—by accident, for five minutes at the church, and don't intend to try to see her until my shit is right. She doesn't need her name dragged into anything. Karen's lawyer already got the no-fault papers, and I'm just waiting on a signature and a seal from the judge. She's got everything, except my car, my tools, my albums and me. Even my lawyer said if we both agreed to say we were estranged for two years, we didn't have to wait the full two year separation under no-fault. She wanted out, and handed me papers when I went to go see my kids. So I signed. Dig. I'm trying to keep my life static-free. Took me weeks to get this little bit of livin' back together, and I haven't even put a dent into what I've gotta do."

Jerome looked around at his stunned friends. He knew that more detailed information about the flea market, his next move, or his intentions to rebuild his life would only complicate things, so he let the subject drop without further explanation. "Okay, y'all?" he added for assurance, and stared at them.

Scoop dropped his end of the load and blinked. "For real, man? You mean that I haven't let Tracey call her for nothin'? Damn. If I'da known that shit, Tracey coulda taken her sorry ass over to her girl Toni's house and stayed for all I care."

"Wait," Buddy said, his gaze tearing between both men. "Valerie told me that Tracey didn't want to talk to Toni. She never said you had anything to do with it."

"Get out, man," Scoop argued. "Tracey's been trying to get on the phone to call her girl to find out what's up—but I ain't havin' it. So, I don't know what your wife is talking about. If anything, Val is probably scared that your hard workin' ass will walk during one of y'all's many arguments, like our boy did. Shooot. I can't have Tracey doin' to me what Toni did to her old man—walkin' 'cause she didn't like somethin' I said or did. I'm not havin' that mess come to my house. No way, brothers. I ain't da one."

"You ain't making sense, Scoop." Jerome was incredulous.

"Do your boy ever?" Buddy said, shaking his head.

"Now wait, let me get this right," Jerome said evenly, bending down to stack the boards. "You can come over here, attempt to chase all the booty that you can trap, but your wife can't see her girl, just because her girl—you thought—was dealin' with me?" Jerome stood up and stared at his friend hard. "Talk to me, man. 'Cause, for old time's sake, I need to understand this one."

"Cool down, Jay," Buddy said nervously. "He don't mean nothin'. You know Scoop and his jacked-up logic."

"It ain't personal, man. We boyz. You and me cool. And you a man—gotsta do whatcha gotsta do. But, I just can't have my wife running wit no girl-friend that, for one, left her husband—a brother wit a goood job," Scoop proclaimed, counting off Antoinette's charges on his fingers and leaning back for emphasis. "For two, took his child in a big relocation vibe, three—thinking her wide butt is fine, just 'cause she makes good bread, and four, done rolled up on a stable household, like yours, and snatched a brother out by a ring in his nose. Now, maybe on number four I was wrong on—since you tellin' me you ain't been with Antoinette. But, the rest is enough. Can't have her influencin' my wife to lose her mind, too." Scoop said with a laugh, then reached into his jacket and pulled out a bottle of liquor, extending it to Jerome. "Drink your house-warming present, man. I don't see why you so worried about the woman anyway, 'specially if you ain't dealin' wit her. She ain't all that no more, anyway."

Jerome let the bottle remain extended between them, refusing to accept it. "For one, if Toni did leave her husband, it was probably because he did something stupid to the woman. Plus, she didn't relocate on the man like a fugitive. She came home to her family, and the brother, I bet, knows where she is, if I know Antoinette. Number two, she's always been smart—so why wouldn't she have a good job? And she was never stuck up, okay. The girl teaches in the community, and that don't pay shit. So, you don't know what you're talking about, man. Plus, she might have filled out a little, but she is now, and always has been, fine. Your sorry ass would try her, that's why you don't want your wife over there—'cause you know she's back home and by herself. And, you know for a fact that you don't treat Tracey right—and you scared that Antoinette might one day talk some sense into that poor girl!"

"Aw, man, the only reason that Toni would talk Tracey away from me is so I could make a play for her," Scoop railed in defense. "You had your chance twenty years ago," he chuckled nervously, trying to bait Jerome.

But somewhere in the tension of the exchange, jealousy accosted Jerome's sense of reason and he took a step toward Scoop. "I'll kill you, man, if you even test her."

Buddy took the bottle from Scoop and turned on him. "Look, man," he challenged, coming to Jerome's defense and trying to intervene in a potential fist fight, "You as bad as my wife. Toni has always been real people, man. And you know how our boy feels about her, so why you talkin' about her gainin' weight, and all that yang? Your bald-dome, fat-gut, knuckle-head ain't what you used to be neither! So, ease up. Don't take Jay there about this woman. He ain't seeing her, but prob'ly wish he could—and can't. His papers ain't finalized up in Harrisburg, he needs for 'em to come back from the state before he can totally get it together, gots lots of bizness to handle if he gonna go to Toni right—and that's they only way T would take a man, is right. Just like before. So don't go there, man. Let it rest."

Buddy's comment, while true, cut to the bone.

Just remembering all the reasons he couldn't immediately go and sweep up his Toni-girl, even though he'd prepared a place for her and the kids to be, made him crazy. Jerome stalked away from his friends and went into the kitchen and grabbed a beer. He popped the top back with so much force that the aluminum tab snapped off in his fingers. Flinging the piece of metal into the sink, he took two gulps between deep breaths and wiped his mouth with the back of his hand. To hell with Scoop.

"C'mon, man. Let it go," Buddy soothed, edging into the room. "You know how our boy is. Simple. Can't do nothin' wit him."

"Aw, man. C'mon. I'm sorry, bro. T's cool wit me. I'll let Tracey talk to her girl. Okay, man? And, she ain't fat, she's still fine. Can't call her stuck up, or whatever. Peace. C'mon, Jay. Let's build the bunk-beds for the kids, drink us some liquor—"

"That's all right, man. Keep the liquor. Been cuttin' back anyway," Jerome whispered through his teeth, staring at Scoop and ignoring Buddy. "You helped enough. I got business to take care of before it gets too late."

"Aw, Jay, man. It's Saturday. Miles don't have any more jobs on the list. Damn, man," Buddy argued, turning in Scoop's direction. "See. You done gone an' upset our boy wit your dumb junk. Jerome, man," Buddy implored, his eyes darting between the two would-be contenders like a referee, "we got the day off, the wives let us out, and we got all night. Why'lln'tchu let me and Scoop hit the bar, go get you a fly VCR—one that fell off the truck, you know, for the kids—for only like, fifty bucks, den we can tell some lies, have some laughs, and squash this crap, man? Peace."

"I got somethin' to do, and can put the beds together myself. Don't need 'em till next week, anyway," Jerome replied evenly, then downed his beer. Looking in Scoop's direction, he wiped his mouth again. "Plus, y'all need to go home to your wives— since everybody here is concerned about either Toni or me being accomplices, I'm not giving you a home-away-from-home here. Hell no, so your wives can blame me for your whereabouts—or assume Toni is with one of you. I'm through for the day."

The three men stood their ground, each eyeing the other to see who would speak first, relent first, back down first. Jerome was unmoved by the age-old ritual. This was his space. His boyz had talked about his woman, and had both let him down. No. Oh, hell no!

"Well, whatchu gonna do, man? Damn," Buddy finally blurted out, leaning against the kitchen counter.

"Go to Radio Shack on fortieth before it closes at nine, Jerome growled, looking at Scoop with contempt, "then I'm going to West Coast Video on Baltimore, before I stop by Royal Pizza on the way back, and chill. And, that's the difference. I'm not lying to Karen, I'm not pretending. She knows the deal. The cards are on the table. She's got papers in her hand—exactly the way she wanted it. And, I've never beat her, ain't cheated on her while man and wife, and never shorted her money. That's what I'ma do. Be stress-free this weekend."

"He's serious, man. I know our boy better than you do, Scoop," Buddy sighed, his shoulders sagging from the disappointment. "If you knew 'em, like I do, you wouldn'ta said a mumblin' word about Antoinette. Damn. A Saturday at home, man. I oughtta kick your butt myself, Scoop, wit your signifying, monkey-drama. Damn!"

"What I say, man, dat was so bad?" Scoop implored in Jerome's direction. "How many times I gotta tell your stubborn ass I'm sorry? C'mon, Jay, I'm not trying to go home tonight. My pockets is light 'til payday—can't hang at the bar tonight, brother," Scoop pleaded, exchanging glances with Buddy.

"He ain't hearin' it, Scoop," Buddy said with finality as he walked past him and out into the hall. "Get your hat, man. You really pissed him off, and that's that."

"Where we gonna go tonight then, man?" Scoop hollered in Buddy's direction. "Huh?"

"I don't know, man. I'm going home. Let Jay cool off. All I can say is," Buddy yelled as he went to the door and held it open for Scoop to follow him, "you don't have to go home, but you gotta get the hell outta here."

Jerome stood in the kitchen as he heard the front door slam, Scoop fussing and complaining the whole way down the duplex interior staircase, out to the porch, and finally to the curb. He was worse than a woman. Everything was changing, so maybe it was time to change some of his friends too. Scoop would be the first to go. Crushing the can in his hand, he tossed it in the trash and pulled off another beer from the six-pack. Damn, that mess got on his nerves—bringing that crap about Toni to his door! He walked into the living room, clicked on the stereo, and cranked the volume. Smooth jazz filled the room, bouncing off the hardwood floors, consuming him at an ear splitting decibel. He moved to the center of the room and surveyed his work. Yeah, Stanley Clark was jammin'! Even he had to admit that his spot looked pretty good. Power from the incomparable bass throbbed in his chest. Yeah.

Music that he couldn't listen to in peace at home. This was his place. For the first time in years. A place where he called the shots. Where he owned every stick of the furniture that he'd hauled up the steps and refinished last week. Dark woods and no flower prints and no pink—and nobody to please, but himself. A man's place. A place that he could afford on one side hustle at night with Mr. Miles. A place that didn't have screaming, and fighting, and mayhem. A place where he had garnered the ounce of privacy he needed in order to survive a potentially long wait for Antoinette. A place where he could dream about a life with her, for making love to her, without invasion.

Jerome leaned his head back and closed his eyes. The music fused with his bones, and as Ramsey Lewis came on, he leaned his head forward to take a swig of beer. It had been years since he'd listened to anything from the Sun Goddess album. The opening chorus sung by Earth, Wind, and Fire took him back... back... Jerome opened his eyes, downed his beer, then paced over to the stereo and turned it down, then off. No. Not the EWF and Antoinette Reeves era this afternoon. Damn the ghosts that had come through his Bose speakers! He'd go get a VCR and a movie instead.

CHAPTER 26

Jerome pulled up the zipper on his black leather bomber jacket a little higher, and hunched his shoulders forward, securing his black Hollywood baseball cap that the kids had given him for Christmas. Night March winds bit through his jeans, and whipped his legs, cutting them like a razor. The Hawk was definitely flying high tonight, he observed with a shudder, glimpsing his watch as he made his way across the parking lot to the video store. By nine-thirty he knew all the good movies would be gone--but anything beat a blank. He really wasn't going to watch it anyway, he rationalized, but just stare at the light and go comatose in front of the set. That was a better option than getting wasted at the bar, now that he'd just dropped a hundred-fifty for a VCR, and couldn't even stand to listen to his music.

The wind practically blew him in the door as the vacuum seal from too much heat inside collided with the cold air outside. Caught in the vortex of patrons pushing to get out, and those trying to scramble into the warm interior, he stopped resisting the current and moved with the stream of bodies until he was washed inside a nearby isle. Orienting himself to the new establishment, he scanned the top of the shelves looking for something to hold his interest for an entire night.

The new release rack was practically empty. No problem, he liked old movies, and hadn't seen anything in the theater when it was out anyhow. He was always working, or had to go see what Karen and the kids wanted. Yeah, tonight he would rent *Tusgeegee Airmen.* Maybe, *Full Metal Jacket... Shogun Assassin.* Too bad *Executive Decision* was out, he noted, as he hunted and pecked through the shelves—and stopped. He had to get out of there. His ghost had followed him to the video store. Damn. Not tonight! Not before he got his shit totally right.

But as she hunted and pecked through the old action-adventures and went over to the dramas, he couldn't move much less breathe. She looked so sad, and so intense as she browsed the isles... and she even had three of his choices under her arm.

A thousand approaches besieged his mind. It was like what he imagined flight school to have been. When did he lower his flaps? What about possible turbulence? Was his altitude right? What about wind resistance? When should he drop his landing gear? He was gonna come in without tower support. What was he going to say to this woman?

"Hi," he stammered as he walked up behind her. He could have kicked himself as she startled and whipped around, and blinked.

"Oh, Jay... God, you scared me... I was so engrossed. There's not much left, I got here so late... How've you been? Did the kids like the flea market? Oh, and yeah, thanks so much for the stuff for Lauren, you didn't have to," she said shyly and looked down at a movie box that she had been considering.

He'd made her nervous. Antoinette always rambled and talked in rapid-fire machine-gun when she was nervous. He'd come in without tower clearance, enough advance warning, or runway space—and he'd hit her cold with a weak line, at that! Now he was getting her brand of wind resistance. He'd definitely over-shot the runway, and now he'd have to circle back to try to come in again. Damn, he had to get his rap together.

"The kids loved the winter flea market. Yes I did have to get Lauren something, it helped your student," he laughed, becoming more comfortable as she smiled, while he answered each of her questions in the order he could remember them, "Sorry that I scared you. And, yes, it's late—so you've got all of my movies."

"I'm babbling aren't I?" she laughed easily, her shoulders dropping a few inches with apparent relief. "You could always make me laugh, Jay. Sorry about the movies. I guess since you did my student a favor, the least I could do is give you a couple of these," she added with a wider smile, handing him *Tusgeegee Airmen* without a thought, then displaying the others for him to make a selection.

God, she was so easy to be around, yet so hard to be around at the same time. He took the movie she'd offered from her without removing his gaze from hers. She was beautiful, and this was all he wanted to look at tonight. She had even remembered the way he could make her laugh, and had said she'd loved him—before. He could have stood there all night...

"Go on," she prompted. "I wasn't going to really watch any of these. I was just going to veg-out at home under a blanket. Why don't you try the Kung-Fu one, are you still into the martial arts and meditation?"

Deep within the core of his rusty engine of a brain, he thought that he'd heard an opening. An offer. She'd just said that she'd be home, obviously by her movie choices, not with a child. Alone. Assuming by the fact that no brother seemed to be in her airspace, definitely alone. She was going to do what he had planned to do—veg-out under a blanket. She had even remembered his interests from twenty years ago, and held them out for him to make a selection. A choice. Jerome checked his gauges. He'd approach again, but he'd make it a smooth one. He was going in for a landing.

"I haven't had the time or personal space in a long while to do meditation. But now that I have my own spot over on Forty-second, and nothing else to do but work and see the kids... Yeah, I'll probably get back into it."

Wait for clearance, he told himself. No mid-air collisions.

"I know what you mean," she sighed. "That's all I do is work and take care of Lauren. I didn't feel like going out with the girls tonight. Truthfully, some of the old crew have been getting on my nerves lately."

She'd turned on the runway lights. He had visual.

"Yeah, the fellas were getting on my nerves, and the music was getting on my nerves... so, I thought I'd buy a VCR and hook it up tonight, and have a by-myself-movie-fest."

"Well, if this is your first time, you can only take out two movies—that won't be much of a fest. Usually it takes me three or four to get to sleep," she said lowering her eyes.

Oh, God... the yellow lines were in sight, and she'd given him plenty of room to land. He dropped his landing gear, and put down his flaps.

"Well... if you want to... I could pay for the

movies, if you can rent them. I'll get a pizza, and you could come over while I hook up the new VCR. That is, if you want to?"

He waited for the first bounce then screech of his wheels hitting asphalt.

"Really?" she said, looking up with a smile that created an intense thermal, "I'd love to."

Houston, we have landed!

He tried not to smile too wide, not to let her see just how pleased he was, and he almost dropped his wallet as he removed it from his back pocket and shoved twenty dollars under the cashier's bullet-proof glass window.

She'd said yes, now what was he going to do? He hadn't done this in over a decade and a half. Dating at forty-one. Jesus.

Antoinette steeled herself against the cold and clasped the front of her coat closed as they crossed the parking lot to their cars. Why didn't she listen to Pearline and her mother's age-old wisdom—to never go out looking like a washer-woman because you never know who you're going to meet? If she'd had any inkling that Jay would have been there, she would have definitely put on a little eye-liner, a brighter shade of lipstick, not had her hair in a pony-tail. And she would have definitely not had on an old, raggedy, light gray pair of sweats, with even older sneakers. Maybe that's why Brian was getting married, and she wasn't. Damn. She had to pull herself together.

"You want to follow me?" he said, sounding unsure as they stood by their cars, both trying to decide the logistics.

Antoinette let her gaze move between his car and her's as her mind quickly reviewed the options. She didn't want to tell him to just let her drop off her car at home first, because that would send out a signal that she was planning on staying. She really hadn't quite made up her mind about that yet. Besides, that would have seemed way too forward... And she couldn't impose on the man to chauffeur her back and forth, once it got past mid-night—which it would be, judging by the bag of movies they'd rented. Damn, why was this dating thing so hard? She was supposed to be married, and comfortable, and done with this phase of her life! Never in a million years had she expected to be doing this at her age.

A smile found it's way to her face, it was the only thing that she could think of to do while she weighed the options and Jerome waited for her response. Okay, she told herself, following him in her car over to his place left options for retreat available, especially when this was probably just a friendship move. Loneliness probably had the best of him tonight, but not enough to make him want to deal with a has-been like herself.

"I'll follow you," Antoinette said after a moment, "Maybe we can swing by and pick up the pizza on the way?"

Jerome seemed to be considering her words, and he hunched his shoulders with the movie bag under his arm and put his hands in his pockets. "Damn, it's cold. I don't know, all I do know is, we've gotta get somewhere warm," he chuckled. "Parking is tight on Baltimore—so why don't we park in front of my spot, and walk to Royal?"

Antoinette opened her car door with a laugh and slipped in. "It's too cold to argue. Lead the way!"

It was settled, she told herself. They'd go as buddies, Dutch. It was easier that way.

The cold air, along with the short separate car ride around the corner, seemed to provide her with the needed space to pull herself together. Jay looked good... way too good for the way she was feeling tonight. But, there were a lot of things she needed to know first—like, the status of his separation. When, where, under what circumstances? This thing was too hot to just take it on faith. People changed in a year, much less twenty. What if he'd been put out because he had gotten into chasing women? Or, what if he was a drug addict? Nah... But possible. Or, worse, what if his stint in the military had made him violent, and he'd hit his wife? That, she definitely needed to know.

Every fear, every stereotype, everything she'd

been warned about, suddenly slithered into her mind, taking the enthusiasm for her date away from her, and robbing her of her sudden joy. Plus, there were other considerations. Like the fact that maybe she'd be the one to get crushed if none of her previous hopes about him even being interested in her that way had been true. Then again, what if he was a decent man? What if he was the same Jay she'd known? What if she fell head-over-heels and somehow let him know that she'd used his image to get through many a night... and what if he said, 'thanks, but no thanks'? All of the possible variations on this theme were too risky, she told herself, as they pulled up to his building. She'd just play it cool and follow his moves--with a whole lot of diplomatic questions wedged in-between. She had to interview him first.

Antoinette turned off her ignition, doused the lights, and unlocked her door. When he came to the side of her car and flung the door open for her, she just looked at him for a moment. Check point. Men didn't do that any more. Respect factor was in full effect. Chivalry was a big plus.

"Thanks," she said quietly, trying to find a graceful way to heave herself out of the too small vehicle. When he caught her under her elbow, she wanted to disappear and die. God, why hadn't she dropped that extra weight!

"I don't know how you stand this little buggy, T," he smiled, lifting her to her feet with seemingly little effort.

Her heart stopped beating. He'd probably felt the effects that gravity had on her overweight carcass.

"You always had those long legs," he murmured with a tone of appreciation, "too long for this little car."

He was a gentleman and a diplomat. She relaxed and said a prayer of thanks.

"It was all I could afford," she replied quietly as he escorted her to the curb and walked toward the outside of it. Oh, yes, he was trained in the basics and hadn't forgotten—unlike many of the better-dressed men she'd met in her sifting process.

"I know what you mean, T. This was all I could afford," he said in a shy schoolboy tone, motioning toward his building. "I hope you don't mind? I'm on the second floor."

And he had humility. Big check point. He wasn't an arrogant show-off like the other guys she'd unfortunately met. This was scaring her. Jerome had not just stoked her libido, but had seeped back into her brain as a potential life partner, taking her memory back twenty years. This is what they used to do before... dream of places they'd live, and things they'd do. Oh my God! No. She had to keep herself in check.

Antoinette stood back and marveled at the building and let her gaze sweep the block. "Oh, Jay. This is gorgeous. They don't make buildings with all that detail and fretwork anymore..." her voice

Leslie Esdaile

trailed off in abject awe. "Look at them all... they're hand-laid stone... and you're right down the street from Clark Park. Have the kids seen it yet? Wow, this was made by real union craftsmen. Artisans."

And he still had understated class...

CHAPTER 27

He could tell that she liked his new location—it was the way that her smile broadened slowly when she gazed at the duplex. Immediate relief passed through him. She was still his Antoinette, his Toni-girl. A woman who could spot quality a mile away. It didn't take her thirty-seconds to see the real value, or the labor that had gone into the architecture. She could see something old and still see the beauty in it. He could feel himself stand a little straighter. The fact that she approved made all the difference in the world.

"Let's walk and talk," he said with a smile, guiding her down the block. "The kids haven't seen it yet. Other than Scoop and Buddy, you'll be the first person close to me to see the inside."

She smiled and looked away. He was glad that

she'd caught his true meaning, and could tell that she was pleased to have been the first female to see it.

"I want to get one of these, one day—to own," he pressed on as they rounded the corner. "Something that I can fix-up myself. You know, maybe live in one part and rent out the other."

"I know you'll do it, Jay. You've always been a hard worker, and have always been good with your hands. You pay attention to details. I've always liked that about you."

He was glad that the pizza shop was within sight. It helped him to focus on patience. He was now hearing everything she said with double meaning. He would definitely pay attention to her details, if she'd let him. Antoinette Reeves could have anything he had to give her—anything she wanted him to get for her.

As he opened the door he checked himself mentally. Remember what old man Miles said, he told himself, call her soft and low and wait...

"Can I help you?" an older Greek woman said cheerfully. "You a new customer? Haven't seen you before," she smiled.

"Yeah," Jerome said pleasantly, glad to have any distraction away from Antoinette. "Just moved in not too long ago."

"Oh, this is good," the older woman said, her eyes glancing brightly in Antoinette's direction. "I like to see new people. New young couples. How long you been married?"

The look of pleased shock on Antoinette's face filled him with a sense of pride, and he cut off Antoinette's confused explanation with a simpler version of his own. "We've been together for about twenty years."

"Oh, this is so nice!" the woman behind the counter exclaimed, as she spun around toward a younger, olive-complexioned girl with dark hair. "Anna! Anna. See. These people marry young, look happy. See. All school and no husband, is no good."

Something in the girl's pretty face looked so sad, and he knew it would draw Antoinette's attention like a magnet. He stared at the girl and Antoinette at the same time from his peripheral vision. Deep down he wondered if Toni still had the same soft heart after going through a divorce. He needed to know that. But he also wanted all of her attention tonight, and wondered if she had ever learned to resist helping what couldn't be fixed? But, he told himself, knowing Toni, they'd be there all night trying to find out what was behind the sad girl's eyes.

"What would you like?" the girl named Anna said, not looking up from her pad.

"I don't know, Jay? Pepperoni, mushroom? You call it."

"How about pepperoni and mushroom? A large, and a two liter Coke," he said, remembering her favorite combination, and the only kind of soda Toni ever drank. "Plus a large bag of barbecue chips," he added with a smile. "That okay with you, T?"

"Uh huh... That's cool."

"Want anything else?" he asked growing wary as Antoinette continued to stare at the girl and had answered him in a far off way. He hoped that she wasn't going to get into these people's business tonight, to prolong a trip to the pizza shop. Tonight, he wanted her all to himself.

"Nope... ah, no thanks."

When Antoinette didn't look at him, and had only answered him with a distant, negative half-grunt, his hopes sagged. She was being drawn to this young woman—it was in her eyes.

"You go to school?" Antoinette asked cheerfully in the girl's direction. "That's good," she added when the girl nodded and smiled.

"Yes, good, but no husband," the older woman cut in, as she slapped a pile of meat for cheese-steaks on the grill. "Don't want her to end up like me. To work, and work, and work, and smell like onions. She's young, and beautiful. Should be out like the ladies I worked for, before my store."

Jerome paced to the window. Antoinette had taken on their case. He could feel it in his bones. He only hoped that Toni could issue a prescription by the time their pizza was ready. It was just like when they were kids. Then, a dawning thought made him smile. She was afraid. It was just like her first time where she made up a million excuses and diversions to keep from being anywhere alone with him—fully knowing that their relationship had reached a decision-point. The memory made him draw his breath in through his nose. Patience, with this new knowledge, was going to be very difficult to summon.

"You know, Ma'am," Antoinette said, "you should be proud to have a daughter who will work in this business with you. "What are you in school for?"

"Accounting," the girl answered with a smile of satisfaction, issuing her mother a look to let her alone.

"One day, my daughter will have a big, fancy job and can live like my pretty ladies."

"But, Ma'am," Antoinette countered, addressing the older woman, "small businesses—especially a well established one like this, are more secure than any job. She can do your books, help you expand."

"That's the truth," Jerome cut in, aware that their pizza would be out of the oven in minutes. When Antoinette peered at him nervously then at the pizza oven, he stifled a chuckle. There were no words to describe how this zaney woman made him feel.

"This is true?" the older woman asked with astonishment. "But the people look so beautiful... like, I cleaned a house in New Jersey. No good money, but honest work. There was a girl from... from... Anna, help me with words,"

"Pakistan," Anna said quietly. "She watched the

woman's children, Momma cleaned, and an Asian man did the lawn, a Latino girl helped Momma clean, and a black lady did cooking and laundry. Momma thinks I should get a good job and live like this woman who hired all of these people."

"This is what we fight about all the time," the girl's mother said, throwing up her hands and letting them drop heavily to her cutting board.

"Did this woman work?" Antoinette asked, her gaze narrowing on the two women.

"Oh, no!" the older woman exclaimed, pulling their pizza from the oven. "Never. She was rich."

Jerome groaned inwardly. This was a multi-ethnic case, with complex issues. His first date was going to be held all night in a pizza parlor. History was repeating itself.

"Did you ever see her husband... and did she look happy?"

"Not much..." the older woman said, glancing at her daughter.

"Then for one," Antoinette said with conviction, "that was not her money. So, she had to do what he said, that's not free. It wasn't her money," she repeated, "Not like you earn here. For two, she has hired all of these people, which will only give her more time to think about how unhappy she is, and for three, you probably make a solid living from this pizza shop. I bet you buy everything cash? Right?"

Both women behind the counter nodded.

"And look at your daughter," Antoinette continued. "She's beautiful."

When Antoinette reached for his arm, he was surprised but pleased.

"Oh, Ma'am, you have the American dream, and don't even know it," Antoinette pressed on, getting wound up in her own momentum. "You don't owe creditors. You work hard for what you have. You don't have to worry about anybody telling you that you haven't done a good job, and firing you. And your daughter is learning, like an apprentice, right by your side. This is what helped build this country. Small businesses, like yours. Shops like yours hire more people than the big companies—it was in the newspaper, if you don't believe me. So, don't let what you see on TV make you feel bad, or let rich people with no values make you lose yours. You should pray that your daughter finds somebody who will not be ashamed to continue your business."

He watched the older woman stand a little taller, and her gaze soften as she looked at her daughter. Antoinette had a way of making people feel special. He sure felt that way as she clung to his upper arm and smiled at the two women, her gaze full of passion and belief. He loved her passion. He loved that she could accept hard, honest work... and somehow, this conversation, though not directed at him, made him understand something about her that had haunted him before now.

"My grandmother was a domestic, and she saved her money and bought her duplex—cash, right,

Jerome?" Antoinette said, giving him a little squeeze until he nodded yes. "She worked for them, but also for herself. An early entrepreneur. Her husband ran a hucksters truck, sold fruit and vegetables as a side business, and worked a job during the day. But when they closed their eyes, they had bought their homes, owned all of their furniture... had good lives."

"This is true?" the older woman asked quietly.

"Yes," Antoinette replied. "Read the history here. All inventions, all big stores came from small businesses, entrepreneurs, and slavery—people even invented while they were prisoners of war, slaves."

"Tell me this," the old woman said, neglecting to cut their pizza that had cooled considerably. "Why do black people rob, and steal, and say mean things sometimes?"

He could feel Antoinette's grip tighten on his arm. They were definitely going to be here for a while.

"If you go into any poor neighborhood... Kensington, with its poor whites, or around Wyoming, where there's poor Latinos, or around on Chestnut where there are poor Asians, parts of South Philly with poor Italians, or Port Richmond section and Grays Ferry—you will see people who have lost jobs. Or, couldn't get jobs. People who are angry and have lost hope. That's when there's crime. But take the little neighborhood pockets where small businesses thrive—crime goes down.

People don't rent, they own their homes. Therefore, they sweep their steps off with bleach, pick up their trash, and get to a graffiti artist before the cops can. See. Businesses stabilize a community better than jobs do, but people have been trained to work a job, so they often don't have the work-ethic anymore to put in an eighteen hour day like working for yourself requires. This was all by design," she flipped, and let go of his arm to lean on the counter.

Her assessment told him all that he needed to know. She could definitely appreciate hard work, an honest dollar, and wasn't going to let his blue-collar scare her away. This was not Karen. Maybe there was a reason they'd come in here, he wondered, gaining appreciation for the shop.

The old woman smoothed her apron and hesitated, looking at Jerome as she began. "I have been robbed twice. By teenagers... I thought..."

"That all black men were thieves," Antoinette said quietly as she stared up at Jerome. "That's also by design," she said quietly. "When a white man commits a crime, you don't see his picture flash up immediately on TV. If it's one of us, they blaze it across the screen."

"It was the same in my country," the woman admitted, laying their pie in the box and cutting it slowly while her daughter turned the over-done meat on the grill. "Poor always got treated different. That's why I come here. But they make you think it's colors, not money. I don't understand this before."

"It's always been that way, Ma'am," Jerome finally interjected, hoping that the old woman would close the pizza box, hand him the pie so he could begin his date. "I get off late from work at night, and will stop in and check on you from time to time. Neighbors used to do that, but don't any more."

"Yes! Yes! This is like in my old country. Nobody had to lock the doors. Everyone looked out."

"I know what'cha mean," Antoinette sighed, and her body froze.

Jerome's trouble radar went up too as a group of young boys burst into the store. He stepped around them and hesitated by the door. He could see Antoinette from the corner of his eye. The two women behind the counter looked around nervously, begging him with their gaze not to leave. Instinct coiled within him, and he handed the pizza to Antoinette. "I might want some dessert. Let me see what they have." When she accepted the pizza from him, he gave her a glance to stay put and stay quiet. He was glad that she could read his mind and sense danger.

"Gimme a hoagie, wit mayo and oil," one of the teenagers yelled at the older woman, "Don't take all fuckin' night, either!"

Jerome could feel his blood pressure going up. He didn't care what color this woman was, or what language she spoke, it was ignorant. But he needed to size up the group, and not make a move that would cause the woman later retaliation. He surveyed the dessert choices with disinterest, watching the young boys from his peripheral vision.

"Yeah, gimme a cheese-steak, wit fried onions, old lady," another yelled. "Hurry up. We ain't got all night!"

"Look," Jerome said, walking over to the front counter very slowly, and making sure that his command had been issued from the deepest bass-line in his throat, "you don't need to talk to her like that. Order your shit, pay the woman, and roll."

"What's it to you, man? Mind your business—"

"What if I told you this was my business, and that was my grandmother? Would you kill somebody over your grandmother?" Jerome asked very slowly and not moving.

Nervous glances passed between the four boys.

"Damn, man," the obvious leader said with a confused look, "I thought the Greeks owned this joint?"

"Deep. Dat's his gran'mom. Chill. Sorry 'bout that, bro. No offense. We thought The Man owned da joint," another said.

"Damn," another mumbled, handing the older woman his money in a much more respectful way.

"Let your boyz know the deal. Everything will be chill then. If I see a name on her grate, I'ma look for dat name? Cool?" Jerome said, puffing himself up and slipping his hand into his jacket for effect.

"Cool, man. Ain't no problem," the first one grumbled as they collected their food and split.

"Damn, dats his grandmom..." He could hear one of them say as they door closed.

Relief swept over the women's faces, and over his body. He hated the adrenaline rush that being out in the street always created. What the hell was wrong in the world! Couldn't a brother walk his woman to the pizza store any more? What was it going to be like when Patsy started dating? Was he going to have to chauffeur his kids in an armored car to keep them from getting hit by a stray bullet from some dumb shit?

"Damn!" Jerome yelled as he slapped his hand on the counter. "I hate this crap! Young punks ain't got no respect. This woman could have been my grandmother, mother—that could be my sister back there working, or my daughter trying to make a little school money!" Rage propelled him around the shop, and he paced from the soda refrigerators and back to the counter.

"Thank you, thank you so much. You are like policia. You no pay. When you come in, you eat free... Neighbors," the older woman said, her voice full of gratitude.

He was too angry to put together what she was saying, but it was Antoinette's gentle tug on his arm that helped stop his pacing.

"Oh, no, Ma'am," he said shaking his head as Antoinette tried to hand him back the five and ten dollar bills he'd given the woman for his order. "That was only right. They have no cause to come bustin' into your store like that!"

"You are my Grandson now," the old woman chuckled. "Your wife is right, Anna needs a good, strong, policia man to protect this store—not a soft man who rides a fancy car while her Momma gets killed. Wise. Very wise."

Antoinette chuckled and tried to pull him toward the door. "I have a lot of students who could use a job. Some of their boyfriends are from the neighborhood. Maybe we could work a deal to get you security, and get them paid under the table?"

"Yes. That is good," the old woman beamed. "Next time, no charge. But, take two slices of cheesecake—Anna, one with cherries. Picka good ones."

The woman's offer made him smile and think of Pearline. She would have done that. All grandmothers did that—no matter what color. He'd traveled enough in the service to learn that much. Jerome nodded as he accepted the desserts, while trying to coax Antoinette out of the door before she got onto another tangent. All he'd planned to do was to bring her to his apartment, and try to get next to her. But, in a few short minutes, he'd had to become a gun for hire—without a gun.

"Those young boys could have glocked you, Jay!" Antoinette practically yelled once they hit the sidewalk. "Are you crazy?"

He had to laugh to release the tension. "Yeah, girl," he admitted, "I'm too old for this, T. In the day, you could duke it out in the streets. But, damn, everybody's packin'—'specially the young boys. They're all punks, that's why they pack—can't fight man-to-man, and don't respect a soul."

"Look," she said quietly as they made their way up the street, "I don't want you to get hurt. No more heroics. Next time, call the police."

He smiled as he opened the front door. She was worried about him, and he had done well, shown her that he could protect her—that he wasn't no punk... even though he would have done the same thing he did if Toni hadn't been there. However, her presence did help his grit, and he knew the young boys understood that he'd have to fight to the end if they'd embarrassed him in front of his woman. It was the law of the jungle.

"All right, all right," he conceded as they made their way up the steps and a new concerned came over him. What if she didn't like his place or, what if she'd been so unnerved, and put totally out of the mood by the incident? Damn. He'd have to start from ground zero, just like Miles had told him. But as she stood in the dim light, waiting for him to turn the locks, her hair just inches from his face, with her cheeks flushed from the cold and the excitement... He knew. The testosterone rush had turned her on.

Almost dropping the pizza, he fumbled for his keys and got the door open, kicking it wider with his foot.

"Jay!" she said with a gush of breath. "This is magnificent."

Antoinette turned her face to the ceilings. "Twelve foot..."

"Go ahead," he said, feeling very pleased and relaxing considerably. "Check out the living room."

He followed her, forgetting to set down the pizza, or take her coat until she began removing it herself.

"Oh, here, let me get that for you," he said quickly, trying to manage the soda bag, cheese cake, potato chips, and pizza—almost dropping the whole payload. He had to get hold of himself. He was literally becoming a clumsy teenager!

"'I've got it, that's okay," she protested, grabbing a sliding bag from the bottom to help him. "C'mon, you've got your hands full." Antoinette dropped her coat on the sofa and marched ahead of him with one of the bags. "Why don't we put this in the kitchen so it doesn't mess up this beautiful table? I haven't seen woods like this in so long, Jay. They're exquisite," she murmured as he followed her to the kitchen.

It was eerie. It seemed like she felt at home. She appeared so comfortable with his space, and yet, unlike Karen had done in the hotel, she didn't stake out boundaries. His pulse raced as he entered the kitchen and turned on the light.

"Wow, may I?" she giggled with a grin, opening

his cabinets. "A bachelor with a clean kitchen?"

"That's because I don't eat here," he laughed. "I open a hoagie on the coffee table and that's it. Nothing I eat requires a plate."

"Uhmph, uhmph, uhmph," she muttered, shaking her head with a smile as she checked out his space. "Gonna have to do better than that and take care of yourself, Jay."

Her warmth was having a dizzying effect on him. He set down the pizza on the table and unzipped his jacket. "Wanna see the kids' room?" It was his pride and joy showcase, because he'd made it himself. Remembering the old man's words, he held out a little bit of sugar to her and hoped that she would follow.

"I would love to," she said with a new shine of excitement in her eyes.

"C'mon, it's back here."

He stepped into the room first, then stood aside, turning on the light. He held his breath and waited.

"Oh, Jay, look at this!" Antoinette spun around and ran over to the bed frames, running her hand over the wood like cool water. "Look, you even did the walls with a border... Mickey and Minnie with spray paint. This is wonderful!"

He leaned back on the door molding to keep his chest from bursting with the pride her admiration created. "My days as a knuckle-head, spray painting buildings, finally came in handy," he laughed. "This old-dude had to give up exteriors, and work the interiors. You think they'll like it?"

"Are you kidding? They're all wearing cartoon gear. The fact that you did a graffiti version will knock 'em out! Their Dad can do something the kids can do—you mean he wasn't old, forever?" she laughed, drawing him into her mirth and making him chuckle. "That's why they flipped when I told them I could jump rope. This old woman givin' 'em fever in double-dutch?" she laughed again, "They just couldn't see it."

"That's cause they're blind," he said, feeling himself stir at the thought of her bouncing up and down with her luscious breasts bobbing. When she looked away shyly, he knew he had to keep her moving. Maybe she'd read his mind?

"C'mon. But, by-pass the bathroom, that's not up to military code," he added, checking it himself, "I'll show you my room, then we can go back to the living room and decide what to watch first." He had to leave her an out—to show her his room, but not make her feel trapped in it.

"Okay?" she said easily, and waiting for him to lead her there.

He took a deep breath through his nose to steady himself and led her down the hall. Twenty years... He was definitely out of practice.

"Well, this is it," he said as casually as he could. "Not much to look at." He waited. He watched. She didn't move at first, but just stood in the doorway, then slowly edged her way inside. He remembered her doing that before... entering the room slowly, looking around, and trying to decide if it would be the day to allow him to be with her.

"Not much?" she said quietly, her renewed admiration holding him for ransom. "Look at this dresser... it must be a hundred years old... and this mahogany sleigh frame. Where did you find it, Jay?"

When she turned around, the look on her face made speech too difficult for him to manage. So he shrugged his shoulders instead.

"This is lovely." Antoinette edged to the bed and bent to run her hand over the crocheted spread that he had fought with Mr. Miles about taking. "This is hand made, Jay."

The old man had been right.

"And you have plants in here, and pictures, old built-in closets. Are they cedar lined?"

"Yup," he said feeling totally overwhelmed by her attention to the details in his room. He knew she really liked it, and might consider laying her head down beside his, one day—if not tonight, just like old man Miles had told him she would. Next to the kids' room, this had been the most important room to complete.

Tension crept down his back. She hadn't moved, but let had her line of vision roam throughout the room, perhaps checking for signs of another woman, or signs of danger. He knew better than to approach her at this point. Just hold out some sugar, and call her with a soft tick to follow.

"How about those movies?" he asked quietly. "You can turn on the stereo, while I go get the VCR—before the crack-heads break my car window and jack it."

"Sure," she said in soft murmur, hesitating for a moment before she followed him down the hallway. "You look really settled-in, Jay. This is nice."

"Be back in a minute," he whispered as he passed her in the hall.

"Okay. Whatever you want."

The sound of her quiet affirmation sent a shudder of anticipation through him. It was in the way she had practically breathed the words "Okay, whatever you want." She seemed so relaxed. She seemed to approve of his environment. More importantly, she seemed to approve of him. She'd even hovered in his bedroom. And she looked so good. God, he wanted this woman. Tonight. Not later. The goal to be patient was wearing on him. Maybe, he thought, as he dashed down the steps, opened the car, and collected his VCR, just maybe... there was so much he wanted to say to her, too. So much water under the bridge between them that she'd become the river of his soul. So much he needed to apologize for from those early years of not understanding that her going to college didn't mean she'd leave him.

As he came up the stairs, he could hear Joe Sample blaring. She still liked jazz piano. Tension locked between his shoulders, and settled in his groin. He had to be cool, and he reminded himself of that fact as he made his way through the door and dropped the VCR on the coffee table. Standing and stretching out the taunt muscles in his back, he took off his jacket and cap, and tried not to look at her.

From the corner of his eye he glimpsed her. She was sitting cross-legged on his floor with a pile of albums on her lap. Her head was thrown back, her eyes were closed, and ecstasy graced her lips with a slight smile of contentment. If only he could make her look like the music had... after...

"I have to get some pictures up in here—of the kids," he said, trying to wrest his brain away from its single focus. "Maybe I'll take 'em to Sears?"

"That'll be nice, Jay..." she said drifting in a sexy tone without opening her eyes.

God, she was making it tough for him to think.

"What else do you want to hear?" he murmured, becoming mentally challenged as he allowed his gaze to sweep over her.

"I want to hear what happened to us, Jay-bird."

She'd opened her eyes and had made the request just above a whisper.

"I was foolish, and thought... I listened to my boys, who all said you were hours away at school, and would trade me in for an educated model. Youth. Gurl, you have no idea how many nights I regretted what you saw when you came to visit me on base that day. You also have no idea how many nights I thought about us..."

"Yes, I do," she whispered. "I'm sorry, too. Youth. A time when things were black and white, and never room for shades of gray."

"Yeah," he murmured, watching the light shimmer in her liquid brown eyes. "I just never thought we'd have a chance to say these things to each other... time goes by, lives get built... all I ever wanted to tell you, Toni, was how sorry I was. Can't blame you for listening to your dad. He was right, and—"

"—No, he wasn't, completely," she said, softly cutting him off. "He'd planted the seed of doubt, but seeing you with all your boys, drinking, and carousing, and gambling... I just looked at that and ran from it. I never even gave you a chance to explain, and I never even imagined that any of it had to do with your being afraid of anything—least of all afraid of what I was going to do. Guess we all have things inside us to heal."

Jerome shook his head, now feeling renewed tightness in his back beginning to strangle his spine. He'd hurt her so badly, then. How would she ever trust him again, especially after being hurt by her former husband? "I am so sorry, baby," he whispered. "This time, I'm trying to get it right, if I even have a chance to try?"

"But..." she said shyly, looking around then down at the floor.

"I signed my divorce papers already, and they're

on the way to a judge," he stated plainly, reading her thoughts and knowing she required an explanation. "Me and Karen's break-up was a long time in the making. I'm not playing games with you, Toni. I want to take it slow, get to know who you've become in the last twenty-years, and start again from scratch."

"Everything around us is changing," she whispered without looking up at him. "Everybody we knew has changed. Some days, I'm not even sure of who I am any more."

He chuckled in acknowledgement of her statement. "Can I tell you the truth?" he asked, causing her to look up at him with a slow smile. "I don't know what is going to happen in my life from one day to the next. But, I am sure of one thing," he added, growing suddenly serious as her sad smile ignited another memory within him, "I am so glad I went to the video store tonight. Call it serendipity, or Divine intervention."

She blushed and looked away, and the simple action felled a domino-chain reaction within him. God, he remembered that look of hers. It said everything and nothing and promised so much at the same time. He let his breath out slowly, and tried to again wrest his mind away from the image of joining her on the floor.

He had to remember to take it slow, though. That meant changing the subject. It was getting thick in the room between them again.

"What else do you want to hear?" he said, as he heaved the VCR next to the television. Turning quickly, he bent down to his stack of albums on the floor—and stopped abruptly.

"Shit!" he whispered.

"What?"

"T, it's my back." Horror locked the muscles around his spine. He couldn't straighten himself up. "I'll be okay. Just give me a minute." He shut his eyes to avoid seeing her look of pity.

Not now. Not tonight!

"Wait a minute, let me help you," she said quickly, standing and pacing to his side to assist him. "You got any Ben-Gay, or Heat in the house? Want me to run to Seven-Eleven and get you something?"

"Naw, I'll be all right," he insisted, watching his bachelor pad turn it into a convalescent home. "I've just been hauling furniture, working crazy hours on no-sleep... ain't what I used to be, Toni. Damn!" he exclaimed as the knots wound around the small of his back and punched at his kidneys. "I'll be okay, though. Won't have you out at night alone," he winced, wanting to kick himself.

"Can you get down on the floor? The sofa isn't wide enough. I can try to work it out, like when you showed me how to do when you'd get a leg cramp sometimes after track?"

He considered her proposition as the pain connected to his shoulder blades. This was not how he imagined being with her on the floor. "If I get down there, honey, I might not be able to get back up."

"Let me get the blanket from the other room. I'll help you get out of that sweater and get your boots off. Do you have any lotion, or Baby oil?"

"Got some lotion in the bathroom," he grumbled, giving in to the pain. Of course it would be in the last place he'd wanted her to see—the bathroom.

Antoinette walked away from his side briskly, and returned after a moment with a bottle of supermarket brand lotion and the throw from his bed. What a date. A beautiful woman, possibly a willing one, all night to show her how much he'd missed her... and his equipment had failed. Somebody shoot him, and put him out of his misery.

"I can't even raise my arms" he admitted, "or bend down to untie my boots."

"It's okay," she said softly, spreading out the blanket and helping him out of his sweater and t-shirt. She then squatted and unlaced his boots. "Step out, and I'll pull them off."

He looked down at her and followed her directions. Karen most assuredly had to have cursed him, he thought, as he stared at Toni's wide, brown eyes. Her cowboy had fallen, and she was there nuzzling him to get up. Jerome shook his head and laughed as a hundred old black-and-white movies crossed his mind. Some jockey. You had to be in shape to mount a thoroughbred, and he couldn't even swing his leg over the saddle if she'd let him.

"Toni, I'm sorry about this, baby... I wouldn't

have asked you over here to care for this broken down old man if—"

"Hush. That's what's wrong with you," she said with a smile, pulling off his other boot. "Tension. Over-work. And stress."

"Yeah," he admitted with a grunt, as she helped him onto the floor. "The last few weeks have been hell."

"I know," she said quietly, straddling his back, and rubbing her hands together to warm the lotion. "I'll tell you, I've already gone through phase one of the divorce thing—that's the part that locks up backs, brings on the flu, migraines, and takes a general toll on your health. Phase one is the, I'm-freaked-out-because-this-cannot-be-happening-to-my-life phase. Phase two, which you are about to embark upon, takes your spirit. That's the, oh-God-I-am-now-officially-a-national-statistic-and-I-never-saw-it-coming. I don't even know what phase three is like, and really am not looking forward to it. Hopefully that will be permutated into you either being bitter, or becoming a Zen Master. Me, myself, I'm angling to grab the stone of wisdom from the hand—so I never have to deal with this again."

"I hear you, baby. If this is just phase one... whew." Somehow, the hard facts seemed to go down his ear canal so much easier when floating on Antoinette's voice while she worked on his naked back.

"It ain't no joke. Nobody wants to do this, even

if you're with a crazy person—you'd rather resolve it some other way," she insisted, putting her weight into an obstinate muscle group.

"You ain't said a mumblin' word!" His voice had come out as a cross between a grimace and a forceful moan. God she was workin' him.

"You sound like Pearline," she laughed.

"Folks around you get strange, Toni. I don't know what it is—shift in the world order, or what—but, they're trippin'."

Antoinette let out a chuckle with a sigh, then reached for the bottle of lotion to refill her palms. "Truth. Since I've been back in Philly, seems like everything has changed. What's going on, Jay?"

"I don't know?" he murmured as her soft, crème-laden hands made contact with his skin again. "Seems like everything came to a head and exploded."

"How long's it been? Be honest."

"Since I left?" Her attention to the throbbing lobes on either side of his spine felt so good that his mind drifted with her steady pulls and thrusts—and, she'd diplomatically ignored his double entendre about things building up. "Almost a month." He let out a low groan of appreciation as her hands worked magic against his skin. "How the hell can your entire life change in a month? Tell me that, T... 'cause I'm still reelin' from it."

"I don't know," she admitted, working hard against the muscle groups as she pondered the question. "How can a split second choice of whether to go one in direction or another change a life? Happens everyday, we see it on the news, right... a person makes a choice to go down a certain street and boom, their life is changed by a speeding car, or something."

Even though his back was still killing him, she'd made him laugh hard. "All right, Antoinette Reeves. But, why can't you use a positive example? Like, why does the guy have to get hit by a SEPTA bus because he crossed the wrong street at the wrong time? Why couldn't he, in your hypothetical case, have picked the right lottery ticket?"

"Because, the odds are, and we hear it everyday that, more bad stuff happens like a car accident, or getting hit by a train, than people hitting the lottery, Jay."

She had thrown her head back and laughed, and it made him chuckle with her.

"True dat. So," he queried her in an amused tone, "is that why all of our friends are putting up barricades and telling us we're kicking up too much dust?"

"I'm not sure of what you're talking about," she said a little too quickly, which belied her position.

"They're scared to death of this thing, T, and you know it."

"Now, why would they be scared, A? And, for B, what thing?"

"A—Scared that there really is something called

a soul-mate, because if that's true, in the cases I've seen, they aren't with theirs. Soooo, that means that there's always a chance of instability. And, for B, the thing that has you sharing a pizza with me, trusting me enough to come home with me, to sitting on my back talking to me like old times, knowing exactly where every muscle still is under my skin, even though you and I haven't seen each other in twenty years. That history thing."

"Oh," she said quietly, moving her hands a little slower. "Well, everything is subject to instability— even with one's soul-mate, so I still don't understand what all the ruckus is about. Especially since I assume your break-up had to do with issues going awry in your household—not anything we did, correct?"

"Correct. But, did you realize that you get very deep and philosophical when you're scared to death? You used to do that when we were kids."

"I do not," she laughed, slapping more lotion between her palms but failing to warm it up first before applying it to his back.

"Yow! That's cold!"

"Serves you right," she giggled. "And, did you know that you make grand, sweeping assumptions when you're afraid? Hmmm? You do, you know."

"Gurl, no I don't."

"Yes, you do."

"Like what?"

"Like thinking all of our grown, married, harried, busy friends care about whatever we're doing. People are way too busy leading their own, hectic lives, Jay."

"All right, if you say so. But, I know that you're scared of this."

"What makes you say that?" She'd stopped rubbing his back, and he'd glimpsed her wide smile from the corner of his eye as she tilted her head.

"'Cause I'm scared to death of feeling this good around you again, girl."

"I'm scared, too," she whispered, now applying too much lotion to his back in jerky, nervous movements.

"All right, let's not rehash the past any more for the moment, or my back will never unlock. You're safe. I can't do you any harm lying prone on the floor. Plus, I'm way out of practice."

"How did it all happen? For real. I mean, how long's it been?" she laughed as she asked the question in a good-natured tone.

"Hurt my back last year doing a small contract. Nothin' serious—but, from time to time, especially when I'm sorta tired, or tense, it acts up."

"Yeah... and the follow up to that question is, you know what I meant."

He chuckled. He did know what she'd meant, but didn't want to answer the second question. If it had been so obvious to her that he hadn't been with a woman in a very long time, then he wasn't going to confirm it. Nor was he about to explain the messy

Leslie Esdaile

situation that had happened in Atlantic City. As far as he was concerned, that didn't even count as love-making—so, in reality he was pushing up on eight months, by his way of looking at things.

That last time with Karen was a finale, something that happened, like an argument with bodies, which finally buried his marriage. What had happened in that hotel had gored him... No, it was not a satiating kind of groove that left one feeling whole and mellow. Besides, if he went into all of that, she'd probably think he was desperate, or something, and he didn't want to have to find out that she wasn't— which was probably the case. He couldn't take news about a boyfriend—not while lying down crippled like this.

"A while," he finally said as her hands wound around a large walnut and dispersed it. "God, that feels good, woman... you have no idea."

She had no idea? Every heavy breath that he expelled, with a baritone groan behind it, made her check her sanity as it ignited her memory.

"And you? You seem pretty relaxed," he murmured.

She could feel the question hesitate and linger in his back as a new ball of knots rose under her fingers. "I'm relaxed, because I'm in the company of an old friend... and after two years, you sort of get used to... well, to the platonic aspects of life."

The muscles relaxed in his back as he breathed out hard. "Two years... damn, eight months had me near tears, baby, till I couldn't take it anymore."

His honest admission drew her to his shoulders, and she worked the sinewy cords between them, down either side of his spine to the deep valley in the small of his back.

"Oh, Jesus, woman, that feels so good..."

She had to close her eyes as she worked. His voice vibrated through her thighs creating a wet spot between them. Embarrassment swept through her as she realized that a river was threatening to pass through her underwear to leave evidence of her arousal in the center of her light-gray sweat pants. His breathing was no longer spasmodic, followed by a wince every time she found a new tangled muscle group. It was now deep and heavy and came up from beneath his diaphragm—just like she remembered. Goose bumps pebbled her arms as she worked, drawing every pore of her skin into a tingling, alive-till-it-hurt pulse that matched his breathing. She'd never get out of there without giving in. Never. No matter what Pearline said about patience. This man had snapped and dragged her suspicions into his lair... a beautiful lair... a place that she didn't mind being held hostage in all night long.

"Jay," she said quietly, trying to make her own breaths sound normal, while desperately trying to figure out how not to let him see the wet spot in her pants when she raised up on all fours over him. "You feel any better?"

He didn't answer, but kept breathing. God, help

her, she'd climb down there and do whatever he wanted her to.

"Jay," she said again, growing concerned, then suddenly realizing that he'd fallen asleep. "I guess you do feel better, honey," she whispered, allowing the wave of disappointment to engulf her as she stood. What had she expected? The man was obviously tired. She was obviously no longer attractive to him. He'd hurt his back.. They were just friends—and that was all he wanted to reestablish not a relationship. Was she crazy? Didn't the man just say he had only been out of his marriage for a month? The discussion about the controversy amongst their friends was just that—an interesting conversational juncture. It was like a generic political topic to discuss when there is nothing of mutual interest to really to discuss... because you don't know the other person's mutual interests any longer. It was time to go. Yeah, this was the vulnerable, break-your-spirit-phase of being newly divorced.

Antoinette tiptoed around the sleeping giant on the floor and slipped into his bedroom and grabbed another blanket. She returned quietly, bent, and tucked the thick wool around him, brushing his cheek with a kiss. At least he'd been a gentleman— even though he claimed that he hadn't had a woman in months. The fact that she couldn't even get a rise out of a starving man pierced her heart with a truth-dipped dagger. Maybe Brian had been right— nobody would want her. Either that was true, or

Jerome was a kind liar. Antoinette looked down at Jerome's prone body, and studied the unconscious smile on his face. Brian had obviously been right, because Jerome slept like a baby—a person without lies.

She let out her breath with despair and looked at her coat and her purse. There was only one diplomatic solution. To leave a note, go home, and let sleeping dogs lie. Then she could take a hot shower, and rinse her embarrassing stain out of her pants so it didn't leave a trail in her laundry hamper. Then, she could watch TV until dawn. Maybe it was for the best, because she hadn't even interviewed him completely. Anyway, it was too soon...

But, God, she wanted him.

CHAPTER 28

He stretched, yawned, and rolled over on his back. For the first time in what felt like ages, total relaxation had consumed him in a drifting semi-consciousness. This was certain peace.

Jerome kept his eyes closed as he listened to the stillness. Maybe she had eaten a little pizza and gone to sleep? He'd just go into the bedroom and wake her up, and climb under the sheets beside her. As the thought assembled in his mind, it hit a brick wall.

Wait a minute... Toni didn't live here. She wouldn't be that bold, not after all these years...

Rolling himself up slowly, he looked at his watch, and panicked. One o'clock in the morning? Jesus. He'd been asleep for almost two hours!

"Toni?" he called out softly, hoping that she'd

read his mind and had stayed. "T...."

Resolved by her no-answer, he pulled himself all the way up and stretched, cursing himself as he did so. How could he have been that lame?

"Damn," he muttered as he looked at the VCR, which hadn't been connected to the television, and over at the stack of movies they hadn't watched. Renewed disappointment filled him as he cast his gaze toward the sofa to the spot that her coat and pocketbook had once occupied. Making his way down the hall, he stopped in every room—just in case she might have hung up her coat, then cursed himself again for his foolish, wishful thinking when he clicked on the bedroom light to find the room vacant. He'd blown it. Totally, entirely, literally blown it.

"Aw, Toni..." he sighed as he shook his head and walked back into the living room to flop on the sofa. Damn, what was he going to do to fix it now? He'd have to wait another two weeks until he had time alone to really pursue her. His kid-weekends were out of the question. That's all he'd need was for them to take a story about some woman back to their mother. With that info, Karen might even try to use Toni as some misguided reason to keep the kids away from him. Custody issues were never settled until the kids were grown. No. He'd have to wait until the ink was dry for any formal introductions. There was no reason to cause unnecessary risk to his parental custody, or for Toni.

Tonight he'd have to settle for cold pizza, and a cold bed. Perhaps he could call Antoinette in the morning, and set up a real date for two weeks from now, one with wine, roses--the works? Maybe, if she wasn't too pissed off?

But, the thought of surviving on only the memory of her touch for another two weeks was totally depressing—especially since she'd reawakened his cellular memory of her with her hands. It had been bad enough working like an ox for Mr. Miles to keep her out of his dreams at night, and worse yet was not being able to get any sleep in the new apartment because of her. Of all the times in the world, she'd relaxed him so, and made him feel so totally safe in her company that, he'd given in to months of sleep deprivation. Now, this new private space with no intrusion only seemed to make his ache for Toni more unbearable. He was sure that he'd never be able to withstand it.

"Damn!" he yelled again into the empty space, kicking the coffee table away with his foot. "Stupid! Pitiful!" Jerome let his head drop back on the sofa and looked up to the ceiling. "What can I tell this woman? Will ya give me a break!"

Too agitated to sit, he stood and paced, then went to the kitchen and flung open the pizza box and grabbed a piece of the cold, coagulated pie. A slip of paper that had been resting on the top of the box floated across the room. Growing more irate, he paced over to the receipt and snatched it up and crumpled it in his hand as he took a large bite of the food he held. Nothing ever went right. Ever! He walked back into the living room and kicked at the litter of blankets on the floor, then went into the kitchen to find a beer to chase down the dough in his throat. Popping off the tab with one hand, he looked at the crumpled paper in his palm using only the moonlight to see it. All this grub to eat by himself, he thought, becoming surlier as he gulped down his brew. A total waste of money that could've gone toward more paint and supplies for the kids' room... he would have never bought that much food to eat alone. For her, he would have taken her to La Bec Fin, the finest French restaurant in the city. But, for himself, he would have opened a can of pork-n-beans!

Jerome set his beer on the counter and leaned against the sink as he unfolded the paper. He needed to look at the hard evidence himself—anything to stay focused on his goal to be patient, practical. This would never happen again. Falling asleep on a date?

Fully expecting to see rows of numbers, he stopped, then looked hard at the feminine handwriting. She wasn't angry. Antoinette had apologized for intruding on his evening, when he was tired. A new wave of shame clawed at his ego. It was worse than he'd thought.

Taking two more deep gulps of beer, he went to the phone by his bed and sat down. Looking at the paper again, he began dialing the telephone number she'd left him.

He could only pray that the right words would come. To hell with patience. He had to see her tonight.

Antoinette yawned, snuggled down deeper into the blankets, and flipped the channels with the remote control. She should have taken at least one movie to occupy her mind, she thought, staving off the gnaw to be with Jerome. But, then again, maybe not, she told herself. It probably would have only reminded her that she was supposed to be on an accidental date—that wasn't. And, although the warm shower had offered some relief, making her sleepy, nothing on the set could eclipse him from her mind. Sitting on his high-firm backside and touching his muscular back...

Antoinette shook the vision from her head as she felt herself begin moisten again at the mere thought. She had to let it go. The man had issues to deal with in his phase one process. They might have had a history, but a lot of years had intervened. They probably weren't anywhere near the same people they had been years ago. This had no future and could never work. No need in ruining a perfectly good memory. If she could just get her mind off making love to him, find some significant flaws to quell how very aroused he'd made her.

Again, she attempted to shake Jerome Henderson out of her mind. It would be tomorrow soon. Maybe she could visit Pearline... or go see her father... or finish up some chores... Her breasts were becoming more weighted and the tips of them stung as she took in each slow breath. The ache between her thighs literally made her hands tremble. No. She had to cold turkey this out of her system. Think of something else!

Anything to keep her head on straight until Lauren came home.

When the phone rang, she looked at it with disinterest and slowly left the warmth of the sofa. "Okay, okay, I'm coming," she sighed. "Yeah, Yeah... tell me about all the fun I missed by not going out, y'all," she muttered, letting out her breath as she picked up the receiver. Yup, she told herself, she should have gone out with one of her girlfriends.

"Hey, lady," Antoinette sighed in a bored voice, "Whassup?"

The lack of response annoyed her. If Brian was calling to bed check her, or some fool was calling with a wrong number...

"Toni," a warm, male voice began, "let me first apologize."

Frozen mid-way between the living room and the kitchen, Antoinette let her breath out very slowly as her body pulsed more alive.

"You don't have to apologize," she said quietly. "I know you were tired, and besides, it isn't like that with us anymore. I—"

"—Can I come over?" Jerome nearly whispered.

"You're wrong, and I need to show you that. I fell asleep because I haven't slept good in months, and especially not in this last month since I heard you were back in town. You've been in my dreams, robbing me of peace and making my hands shake 'cause I've wanted you so bad. Then with you petting me and talking to me tonight, like old times, I drifted off in the most exquisite rest I've had in years. But, it wasn't because I didn't want you."

For a moment, she couldn't speak. The hoarseness and depth of his voice... He'd just flat out said it—confirmed it. No pretense. No suave manipulation. Just straight up without a chaser. Just like the first time. That was her Jay.

"I'm sorry, Toni," he stammered when she took too long to respond, "I have no right to.... I just really want... I mean... God, girl, if you only knew."

His latent desire came through the phone and wrapped itself around her. The way he'd said her name...

"I know what you mean. I just thought that—"

"—You thought wrong, baby. I need to see you. Now. I repeat. Can I come over?"

She swallowed hard, and her gaze tore around the living room as a hundred thoughts raced through her mind at once. "Okay," she murmured, "I'll see you in a little bit. Bye."

"At your side in five," he whispered, then hung up.

Antoinette covered her mouth and took a deep

breath. He'd given her their code phrase—'at your side in five,' just like in high school. He'd remembered. She also allowed herself a moment to remember the passion that always followed those words—then she sprang into motion. Five minutes! She had five minutes to pull off that old robe, kick off her fluffy slippers, straighten-up the bedroom, and find a dash of perfume. If she could only twinkle her nose like Samantha on the old show *Bewitched*, or fold her arms and blink herself beautiful like on *I Dream of Jeanie*. Five minutes! Not a bit of make-up on, she had a newspaper on the foot of the bed, with a damned doll and stuffed animals from Lauren in it!

She tore around the condo like a mad woman, dropping the telephone twice before she could get it to stay in the wall mount. Rushing to the bathroom, she took a swig from the bottle of mouthwash and spit out the mint-flavored liquid while flinging her old robe and slippers into the laundry area. Streaking into her bedroom, she found an old silk Kimono--the one that Brian used to call her moo moo. Too bad. It would have to do. She didn't own anything from Victoria's Secret that fit any more. The bed grabbed her attention next, and she collected up everything in one scoop, then dumped it in the bottom of her closet—pulling her hair out of the pony tail scrunch at the same time. Perfume! Jesus, what kind of perfume? Running over to the vanity, she almost tripped on the edge of the comforter, catching her fall on the dresser as she made a selection and fluffed up any residual body that may have mercifully stayed in her hair. Okay. Red.

Her gaze scanned the bedroom like a hawk with night vision. Cool. It passed inspection. She then ran into the bathroom and gave it a quick-once-over-lightly. Cool. The living room was okay—all except the blankets on the sofa and the melting pint of Hagen Daas—that had to go in the trash. Scooping up the almost-empty carton with one hand, and the blankets with the other, she ran over to the garbage can and pushed the wet container down deep—hiding the evidence of her sin. He could already see that she was way over-weight, that's all he'd need was to see how she'd gotten that way.

Morose thoughts stole her thunder as she walked more slowly back to the bedroom. Who was she fooling? She wasn't a genie, capable of making layers of body disuse and misuse go away in five minutes—no matter how clean her place was.

Antoinette heaved the blankets on the bed and spread them out slowly, waiting for the bell. He was remembering something she wasn't anymore, and once he put his arms around her, he'd feel the truth for himself as her layers got in the way of his memory. This room wouldn't be seen.

When the interior doorbell chimed, she looked at the clock and stood away from the bed. He'd made it over in five minutes—only to be disappointed. Okay. She knew the look. Her husband had shown it to her on too many occasions to mistake it. One peep into Jerome's eyes, and she'd know. Antoinette took her time and steadied her breath as she approached and opened the door. She had her face-saving line already rehearsed.

"You didn't have to come over here, Jerome," she said quietly, as he stepped into the foyer and she shut the door behind him. "Like I said. I understand."

He just stared at her, then touched her face. His fingers trembled as they lit her cheek with fire, and his steady gaze held her tumble of awkward words.

"No, you don't understand," he whispered, moving in closer as he stared at her. "You couldn't possibly know."

She scanned his face for any sign of pity, for any sign that his words of kindness were false. But his eyes spoke volumes as they bored through her.

"I've changed, and I'm sorry, Jerome. I'm not what—"

His mouth found hers, cutting off her awkward explanation. The warmth that emanated from the inside of it captured her lips and a hot breeze danced across her tongue as his circled hers. The once gentle touch that had held her cheek became firmer as he brought his other hand up to her face and pulled her to him with more force to deepen their kiss. Wide hands slid down her neck and shoulders and wrapped around her back, crushing her to his body. She could feel the want in him as his hand slid down to the small of her spine and pressed her between his legs. The effect was dizzying, wondrously mind-altering as she remembered.

Breaking momentarily from her mouth, rough stubble from his jaw grazed her neck as his mouth planted a series of memories next to each sensation. His groan felt like it had come up from the bottom of his soul as he found her mouth again, harshly pulling a returned sound of longing up from hers.

"Don't apologize to me anymore for being beautiful, woman," he said in a ragged breath against her hair. "I want you so bad, it hurts. Twenty years of wanting you again like this. C'mon. Let me show you." He eased his embrace and let his hands slide down her backside then he closed his eyes. "Please, Toni," he whispered. "We've got a second chance."

Their mutual reservations gave way to a slow retreat, eroding layers of fear in an unsure stop-start dance. Hands hovered above skin, tentatively grazing it before committing to follow through with a touch. Within those slight hesitations, years of doubts cast upon already damaged self-esteems lingered. Ghosts of wrong lovers that had spoiled spirits and hurt hearts slithered into the smallest spaces between skin and fingertips. Yet, he'd already shown her much of what she needed to know. This was the Jay that she'd remembered—gentle, but passionate—waiting for her readiness.

Taking his hand she led him to the bedroom, and waited as he stood only inches before her.

Within the small space between them she could feel all the unspoken questions dance against their clothing; will I be accepted, has too much time passed? Each wanted as much as the other to create a new memory without extinguishing the cherished fantasies of their history. They waited and watched each other intensely, hoping that the invisible wall of trepidation that held them for a moment would dissipate under the desire that had begun to crumble its foundation.

"I missed you, Jay," she admitted quietly, touching his face.

Covering her hand with his own he stared at her in the moonlight, and shook his head. "I feel like I'm eighteen again. I'm almost afraid to touch you. I can't tell you how many nights I've thought about this."

"You too?" she breathed against his neck, relaxing from his admission. "I used to think about this all the time."

She looked up, needing to see his expression, needing to know that it had been all right for her to hold him in her heart that long like this. His smile greeted and warmed her, and he stepped closer to pull her into an embrace again.

What started out as a slow dissolve of her sanity, again became a sudden impassioned rush of tangled arms and legs. Chuckling at her inept attempt to unfasten his belt, she stopped kissing him and looked into his eyes.

"I haven't done this in a while," she admitted with a whisper as a wide smile overcame his face.

"Me neither. That's why you're robe is all in a ball around your neck," he chuckled softly, brushing her lips with his own and seeming relieved. "Maybe you'd better do it? It's not as easy as they make it look in the movies."

She pulled her robe over her head and waited as he snatched off his baseball cap, then fought with his jacket, sweater, pants, and boots, finally freeing himself from the twisted clothing. As a pile of clothing mounted on the floor, they both laughed and fell into an easy embrace. And just as immediately, their mirth dissipated the moment their skin came together. His sudden shudder connected to her own and released another warm valley-stream within the boundary between her thighs.

"I'm glad you don't know how to do this," he whispered.

She knew exactly what he meant, and shared the satisfaction of knowing that this was not something he'd mastered with several others before her. She loved the exquisite quality of being special, different—cherished. "Let's go and lay down, Jay. I think we're too old for mid-floor acrobatics."

He didn't laugh, or smile, but followed her to the bed with a singular intensity reflecting in his eyes. She definitely remembered his serious look—the one that meant he couldn't take it any longer. She shivered at the thought, and popped under the blanket with anticipation while she watched him slowly join her under the covers. All the years of waiting... needing... hoping... conspired against her fears and fought their way to the surface of her desire when he lowered himself to enter her.

She felt so good. Too good. Thick fleshy, folds of wet woman. Soft, lush breasts broke his fall and supported his chest, as delirium from her scent filled his nose and wound itself around the base of his brain. He sank his hands into the deep, sumptuous valleys of velvety skin that separated her waist from her hips, coaxing her bottom to respond to his rhythm as his palms found the roundness of her behind. A shudder claimed him, as did the heat that created a vacuum between their bodies. It had been so long...

"Oh, girl..." he whispered, the words dissolving into a guttural moan when he shuddered again hard, and found himself quickly approaching. "Is it okay?"

"No," she whispered back in immediate panic, her body freezing his with its sudden stillness. "I'm not on anything. Oh, my God. We have to get up."

All he could do was fill his lungs with air and beg his body to stop moving. Never in his adult life had he been forced to fight against his nature like this. When he felt her clamp around him and pulse with want, he withdrew. Her quiet gasp of pleasure slashed at his reason as he looked down at her. Her face was covered with a glistening sheen. Her ample breasts swayed as she took each breath, and her nipples pouted and begged him to kiss them. He could feel a bead of sweat roll down his temple. He prayed for strength as his arms trembled under his own weight. He had to get up.

"Do you have anything in the house?" he breathed against her cheek, summoning logic, and trying desperately to ignore the way his groin throbbed out a request that he dared not respond to. Pulling himself back, he crouched over her on his hands and knees. He had to keep his distance. Paradise was too close.

"No. I mean, they're dated—I think they've expired. I never even opened the box when the girls gave them to me a couple of years ago," she whispered, closing his entry to Eden as she slipped under and around him to the side of the bed. "I am soooo stupid! What was I thinking?"

Pleased beyond measure by her admission, despite the heavy-laden pain in his groin, he thought better of introducing the possibility of the two condoms he still had in his wallet from Atlantic City. Bad move, he told himself, requiring too much explanation. Not now. Later. If ever.

"It's not just you, baby. I'm the one with four kids who oughtta know better. I wasn't thinking about anything, but this," he whispered in haggard spurts, pulling her against him again. "I'll go get something, if you promise to still want to make love as much as you do now when I get back."

"You can count on it," she whispered, sending

another shudder through him as her palm slid between his thighs.

"I can't... not yet... not when you do that. Just once more, before I go, baby," he moaned as the heat from her hand collapsed his judgment.

"Are you sure? You won't have an accident... will you, Jay?"

"Yeah... No. I mean... I always took care of you, right? No accidents, baby, just one more time."
Pulling her to lay under him, he kissed away her fears and sank into sheer oblivion. But her subterranean temperature released a spasm that traveled up his spine and past his lips, "Dear, God in Heaven..."

Instantly, his own words brought back his reason, and he withdrew sharply, panting from the wall of pressure that had spiked in two strokes. "I'm beyond the point of promise, I gotta get up."

Her eyes searched his face, and she slipped from his hold and stood up. He rolled over on his back and began counting in his head backward from a hundred. He had to get up. She was the only one making sense as she put on her robe and sat down on the side of the bed. He could feel her presence looming next to him. A woman that wanted him. One that he'd fantasized about in the shower, on the sofa at the old house, sleeping on an old cot in a dingy basement, the woman who'd made him wet dream like a schoolboy... the one who stole his sleep when he got his own apartment, the one that had almost made him lose his mind in the barracks.

"C'mon, Jay," she whispered as she brushed his mouth with a kiss. "The longer you wait, the harder it will be to go."

"It's already too hard," he whispered and returned her kiss with force, then let her slip away from him so he could get up.

Tugging on his pants and his sweater, he tried to painfully zip his jeans around the lead-pipe that protruded from them. "Damn... I can't get 'em closed," he winced as he forced himself into his pants. "This is crazy."

"You gotta put on some socks and some underwear, honey," she chuckled. "You're gonna catch a death of cold."

He didn't look at her as he put on his jacket, and grabbed his cap. "Not with this much thermal. I'm not going to be outside that long."

Swiping her mouth with another quick kiss, he bolted for the door and slammed it behind him. He took the steps by twos, unable to wait for the building's slow elevator, until he hit the pavement, and tried to half-walk, half-cool-run to his car. Pulling out of the space with one motion, he reached into his jacket, dumped out a cigarette and lit it, then crushed it out after three puffs, swerving into the parking lot of the Seven-Eleven. Too distracted to care, he left his car diagonally slanted in an open space and bound for the store. His heart slammed against the inside of his chest as he waited for the short line to move.

Damn, people were slow! Finally reaching the counter, he ordered two three-packs of Lifestyles, ignoring the sly glances that the brothers in line gave him. Accepting his change, he jumped back into the car, pulled the two unopened condoms from his wallet and tossed them out of the window—banishing the end of his bad luck. He waited impatiently for an opening to the traffic pattern on Chestnut, then pulled off on two wheels.

Antoinette paced in front of her door with the window ajar until she heard what had to be Jerome's car pull up. Despite the Saturday evening traffic, one car stood out in her mind as she listened for the vehicle door to slam, then heard someone take the steps in three strides. She leaned back on the wall and giggled. It was just like high school, when they'd have to find a way, any way, anywhere, to get together. Hearing Jerome hit the landing in the hallway she opened the door for him.

The look on his face widened her smile, yet his intensity stopped her advance toward him. The primal haunt that his eyes held stilled her. She couldn't move as he slammed the door behind him, reached for her, and almost pressed the life from her against the wall. Not fumbling this time, he dropped his jacket and cap without ever breaking the seal of their kiss. Pulling her by the hand, he nearly dragged her behind him into the bedroom, only stopping to slip her robe over her head.

Leslie Esdaile

Resealing their kiss, he brought one knee up then the next to unlace his boots. Still kissing her, he stepped out of them and dropped his jeans, leaving her lips only once to pull off his sweater.

This time when he joined to her, they almost fell, and she had to laugh as they tumbled on the bed. "Your package," she protested. "The reason you went to the store... remember?"

"Oh, yeah. Damn," he chuckled, briefly leaving her to grab his jeans. Pulling out two packs of latex-wear, he threw one on the nightstand and fiddled with opening the other.

"Two three-packs?" she whispered in awe, covering her mouth with her hand.

"They don't sell the boxes of twelve at Seven-Eleven," he murmured, tearing open a foil wrapper with his teeth, then turning away from her.

"You would have brought a box of twelve?" Antoinette let her question trail off as he turned to face her and slipped under the blanket with her.

"I missed you, baby," he whispered, kissing down the center of her chest and stopping along the way to pay homage to her belly-button before he nipped the inside of her thigh. "I've got twenty years to catch up on. Lay back, and remember."

She followed his lead down the trails of ecstasy that he reawakened, past all of the hurts and fears, connecting to their once love with both reverence and the new skill of age. His mouth made her remember the definition of being cherished, as it

512

dropped molten kisses against neglected membranes, siphoning her cries, which he answered with his tongue. Each time, he was more gentle, each time he rediscovered terrain that had not been explored since their youth, and each time he found a secret well of pleasure that poured forth appreciation as he found those caverns that had been locked away within her. He tasted her until her voice filled the room, and he blanketed her hard, fast, and immediately, unable to deny himself sanctuary any longer. And, each time as her legs locked him against her in protective warmth, his voice thundered behind hers in a sonic boom that always came from his depths, until only the stillness of the night and their breathing could be heard.

Winded, she rolled onto her side, and peered at him. Jerome lay on his back taking in life-sustaining gulps of air. She smiled with a satisfaction that went far beyond her sated body. He had touched her soul.

"Oh, my God, woman," he whispered raggedly. "I haven't been able to hang like this since high school."

Antoinette peeped over towards the pile of foil clutter that lay on the nightstand and lowered her eyes. "Jerome Henderson, we've got a problem," she chuckled. "I'm addcted. No doubt-about-it."

"Good," he murmured, filling his hand with one of her breasts, "I've got one more left before I have to go back out for ammunition."

"That's only 'cause it's been a while," she whispered sadly. "When this wears off... when reality hits.... but this was wonderful, tonight."

Her sad eyes drew him, and he looked at the shine from them as the moonlight draped over her shoulder. Never in his life had he been so content. Never since before, when she was all his. "What did your ex do to you, baby... to make you feel this way about yourself?" Emotion constricted his chest as the question battered his mind.

"Oh, Jay... you have no idea," she whispered, her eyes casting a sheen before she lowered them. "It wasn't just him. It was a lot of things. The men in my life that came before him, like my father's opinion of me—always wanting me to be some petite little doll that blindly obeyed... and the ones that came after him—the lovers I took in anger right after the divorce, but who never really knew or cared about me. I haven't felt pretty since I left your arms, Jay. Men don't treat a woman like this any more. They just don't. Not after you lose your figure, and have bills to worry about—when life gets real, honey. That's just the way it goes."

Her admission broke him. How could this wonderful woman believe such a lie?

"You said we have a problem," he murmured so low that she had to look at him. "We do." He waited until her gaze searched his face before he continued. "The problem is that I love you," he whispered. "And, I can't let this go a second time around. We have to make this work some kinda way."

"Men, sometimes think they want one thing, then change their minds later, especially when the packaging is better. I can't take my little girl through that."

"That's because we're fools," he whispered, leaving her breast and following the curve of her hip with his hand. "Too many of us want what we've been shown in the magazines and on TV—skinny girls, too young and too stupid girls. We don't know what a real woman can be like... sometimes until it's too late—unless we've been to the valley without water—to the rock. I've been to the rock, Toni. Trust me."

He let his hand rest on her belly, and he shook his head no when she tried to pull away, allowing the tips of his fingers to trace a pregnancy stretch mark before he bent his neck to kiss it. "No. Don't," he whispered against the soft skin at his cheek. "Rembrant drew women right, fleshy, all woman, voluptuous. The masters knew," he said gently, running his palm down the outside of her thigh and back up the curve of her hip as he stared into her eyes. "Real. Warm. Mysterious beyond imagination. Worth respect, and praise, capable of unspeakable pleasure, or wrath. Woman. Real woman. And smarter than any of us, beyond our greatest fears," he whispered near her mouth.

"You're biased," she whispered, brushing his lips and tracing his brow with her fingertips.

"You're right," he whispered back. "Because you are the river of my soul. I tried it the other way—living without you. It didn't work. My spirit almost turned to dust and died without you, my healing river. I've been to the rock, trying to forget about you. No more. Marry, me, Toni. I don't have to wait to know what's real."

He felt her hesitation as he brushed her mouth. "Just say yes. Tomorrow, we'll talk about it. Tonight, just let me keep loving you like this," he urged, and found her tongue. He didn't want to hear her answer, or any excuses about legalities, children, ex-wives, or bills. He only wanted to feel her response beneath him. That would let him know. He'd wear her down later, and argue with her in the cold light of day over breakfast tomorrow—if necessary. They could decide about how to incorporate the children into this, and figure out what to tell their family and friends—tomorrow… They could work out how they'd see each other, and figure out the finances, and such—tomorrow. If he had to get a third job, he'd look for it—tomorrow.
But, not now.

Not when she flowed through every cell in his body. Not when he'd been without her for so long. And, not when she was trembling in his arms like the shy girl of fifteen that he had once made woman.

Sequel Excerpt
For

Still Waters Run Deep

Is there such a thing as a soul-mate and can friendships withstand the test of time? And, what really broke up Antoinette and Jerome in the first place—what was the sequence of events that fractured their young love? "Rivers of the Soul" merely scratched the surface of what Toni saw when she went down to Dover Air Force Base. Only Buddy and Jerome really know.

Explore these age-old questions about friendships that defy answers in "Still Waters Run Deep," where the truth is revealed about Jerome and Antoinette's early relationship, and the impact that it now has on their children—and upon the marriages and bonds of their closest friends.

Don't you want to know how the relationship with Antoinette and her stepmother, May, evolves? How does Antoinette deal with her sister, once and for all? What happens with each member of the girlfriend crew, and childhood buddies that have sworn to be together until the end? What happens to Valerie and Buddy, Tracey and Scoop, Cookie, and Francis? Why is Toni so indebted to her cousin, Vanessa? It goes beyond babysitting help. And, let's not forget about all of the young women from Antoinette's class... what happens to them, and how are their lives transformed?

Can five children thrown together in a blended relationship actually bond? What happens when one spouse opens a custody battle to try to keep Jerome's children from him? And, what is Brian's story? What happens to Antoinette and Jerome when her ex-husband makes a play to reclaim what was once his? Can Antoinette and Jerome pull this off without losing the magic that held them together in an emotional connection for twenty years? How can they support all those children and still build the life they had hoped for? What happens when jobs get shaky, and friends die suddenly? What happens to Jerome when he discovers who Antoinette really is—not a wounded little girl, but a confident, successful woman. And, what happens between Jerome and his father? What happens when life gets real?

And, of course, what's in a vision sent from the realm of the spirit? Could it be that the ancestors are still with us? Just ask Pearline.

Join this communion of spirits in *Still Waters Run Deep*. The first book is only half of the story!

Indigo Novella's
by
Leslie Esdaile

Midnight Clear, an Indigo holiday anthology.
ISBN 1-58571-039-3

In the small town of Mystic Ridge it is said that the spirits of the ancestors watch over the townsfolk, causing mischief, setting old wrongs right and healing wounded hearts. Maybe it's rumor, or maybe it's not. But one very special winter night, magic truly comes to pass, and four of romances' richest voices spin the enchanting tales of what happened on a Midnight Clear...

In Leslies Esdaile's *Home for the Holiday's*, returning to Mystic Ridge should be a special time for Colette and Franklin. Instead, their homecoming is filled with sorrow over the loss of Colette's grandmother, and doubt about the future of their marriage. Neither of them is prepared for the magical spirit that will change their lives, heal their family, and mend their hearts one snowy winter's night.

"Midnight Clear, captures the essence of the holiday season: love, family memories, laughter, hope, and spiritual renewal. Leslie Esdaile, Carmen Green, Gwynne Forster and Monica Jackson have given readers a wonderful gift. Thank you for this collection."
Gwendolyn E. Osborne-The Romance Reader

Time Enough to Love
by
Leslie Esdaile

After The Vows, an Indigo Anthology
ISBN 1-58571-047-4

Aruba, a lover's paradise, is the perfect place for a couple to rediscover each other and reaffirm a relationship that's headed for meltdown.

For Better, For Worse takes on a whole new meaning for Alexandra and Edward. They thought this second marriage would be their second chance, an opportunity to get it right this time. So they pooled their hearts, their resources and their families, but forgot the true reasons they walked down the aisle—forgot how to make Time Enough to Love. It's going to take a fanning of the flames to rekindle the old fires and a sacred promise remembered to see them through.

INDIGO

Summer & Fall 2001

July

Love Doesn't Come Easy · Charlyne Dickerson · $8.95

August

Yesterday's Dreams, Tomorrow's Promise
Reon Laudat · $8.95

September

A Dangerous Deception · J. M. Jeffries · $8.95

October

Illusions · Pamela Leigh Starr · $8.95

November

The Love We Had · Natalie Dunbar · $8.95

December

Rivers of the Soul · Leslie Esdaile · $8.95

OTHER GENESIS TITLES

A Dangerous Love	J.M. Jefferies	$8.95
Again My Love	Kayla Perrin	$10.95
A Lighter Shade of Brown	Vicki Andrews	$8.95
All I Ask	Barbara Keaton	$8.95
A Love to Cherish (Hardcover)	Beverly Clark	$15.95
A Love to Cherish (Paperback)	Beverly Clark	$8.95
And Then Came You	Dorothy Love	$8.95
Best of Friends	Natalie Dunbar	$8.95
Bound by Love	Beverly Clark	$8.95
Breeze	Robin Hampton	$10.95
Cajun Heat	Charlene Berry	$8.95
Careless Whispers	Rochelle Alers	$8.95
Caught in a Trap	Andree Michele	$8.95
Chances	Pamela Leigh Starr	$8.95
Cypress Whisperings	Phyllis Hamilton	$8.95
Dark Embrace	Crystal Wilson-Harris	$8.95
Dark Storm Rising	Chinelu Moore	$10.95
Everlastin' Love	Gay G. Gunn	$10.95
Forever Love	Wanda Y. Thomas	$8.95
Gentle Yearning	Rochelle Alers	$10.95
Glory of Love	Sinclair LeBeau	$10.95
Indiscretions	Donna Hill	$8.95
Interlude	Donna Hill	$8.95
Kiss or Keep	Debra Phillips	$8.95
Love Always	Mildred E. Riley	$10.95
Love Unveiled	Gloria Green	$10.95
Love's Deception	Charlene Berry	$10.95
Mae's Promise	Melody Walcott	$8.95
Midnight Clear	Leslie Esdaile	$10.95
(Anthology)	Gwynne Forster	
	Carmen Green	
	Monica Jackson	
Midnight Magic	Gwynne Forster	$8.95
Midnight Peril	Vicki Andrews	$10.95
Naked Soul (Hardcover)	Gwynee Forster	$15.95
Naked Soul (Paperback)	Gwynne Forster	$8.95
No Regrets (Hardcover)	Mildred E. Riley	$15.95
No Regrets (Paperback)	Mildred E. Riley	$8.95
Nowhere to Run	Gay G. Gunn	$10.95

Passion	T.T. Henderson	$10.95
Path of Fire	T.T. Henderson	$8.95
Picture Perfect	Reon Carter	$8.95
Pride & Joi (Hardcover)	Gay G. Gunn	$15.95
Pride & Joi (Paperback)	Gay G. Gunn	$8.95
Quiet Storm	Donna Hill	$10.95
Reckless Surrender	Rochelle Alers	$8.95
Rooms of the Heart	Donna Hill	$8.95
Shades of Desire	Monica White	$8.95
Sin	Crystal Rhodes	$8.95
So Amazing	Sinclair LeBeau	$8.95
Somebody's Someone	Sinclair LeBeau	$8.95
Soul to Soul	Donna Hill	$8.95
The Price of Love	Beverly Clark	$8.95
The Missing Link	Charlyne Dickerson	$8.95
Truly Inseparable (Hardcover)	Wanda Y. Thomas	$15.95
Truly Inseparable (Paperback)	Wanda Y. Thomas	$8.95
Unconditional Love	Alicia Wiggins	$8.95
Whispers in the Night	Dorothy Love	$8.95
Whispers in the Sand	LaFlorya Gauthier	$10.95
Yesterday is Gone	Beverly Clark	$10.95

All books are sold in paperback, unless otherwise noted.

You may order on line at www.genesis-press.com, by phone at 1-888-463-4461, or mail the order form in the back of this book.

Love Spectrum Romance

Romance across the culture lines

ORDER FORM

Mail to: Genesis Press, Inc.
315 3rd Avenue North
Columbus, MS 39701

Name _____

Address _____

City/State _____ Zip _____

Telephone _____

Ship to (if different from above)

Name _____

Address _____

City/State _____ Zip _____

Telephone _____

Qty.	Author	Title	Price	Total

	Total for books _____
Use this order form, or call 1-888-INDIGO-1	**Shipping and handling:** $4 first two book, $1 each additional book _____
	Total S & H _____
	Total amount enclosed _____
	Mississippi residents add 7% sales tax